This Books Belongs To:

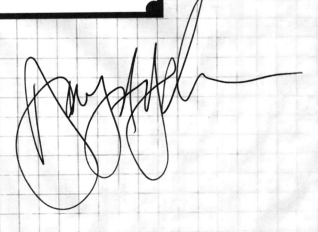

OTHER BOOKS BY BEN BEHUNIN

Remembering Isaac

Discovering Isaac

Becoming Isaac

Forget-Me-Notes

Borrowing Fire

Put A Cherry On Top

The Lost Art of Wooing Rabbits and Other Wild Hares

Ben's books are available from his website,
www.potterboy.com, www.amazon.com and
wherever above average books are sold

THE DISCIPLE OF THE WIND

A novel by

Ben Behunin

The Disciple of the Wind

First printing, November 2017

Published by
Abendmahl Press
P.O. Box 581083
Salt Lake City, Utah 84158-1083

ISBN 978-0-9838025-3-2

Photography Ben Behunin, Bert Compton and Quin Boardman
Designed by Ben Behunin and Bert Compton
Layout by Bert Compton

For Sabato, Sam and Simon.

Thanks for showing me that a humble, broken man can
still be useful, productive and inspiring, and for giving
me the hope to try.

We have come from God,
and inevitably the myths woven by us,
though they contain error,
will also reflect a splintered fragment of the true light,
the eternal truth that is with God.
Indeed only by myth-making,
only by becoming 'sub-creator' and inventing stories,
can Man aspire to the state of perfection that
he knew before the Fall.
Our myths may be misguided,
but they steer however shakily towards the true harbour,
while materialistic 'progress' leads only to a yawning abyss
and the Iron Crown of the power of evil.
— J.R.R. Tolkien

TABLE OF CONTENTS

PRELUDE TO THE WIND

The seed for this book blew in on a gentle breeze ten years ago, landing in the fertile soil between my ears as I worked quietly in my studio. This isn't entirely unusual. For the past twenty years, seeds have blown in and out of my head on a regular basis, vying for my attention as I commune with the clay. Many seeds have tumbled onward in search of other, perhaps more fertile ground, while others have germinated, sending shoots deep into my heart.

There are some things we learn in life that become such a part of us that we don't remember ever not knowing them. For this last decade, I have tried to learn all I could about the Watts Towers and their builder, Simon Rodia. My admiration for this man's work has influenced so many of the details of my own work and life and home. It feels like he's a friend I've known forever. But still, if I strain my mind, I can remember there once was a time when my only association with Watts was the Rodney King riots that erupted in the spring of 1992. I was a senior in high school at the time. I remember the chaos and anarchy I saw on

TV. It was a dark time in the history of justice and race relations in the United States. My wife, Lynnette, remembered that era, too. That might have been the reason she wasn't thrilled with the idea of us driving into Watts with our young children on our next trip to beach. That was the summer of 2007.

GPS was still fairly new back then. We didn't have one. And despite Lynnette's best efforts at navigation, I got us lost, somewhere in South Central, L.A. I stopped at a service station to ask for directions. The mechanic was helpful, but did nothing to ease her concerns.

"Boy, you're drivin' a minivan into Watts? I sure hope you're packin' heat."

I wasn't.

I recently returned to Watts—probably my tenth visit in as many years—this time to collect photos for this book. I'll admit that driving through the neighborhood can still be a little disconcerting. You'd be hard-pressed to find a yard that isn't guarded by a tall, iron fence, or a window that isn't barred. But somehow, as if by some beautiful, unseen magic, in the middle of this unease and disharmony shines a bright oasis of hope and love. Like the sails of a giant pleasure ship, the towers invite you to cast off the bowlines and head for brighter shores and nobler lands.

Over the years, trips to Simon's towers have nourished that tiny seed, encouraging it's growth. I've decided the world needs places like this—places where we can slow down long enough to listen to the wind whispering gently through our souls. They've inspired me to do all I can to turn back the tide of darkness and try to offer light, love and hope as a remedy. I believe that was Simon's intention.

This is not only a book. It's a seed. It's an invitation. I invite you to begin with an open heart and proceed as the way opens.

Cheers to your journey.

CHAPTER 1

A NEW WIND

Nothing in life is to be feared, it is only to be understood.
Now is the time to understand more, so that we may fear less.
—*Marie Curie*

The sun was hot on Kate's neck and shoulders as she peddled the rusty beach cruiser down the boardwalk, lost in thought. It had been just over a week since her arrival, and she wondered to herself why she hadn't done this before now, feeling so much better about her decision to move to Newport Beach after spending the morning with her toes in the sand.

Passing a pair of middle-aged women in bikinis with bronzed, leathery skin, Kate glanced at her own sunburned shoulders, wishing she had remembered to grab the bottle of sunscreen she'd seen in the garage the night before when she'd discovered the old beach cruisers. Distracted, she swerved to narrowly miss a happy couple on a tandem pedaling in the opposite direction. The jerking of the handlebars upset the collection of seashells she had carefully nestled in her beach towel. She grimaced as a few of them slid through the rusty wire basket, landing on the sandy boardwalk. She considered going back for them, but the crowded boardwalk dissuaded her. Instead, she carefully reached into the basket to cover the remaining shells with her towel, making sure the notebook—the main reason for her early-morning beach excursion— was also secure.

She felt a little silly about the shells, not to mention the fact that she'd had to compete with a couple of six-year-olds to collect them. Other than a brief walk along the boardwalk with her sister, Jill, the night she'd arrived, this was Kate's very first trip to the beach in her twenty-two years; her first time to collect sea shells; her first time to dip her feet in the Pacific. She had considered going in deeper, but her curiosity about the notebook had driven her back from the water's edge. Instead she spent the morning on her beach towel, flipping through page after page of handwritten notes, compelled to continue reading long after her stomach began growling.

The notebook had piqued her curiosity since the moment she had found it—buried under a stack of obsolete phonebooks in the bottom drawer of her new desk. After spending the first four-and-a-half workdays cooped up in a converted janitorial closet, she was thrilled when, on Friday afternoon, she was finally given a real office.

Kate had found the notebook just before leaving for the weekend. With the name of its owner scrawled on the cover in black marker, there was no mistaking who the book belonged to: Dr. Leslie Hermansen. Kate had heard the doctor's name dozens of times that week. She'd inherited many patients—and their associated files and paperwork—that the doctor had left behind eleven months earlier when she'd accepted another position. Kate had heard only good things of the doctor—her professionalism and her strict attention to detail. And so it had surprised her to find Dr. Hermansen's notebook forgotten in the bottom drawer of her vacated desk.

Kate's surprise had only grown, however, when she opened the cover of the notebook and found Dr. Hermansen's note.

During orientation on her first day, her supervisor, Dr. Cartwright, had stressed to Kate that she was strictly forbidden from removing any medical records from the premises. But after five days of sorting through dozens of file boxes stuffed with official records and manila folders, she knew this notebook was obviously something quite different.

As she pedaled down the boardwalk, Kate smiled to herself, remembering her pulse racing as she drove past the guard shack just the evening before, the notebook secretly stowed in her bag. It had felt so clandestine, yet the doctor's note left her feeling that she had no other reasonable choice. Even then, however, she had been paranoid the whole way home, continually looking in her rearview mirror while her hyperactive imagination led her to believe she was being followed.

With those fears still fresh in her mind when she arrived home after the long commute, she had stowed her bag behind her makeshift bed and tried to forget it, busying her mind instead with a week's worth of laundry.

And that was when she found the note—for the second time. She'd gone to her Subaru, looking for quarters to run the coin-operated washing machine in the garage, but instead she found the note, crumpled up like the piece of litter she thought it was when she first found it—clinging to her windshield at the end of a long, awkward, first day at the State Hospital.

She hadn't been able to make heads or tails of the illegible writing that first time, but something big changed in the waning light of Friday evening as she sat behind the wheel of her car, feeling overwhelmed. Tired and frustrated by a difficult week filled with hard realities, she'd found herself thinking she'd made a colossal mistake in coming here, so far from her comfort zone. She was sorry she'd come all this way; sorry she'd accepted a job she already knew was going to be impossible to love; sorry that she didn't even have enough quarters to do a load of laundry. She felt even more pathetic when her tears began falling and she caught a glimpse of herself in the rearview mirror, her drugstore mascara forming dark rivers down her cheeks. She reached for the crumpled napkin on the floor when she saw the scribbled writing. She unfolded it, flattening it out on the steering wheel before attempting to decipher its meaning. Over and over she tried to read the words, even turning it upside down more than once to see if it might help. Finally, when she'd closed her eyes and listened to the words in her own voice— so strangely strung together—understanding came. It was an answer, but more than that, it was *the* answer she had been waiting on for months. And as her tears continued to fall, she realized this message, wherever it came from, would change everything.

After walking to a convenience store to get quarters and clear her head, she'd returned to the house with new determination. If she was going to stay, she was going to do more than simply survive. Her sister had been kind enough to offer her a ratty couch in the dated, third-row beach house she shared with three roommates and untold numbers of couch surfers, beach bums, and freeloaders. There was much about her environment that she couldn't change, but she also knew she didn't have to live in squalor either. By the time she fell asleep, several hours later, she had singlehandedly whipped the place into decent shape and in the process, changed her entire attitude from one of despair to one of hopefulness.

That hope had only multiplied in the hours she had spent this morning on the beach reading through Dr. Hermansen's notebook. Unexpectedly, Kate had discovered the source of the note she found on her car: a patient with what can only be described as either unusual gifts or eccentric disturbances. What she learned from the notebook had left her with more questions than answers, but she was excited and hopeful that the skills and talents she'd been acquiring over her lifetime might come to some use in understanding and helping this unique patient. For the first time in her life, Kate felt like she might just be at the right place at the right time. And though her mind was filled to overflowing with questions surrounding her discoveries, her heart was filled with an unparalleled calm.

Kate smiled contentedly to herself now, the sun beaming brightly on her face, and the rich scents of life by the sea whirling about her as she glided almost effortlessly over the boardwalk.

But that feeling did not last for long. Distracted by two tan, surfboard-toting beach bums walking shirtless down the boardwalk, Kate drifted into the oncoming traffic. She responded quickly, hitting the brakes hard before skidding out of control on the sandy surface. Veering right, she became airborne as she launched herself off the boardwalk.

There was no time to be scared. For a very brief moment, she was even overcome by a state of euphoria as she and her bike seemed to soar over the sand. But that sense of splendor was short-lived as gravity reached up to grab hold of her tires, yanking her forcefully back to earth. Over the handlebars she flew, sailing spread-eagle onto the sunbaked sand. Getting her hands underneath her, she lifted her head and torso off the sand, not knowing if she should laugh or cry as she spit the sand out of her mouth.

"Are you okay?" a man asked from behind her.

She nodded but said nothing, her mouth still too full of sand for her tongue to function properly. She wondered how many people had seen her. And as she saw the shadows of people coming toward her, she quickly checked herself to make sure her tank top was still covering the essentials.

"I think she's hurt," she heard someone say as she rolled over; feeling like the wind had been knocked out of her. Slowly, she sat up on the hot sand, feeling dazed and embarrassed. Two hairy-chested men left their patio and rushed to her aid, each taking one of her hands and lifting her to her feet. A girl about her age lifted her bike out of the sand while several other people gathered up the collection of shells that had flown from their place in the handlebar basket. When it was clear that she was okay, the crowd quickly dispersed.

"Hey, this might sound kind of a crazy, but I'll give you fifty bucks to do that again," she heard a male voice say.

Kate looked around, wondering who would make such a ridiculous offer. She noticed a young man coming toward her, a camera hanging from his neck.

"That was awesome!" he exclaimed, smiling broadly. "I know millions of people would laugh their butts off if we could get that on YouTube."

"Really?" she said sarcastically, shaking her head.

"Absolutely! That was one of the best wipeouts I've ever seen! I've got my own YouTube channel, and...if you could do that again, I could..." He trailed off as Kate scowled, trying to ignore him as she spit another bit of sand from her tongue.

"Hey, don't I know you?" the annoying man asked.

"I hope not," she muttered, not looking up.

"Yeah, we met last night, remember? Betsy? No, wait, didn't you say your name was Betty...Betty the laundry girl?"

Surprised, Kate looked up, recognizing the man as the clerk from the convenience store where she had gone for quarters the night before. "This isn't a good time, Dirk," she said, brushing sand off her elbow to expose a painful patch of road rash.

"What...no, my name's not Dirk."

"Oh, did I say Dirk? Sorry, I meant *Jerk*!"

He laughed. "Sorry...I guess maybe I was a little insensitive?"

"*A little insensitive*? Are you kidding? You just asked me to repeat probably the most embarrassing minute of my life."

The man smiled. "I told you there'd be money in it for you, right? We could negotiate for more if it's as big of a hit as I think it'll be."

She glared, shaking her head. "I'm not even going to respond to that." She turned away and began pushing her bike back the way she had flown.

"Hey, listen," he said, following her. "I...I'm sorry. Let's just forget it."

"Easy for you to say."

"Hey, I was just thinking..." He stopped, bending down to the sand.

Kate took advantage of the opportunity to lose him and kept walking.

"Hey, is this yours?" he asked as she struggled to get her bike back up on the boardwalk.

She turned to see him pulling the half-buried notebook out of the sand. Immediately she ditched her bike, the contents of the basket spilling out again onto the beach as she turned to retrieve the notebook. "Yes, that's mine," she said, stooping down to reach for it.

"Whoa!" He said, pulling it away from her. "How do I know it's yours?"

She watched him as he brushed sand from the cover, and she immediately began to worry.

"There seems to be at least one minor inconsistency in your story." He smiled playfully, but she offered only a scowl in return.

"I thought you said your name was Betty? This says Dr. Leslie Hermansen."

"Just give it to me!" she barked, feeling more like she was confronting a sixth-grade playground bully than conversing with an adult.

"Why should I?"

"Are you really going to act like a twelve-year-old? I told you it's mine. Isn't that enough?"

He smiled wryly. "I'm not so sure it is."

Kate felt her face flush as her anger began to boil. "Look, it's a book about one of my patients. Now, please, just hand it over and no one will have to get their eyeballs scratched out."

The man laughed. "Take it easy. I was just kidding. Are you a doctor?" he asked, handing her the book, which he pulled back just as she reached for it.

"No, I'm...I'm a social worker."

"Are you sure? You seemed a bit hesitant there. How do I know you're not trying to cheat me out of a map that leads to buried treasure?"

"Is it all about money with you?" she asked, lunging for the book and missing.

"Isn't it all about money for everyone?" he asked, offering her a toothy grin.

"No! For some of us, it's still about principles, like being kind, and not stealing, and not taking advantage of someone who has just flown off her bike and lost whatever dignity she had."

He smiled and nodded, extending the book to her again, and she started to think she was making some progress with him. But before she could reach it, he pulled it away again, hiding the book behind his back.

Kate tasted the venom gathering in her mouth. "Listen, Jerk, I don't know who the heck you think you are, but I'm in no mood to play this stupid game with you. Just give me my notebook so I can leave."

He laughed again. "Did you just say heck? I don't remember the last time I heard anyone use that word."

Kate bit her cheek, trying not to smile. "Why don't you just hand over my notebook so I don't have to kill you."

"This is starting to sound serious."

"Oh, it was serious the second you opened your ignorant mouth."

He laughed. "Technically, wasn't that last night, Betty the Laundry Girl—if that's *really* your name?"

Kate spit sand from her tongue again, unable to keep from cracking a smile. "You were much nicer last night. Almost charming."

"Really?"

"Almost. Now can I have my book?"

"Not yet."

"This is harassment. What do you want from me?"

Her question seemed to surprise him. "The truth," he finally said after an uncomfortable stare down.

"What do you care about truth? I thought you were just after a quick buck."

"I am, but the truth is still nice sometimes."

"The truth is you're a pain in the butt."

"You're not doing a very good job convincing me that this is your notebook."

Kate ran her fingers through her hair, worried, knowing she had to get the notebook back. Searching her mind for ideas, she was distracted when a small piece of paper fell to the sand as the jerk held the notebook behind his back.

"Will you please be careful!" she pointed. "You're already losing stuff."

Keeping the notebook behind his back as if he were expecting a surprise attack, he stooped over to pick up the small piece of paper. He examined it quickly before looking up at Kate as if for the first time. "You've been to Watts Towers?" he asked, a totally different tone in his voice than had been present just a moment before.

"Yes. Why?"

"When?"

"On Monday. What do you care?"

He looked up from the piece of paper, shaking his head. "Do you have any other answers?" he asked smartly.

"What do you mean?"

Watts Towers of Simon Rodia
State Historic Park
Watts Towers Arts Center Campus
City of Los Angeles Department of Cultural Affairs
GENERAL ADMISSION $7
010419

"Watts Towers is only open for tours Thursday through Sunday."

"Yeah, I only got to see it from the outside."

"Outside of what?" he asked snidely, as if he were trying to catch her in a lie.

"The tall fence."

"So what's this?" he asked, holding up the piece of paper that had fallen from the book—a ticket for the Watts Towers tour.

Kate shook her head. "That was in the notebook when I got it. I…"

"So, I was right. This isn't your notebook?"

"It belongs to my colleague, Dr. Hermansen."

"So why do *you* have it?" he asked, taking a closer look at the cover.

"Are you some kind of notebook police? Why is this any of your business?"

"You don't need to get all huffy about it. I'm just wondering?"

"It's a long story, and I'm sure you wouldn't be interested. Now just give me my book so I can leave, please."

He handed her the book, and this time he didn't pull it away. She waited with an outstretched hand for the ticket as well, placing it back in the book before turning on her heel and walking back to her bike at the edge of the boardwalk.

"Hey," he called out, "you're just gonna leave?"

She didn't respond, putting the notebook into the basket and choosing to forget the shells that had fallen out. She lifted her bike out of the sand and muscled it onto the boardwalk without looking back.

"Wait, you can't just take off like this," he said, racing alongside her and taking hold of her handlebars.

"Watch me," she said, swatting his hand. She threw her leg over the bike and pushed off, not even glancing sideways at him. She had pedaled only two rotations when she knew the bike did not feel the same way it had before, and she rolled quickly to a stop.

A very little key will open a very heavy door.
Charles Dickens

CHAPTER 2

NEGOTIATIONS

There is no easy way from the earth to the stars.
— *Seneca*

"You're tire's flat," the man said. "I can help you with that."

She tried pedaling again, but it was no use. The old tire had partially separated from the rusting wheel, exposing the deflated inner tube. Kate wasn't going to let this stop her from getting away from the most annoying guy she had ever met. She gracefully dismounted and began pushing the bike without even looking back to acknowledge him.

"Wait," he called out, but she didn't. He ran to catch up to her then walked alongside her. "I've got tools," he said. "I can fix this."

"I can fix it myself, thank you," she retorted, looking straight ahead.

"Listen, I'm sorry. I was just looking for an excuse to talk to…"

"I don't have the time for dumb, rude boys," she said, cutting him off.

"Come on, Betty."

"That's not my name."

"Well, I'd be happy to call you by your real name, if I knew it," he responded, walking quickly to keep up.

"Mmm, let's not do this. You go your way, and I'll go mine. We'll just forget this whole thing happened and the world will be better for it."

"We could talk about it over lunch."

She laughed. "There's nothing to talk about."

"What about laundry? We could talk about laundry. I've been doing laundry for like...ten years almost. I'm practically an expert."

She couldn't keep from laughing, in spite of the anger she still felt.

"Or we could talk about Watts Towers."

"What about them?" she asked as she continued to push her bike. She was curious what he might know, but after his cheeky shenanigans, she wasn't about to give him the time of day.

"What do you want to know? I know like, basically everything there is to know about the towers."

"Wow! And you're humble to boot!" she said sarcastically.

He laughed, undaunted. "No, but really. I made a documentary about the towers for my senior project. I've done a ton of research up there. Maybe I could show you my movie sometime."

"Yeah, tempting, but I have boatloads of laundry to catch up on."

"So, I'm not going to get a second chance?"

"Uh, I think that was your second chance, and if you didn't notice, you totally blew it. You should know that I work with mentally ill people all day long. I kind of know one when I see one, and just so you know, you might want to have yourself checked out."

The man laughed. "That's a new one. Do you say that to all the guys?"

Kate shook her head. "You don't give up, do you?"

"Not when I meet someone interesting."

"No, then you just steal their stuff and act like a jerk."

He laughed unapologetically. "Hey, I just live a few blocks away. At least let me help you fix your bike and then you can decide if you'll let me buy you lunch."

"You're kidding, right?"

"No. And then after lunch maybe I can show you my film. If you still think I'm a jerk after that, then I'll leave you alone."

She shook her head, not believing his inability to take a hint. "I don't even know your name."

"Yeah, I know. I have a feeling this would have started out a lot differently if you'd asked me my name last night when you came in for quarters."

"Oh, really?"

"Sure, I would have told you my name, and then you would have asked for my number, and then you would have called me this morning and asked if I wanted to go for walk on the beach or fishing on the pier, and we'd have spent the whole morning talking about your favorite... fabric softeners...and we'd have discovered that our cousins went to high school together and that we're both Scorpios, and the day would have been much better."

She shook her head, laughing. "I'm actually a Libra, but nice try."

"Me too, come to think of it. What does that mean—nice try?"

"It means I wish I would have seen this side of you instead of your jerk-faced side. You're actually almost funny."

"Is that good? You like funny?"

She smiled. "Compared to the alternative, yeah."

"Well, like I said, if you'd asked my name instead lying to me, this all would have been different."

Kate smirked. "Let me guess," she said, turning to him as she continued pushing her bike down the boardwalk. "I bet your name's Brad."

"Brad? Pshaw! Why would you say Brad?"

"You look like a Brad, with your surfer hair and your tan and your smooth ways with the ladies."

"Well, Miss Smartypants, my name isn't Brad, and if you can believe it, I'm not always this smooth with the ladies."

"Wow! I'm glad I caught you on a good day."

He laughed. "I'm sorry I didn't introduce myself last night. My name's Charlie. Charlie George."

Kate snickered "Charlie George what?

"No, that's it. Charlie A. George."

"My dad always told me to never trust a man with two first names. What does the A stand for anyway? Astronaut?"

"I wish. What's *your* name, I mean your *real* one?" he said, an obvious and lame attempt to turn the attention away from himself.

She chuckled. "You think I'm letting you off that easy, Mr. Astronaut? What's your full name?"

He took a deep breath and lowered his voice. "Charlie *Aurora* George."

"Haw! No wonder you're so mean—you've had to put up with a name like Aurora your whole life."

"Yeah, that's hilarious."

"Were your parents hippies or something?"

"Close enough. They were going to name me Aurora if I was a girl and Charlie if I was a boy."

"Oh, that's too bad they couldn't decide which one you were."

"Easy!" he said smiling. "So, what's your real name, Betty?"

"I'm Kate. Kate Larsen."

"Just plain Kate Larsen? There's no embarrassing middle name?"

"Nope."

"Where are you from, Kate Larsen?"

"Oh, I'm pretty sure you wouldn't have heard of it."

"Try me."

"A little town called Preston, Idaho."

Charlie laughed. "Are you kidding? Of course I've heard of it. That's where Napoleon Dynamite's from, right?"

Kate shook her head, laughing. "You know it's not really like that, right?"

"Yeah, that's what I heard. One of my roommates used to date a girl from Preston."

"*Really?*"

"Yeah, she was the craziest girl I've ever met. She used to talk about going cow tipping on the weekends and getting out of school every fall for like a month to pick potatoes. Oh, and she could burp louder than most guys. I think her name was Jane or maybe Jill or something like that. Do you know her?

"That sounds a little bit like Jill Larsen," Kate replied.

"Yeah, I think that's it. Do you know her?"

"As a matter of fact, I do. Jill's my sister."

"No way!" He laughed. "You don't seem anything like her. Was she adopted?"

Kate smiled. "I think my mom wishes she was, but, no, she's my baby sister."

"Different strokes for different folks, right?"

Kate nodded, but didn't respond otherwise, continuing to push her bike down the boardwalk."

"So, if you're a social worker, I'm guessin' you went to school instead of partying, huh?"

Kate smiled, nodding again.

"Yeah, well, I guess there's probably a better future in that, right?"

"That's what they tell me. Isn't that why you went to school?"

"Me? No, I went to school to meet babes."

"You couldn't do that out here? I mean, it seems like a pretty easy way to meet girls, walking around with a camera, asking chicks if they want to star in your next YouTube video."

"Yeah...well, that hasn't worked out so well for me."

"Really? That surprises me," Kate responded sarcastically.

"Yeah, I tried to get a video of your sister burping the alphabet, but she always refused—something about her family seeing it back home."

"So, you weren't kidding, then? You really do make YouTube videos."

"How do you think I pay for my student loans?"

"What about your job at the convenience store?"

"Yeah, that almost covers my rent. In my spare time, I run an underground bike shop with my roommate out of our garage to pay for my other expenses."

"Wait a minute," she said, slowing down, "you really do know how to fix bikes?"

Charlie laughed. "Didn't I tell you?"

"Where's your garage?

"Three blocks back the way we just came."

"What? Why didn't you say something?"

"You looked like you knew where you were going. I didn't want to get in your way."

She shook her head. "You have wrenches and stuff?"

"Of course."

She stopped suddenly midstream on the boardwalk and turned around, crossing the dotted yellow line that formed a pervious divider between the north and southbound traffic. "If you're going to show off your fix-it skills, you might as well push it too," she said, leaning the bike toward Charlie.

He secured his camera around his shoulder before taking the handlebars.

"So, have you always aspired to being a YouTube movie producer?"

Charlie forced a smile. "It's just kind of a starting point, I guess— you know, to keep my skills up until I get my feet on the ground."

"I thought California's where dreams come true for movie people."

"Yeah, well, the economy isn't what it used to be. I didn't want to sell out and spend my life making movies I don't believe in. At least this way I get to call my own shots."

"Right, so instead of making movies you believe in, you're what... justifying the time and treasure of your education by fixing bikes, running a cash register, and accosting strangers on the beach with your camera, hoping to make a quick buck on YouTube?"

"And I suppose your life turned out just the way you figured it would?" he responded defensively.

Kate laughed out loud. "How long have you been done with school?"

"It will be three years in December. It's definitely not what I had in mind when I got started, but it's not bad. I'm sure there are probably easier ways to make money, but most of them aren't legal."

They veered off the boardwalk and down 32nd Street, turning their backs to the beach.

"So, how about you? How's it bein' a social worker?" he asked.

"I haven't decided yet. I just started on Monday, but it's already way different than what I thought I'd be doing."

"How so?"

"I guess I thought I'd be working more with people, not just sorting through papers and files. The economy's been tough on my field too, and the State Hospital in Watts was the only offer I got. They're going through some major financial cuts. They've had to let go of a bunch of doctors and hire interns like me to replace them."

"They can do that?"

"I guess so. They wouldn't have offered me the job if it wasn't legal, right?"

Charlie shrugged. "I don't know anything about that kind of stuff. They must be payin' you all kinds of money to leave a pretty place like Preston, Idaho, for the ghetto."

"I wish. It was more like desperation. I've got a boatload of student loans...and I was looking for a new adventure."

Charlie raised an eyebrow. "I'm guessing Watts hasn't disappointed you?"

"How much farther is it?" Kate asked impatiently, deciding not to answer his question.

"It's just right there," he said, pointing across the street. Kate probably could have guessed once she saw it. The gray-colored garage door looked like it had been spray-painted using bikes as stencils. The entire door was covered with the outlines of bikes and bike parts in various shades of gray.

Charlie rapped on the door with his knuckles. The sound of a sliding bolt was heard before the door lifted, exposing a small work space filled with bikes of all sizes and colors.

"Kate Larsen, meet my roommate, Andy Kafusi."

Kate turned to meet a handsome, muscular, dark-skinned man with a big grin. His chest was bare except for the greasy shop apron he wore around his neck, which draped his front to just above the hem of his board shorts.

"Nice to meet you," he said, his voice deep and low. He put forward his greasy, scarred fist to offer a fist bump, which Kate returned graciously.

Charlie removed a bike from the jaws of a bike stand, putting Kate's beach cruiser in its place. She watched as he removed the wheel, checked the tube, and replaced it with a new one after discovering the old one was cracked and rotten. Before replacing the wheel, he tightened the rusty spokes and lubed the chain.

"You're really fast," she said as he tightened the axel nuts. "It would have taken me twice as long—if I could have found the right wrenches."

Charlie looked up and smiled. "I don't know many girls that know the difference between a wrench and a pair of pliers."

"Maybe you need to get out more," she teased.

"What's this?" Andy asked, holding up an L-shaped tool he was using to tighten the handlebars on the bike he was working on.

"It's an Allen wrench," she fired back without hesitation.

"Impressive. What about this?" he asked, grabbing a small T-shaped tool. "Bet you five bucks you don't know what this is."

She looked at it for a minute before handing it back to Andy. "Tell ya what. If I get this right, you pay Charlie for fixing my bike."

"And if you don't?"

"Then I'll buy you both lunch."

"It's a deal," Andy responded confidently. "There's no way you'll get that one."

Kate smiled, taking a second glance at it, just to be sure. "It's a valve stem remover."

"No way you got that! Are you a grease monkey or something?" Andy asked.

"I used to help my dad fix stuff at home."

"Do you know how to fix bikes?"

"As long as they're made by John Deere."

Andy smiled. "If you ever want a part-time job, let us know. We'll put you to work."

"I don't know if you can afford me," she joked. "Since I graduated, I bill out at fourteen bucks an hour."

"Shoot, if you're any good, we'll pay you twenty bucks an hour," said Charlie.

"You're kidding, right?"

"No. We have bikes lined up for the next two weeks. There's kind of a never-ending supply of broken-down bikes and people who want to throw money at us to fix 'em."

"So what are you doing hanging out on the beach? I thought you were all about money."

"I am. I was just walking home from taking some bridal pictures when I ran into you," Charlie explained. "Besides, if we crank 'em out too fast, people will start expecting it. We're still faster and cheaper than the big bike shops anyway."

"Maybe I'll just quit my job and work here," she mused.

"Where do you work?" asked Andy.

"Dude, she works in Watts, at that big state hospital," Charlie answered for her.

"Wow, are you a doctor or somethin'?"

"Or somethin'," Kate replied.

"Have you seen Charlie's movie yet—the one about Watts Towers?"

Kate shook her head.

"Oh, you gotta see it. That kid has talent comin' out of his ears—if he'd only apply himself."

"Thanks, Dad," Charlie responded sarcastically.

"I'm just sayin'."

"Well, at least I have one fan, right?"

"You'd probably have a lot more if you'd ever finish it."

"Be nice!"

"Why don't you see what Kate thinks?"

"I don't think she's interested."

"Did you ask her?"

"Not exactly," Kate replied. "After he accosted me with his camera, trying to get me to launch myself off the boardwalk a second time for the benefit of his millions of YouTube viewers, he then told me my life wouldn't be complete until I had seen his masterpiece of a movie."

Andy raised one eyebrow as he turned to look at his friend. "Yeah, probably not the best way to get people interested in your stuff."

"Right?" Kate responded.

"So, how would you have done it different?" Charlie asked, looking to Andy for advice.

"If you haven't noticed," Andy whispered, as if lowering his voice meant Charlie wouldn't hear, "he's not very slick with the ladies."

"Yeah, I kinda got that impression," Kate replied.

"You can't blame him entirely."

"No?" Kate played along.

"No, his mother once found him stuck under the couch cushions when he was three, all blue and starved of oxygen."

"That would explain a lot."

"Oh, knock it off," Charlie responded.

"So, you think it's decent—his movie, I mean?" Kate asked.

Andy nodded. "I never would've believed such a place existed if it hadn't been for Char's movie. I've been up to Watts a bunch o' times since. There's somethin' really...I don't know...different about that place. You ought to check it out, though, if he ever finishes his movie."

Kate raised an eyebrow as she turned to Charlie. "Didn't you say it was your senior project?"

Charlie nodded.

"What kind of grade do you get on a senior project that's not finished?"

Charlie frowned. "An incomplete," he said, tossing his wrench onto the workbench and turning away.

"So...you didn't really graduate then?"

Andy smiled coyly and turned back to the bike he was repairing, leaving Charlie to defend himself.

"I...pfff. No, I'm three credits shy of a diploma. I...I never finished my project."

Kate nodded. "Are there any more lies you want to admit to while you're on a roll?"

Charlie rubbed his hands on a dirty rag before tossing it aside. "These aren't my real calves. I got implants."

"Really?" Kate asked, looking at his nicely shaped calves for the first time.

"Nope. That was another lie, but I think you now know all my secrets."

Kate smiled. "Okay."

"What does that mean?" asked Charlie.

"Well, I guess it means that maybe you're not as big of a jerk as I thought you were."

Andy snickered.

"Am I wrong?" Kate asked.

"No, there just aren't many ladies who put up with Charlie's BS long enough to discover he's a really good guy."

Kate nodded. "He wanted to buy me lunch earlier, Andy. Do you think I should forget all those lies he told me and go with him anyway?"

Andy looked like he was carefully considering the question for a moment before he smiled. "Yes, but keep him on a short leash, and don't be shy about calling his bluffs."

Use what talents you possess; the woods would be very silent if no birds sang there except those that sang best. —Henry Van Dyke

CHAPTER 3

PASTRAMI ON RYE

We are all cells in the body of humanity—
all of us, all over the world.
Each one has a contribution to make,
and will know from within what this contribution is.
—Peace Pilgrim

"Where are we going?" she asked, pulling up alongside Charlie as they pedaled south down the boardwalk.

"Have you eaten at the *Stuft Surfer* yet, down on 15th Street?"

"No. Why?"

"Do you like pastrami?"

"Who doesn't?"

"Yeah, well, the *Stuft Surfer* has the best pastrami on rye in Orange County."

The afternoon was clear, and the boardwalk was crowded with

people walking, biking, pushing strollers, and rollerblading. Weaving through the slower traffic, they soon arrived at the cafe.

"Hey, Charlie." A brunette with an unnatural shade of eyes spoke through the screen at the off-boardwalk counter, her voice laced with flirtation.

"Oh hey, Stacy. How's your ride treating you?" Charlie responded.

"Good, thanks to you. Did my friend Vanessa come and see you yet?"

"Yeah, yesterday. Thanks for sending her my way. She's crazy, right? I told her it would be cheaper to buy two new bikes with all the stuff she wants done. Did she tell you she wants the whole frame bedazzled with hot pink rhinestones?"

"Yeah. It's gonna to be so cute."

"Uhh, I guess. Hey," he said, lowering his voice and stepping closer to the screen, "is it okay if I use some of my credit?"

"Sure, what do you want?"

"Two pastramis with chips, pickles, and lemonades."

"Sure thing," she said, glancing up at Kate, who stood behind him clutching the notebook to her chest. "You got a date, Charlie?" she asked playfully.

"Uh, yeah...I...this..."

"Actually, no, he doesn't. I'm Kate," she said, cutting him off, not wanting anyone to get any ideas.

"Right. Well, I'll call your name when your order's ready," Stacy said, looking at Kate with just the slightest hint of stink eye.

"You know all the girls?" Kate asked as they took a seat at one of the umbrella-covered picnic tables on the sand just across the boardwalk from the cafe.

"Yep, pretty much," he said, avoiding the bait. "So, tell me more about your book," he said, pointing to the notebook she'd carried with her even though their bikes were parked no farther than ten feet away.

"There's not much to tell, really."

"So why didn't you leave it in the basket?"

"Why don't we start with you telling me about your documentary?"

"Sounds like you're avoiding my question."

"You got that, huh?"

"Why?"

"Why what?" she asked, playing dumb.

"Why won't you tell me about your book?"

"Because it's...I don't think you'd understand."

"Try me."

"You first."

"What?" he asked.

"Tell me about the towers."

"That's a pretty broad question. What do you want to know?"

Kate opened the book and removed the Watts Towers ticket Charlie had seen before. "I want to know why—when you were holding my notebook hostage on the beach back there—why everything changed as soon as you saw this and found out I'd been to the towers."

Charlie looked surprised by the question. "I don't know...it just seemed like a crazy coincidence."

"A crazy coincidence?"

"Yeah, well, there aren't many people who've even heard of the towers—far fewer who've seen 'em. I spent almost every Friday for close to three years up there, working on my film, trying to figure it all out."

"What's there to figure out?"

Charlie shrugged, looking as if he wanted to say more, but didn't.

"Andy said something curious earlier, something about the towers being...I think he said *different*. But the way he said it—I don't know—it just feels like there's something bigger going on up there than just a bunch of funky towers."

Charlie's look of surprise only deepened with this disclosure. "You said you were there on Monday, right?"

"Yeah, why?"

"Why'd you go?"

"I didn't really mean to...I got lost, and..."

Charlie smiled but said nothing, encouraging her to continue.

"I was on my way back to the freeway, or so I thought, and I guess I just kind of stumbled upon them."

"So did you just drive past them?"

"Well, no, I...there was something about them...I was curious, I guess. I got out and walked around."

"Was anyone else there?"

"Yeah, probably about a dozen people. Why?"

"Did you talk to them?"

"Yeah, I mean, not all of them. It was kind of crazy."

"Crazy?"

"Yeah, I felt like I was the only one who wasn't there on purpose. And the crazy thing is, they were from all over the world, like this was some kind of destination I'd never heard of. I met some girls from France who were pretty upset that they'd come all this way and it was only open for tours a few days a week. There were a couple of people from South Africa and another group from Australia."

Charlie smiled and nodded again as if he'd expected her answer. "Did you happen to see any children there?"

Kate was surprised by the question but remembered the young family from Minnesota who agreed to show her the way back to the freeway. "Yeah, I met a couple who was there with their daughter— probably about six years old. Why do you ask?"

"She liked it, didn't she? The towers, I mean."

Again, Kate was surprised by his question as she remembered the little girl's reaction. "Yeah, she liked it a lot. Her parents told me they'd spent a couple thousand dollars on flights and tickets to Disneyland and that their daughter asked them if they could just come back to the towers instead of going Anaheim."

Charlie nodded again. "What did *you* think of the place?"

"I don't know. It was crazy and beautiful and so...unexpected, I guess. What about you? What got you interested in the towers?"

"How much time do you have?"

"It depends on how good your story is. Your questions make me curious."

"Yeah, me too."

"So?"

The girl at the café window called Charlie's name.

"I'll be right back," he said, getting up and crossing the boardwalk. A minute later he returned with their order on a plastic tray. He set one of the giant sandwiches down in front of Kate, and her mouth immediately began to water as she looked down at the marbled rye bread.

"Thanks, I'm starving."

"You're welcome. Consider it a peace offering for the way I acted earlier. I'm sorry."

"Apology conditionally accepted," she said, taking a big bite of her sandwich.

He looked confused. "What are the conditions?"

"That you stop avoiding my questions."

"That hardly seems fair...if I'm the only one giving any answers," he said, glancing down at her notebook.

Kate swallowed hard. "Look, Charlie, the timing's just not right. Maybe we can talk about it after we build a relationship of trust."

"Now you've got me even more curious."

"Sorry." She moved the notebook onto the bench next to her, out of his sight. He looked disappointed.

"So, Miss Social Worker, how do you propose we build a relationship of trust in the next ten minutes?"

Kate laughed. "That usually takes *way* more than ten minutes, especially when one party has legitimate reasons for not entirely trusting the other party."

"Who said anything about a party? And besides, that was so sixty minutes ago. Oh, and just so you know," he said, taking a big bite of his sandwich, "I've been counting, and you lied to me at least as many times as I lied to you," he sputtered through a mouthful of sandwich.

"It might be best if we didn't dwell on who lied the most, even though we both know it was you. Besides, I thought you were about to tell me why you started going to Watts."

"You're not going to tell me about your notebook, are you?"

"Not today. I don't want to interrupt your story."

He smiled, conceding he wasn't going to get anywhere with his continual inquiries. "What do you want to know?"

"I want to know why someone like you would spend enough time in Watts to make a documentary about it...or at least most of one."

Charlie ignored the jab. "I guess I first got interested when I was a senior in high school. There was picture of the towers in my humanities textbook. It's kind of become an obsession, trying to understand what they are."

"Aren't they a work of art?"

"Sure, but...it's more than that."

"What do you mean?"

"You've been there. You've met people who came from far away to see it. It's almost like the towers have some strange gravitational pull that draws people in from all over the world; not in huge numbers, but regular people who just up and decide one day that they're going to travel to the other side of the world to see 'em."

"So...what is that gravitational pull?"

He shook his head. "It sounds kooky, but it's almost like there's some kind of...supernatural connection that people have with the place. At least that's the way it was for dozens of people I interviewed for the documentary."

"What does that mean—supernatural connection?"

Charlie shrugged. "Something happens to some people when they're

there...they leave...different than when they came, somehow transmuted into something...I don't know...different...like a better version of themselves. Andy used to be a big partier when I first met him. But after joining me on a couple of trips to the towers, he quit drinking and doing pot and started doing his art again. He's a totally different person than he used to be."

"Do you know what it is?"

"I...it sounds weird. I..." He trailed off, unable to find the right words.

"I think I might get it. It was kind of like that for me. I..." she hesitated, trying to remember the exact order of events. It had been her first day at the hospital. She remembered walking to her car in the parking lot and finding the strange note on her windshield. Distracted by the note, she'd pulled out of the parking lot, unsure of which direction she needed to go.

"Tell me about your experience," he encouraged.

She decided to skip the bit about the note. "I remember feeling disoriented as soon as I left work, so I tried to turn around, but I got stuck on a stupid one-way street. By the time I got off it, I was surrounded by blocks of run-down houses and vandalized storefronts. It kinda felt like nobody cared."

"Did you end up in Compton?"

"I have no idea. I just kept driving, trying to find anything that looked familiar."

Charlie smiled.

"No, I'm usually pretty good at this kind of stuff," she said defensively. "I've never gotten lost in my life, at least not like that. I just couldn't figure out what direction I was going, and my boss had warned me about stopping to ask for directions. It was like, no matter where I turned, I didn't feel like I was getting closer to the freeway or anything else that looked even vaguely familiar. I didn't think anything really scared me anymore. But my boss, he kinda spooked me," she shook her head. "He made it sound like I'd gotten a job inside the gates of hell."

Charlie laughed. "Did he tell you that before or after you accepted the job?"

"After, of course. He did tell me to get a GPS so I wouldn't get lost, but I didn't really listen and...well, it was pretty embarrassing, showing up late on my first day of work. My sister talked me into getting a smartphone that night when I finally got home. I guess there's an app for everything, right?"

"If it makes you feel any better, I still make sure I have Google Maps on whenever I drive into Watts."

"You don't know the way?"

"I do, but I can't tell you how many times I've been stuck in my own head and missed my exit. Watts has been a really tough neighborhood for decades. I've never witnessed any violence myself, but I've interviewed lots of people who have. I've spent enough time in neighborhoods surrounding the towers to know that's not a place to get stuck in the crossfire. How'd you end up finding your way out?"

"I just kept driving until..." she trailed off, remembering.

"Until...?"

"I must have seen the towers—sticking out above the trees. I was curious. I just drove down the street and there they were."

"And after that...after being lost in the grit and grime of Watts, you didn't hesitate to get out of your car?"

"Come to think of it...no. Crazy, right?"

"Hmmm."

"What does that mean?"

Charlie shook his head, smiling. "You felt something, didn't you?"

She raised one eyebrow. "What is it you think I felt?"

He took a deep breath. "Hope! Almost like getting washed up on a lush island in the middle of a huge, turbulent ocean and you can finally come up for air and breathe and experience something beautiful. Or maybe it was a strange, totally surprising feeling of peace."

She smiled. "Yeah, that's actually exactly what I felt," she admitted, remembering the feelings of awe she had so unexpectedly experienced along with hope and peace.

Charlie was smiling when she looked at him, but his smile somehow made her feel uncomfortable—exposed—somehow too familiar with a guy she had really only met just an hour before.

CHAPTER 4

THE MESSAGE

Everyone thinks of changing the world,
but no one thinks of changing himself.
—Leo Tolstoy

"Why are you smiling?" Kate asked.

"Sorry," he said, looking more serious. "I...what you experienced is basically what I've tried to capture in my documentary."

Kate looked surprised. "How do you capture a feeling like that on film?"

Charlie shrugged. "Maybe that's my problem. I haven't been able to define it or put into words what happens there. Nothing has really gone the way I planned."

"How did you want it to go?"

"I don't even know anymore." He looked away, but there was something about the way he said it that made Kate wonder what he wasn't saying.

"Do you think that's part of the problem?"

Charlie shrugged. "I think it was more that my professor didn't understand the ethereal ramifications of artistic expression."

"Kinda sounds like a cryptic cop-out," Kate responded.

"Maybe it is. The only thing I know for sure any more is that not only has this been the most frustrating experience of my life, it has also become one of the most sensitive."

"Is that why you didn't finish it?"

He shook his head, but the frustrated look on his face made it clear that this was indeed a sensitive subject. "It's just that this film was kind of my baby, and I don't think anybody really likes to be told that they have an ugly baby."

Kate laughed. "No, I'm sure that's probably true. How much time did you spend on it?"

"Almost five years, I guess. I actually started researching at the end of my sophomore year, and I guess it's still a work in progress. I never really intended to use all that research for a film, at least not in the beginning. But I found that my fascination with the towers was so consuming I figured I better find a way to justify all the time I was spending there."

"I'm sure you figured out why people built them?"

"People?"

"Well, yeah, I assume a bunch of people built them, right?"

Charlie smiled. "I forgot. You didn't do the tour, did you?"

"No. Why?"

"It's just as well. The tours really only tell the basic story anyway and skip most of the good stuff."

"Like what?"

"Like all of Sam Rodia's back story. Like why he built them in the first place."

"Did you say *Sam* Rodia?"

"Yeah, why?"

"Oh, nothing. Who was he?"

Charlie looked surprised. "He's the guy who built the towers."

"You mean with a lot of help, right?"

Charlie shook his head. "He built them all by himself."

"What? That's crazy. That must have taken fifty years!"

"Almost. He worked on the towers for thirty-three years."

"Wow! Is he still alive?"

"No, he died in 1965."

"Seriously? That was more than fifty years ago!"

Charlie laughed. "I know."

"How did he die?"

"Old age. He was eight-six."

"What? Was he working on the towers until he died?"

"No, only until he was about seventy-five. And then he just walked away. He deeded the property to a neighbor and moved up north to Martinez to be near his sister. He never came back."

Kate looked at him incredulously. "This story only gets crazier. Who was he?"

"That's the thing—he wasn't really anybody, just an Italian immigrant who came to America looking for a better life. He was only fifteen when he ended up in the Pennsylvania coal mines. I don't think he ever had more than a third-grade education. The people I interviewed who knew him said he was probably illiterate, maybe dyslexic, and he wasn't even five feet tall. He had every reason for history to forget him, but instead people come from all over the world to see his towers."

"So...was he an artist or a madman?" she asked, looking confused.

Charlie laughed. "I think he must have been a genius, which, as I've researched it, is probably some kind of artist-madman hybrid."

"But wouldn't you have to be more than a little bit nuts to go to all the trouble of building something like that in the middle of a ghetto? I mean I could understand it better if he'd built them on the beach or at Disneyland or someplace where people wouldn't have to drive through the gates of hell to find them."

Charlie smiled. "How do you know that wasn't part of his genius?"

She gave him a funny look. "What kind of artist-madman hybrid are *you*?"

"I haven't decided. But before you say anything else, you should know that he didn't build the towers in a ghetto."

"What?"

"I know it doesn't look good now, but Watts hasn't always been that way. I mean, it was never Beverly Hills, for sure, but when he bought his property back in the twenties, Watts was a respectable working-class neighborhood. The streets were clean, and the houses didn't have bars on every window. I've seen pictures of the neighborhood from the time he was working on the towers. You wouldn't recognize it."

"So what happened?"

"Watts has gone through many cycles of change in the past ninety years. Racial tensions have played a big role, but drug abuse, poverty, and crime have all led to its decline. I interviewed one resident who'd lived in Watts for more than ninety years, and she blamed its decline on the welfare system."

Kate looked surprised. "What does that have to do with anything?"

"Like I said, Watts used to be a working-class neighborhood, filled with immigrants who were trying to live the American dream— you know, provide a better life for themselves and their children than whatever they'd left behind. According to this lady, in the early days of Watts, people worked hard at their jobs and then they came home and worked hard on their yards and houses. They planted gardens, kept their homes in good repair, picked up their garbage, and were concerned about their community. When you rent your home, or when the government pays your rent, most people don't care much about planting gardens and keeping the house painted. It was her theory that when people aren't working, either because of choice or lack of opportunity, they have a whole lot of time to get into trouble.

"She said that when you look next door and see that your neighbors look a little scary, you build a tall fence around your yard and put bars on your windows to protect yourself. Your neighbors do the same, and pretty soon you're afraid to walk down the streets. When people don't get to know their neighbors, it's not usually very long before everyone looks at everyone else with suspicion. From there, it seems like fear and apathy pave the road into darkness. She was mad as hell at what the government had done to her people and community—giving them fish instead of providing opportunities for them to catch their own. And the problems only multiplied with each generation. For a while, I considered doing a whole documentary about the messes the welfare system has created, based on my interviews with Shirley."

"Why didn't you? That seems like a pretty compelling story."

"I might have if Shirley hadn't died. Plus, it didn't feel like that was the story I was supposed to tell."

"And what story is that?"

He sat silent for several seconds, turning to look out at the sea. "Have you ever felt like you're supposed to do something—something big—but you get nervous about doing it and…I don't know…you get scared of putting your baby on view…afraid of people thinking you're a fanatic—a raving lunatic?"

Kate waited for more, but he didn't seem anxious to go further. "If it's any consolation, I know what a lunatic looks like, and though you seem more than a little odd, I think we can safely rule out lunacy."

Charlie laughed. "So, I've told my story. What about yours?"

"I don't think you're done."

"What do you mean?"

"You said you were afraid, but you never really said of what. What story is it you're supposed to tell? What is it you're afraid of?"

"You're not going to let this go, are you?"

"Can you let it go?" she asked

"Huh?"

"This has obviously been eating at you for a while. I don't blame you. I think if the ending to a film I'd been working on for five years was the only thing that stood in the way of me graduating, it'd be eating me up too."

"You have no idea."

"You're right. Why don't you tell me about it?"

He smiled. "You're not on the clock, Miss Social Worker. You don't have to take me on as a special project."

"Oh, good! Thank you. I was worried that you were getting the wrong idea and I'd have to listen to you for the rest of the weekend," she teased.

"Is everything a joke to you?" he asked, smiling but obviously bent.

"No, but maybe you do need a social worker. When was the last time you talked to anyone about your fears?"

Charlie laughed out loud. "Never."

"Never? Really?"

"Yeah, what's there to talk about? I already know I'm a chicken. I don't need to open my big mouth and let everyone else know that I can't face my fears—that I've wasted the last two and a half years trying to find a way around what I know I'm supposed to do. I already know the answer to my problem, and a lot of good that's done me. Thanks, but no thanks. I don't need your help."

"So what is it you're afraid of?" she asked, undaunted

He shook his head, looking away. "Telling a story that needs to be told."

"And what story is that?"

"It just feels like there's something more—something I haven't seen yet—something I haven't been able to understand. I know there's something there...something that haunts me."

"Tell me about it."

He shook his head, but didn't reply.

"What's haunting you?"

"That's the thing—I don't know. Part of me wants to run from it, and part of me wants to dig deeper and figure it out—whatever it is."

Kate watched him, waiting for more. "It looks to me like fear's winning this fight."

He looked up, surprise in his eyes.

"This isn't my first rodeo. Fear holds a lot of people back."

"Okay, so if you're so smart, what am I supposed to do about it?"

"That's a good question. What *are* you supposed to do about it?"

"I don't know anymore," he muttered.

"That implies that you once did."

He looked surprised again before turning away.

"What are you afraid of, Charlie?"

"Lots of things. I don't know what's down that rabbit hole."

"It could be a great adventure."

"Yeah, maybe. But it could also be death."

"Really? Aren't you being a little dramatic?"

"Okay, so maybe not death in the way you're thinking, but death in a very real professional way. Making a film—even a low-budget documentary like this one—people see it."

"Isn't that what every filmmaker wants?" she laughed

"Yeah, but if it sucks, it's death."

"What are you talking about? It's a movie."

"Look, you live in a different world. As a social worker, I'm guessing you don't have to worry about Snapchat and Twitter feeds with your name on them. I've seen it happen—people say or do something stupid, and the next thing you know, Facebook lights up and the storms of hate brew into a hurricane while they're sleeping. People in my industry get crucified in cyberspace all the time for small, stupid stuff. If my film sucked, I might never get another chance to work."

"So let me get this straight—you're letting your fear of what strangers might tweet about you shut down the opportunity of success and adventure and keep you from even trying?"

He shook his head. "You don't understand."

"You're right. I don't. I don't understand why you'd let fear of what someone might think keep you from following your dreams. Haters are always gonna hate, right?"

He shrugged.

"Where did all of this angst come from?"

"Uhh, are you talking about *all* my angst, or just the angst specifically tied to this film?"

"Let's start with your film."

"Okay, well, to begin with, my professor thought it was stupid."

"Really? Your professor told you your film was stupid?"

"Uhh, well, not exactly. I think his exact words were 'irrationally delusional.'"

"Wow! Nice professor. But you do know there's a difference between 'irrationally delusional' and stupid, right? At what point in the process did he tell you that?"

"Pretty early on, actually."

"And you went ahead with it anyway?"

"I tried not to. I mean, I did. Kinda. It's complicated."

"I'm listening."

"You don't have to do this."

"I know, and I'm still listening."

He shook his head. "Every time I thought about doing something else, a voice in my head screamed out at me that..." He trailed off.

"Screamed out at you that...? I don't know if you noticed, but you didn't finish your sentence."

He sat up, resting his elbows on the table. "It screamed out at me that the towers had chosen me to tell their story."

"Interesting," she said, thinking of the things she had been reading in the notebook. "What else did it tell you?"

"What do you mean?"

"It just seems like if the voice in your head was telling you something that specific, maybe it would give you a little more direction—maybe be a little specific."

He stared at her for a moment, looking surprised. "It did. I felt like I was supposed to tell Rodia's story."

"Has no one told his story before?"

"Sure, parts of it, but not the same parts."

"How is your movie different?"

"You really don't ask any easy questions, do you?"

"Charlie, your story's compelling. I want to know more than what you're telling me. It's almost like you're afraid to let it out."

"Absolutely!"

Kate nodded thoughtfully. "Maybe we could help each other."

He raised an eyebrow. "How?"

"I'm not sure. I'm a pretty good listener, though. My dad used to say that most of us already know the answers to our big questions but we have to hear ourselves say them out loud before they make any sense. I think maybe sometimes we just need someone to listen."

"So what do you get out of the deal?"

"Information. I want to learn more about those towers and what would inspire someone to build something like that."

"If I say yes, are you going to tell me about your notebook?"

"When the time's right, maybe."

"What's going to keep you from taking all my information and running away?"

"I could get my information from someone else," she answered, playing it cool.

He laughed. "That would require a minimum of five years of research and the resurrection of at least three people."

She thought about that for several seconds, realizing he was probably right. She didn't have a ready response, and she was distracted when she looked over his shoulder to their bikes. Her eyes were drawn to a white piece of paper that was wrapped around a spoke on her bicycle's wheel, fluttering in the coastal breeze. She knew it was probably just a piece of garbage, but she couldn't keep from looking at it, curiously drawn to it. Without a word, she stood and walked to the bikes.

"So...that's it?" he asked, turning around. "Not even a thanks for lunch?"

She ignored him, stooping over to pull the paper from the spokes of the wheel.

"There's no way that tire's flat," he said defensively. "It's a premium tube."

"Relax. There's just something here on the wheel."

He walked next to her, standing over her as she untangled the paper. "What is it?"

"It's just a scrap of garbage," she said as she stood, walking to the trash can to throw it away. But before she could let go, she noticed that something appeared to have been written inside the folds. She opened it up, staring at the writing.

"Is this some kind of trick?" she asked, turning around to face Charlie.

"What are you talking about?"

"This!" She handed him the napkin and waited for a response.

Charlie looked down at the napkin. "What is this?"

"You don't know?"

He stared back at her like she was crazy. "What are you talking about?"

"You honestly don't know?"

"What should I know?" He laughed. "It's just a napkin with some scribbles on it."

She stood in front of him and looked him in the eyes. "You didn't put that on my bike?"

"Why would I do that?" he asked incredulously.

She took the napkin back from him and turned it over again, stopping to stare at the iconic logo emblazoned on the underside. Jack in the Box. She walked back to the table and sat down, continuing to stare at the napkin.

"You know, I thought your sister was pretty trippy, but I'm pretty sure that she's nowhere near as tripped out as you are."

"What are you doing tomorrow?" she asked, ignoring his insult.

"My laundry," he lied.

"That's too bad. It would be fun to have you show me around the towers."

"You wanna go to Watts?"

"Yeah, I'll drive if…"

Charlie cracked a smile. "What time do you want to leave?"

CHAPTER 5

STEPS INTO THE DARK

The ability to ask questions is the greatest resource in learning the truth.
—Carl Jung

Kate wasn't sure if she should honk, it still being early on Sunday morning. She knew she was a few minutes early, but she'd been awake almost three hours already and was feeling anxious to get on with the day. She had written down at least a dozen questions for Charlie but guessed there would probably be many more before the day was over.

She glanced down at the notebook sticking out of the top of her bag resting on the passenger seat. She had stayed up late reading, finishing up the last pages just as her sister got home at one-thirty a.m. Jill had laughed when Kate asked about Charlie.

"He's clueless about girls, but he's a really good guy," Jill had said, both confirming Kate's suspicions and setting her mind at ease. In spite of all that, however, she still couldn't get over the fact that she had committed herself to at least a handful of hours with a guy who had infuriated and lied to her more times than she could count just under twenty-four hours earlier.

"Have you been waiting long?" Charlie asked through the open window, startling her.

"Just a few minutes." She moved her bag, making room for him to sit down.

"Sorry." He climbed in beside her, setting his backpack on the floor in front of him.

"Charlie, I have just one question for you before we leave."

"Okay."

"Can I trust you to not lie to me anymore?"

He smiled, his tired eyes sparkling playfully. "Scouts honor," he said, holding up two fingers.

"I assume you know that's the Cub Scout sign."

"Yeah, well, I never made it to Boy Scouts. In fact, I got kicked out of Cub Scouts for playing with gasoline."

"Why doesn't that surprise me?"

"It was awesome, actually. I mean, we all should have died, but..." He stopped mid-sentence when he saw that Kate was obviously not amused.

"Yes, you can trust me," he said, deflated.

"Okay, then you can hold this." She pulled the notebook from her bag and handed it to him.

"So, you're finally going to tell me what this is?"

"Against my better judgment, yes."

He looked down at the book. "Can I ask a question before we go any further?"

"Sure."

"Does this change of heart have anything to do with that napkin you found on your bike yesterday?"

Kate was surprised. "It might, why?"

He opened his backpack and removed an iPad covered in surf stickers. He clicked it on, running his fingers over the cracked screen several times before he stopped, turning the screen to face her. "Do you think it might have been written by the same person who wrote these notes?"

Kate looked down at what looked like a bulletin board—close to a dozen notes scrawled on various shades of paper, pinned and stapled to a wall. She immediately recognized the nearly illegible script on many of the notes.

"Where did you get this?"

"I took that picture three years ago when I was interviewing the night watchman at the towers."

"Where'd he get them?"

"I never asked. I'm not even sure why I took this picture. I just found it last night when I was sorting through my photos. The scribbles reminded me of the scribbles on that napkin."

Kate smiled nervously. "It's inside the notebook."

Charlie opened the notebook, finding the folded napkin just inside the cover, the handwriting plain to see. "Do you know what this is?" he asked.

"Yes."

Charlie looked closer but still couldn't see it.

"Can you read it?"

"You mean it's supposed to be read?" He chuckled. "It just looks like a chicken was playing around with a Magic Marker."

Kate laughed. "That's because it's upside down."

He nodded, turning it around. "Yeah that's better. Now it looks like a four-year-old was trying to write with a chicken with a Magic Marker in its beak."

"Can you read it?"

He shook his head. "*Can you?*"

"I've had a little bit more practice." She read it aloud.

USE CAN TRUSSEMN EES
POST ABE PXROVIT
BREENEM TOOOA
TONRZ WICNEW

"What?"

"Listen closely." She read it again, a little slower.

"Kate, those aren't words—at least not English words."

"Try it again. But close your eyes this time, and listen hard."

He nodded but looked dubious before shutting his eyelids tightly.

She read the words a third time, slower, deliberately.

"Are you trying to tell me that that note says, 'You can trust him. He's supposed to be part of it. Bring him to the towers with you?'" he asked, his eyes suddenly wide open.

"I think so."

"What in the world does that mean?"

Kate laughed. "I have no idea, but when I saw this yesterday, I knew I needed to get back to Watts and that you needed to come with me."

"But what does...? Do you know who wrote this?" He looked flustered and confused.

"I think so. I think it must be the same guy who wrote those," Kate said, pointing to the iPad.

Charlie looked down, shaking his head. "Okay, you're totally freakin' me out. What the..."

"I don't know," she responded, shaking her head.

"But...Why...? How did you...whoa, this is totally crazy."

"I know."

"Why aren't you freaking out?"

"Oh, believe me, I was yesterday. I got a head start, remember."

"Yeah, but...dude, this is totally not what I expected."

"What did you expect?"

"Not this. Definitely not this! I don't even know what *this* is. Do you?"

"No."

"So, what are we supposed do with it?"

"It feels crazy taking instructions from a napkin, but the only thing that comes to mind is to drive to Watts and...I don't know. I don't know what to do after that. Maybe something else will happen there."

"But how did this napkin end up...?"

"Charlie, believe me, I have no idea, but I've got a hunch that we'll both have some answers by the end of the day."

"Then drive," he said, laughing. "I've been trying to find answers in Watts for the last five years,"

Kate nodded and started the car.

"What else is in this notebook?"

"A bunch of stuff about Sammy."

"Who?"

"Sammy. He's the one that notebook's all about. I think he's also the one who wrote those notes."

"How do you know that?"

"I watched him put a note on my car on Monday. It's at the back of the notebook."

Charlie flipped to the back cover and pulled out the wrinkled napkin. He stared at it for a long moment. "I can't tell what it says." He turned it sideways then upside down, but it didn't seem to help.

"You is where you is supposed to be."

"And that means something to you?"

"I didn't understand it at first—it just looked like

a bunch of nonsense, like you said. I didn't figure it out until Friday when I found it again under the seat when I was looking…for quarters."

"To do your laundry?" he asked thoughtfully.

Kate smiled. "Yeah. That was right before I met you. The thing is, before I found that note, I'd been feeling like I was wasting my time, coming all the way here to do a job I really wasn't liking. I was feeling totally overwhelmed, having to live in a crazy, dirty party house filled with strangers and not feeling like I was making any difference at all in the world. And then I stumbled on this note—and it finally hit me what it says—and I've spent the last thirty-six hours feeling like…maybe there's way more to whatever this is than I bargained for when I moved to the other side of the universe for the promise of fourteen dollars an hour."

"So, is this guy Sammy…is he one of your patients then?"

"I don't know."

"What do you mean?"

"Technically, I'm not sure if he even *is* a patient."

"*What?*"

"It's a long story."

"Why doesn't that surprise me?"

Kate took a deep breath. "Listen, I'm trying to figure this out too. I have no idea where this is going or what I'm supposed to do with it. But I've pretty much come to the conclusion over the last thirty-six hours that I'm supposed to be here. That's really all I've got—that and about a million questions."

"So catch me up," he said, laughing nervously as they pulled onto the freeway.

Kate nodded. "From all that I've read, Sammy has some unique challenges, but he also has some very unique gifts."

"Such as?"

"Have you ever heard how blind people often develop an unusually strong sense of hearing?"

"Sure."

"I think Sammy's gifts are something like that."

"How so?"

"I get the impression from reading that notebook that Sammy has a very unique ability to hear."

"Is he blind?"

"No, I don't think so. I'm still trying to figure this out myself, but it's like he can hear things most of us can't...or don't."

"You mean like how a dog can hear high-pitched sounds that humans can't?"

"Yeah...maybe...I don't know exactly what it is or how it works, but there seems to be some kind of a connection between Sammy and...and the wind."

"The wind?"

"That's what Dr. Hermansen said," Kate responded, pointing to the notebook.

"Interesting."

"What?"

"Well, one of Simon Rodia's neighbors told me that every night he used to climb up to a perch he built onto one of the towers to...listen to the wind."

"Did they say why?"

"No. There were all sorts of rumors that circulated over the years. One of them that got started during World War II was that the towers were some kind of secret radio antennas and that Simon was a spy, transmitting secret messages to the Nazis."

"Is there any truth to that?"

"Not at all. Simon was a pacifist. He avoided conflict of any kind. I think that was one of the reasons he left Watts."

"I don't understand."

"I guess back in the early Fifties, some of his neighbors ratted him out to the FBI. When he came home from work one night, his house was surrounded by federal agents who were poking and prodding the towers to see what he was up to."

"Did they find anything?"

"No. The records of their investigation, if there ever were any, must have been destroyed. I spent a lot of time searching through old archives and only found a short article that suggested suspicion. The Feds left him alone after that, but some of his neighbors started a witch hunt of their own."

"What?"

"Yeah, Simon was always a bit different, but after the war, when Hispanics and Blacks started moving into Watts, he started sticking out more and more. His English was never very good, and I don't think he ever gave the same answer twice. Plus, it's kind of hard to fit in when you have the tallest structure for miles around in your backyard. After the Feds came and went, the neighbors began picking on him. Several of the young boys in the neighborhood started shooting the towers with their BB guns, breaking the bottles and pottery shards. He'd come home from work to find kids climbing on the towers, ripping things apart. He did what he could to keep them off, afraid the kids would get hurt and he'd get in trouble."

"How'd they get through the fence?"

Charlie smiled. "That fence was built only about twenty years ago. Before that, people could come and go whenever they wanted. There are still plenty of people who grew up in the neighborhood who used the climb the towers for fun."

Kate smiled. "That actually sounds pretty cool. I bet the view from the top is impressive."

"Yeah, well, it's probably also pretty dangerous. Some of the cement is crumbling, and there's not a single weld on the whole thing. Simon actually fell from the towers back in the Fifties, and they say he was never the same."

"Wow! How far did he fall?"

"No one knows for sure. A neighbor girl found him one morning at the base of the first tower, moaning incoherently. I think he probably had a traumatic brain injury, but he never went to the hospital. He laid in his bed for a few days, then he got up and packed his bags and left."

"So, do you think he left because of his injuries?"

"I'm sure that probably had something to do with it, but I interviewed a really old woman a couple of years ago who told me Simon left because he had finished his work."

"What does that mean?"

Charlie shook his head as he looked away. "I don't know for sure, but I think that might be part of the story I'm supposed to tell."

No one can lead a happy life, or even one that is bearable, without the pursuit of wisdom, and that the perfection of wisdom is what makes the happy life, although even the beginnings of wisdom make life bearable. Yet this conviction, clear as it is, needs to be strengthened and given deeper roots through daily reflection; making noble resolutions is not as important as keeping the resolutions you have made already.

Seneca the Younger

CHAPTER 6

QUESTIONS

Mankind suffers from two excesses:
to exclude reason, and to live by nothing but reason.
—Blaise Pascal

"So who's Dr. Leslie Hermansen?" Charlie asked, looking down at the notebook.

Kate knew he was avoiding her question, but she decided not to press him, anxious to share some of the things she had gleaned from the notebook.

"She used to work at the state hospital. She compiled that book while she was trying to figure out who Sammy is."

"What did she find out?" he asked, letting the book fall open toward the end, where another hand-scrawled note had been stapled to the page. "What's this?"

Kate glanced over quickly, trying to keep her eyes on the road. It was one of Sammy's notes, written on the back of a long sales receipt.

"That's the note that made her decide to leave."

"Wait, where did she go?"

"To the University of Michigan."

Charlie looked down at the note.

"And this note made her decide to move to Michigan?" he asked after looking at it for thirty seconds and not being able to make heads or tails of it.

Kate nodded. "Call your friend. He has a job for you."

"I see that now that you say it, but how do you decipher that without any help?"

"It's a lot easier when you have a few letters to compare and a little time to think about it."

"Okay, but she must have had more than one friend, right? How would she know which one to call?"

"She wrote that she knew who it was referring to immediately."

He looked at her incredulously.

"Yeah, I know. I'm still trying to work through that in my head."

Charlie flipped through the pages to find Sammy's notes scattered throughout the notebook. "I take it she called her friend and he offered her a job?"

"That's what it says," Kate said, pointing to the notes Dr. Hermansen had written on the pages following Sammy's note.

"How did he know about the job?"

"Sammy?"

"Yeah."

Kate shrugged. "I have no idea. After reading the whole notebook, I think it sounds like Dr. Hermansen found a few answers, but there were still tons of unanswered questions. After she got to know Sammy, she started doing some research on auditory hallucinations. From what I can tell, some of that research attracted the interest of a professor friend in Ann Arbor. He's the one who gave her the job."

"Doesn't this seem a little crazy to you?" he asked as he turned the pages.

"No, it seems *a lot* crazy to me!"

"I can probably guess what an auditory hallucination is, but what does it mean to you—I mean in medical jargon?"

"Probably the same thing it does to you—hearing voices—delusions inspired from things you think you hear."

Charlie furrowed his brows thoughtfully. "That seems to be different than whatever this is," he said, pointing to the note. "I mean, these things…each of the notes you've shown me, they're all real, or…true. There doesn't seem to be anything delusional about them at all."

"I know."

"So, what *is* this then?"

"I wish I knew. This is way beyond anything I learned in school. The only thing I've ever seen that's anything like this was a woman I knew at the care center where I worked for the last couple of summers. She was ninety-something years old and as demented as a rabid bat, but every once in a while, she would scream out something crazy that ended up happening over the next few days."

"That could be helpful," Charlie suggested. "It would be nice to take her with me next time I buy a lottery ticket."

"It was never anything like that. Three times, she told us which patient was going to die next. She was right every time."

"Was she a witch?"

"No, she was a sweet old lady who she seemed to have one foot in this life and one foot in the next. She even accurately predicted the birthday and gender of one of her great-grandchildren, a baby girl, whose parents had already chosen to name their baby after her. I had no explanation for that either, but maybe ..."

"Yes?"

"I don't know how to say it without sounding like I belong in a paranormal psycho movie."

"Why don't you try and I'll let you know how it sounds?"

Kate smiled but hesitated, not wanting to sound stupid. "I guess my question is similar to one Dr. Hermansen posed somewhere in there."

"Which is what?"

She took a deep breath. "It sounds weird saying it out loud, but I've found myself wondering if...well...if someone or something is trying to get our attention but maybe only some people are really listening."

Charlie looked thoughtful for a long moment.

"It almost sounds insane, right?" Kate continued. "But judging from just the two notes I've gotten, I have to believe there's something to..." She shook her head. "Look, I spent a whole month before I came here trying to figure out if this was really where I was supposed to be. I grew up with prayer being a part of my life, and I like to think I got a few answers along the way—but this is different. Dr. Hermansen wrote something in the front of that book," she said, reaching over to turn the pages, pointing to it when she found it.

Open your eyes and heart to possibility.

Charlie read aloud. "Sounds like dangerous advice," he mused.

"I know, right? It sounds like one of those trite phrases you read in a greeting card, but in this context, that advice sounds a little bit more important, like you'll never get this if you don't think way outside the box."

"You said something a minute ago," Charlie said, staring out at the freeway. "Something about having one foot in this life and one foot in the next."

Kate nodded.

"Do you believe that? Do you believe there's something...next?"

"That's a pretty personal question to ask someone you just met two days ago."

He nodded, looking thoughtful.

"What about you?" she asked.

"I asked you first."

"Okay. Then, yes. I believe there is something *next*."

"Are you a Christian?"

"Born and raised. How about you?"

He shook his head. "I don't know. I never had any kind of religion growing up. Even the possibility of there being something out there beyond this life—it's all an enigma. I guess I'd consider myself a skeptic on good days and an agnostic on the rest."

"What's the difference?"

"I'm not sure," he said with a little laugh. "I guess that's why I was intrigued by what you said about what comes next. It's not every day I get to talk to a believer."

Kate smiled. "You make it sound like believers are as rare as leprechauns."

"Aren't they? Especially with people in our generation. I heard recently that something like seventy-six percent of Americans believe in some kind of higher being. Apparently even more believe in some sort of an afterlife. But only around forty percent of people ever talk openly about spiritual beliefs. I guess I wonder why, if so many people believe in something...why don't more of you believers talk about it?"

Kate shrugged. "It's kind of a personal thing, don't you think?"

"Maybe," he said, looking thoughtful. Silence fell between them and lingered awkwardly. As they approached a billboard of a busty woman in a bright purple negligee, Charlie broke the silence pointing at the sign. "Underwear's a personal thing, too, but there it is, in your face, like it or not."

She laughed. "This is a topic I never thought I'd be discussing with you."

"Actually, I'm kind of a fan of purple underwear."

She rolled her eyes. "I was talking about faith."

"You wouldn't think a guy like me would be interested in what people believe?"

"No offense, but my first impression of you was that you were more of a self-absorbed beach bum."

"Wow, thanks! Why did you ask me to come with you, then?"

Kate raised her eyebrows, concentrating on the road. "Let's just say that if it wasn't for that note, I'd probably be here alone."

CHAPTER 7

THE ORACLE

We cannot teach people anything;
we can only help them discover it within themselves.
—Galileo Galilei

It was just before eight o'clock when they pulled next to the curb in front of the Watts Towers Art Center on 107th Street. The friendly conversation they had both enjoyed for the majority of the hour-long trip had come to an awkward halt after Kate had called Charlie a self-absorbed beach bum. She had worried about awkwardness, but she hadn't considered that her words might be the cause of it. She regretted her untempered honesty.

"It looks pretty quiet," Kate said, looking around the deserted, verdant grounds.

"Yeah, well, the center doesn't open until ten."

"What? Why did we come so early?"

Charlie laughed. "Because you wanted to."

"Why didn't you tell me?"

"You didn't ask. I figured you had something in mind."

"What should we do now?"

"Come on, let's go look around."

They got out of the car, and Charlie led them to a colorful bench that stood in the shade of a giant eucalyptus tree that grew between the towers and the art center.

"I brought some bagels," he said, setting his bag down on the bench. He reached in and pulled out a plastic bag with a half dozen bagels jumbled inside. "One of my roommates works at a bagel shop and gets to bring home whatever's left on Saturday night. Help yourself." He handed the bag to Kate.

"What are you kids up to?" someone asked from behind them. They turned to see a barrel-chested, black man in a gray uniform standing near the guard shack.

"Isaiah, good morning! Come join us for a bagel."

"That could only be Charlie George," the man said, shielding his eyes from the sun. "Who'd ya bring with ya?"

"My new friend. Come and meet her."

Isaiah laughed out loud. "Boy, how many girlfriends you brought to see the towers so far?"

"None of your business," Charlie responded with a broad smile as if he had been expecting this very question.

"And you brought me some stale ol' nappy bagels again, tryin' to loosen my tongue, did ya?"

"That's right. I saved a garlic one for you."

"Boy, they all taste like garlic after you put one of them in there with the others, even the fruity ones."

Kate watched him move slowly, each step looking painful, like his hip was out of socket.

"This is my friend, Kate Larsen," Charlie said, making introductions.

Kate turned and took the man's giant hand, looking into his bloodshot eyes and his happy face. "It's nice to meet you," she said, offering him a friendly smile.

"A friend of Charlie George's is a friend of mine. And never you mind me teasin' him 'bout bringing ladies here. He's a good egg, and if you know more 'bout the towers than most of the guides, then I guess you oughta show off every now and again. Ha ha." He clapped Charlie on the shoulder.

"How have you been, old man?"

"Better'an some, not as good as others. You finish your movie?"

"Not yet."

"Boy, I've seen tar that's faster than you."

"Hey, I'm working on it."

Isaiah smiled and nodded. "What brings you to the hood today?"

"Kate did, in her Subaru," Charlie reported, pointing to her car.

Isaiah looked up at the car parked on the street. He looked back at Kate then watched as Charlie slid his camera strap over his head. "I'll be right back," he said, turning around to retreat back to the guard shack.

"You forgot your bagel," Charlie called out.

"Keep it warm for me."

"He's been the head security guard here since the center opened back in the early Seventies," Charlie said as he watched Isaiah hobble back to the shack.

"He doesn't look that old," Kate responded.

"I think he was in his early twenties when he got hired here. He grew up just around the corner. His father actually knew Simon pretty well."

"Does he have a family?"

"Yeah, but his kids are all grown, and the towers are pretty much his life. I think there's only been one time that I've been here when he wasn't."

Kate nodded, taking a bite of her bagel as she stared out across the lawn. "This tastes like garlic," she said, laughing.

"Don't you like garlic?"

"Sure, but not usually on a cinnamon raisin bagel."

"You oughta try the blueberry garlic," Isaiah said, coming up behind them. "It sends a jolt through your system. The way I figure, if you start your mornin' with that in your mouth, your day can only get better from there."

Kate laughed.

"Charlie, how long you been comin' here now?" Isaiah asked.

"Almost five years, why?"

"Just wonderin' why it took so long."

Charlie pivoted on the bench, turning all the way around to face Isaiah. He handed him a bagel, smiling. "Are you trying to tease me about girls again?"

Isaiah shook his head. "You know me better 'an that. There's no tryin' 'round here. I do or I don't."

"So which one is this?"

"Neither," he said soberly, handing him an oversized piece of manila-colored paper with a rough, sophomoric crayon drawing covering most of its surface.

"What's this?" Charlie asked. "Are you making art now?"

"Why don't you take a closer look?"

"It looks like a picture of a bake sale," Charlie said, looking up at Isaiah.

"Almost there. Look again."

Charlie looked back at the drawing. On the left side of the picture were the towers, but under a tree, a table was set up with round cookies. A boy and girl sat behind the table.

"It's cute. Did your grandkids draw this?" Charlie asked.

Isaiah shook his head. "You ain't seein' it, are ya?"

"What am I supposed to see?"

"Boy, you're one of the slowest learners I've ever met." He pointed to the boy. "What color hair does he have?"

"Brown."

"Good. What kinda hair does she have?" he asked, pointing to the girl.

"Blonde and curly."

"Very good. What's hangin' 'round that boy's neck?"

"Uh, a big necklace?"

"Close enough. Where's the sun?"

Charlie looked around, finding a half circle of yellow crayon on the far-left edge by the towers. "It's there, just above the first tower," he said, pointing.

"Okay, what's that down on the bottom there?"

"Uh, it looks like an elephant...or maybe a blue car?" Charlie smiled, looking up. "What's this all about?"

At the mention of the blue car, Kate looked over his shoulder and couldn't believe her eyes. There was no mistaking what she was looking at.

"Why don't you turn your blind eyes around and see where you are," Isaiah said, motioning with his hands to the view before them.

Charlie turned around on the bench and looked out across the lawn to Kate's blue Subaru. As recognition began seeping through his thick head, he looked down at the bench they were sitting on, seeing the bagels laid out like at a bake sale. He looked at Kate's hair, then down at the camera that hung around his neck. Then finally he looked up at the sun, just cresting the top of the shortest tower.

He turned around to find Isaiah smiling. "Is this some kind of parlor trick?" Charlie asked, not sure if he should be amused.

"No, it's way better than that."

He looked down at the picture, then back at Isaiah. "What is this?"

"That's something special. I've only seen a handful of 'em. Everyone of 'em has been a good omen so far."

"A good omen?" He turned to Kate. "Do you know what this is?"

"I think I might."

"Enlighten me."

Kate looked up at Isaiah. "I think it's called an oracle or something like that, right?"

"How did you know that?" He paused, looking down at the picture, then back to Kate. "Of course you knew that. That's you, isn't it?" he said, pointing to the picture. "You're the one we've been waiting for."

CHAPTER 8

THE ONE

Pure truth, like pure gold, has been found unfit for circulation
because men have discovered that it is far more convenient
to adulterate the truth than to refine themselves.
—*Charles Caleb Colton*

"What does that mean, '*the one we've been waiting for*?'" Charlie asked, sounding a little upset. "I've been coming here for almost five years, and this is the first I've heard of any of this. What's going on?"

"Settle down, Charlie," Isaiah said, resting his large hand on Charlie's shoulder. "This is good news."

"It is?"

"Yes. It sounds like your friend here might already know why." He turned his head to Kate.

She smiled nervously. "Umm, I don't know much. I...I just got a note yesterday that...that said I was supposed to come here—and bring Charlie with me."

"This is good," Isaiah responded with a broad smile. "What do you know about this picture?"

Kate shrugged. "I assume it must have been drawn by Sammy?"

"That's right," he said, looking a little surprised, his smile only broadening. "How do you know Sammy?"

"I've actually never met him."

"Where did this picture come from?" Charlie asked, interrupting.

"It's been hanging in my office over there for more than a year."

"Seriously? You didn't just sketch it up real quick?" Charlie asked.

Isaiah laughed. "Are you out of your crazy cracker mind?" He turned the picture over and pointed to the top corner where a date had been written in pen.

Isaiah continued. "Sammy brought that to me last year and asked me to keep my eyes open for this day."

"But what does it mean? Why would he do that?" asked Charlie.

"That's the way Sammy works," Kate answered. "He doesn't communicate like you and me. I'm not even sure if he talks."

"If you've never met him, how'd you know these things?" Isaiah asked, looking at her more closely now.

"How do I know I can trust you?"

The big man smiled. He turned his head from side to side to see that no one was watching before holding his fist out for Kate to see. This was the first time she had seen anyone make the sign described in Dr. Hermansen's notebook, but it made it clear that Isaiah could be trusted.

"Wait, what was that all about?" Charlie asked.

Isaiah ignored him and his question. "I've only met a couple of white folk who know the sign. Who are you?"

"Uhh, well, I just started working at the state hospital. I got one of Sammy's letters on Monday and another one yesterday. And on Friday, I found this notebook in my desk," she said, pulling it from her bag.

Isaiah nodded and smiled. "Well, I'll be. You *are* the one we've been waiting for."

"I am?"

"You don't know?"

"I'm not sure what that means," Kate replied.

"Come on. You're pullin' my leg."

Kate looked at Charlie but was surprised to see that he looked even more confused than she felt. "Why do you think I'm here?"

"You're the interpreter."

"I am?"

"That's why you're here, isn't it?"

"Uh…Dr. Singh didn't say anything about that. To be honest, I don't really know what my job is."

"This don't have anything to do with Dr. Singh, but you know how to talk with your hands, right?"

Kate nodded, looking both surprised and confused. "What's this all about?"

Isaiah smiled at Kate before turning back to Charlie. "I've been wonderin' about you since the beginning."

"What do you mean?" asked Charlie.

Isaiah smiled, nodding as he took another look at the oracle. Without looking up, he spoke again. "You got stuck, didn't you? You tried to make your movie, but you couldn't splain what it was you were sposta to be sayin'."

"How do you know that?"

Isaiah laughed, turning his head back to face Charlie. "'Cause you started askin' the right questions but you never finished."

"What aren't you saying?" asked Charlie, his face registering ever-increasing surprise.

"Charlie, the answers you were after have been here all along, but you couldn't see 'em 'cause you were thinkin' 'bout 'em wrong. Obviously the timin' wasn't right either."

"You make it sound like both of those things are now somehow different."

"I can only hope. But Kate needed to be here, didn't she?"

"Why?" they asked in unison.

"That ain't mine to splain," he said, handing the oracle to Kate. "I still don't know how this works, but that ain't never kept it from workin'. By some unseen hand, the world keeps on spinnin' and the universe keeps puttin' the right people here at just the right time. I don't know what kept you from learnin' the stuff you needed to learn, but it's different now, ain't it?"

Charlie laughed apprehensively. "You're making me nervous, old man."

"Why?"

"Because it feels like I'm watching an elaborate conspiracy unfold in front of me. Is this some kind of a gag you two came up with to freak me out?" he asked, looking back and forth between them.

Kate and Isaiah turned to each other and laughed.

"Why would we do that?" she asked.

"I have no idea. So what's the gag?" Charlie asked, trying to smile.

"This aint no gag," Isaiah responded. "I've never talked to this girl in my life."

Charlie looked even more uncertain. "Okay...so...do you have any idea why I'm here today?"

Isaiah nodded. "I think I've got a pretty good idea."

"Really?"

"Sure. You're here to do what you were made to do."

Charlie's only response was a look of confusion.

"Boy, why'd you study film?"

"Because I wanted to tell stories that make a difference in the world."

"So when you gonna start?"

"Excuse me?"

"You heard me. I know what you've been doin' with all that talent inside you."

"You do?"

"I know I'm old, but it only takes a Google search to figure out how you're spendin' your time."

Charlie looked away. "I'm just trying to earn a living."

"S'pose so, but it seems to me you've been takin' the easy way out. You got scared of what you're sposta be doin', and you ran away from it."

"Hey, a man's gotta eat."

"Yeah, we all do. But the thing is, I don't see that gettin' ya any closer to where you're sposta be."

"Since when are you my judge?" Charlie asked defensively.

"Not judgin'—just observin' what's goin' on and seein' someone who's got talent and's been pissin' it away."

Charlie shook his head, looking upset. "What am I supposed to do, Isaiah?"

Isaiah pursed his oversized lips and nodded. "That right there is the question that matters. That's the question you shoulda been askin' all along."

"Huh?"

"We all got somethin' to do, Charlie. We're all here on this big blue planet for a reason. I knew you had somethin' big to do here when you first started comin' 'round. You got a big story to tell. But you stopped askin' questions. You either got lazy or scared or both. The door's been open for a couple of years already, and you've been goin' every way but through it."

Charlie looked thoughtful, but didn't respond.

"It's like this," Isaiah continued. "The hand of Providence opens and closes doors every day, but this door's been waitin' open for you for a long time."

"Do you know what I'm supposed to do with it?"

"Not exactly...but you do."

Charlie looked down at his feet.

"Yep. I saw that light go on in your noggin almost five years ago. You knew then what you were sposta do. What happened?"

"I got stuck," he said defensively.

"I'd say you got stuck! In a big ol' pit of your own silly fears and pride you got stuck!"

Charlie smiled, shaking his head. "Okay, if you're so smart, what am

I supposed to do about it?"

Isaiah laughed. "You know that better'n me."

"I'm not sure I do."

"Maybe not the whole picture, but you know 'nough to take the next step. That's all you need. You probably ain't gonna see the big picture till you're well into it, but you fo' sure ain't gonna see the second step till you take the first. It seems to me that you're sposta get back to what you started and stop lettin' things get in your way. I hope you know the universe don't usually keep doors open like this."

"So, why did it do it for me?"

"I think you must have somethin' big to do here."

"How do you know that?"

"I heard it on the wind, almost five years ago." Isaiah said quietly, almost whispering, his face looking up at the branches overhead.

"If you know what needs to be done, why don't *you* do it?"

Isaiah shook his head. "That ain't my job. That ain't why I'm here."

"Why *are* you here?"

"To protect the towers so people like you two can come and discover for themselves what the universe wants 'em to do."

Charlie nodded, letting out a long, resigned breath.

"Do you know what that means?" Kate asked incredulously.

Charlie grimaced. "That...that's the film I'm supposed to make."

"I thought you said the film was supposed to be about that Rodeo guy."

"Rodia. Yeah, he's a big part of it too."

"Do you also know why I'm here?" she turned and asked Isaiah.

The big man shrugged his broad shoulders. "Not exactly, but the fact that you've got that notebook and that you've already gotten a couple of Sammy's messages—and that you came here with Charlie on this day—that's gotta mean somethin'...somethin' big. I've seen a handful o' Sammy's oracles over the years, but nothin' quite like this. Thing is, nobody comes here by accident. People are either lookin' for somethin' or they're here 'cause there's somethin' for 'em to do."

"Why didn't you tell me any of this before?" Charlie asked, looking to Isaiah.

"Would you have heard it?"

Charlie shrugged.

"I tried—many times I tried. You weren't ready to hear it."

"What makes you think I am now?"

"Can't say for certain, but the universe seems to have been anxiously waitin' for you to get over yourself so you can move forward."

CHAPTER 9

LISTENING

Truth is the offspring of silence and meditation.
—*Isaac Newton*

"So, what's the first step?" Kate asked.

"You came here to see the towers, didn't you?" Isaiah responded.

"Yeah, but they're not open until ten, right?" Kate replied.

"Nope. The center opens at ten. The tours don't start until noon on Sundays."

She looked disappointed.

"But as luck would have it," Isaiah continued with a broad smile, "Charlie here's one of the few people we've ever let in to give his own tours."

"You'd still let me do that?"

Isaiah nodded. "I've been waitin' for this day for a long time."

"And what day is that exactly?" Charlie asked, one eyebrow raised playfully.

"I'm hopin' it's the day that you finally start doin' what you were made to do."

Charlie nodded thoughtfully as he turned to look up at the towers.

"I got a good feelin' 'bout this. This story's been waitin' more than ninety years to be told," Isaiah continued.

"Are you talking about Simon's story?" Charlie asked.

The big man shook his head. "There've been lotsa folks who've come here over the years, tryin' to figure out what this is all about. Most of 'em have focused on Simon or the towers, but not one of 'em have focused on what changed Sabato to Sam and later to Simon."

Kate looked at the men, confused.

Charlie nodded but kept his eyes on Isaiah. "What makes you so sure that's the story I'm supposed to tell?"

"I told you once that if you focus on the man, as others have, your story'll be limited in power. And by so doin', you'll deny the power that can change hearts and minds fo'ever."

Charlie nodded again, but Kate's look of confusion only grew broader. "I'll explain later," he assured her.

"Simon always said that he wanted to do somethin' big," Isaiah continued, staring up at the towers. "The work he left behind's proof that he did what he set out to do. But if you look a little closer—if you open your heart—you'll see these towers were built for a bigger purpose. People come from all over the world to see 'em—they come and are surprised not only by their beauty but, if they've got any heart at all, they leave feelin' somethin'…somethin' bigger. Ever since you started comin' 'round, askin' all your questions, I've been hopin' you're the one who's gonna tell that story."

Charlie looked humble but also hopeful.

"I had to get swallowed by a whale once too before I finally figured out what I needed to be doin'."

"Is that some kind of metaphor?" he asked, looking confused.

Isaiah laughed. "Yes and no. I s'pose we all have our Jonah moments—knowin' what we're sposta be doin' but afraid of doin' it.

You know what I mean? Most of us have to be swallowed by some kind of whale and wallow in our own messes for a while before we're humble enough to listen to that little voice inside our hearts. Fo' me, it was knowin' I was sposta come *back* here."

Charlie looked both surprised and confused. "Come back here? I guess I assumed you always lived here."

"Most of it, 'cept the four years I spent playin' ball at Penn State."

"Wait, you went to college?" Charlie responded, —and immediately wished he hadn't sounded so surprised.

Isaiah nodded affirmatively. "Class o' 1974."

"What did you study?" Kate asked.

"Anthropology."

"You never told me about that. And you played football too?" Charlie responded.

Isaiah nodded. "You never asked."

"What did you want to do with your degree?" Charlie asked, looking at Isaiah as if for the first time.

"I wanted to get a graduate degree, maybe a PhD. But what I really wanted was to do field work—to travel the world and learn to understand people and cultures and their stories."

"Why didn't you?"

"Long story. The short of it is that I was sposta do somethin' different and I knew it. That little voice kept tellin' me to go home—that I was sposta be here." Isaiah laughed and mopped his hand over his face. "There's an old Yiddish proverb I heard when I was livin' back East. "Man plans, and God laughs." I think about that all the time, and I s'pose that's what it's all about—learnin' to know that some plans are better fo' you than others—learnin' how to choose the one you're sposta choose, even when it hurts at first."

"You is where you is sposta be," Kate mused, knowingly.

"Pardon?"

"That was the first message I got from Sammy. 'You is where you is sposta be.'" She opened up the notebook and pulled out the wrinkled note, handing it to Isaiah. He took the note and looked it over, smiling.

"You understood what this says?"

"Yes. I mean no…not at first. I thought it was just scribbles the first time I saw it. I guess…I guess I had to try a little harder to understand."

Isaiah nodded, looking down at the note again. "You had to be ready to hear it."

Kate looked at him, confused, wondering what he meant.

"Lotsa folks would've thrown this away, thinkin' it was only garbage." Isaiah said, handing the note back to Kate.

"Yeah, I almost did."

Isaiah looked thoughtful. "What was goin' through your head when you 'scovered what the message said?"

Kate thought about it, remembering how she had found the note for the second time, crumpled up on the floor of her car. "I…I was feeling overwhelmed; wondering why I came here; thinking I'd made a big mistake."

"And you found that note at just that moment?"

"Well, no. I mean, I first found it on Monday. It was stuck to my windshield when I finished work. I didn't really give it a chance until…" She faded out, looking very thoughtful.

"Until you was good'n ready, right?" Isaiah suggested.

Kate nodded, remembering how she had disregarded the note when she had first found it, but how, just a few days later, it had become the answer she had been looking for—the answer she needed.

"Ain't it peculiar how the message was there, just waitin' fo' you to be ready?"

Kate nodded as she considered his words.

"And you said you've received another message?"

"Yes, just yesterday," she said, handing him the second note.

Isaiah read the second note before looking up with a smile. "What would you have thought if this message was the first message you ever got?"

Kate snickered. "I wouldn't have understood any of it. I'm sure I would have thrown it away, thinking it was just...somebody's litter."

"Yes, and this oracle woulda had to wait for 'nother day—'nother time—to be fulfilled," Isaiah said, pointing to Sammy's drawing.

"What in the world is going on here?" Charlie asked, looking more confused than ever.

"Oh, I think it's somethin' much bigger 'an this world," Isaiah responded, smiling.

"Huh?"

"You may not know exactly what I am talkin' 'bout yet, but you've surely seen enough to know there's somethin' much bigger 'an this world alone goin' on here."

Charlie nodded. "Can you tell me what it is?"

"I think you've known what it is fo' a long time; you've just been too scared to let yourself see it."

Charlie looked away uncomfortably, staring across the grassy field.

Isaiah rested his hands on Charlie's shoulders. "What do you see when you look out there?

"Uh, Kate's car?" he responded lamely, as if he'd just been asked a dumb question.

"Yes, but focus in a little closer."

"Grass."

"Wow! Very observant. What else?"

"Dandelions."

"And?"

"And what? I don't understand what you're asking me."

"I'm suggestin' that you usually see the obvious things—the big things—but you're missin' the fine details. Just a take a minute and look."

Kate turned and did the same, focusing her attention on the lawn in front of them. After only twenty seconds, Charlie interrupted the silence and turned his head to look up at Isaiah. "Is there a point to this?"

"Shhh," Isaiah responded, his eyes closed. "Sometimes you gotta close your eyes in order to see clearly."

Charlie looked at Kate, who smiled before closing her eyes and turning back to face the grassy field. Charlie reluctantly followed suit.

A full minute passed before Isaiah patted Charlie's shoulders. "What'd ya observe?"

"Uh, the inside of my eyelids."

Isaiah pursed his lips and shook his head, looking disappointed. "How 'bout you, Miss Kate?"

"Umm, I heard the rustling of the leaves on the trees behind us and...I heard the sound of a helicopter."

"Very good. D'you observe anything closer to home?"

Kate thought for a moment before shaking her head.

"Let's try this again, but this time, close your eyes and just listen to the sounds right next to you."

Charlie shook his head impatiently, wondering if Isaiah was for real. He turned to look back at him. But Isaiah's eyes were already closed, and a pleasant smile was on his lips. Reluctantly, Charlie closed his eyes and waited for this exercise to be over so he could get on with other things.

After what felt like much longer than a minute, Isaiah spoke again. "What'd you observe this time?" he asked calmly.

"I heard the birds in the tree behind us," Kate offered. "Have they been there the whole time?"

Isaiah nodded. "There's a family of robins in the eucalyptus. The eggs just hatched last Sunday, and the chicks are finally startin' to sing more than just screamin' to be fed."

Kate smiled, imagining a nest full of ugly chicks being fed by two red-breasted parents.

Charlie focused his listening, searching for the sound of birds, and finally heard them for the first time.

"How about you?" Isaiah asked.

"Uh, I heard a motorcycle, probably a Harley or something—must have been a few blocks away."

Isaiah nodded. "Not bad. Let's try this one more time. But this time, I want you to try to block out everything beyond ten feet in any direction."

Kate nodded, obviously much more interested in this exercise than Charlie. Again, a long silence followed.

"What'd you hear?" Isaiah finally asked.

"Bees," Kate said looking surprised. She opened her eyes and saw them, dozens of them visiting the hundreds of dandelions scattered across the lawn. "Have they really been there the whole time?" she asked, surprised by her own inability to recognize what was right at her feet.

"From sunup to sundown every day. I heard there's a man who lives through the block who keeps bees in his backyard. I think these must be his."

Charlie looked at the bees, surprised by both the sight and sound he observed once they had been pointed out to him.

"What did you hear?" Kate asked, turning to Isaiah.

"I've probably had more practice than you."

Charlie nodded, laughing.

"In 'dition to the bees and the wind in the trees, I heard the three of us breathin'. I heard the sound of my own heart beatin'. And I heard Michael Bublé singin' on Charlie's headphones in his backpack."

"Seriously?" Charlie asked, unzipping the front pocket of his backpack, where his iPhone was stowed. He pulled it out to see Michael Bublé's name displayed on the device's cracked screen. He quickly silenced the barely audible sound emanating from his earbuds. "How could you have possibly heard that?" he asked, turning to look at Isaiah.

"I doubt I would've if I hadn't been listenin'."

"Yeah, but it was right next to me, and I couldn't hear it."

Isaiah smiled. "Most of us only hear the loudest things around us, but if we'll slow down and really listen, we'll see there's a lot more goin' on than what we naturally p'ceive. The bees were tendin' to the dandelions when you kids crossed the lawn to sit down here. You walked right through the middle of their breakfast, but you didn't see 'em till you slowed down 'nough to listen. The same is usually true of the most important voices in life, which often get drowned out by the din and babel of our noisy world. Those voices are there all the time, but there ain't many folks who choose to stop and listen."

Kate nodded, remembering what she had read in the notebook. "Is that what Sammy is, then? Is he a listener?"

"What gave you that idea?" Isaiah asked, looking surprised.

"Uh, well, I have the advantage of this notebook."

Isaiah looked down at the notebook in her lap and nodded. "We each got our own set of gifts and weaknesses, don't we? Dr. Hermansen was gifted in many ways, but one's gift can also become one's weakness."

"I'm not sure I understand," Kate responded. "Did you know Dr. Hermansen?"

"We were acquainted, yes. She's a smart gal."

"But?" Kate asked after he offered nothing more.

"But knowledge is limited, ain't it? And just 'cause you got a couple o' letters after your name, that don't mean you understand everythin' there is to know. Some things can't be understood or even diagnosed in a couple of visits. She probably did as good a job as she coulda with what she had, but she limited herself."

"How? What do you mean?"

"It seemed to me that she was tryin' to fit Sammy into a category—somethin' she could label, diagnose, and treat. Some things can't be understood correctly without an open mind. And sometimes the only treatment is reverence and respect."

Kate nodded. "From what she wrote, it sounded like she was frustrated that she couldn't figure him out."

"Oh, she probably did better than most docs, but she had a hard time lettin' go, comin' to grips with the cold facts that many things were beyond clinical understandin'. A lot of docs think they know it all, that all of life can be boiled down to a few common elements. But even though we can temporarily gain some control over a few things, we'll never—with our puny, finite minds—gain control or even understandin' over everything. Some foolishly believe they can play God, but they inevitably lose...or are humbled in the end."

"So, which one was she?" Kate asked after a moment's thought.

Isaiah looked up at the towers and smiled. "Leslie learned to listen."

CHAPTER 10

T H E W I N D

In faith there is enough light for those who want to believe
and enough shadows to blind those who don't.
—*Blaise Pascal*

Kate looked up at him, curious about all his response might entail. She noticed that Isaiah seemed distracted, focusing on something beyond her view.

"My daddy used to tell me that if I was hungry for understandin' and humble 'nough to ask the right questions, then I'd always find teachers who could teach me the things I needed to know," Isaiah reported.

"Yeah? How's that worked out for you so far?" Charlie asked, challengingly.

"Splendidly!"

"I wish I could say the same," he responded.

"Yes, well, sometimes when you don't get the answers right away, you just have to keep askin'. Sometimes it's just a matter of longevity."

"What are you saying?"

"I guess I'm sayin' that when the teacher is ready," Isaiah responded, turning his body and raising his large, fleshy hand to the far side of the towers, "the students are wise to show up."

Charlie's and Kate's eyes followed Isaiah's line of sight to where a man was sitting on the concrete seats that formed the small amphitheater on the north side of the towers. They stood to better see him. He was dressed in faded jeans, and a dark hoodie was pulled over his head, cinched up so only his face was exposed.

"Who's that?" Charlie asked.

"That's the man who's been waitin' for you to be ready."

"Sammy?" Kate asked.

"The one and only."

"Will you introduce us?"

"Perhaps. He may be too busy, but we could give it a try."

Kate and Charlie quickly gathered up their things, and Isaiah led them across the lawn. Sammy's head was raised and turned toward the towers, his shiny, dark face bathed in sunlight. They noticed that his eyes were closed but his hands were busy, scrawling something on a pad of paper with a black Magic Marker.

"Watch him," Isaiah said, stopping a short distance from him.

They watched as Sammy finished whatever he was writing, tore the paper from the pad, set it to his side on a small pile of similar papers, and began again with a new note, never once opening his eyes.

"What is he doing?" Charlie whispered.

"He's listenin'," Isaiah responded, obviously making no attempt to lower his voice.

"What do you mean?"

"He's getting messages."

"What kind of messages?"

Isaiah shrugged.

They watched as he ripped another note off the pad, setting it on the pile at his side as he had before, his pen moving quickly to begin another note. As they continued to watch, a gentle breeze blew past them, sweeping three notes off the top of the pile. Becoming airborne, the papers began to gather height, floating and flying weightlessly before disappearing quickly beyond the tops of the trees.

"What's going on?" Charlie asked, reaching for the lens cap on his camera.

Isaiah stopped him, placing his large hand on Charlie's camera. "This isn't part of your story, at least not yet."

Charlie looked surprised. "How do you know?"

"'Cause I do. If you focus on him, your story'll go the wrong direction. Just watch."

"But what's he doing?" Charlie persisted.

"I told ya. He's listenin'."

Charlie looked confused. "If he's listening, why can't he hear us?"

"Cause he's deaf."

"*What?*"

Isaiah turned to face Charlie. "Sammy was beaten by a foster parent when he was only three. Both of his ears were ripped off, and the infection that came after left him stone deaf."

"Dr. Hermansen said he wears headphones most of the time. Is that to cover his scars?"

"Yes, it's either headphones or a hoody."

Charlie shook his head, looking angry. "Who would do that to a little kid?"

"Someone who didn't want him hearin' what he was hearin'."

"I don't understand," Charlie said as Sammy ripped another note from the pad.

"Me neither, but that don't keep it from workin'."

"Are those notes like the ones I got?" Kate asked.

Isaiah shook his head. "Each one's different."

Kate looked thoughtful, remembering the two notes she had received and the others she had seen in the notebook. "Where do the messages come from?"

"You don't know?"

'No. I mean, Dr. Hermansen thought they were either psychotic babble or auditory hallucinations. I think she thought Sammy was schizophrenic."

"Yes, but she changed her mind, didn't she?"

Kate nodded. "She suggested that in her notebook, but she didn't say exactly how her diagnosis had changed."

"Sammy musta had some kinda major impact on the way she thought 'bout people—the way she thought 'bout life and our place in the universe."

"Tell me about that," Kate responded. "Tell me what it was that changed her mind."

"You don't know?"

"I don't think so."

Isaiah smiled and nodded. "There are only two things that change people's minds—that open them up to learning."

"Truth?" Charlie asked.

"Yes, that's the easy one. But truth alone ain't really ever 'nough, is it?"

Charlie looked confused.

"Truth's all around us, Charlie. We breathe it in every day, but still most of us are still walkin' 'round actin' like ignernt fools. I think it was Winston Churchill who used to say that 'Man will occasionally stumble over the truth, but most the time we will pick ourselves up and carry on.'"

Charlie nodded thoughtfully.

"No, truth all by its lonesome don't have the power to change the human heart. There's somethin' else much bigger that's needed for the kind of learnin' that matters."

Charlie and Kate looked at each other.

"A good teacher?" Charlie asked, looking unsure of his answer.

"That don't hurt, but good teachers often don't get any farther than bad teachers if the student ain't ready."

"Patience?" Kate asked.

"Another helpful ingredient, but not what I was goin' for."

Kate and Charlie looked at each other again. "Can you give us a hint?" she asked.

"Yep, but only a hint. When you discover it for yourself it always means more. Like truth, it's all around you, but you usually don't know it till your eyes of understandin' are open. There're lotsa smart folks who never know it—whose understandin' is limited 'cause they never get it. I tell you, that's the ingredient that changed Sabato to Sam and Sam to Simon. That's why he built these towers. That's why he spent thirty-three years of his life building them as big as he could, hopin' others might come and feel somethin' and learn to know what he knows.

"If you tell folks what it is they're here for, you take away all the fun of 'em findin' out for themselves. But if you plant a seed—if you tell 'em there's more to see than just some happy-lookin' towers, some of 'em will look a little deeper. Some of 'em'll see a little bit more. Some'll walk away and think you're mad. But fo' some," he said, raising one eyebrow, "Fo' some, that seed'll start to grow. It'll grow tall and bright and blossom into a million flowers and bear fruits that nourish and strengthen others. Charlie, you already sniffed those flowers and got a nibble of that fruit."

"I did?" he asked, looking very confused.

Isaiah nodded. "You may not know what it is yet, but you know it's more'n what you see. And there's somethin' in you that's been tellin' you for years that whatever it is, you gotta have more of it and you gotta use your gifts the universe has given you to help others see it too. Ain't that right?"

Charlie looked surprised but nodded. "How come you've never said any of this before?"

"I did."

"When? What are you talking about?"

"Every time you asked, I threw you a bone, didn't I? 'Look here,' I said. 'Think about this,' I told you. 'Talk to this person or that person,' I suggested. Each of those things got you closer to seein' the big picture, didn't they?"

Charlie looked thoughtful then nodded slowly.

"You got closer to seein' the big picture than most, but you stopped askin' questions. How come?"

Charlie took a deep breath and exhaled slowly. "I guess I worried I was going in too deep."

"What were you scared of?"

He shrugged, looking away.

"What were you scared of?" Isaiah repeated.

"I was afraid that people would think I was crazy, that I'd become some kind of an obsessed fanatic. There are plenty of wackos in this world already. I didn't want to lose any chance of getting where I want to be."

Isaiah smiled.

"What's so funny?"

"Did you ever hear the story of the young fool who sold his ranch in Texas and headed to the California gold fields, dreaming of gold nuggets the size of oranges?"

Charlie shook his head, wondering where Isaiah was going.

"Yep, he arrived a little too late. He wasted his treasure and his youth chasin' the dream of fast money. In the meantime, back on his ranch in Texas, the new owner 'scovered a different kind of gold seepin' up through the soil. It turned out to be one of the richest oil fields this country ever knew. The funny thing is, the man who came searchin' for gold thought it was just gunky water. It was right under his feet the whole time—he just ain't never looked close 'nough to see it for what it was. We all do that. We all miss out on what's right in front of us, distracted by our own impatience and pride."

Charlie forced a smile. "What is it that you think I missed?"

"The gold."

"Are you talking literally or figuratively?"

"Both," Isaiah responded without hesitation.

"So, how do I find it?"

The big man smiled. "Well, to begin with, you gotta believe there's more to know than what you got already. And you gotta want a piece of it—not just to know somethin' other people don't know to make yourself look like a smarty-pants or to show off to the ladies. But to want a piece of it 'cause you're gonna use it for good."

"What does he have to do with it?" Charlie asked, nodding at Sammy.

Isaiah turned and looked at Sammy for a long moment before turning back to Charlie. "I don't know. Maybe nothin'."

"But I thought you said he…"

"Yeah, I really don't know what the plan is from here."

"Then how do you know my film's not supposed to be about him?"

"That much I do know. He obviously wanted you here—now—together. I've never known what the plan is, but somehow it always works out."

"So…we're here because of some cryptic note, *and there's no plan*?"

"Of course there's a plan. There's always a plan."

"So what are we supposed to do, wait for the heavens to open and the angels to toot their trumpets?"

"Now you're just bein' sassy."

"Isaiah, I'm looking at the most interesting thing I've seen around here in the last five years, and you're telling me he's not part of it?"

Kate shook her head. "That's not why we came here, Charlie."

"Oh, really? *Why did we come here*?" he asked impatiently.

"We came here so you could show me the towers."

"But what about him?" Charlie asked. "He drew a picture of us being here. He knew we were coming. And here he is, sending letters by… by *wind-mail*, and I'm supposed to just walk away and pretend I'm not seeing it. This is bull!"

"Charlie, you didn't know anything about this an hour ago. I don't know why you're getting so excited about this now. Let's just do what we came here to do," Kate responded.

"You're kidding me, right? You're watching this, and you wanna just walk away."

"No, I don't, but my gut's telling me to stick to the plan. If I'm supposed to be an interpreter, I'm pretty sure we'll get our chance to talk to him."

Another gust of wind interrupted them, tousling the highest leaves on the eucalyptus before bearing down and racing smoothly across the lawn, parting the dandelions in its path. Curiously, it circled Kate, lifting the blonde tips of her hair above her head and swirling them about, then jumped to Charlie, where it quickly rearranged his hair as well before moving on to Sammy. Here, as it had done before, the wind took hold of the pile of Sammy's notes, lifting them into the air like a flock of butterflies.

Charlie instinctively reached for his camera, but Isaiah seemed to anticipate his movement. Again, he placed his hand on top of the barrel of the lens without taking his eyes off the paper notes now swirling in a spiraling tower, rising higher and higher. When the spinning column of paper reached what looked like the same height as the tallest towers, they began spreading out in every direction, tumbling and spinning higher and broader until they had all disappeared.

"You're killing me, Isaiah. What the hell's going on here?" Charlie asked, his eyes wide open.

"I assure you this ain't got nothin' to do with hell," Isaiah responded. "And watch your mouth, young man. There's a lady present."

"I'm sorry, but what just happened?" he responded, pointing to the sky.

"The wind...well, the wind stopped in to pick up the outgoin' mail."

"But, the wind...all those notes...they just...what the...? What just happened here?"

Isaiah turned to Kate. "I assume you know about this?"

Kate nodded. "I read about it in the notebook, but I didn't imagine it being so...beautiful. Is this always how it happens?"

Isaiah shook his head. "I think it must be showin' off for you today."

"Wait a second," Charlie interrupted. "You make it sound like... this...whatever it is, happens all the time."

Isaiah simply nodded.

"Isaiah, I've been around here a million times, and I've never seen anything like this."

"No, but then you haven't been lookin' for it, have you?"

Charlie looked at Sammy, then back to Isaiah. "Would I have seen him before?"

"If you'd been lookin', yes."

"Does he hang out here a lot?"

"You could say that."

"Why? I mean, what is he doing?"

"I already told you. He's listenin'. He's a listener."

"Yeah, but you also told me he was deaf. How can he...?"

"That's the question, ain't it?"

"Well, yeah, I mean...how...what is he listening to anyway?"

"He ain't gettin' this, is he?" Isaiah asked, turning to Kate.

Kate shook her head. "I don't know if I'm too far ahead of him."

"But you know what he's listening to?"

"Uh, I'm still trying to wrap my head around it, but yeah, I think so."

"Then please tell me," Charlie pleaded.

"Well...I only know what I've read, but it seems like...like Sammy has some kind of a connection to the wind, right?" she asked, looking to Isaiah for reassurance.

He nodded encouragingly.

"Dr. Hermansen said that he's been hearing voices since he was a little kid."

"That's right."

"What kind of voices?" Charlie asked.

"There are really only two kinds," Isaiah answered.

"The kind you can hear and the kind you can't?" Charlie guessed, looking impossibly confused.

Isaiah shook his head "Good and evil. Sammy hears both kinds, but unlike the rest of us, he's learned to keep his ears tuned to the good."

Charlie looked confused. "But if he's deaf...I've heard of people losing an arm or leg and feeling phantom pains in their missing limb. Is it like that? Does he hear phantom voices?"

Isaiah shook his head. "It ain't nothin' like that. To be honest, like I said before, I don't know how it works. I've got my theories, but I got no way of provin' 'em."

"What's your theory then?" Charlie asked.

"I think Sammy's listenin' to the same wind that 'spired Simon to build those," Isaiah responded, turning his head to look up at the towers.

Charlie turned to look at the towers also, the sun blinding him. "What does that mean?"

"It means they still work," Isaiah responded, smiling broadly.

"I don't understand," Kate said. "There's obviously some kind of connection between Sammy and the towers, but tell us what's going on here."

"Do you know the history of this place?" Isaiah asked, looking at Kate.

She shook her head.

"But you know 'bout Simon Rodia, right?"

"Uh, not really. I just know that he built the towers, right?"

Isaiah turned to Charlie and shook his head. "You ain't much of a tour guide, are ya?"

"I was getting there," Charlie laughed.

"Then you should start there," he replied, reaching deep into the pocket of his gray uniform pants and producing a keychain, which he tossed to Charlie. He glanced at the gold watch on his wrist before looking up. "Folks'll start arrivin' soon. You best get movin' if you want any privacy."

"But what about him?" Charlie asked, pointing to Sammy.

"If he wants to meet you, he'll be here when you're done. Otherwise, you'll have to get acquainted some other time."

"But..."

"No buts. Best just to get on with what you came here to do."

Charlie looked reluctant to leave, watching Sammy continue to write the notes, apparently oblivious to his surroundings and the conversation that had taken place only twenty feet from his side.

Kate slid the notebook into the bag slung over her shoulder while Charlie thanked Isaiah for letting them in. As they walked across the lawn to the tall gate, Kate noticed that Charlie's eyes were glued to Sammy. "What are you thinking?" she asked as they reached the fence.

"I'm trying to figure out if Isaiah is protecting him from me or me from him."

"Why does it need to be either one?"

"You saw how guarded he was. He's never stopped me from taking pictures of anything. I've got thousands of pics and dozens of hours of footage of this place and the people who come here. I'm just wondering why this is any different."

Kate nodded, remaining silent. As Charlie inserted the key into the lock, she glanced back at Sammy, who, for the briefest moment, opened his eyes and looked their way before resuming his previous stoic posture, staring up at the sun with his eyes closed as he had been before. But this time, his large lips were drawn up in a smile.

A grateful heart is a beginning of greatness. It is an expression of humility. It is a foundation for the development of such virtues as prayer, faith, courage, contentment, happiness, love, and well-being.

James E. Faust

CHAPTER 11

SLOW STARTS

The unexamined life is not worth living.
—Socrates

"I really can't believe I'm walking away from that," Charlie whined, closing the tall gate slowly behind them. Pressing his face to the gate, he looked to see Sammy still sitting with his face toward the sun, his hand busily writing notes. Recognizing that Isaiah had disappeared into the guard shack, he raised his camera to his eye.

"That's not why we're here," Kate said, resting her hand on his shoulder.

"I can't let this go."

"Yes, you can. It will only distract you from the story you're supposed to tell."

"How do you know?" he asked defiantly, his eye glued to the viewfinder and his index finger resting haltingly on the shutter button.

The lens spun and hummed, unable to focus on the man, the tight wire of the gate confusing the camera's focus. Charlie adjusted a knob and tried again, but the camera refused to focus on Sammy.

"Charlie, that's not why we're here," she repeated. "Don't get distracted."

He took a deep breath, frustrated, before lowering his camera. "I've never had this problem before. My battery must be low," he said, turning his back to the gate, staring down at his camera. He made another adjustment and lifted the camera to the towers. Immediately the shutter clicked multiple times. Quickly, he swung back around and went back to the fence, intent on capturing a picture of the man. But just as it had before, the lens refused to focus on his desired subject.

"Charlie, don't get distracted," Kate repeated. "We came here for a tour. Come on, let's get on with it."

The lens purred as it zoomed in and out, refusing to focus. Charlie cursed under his breath, his frustration growing.

"It's not going to work, Charlie."

"I've got to get this," he responded, leaning his shoulder against the fence for stability. He wrestled with the camera for another full minute, making several adjustments, but to no avail. The lens simply refused to focus on the man on the other side of the fence.

"Charlie, stop this!" she said forcefully. "We're wasting time."

"I know what I'm doing," he said, pointing to the camera. "Why won't it work?"

"Maybe for the same reason you haven't been able to finish your documentary."

He looked up, his eyes wild, almost scary.

"Maybe you've been focusing on the wrong thing."

He shook his head. "And how would you know? You hadn't even heard of the towers a week ago. What makes you think you're an expert?"

"Whoa, calm down. I never said I was."

"So how do you know it's not about him?"

"You mean other than the fact that Isaiah didn't leave any question about that? My gut's telling me that we should listen to him and do what we came here to do."

He shook his head again, still fumbling with his camera. He raised the lens once more to the towers and pressed the shutter button. The camera responded as it had before, firing off several frames. For a third time, he returned to the gate, aiming the lens in the direction of the peculiar man. And for the third time, the camera refused to focus. "Stupid piece of crap!" he muttered angrily.

"My dad used to always say that it's a sad man who has to blame his tools for his own ineptitude."

Charlie laughed out loud. "Are you always so infuriating?" he asked, turning again from the fence.

"Only when I don't know how else to get someone's attention. Look, if he's supposed to be part of the story, he'll still be here when we finish what we came here to do."

"Kate, you saw what happened out there. Doesn't that scream for your attention?"

"I'm not saying it doesn't. Whatever it is that's going on there, it's compelling and definitely one of the more intriguing things I've ever seen. But what were you planning on doing? You can't just accost him with your camera and expect him to tell you how all that magic works with the wind and his letters, and…" She looked up, distracted as several more pieces of paper tumbled acrobatically through the air overhead, carried aloft by some unexplainable, unseen force.

Charlie quickly raised his camera to his eye, but the papers were gone before he could find them in his viewfinder. "You know what I can't believe?"

"What?"

"I can't believe Isaiah never told me about this."

"Maybe he's protecting Sammy from people like you."

"What's that supposed to mean?"

"Charlie, could you imagine how much trouble and chaos you would create for a guy like Sammy if you opened this up to the world? I know enough from reading this notebook that there are a lot of people who are trying to protect Sammy."

"From what?"

"From people like you who would throw a video up on YouTube and ruin a guy's life."

"Are you kidding? He'd be famous before the sun set."

"Being famous isn't always a good thing."

"Speak for yourself. Would you deny this guy the opportunity to be rich—to get out of this hell hole—to live a better life?"

"No, I wouldn't want to deny him any of that. I'm just saying I don't think you're the one who should get to make that decision for him. And besides, I don't think he needs you. He seems to be doing just fine on his own."

"Pssshh. Look around you. We're in the middle of a freakin' slum. We could take this show on the road—get him out of here."

Kate shook her head. "Are you listening to yourself? You don't know anything about him, and from the sounds of it, you're making this way more about you than I think you probably should. No wonder Isaiah didn't introduce us."

"What do you mean?"

"My notebook says this community has been protecting Sammy for most of his life. They're definitely not going to let someone like you sweep in and carry him off to the circus like he's some kind of freak show."

Charlie shook his head and looked away. "So if you have all the answers, why am I here?"

"I'm not sure what you're asking."

"I'm a filmmaker. I try to make films about compelling stories. Yeah, if I'm lucky, I make a few bucks along the way. There's nothing wrong with that. A guy's got to live, and I know a good story when I see one. I'd make him the same offer I made you yesterday when you went sailing off the boardwalk. We could all benefit from it."

Kate looked disappointed. "Do you ever do anything without thinking about the money—about what's in it for you?"

He laughed. "Ya know, I've met plenty of starving artists, and as far as I can tell, the lifestyle is totally overrated. Besides, it's a terrible business model. There's not a lot that I learned from my old man, but he did teach me that you should never leave money on the table. You either got to run with it yourself or expect someone else will."

"What about doing something for the better good of society? You know, help out your fellow man. If nothing else, what about karma?"

"Yeah, well, if you haven't figured it out yet, karma's for chumps. Money makes the world go round. That's one thing that's never gonna change."

She looked away, feeling disheartened. "I thought it was love," she said under her breath as she turned away to face the towers.

"What was that?"

She shook her head. "Forget it. I think we'll just have to agree to disagree."

"Whatever."

"Is it always going to be like this?"

"What are you talking about?"

"I'm just trying to imagine a scenario where we can work together where I don't want to hurt you."

Charlie laughed. "Excuse me?"

"I don't know if it's the fact that I got up early and hardly slept for the last two nights, but I really just want to leave right now and say if you ever decide to not be such a mammoth jerk, give me a call."

"What?" he asked, looking oblivious.

"Yeah, I think I'll just go. I'm not doing this with you," she muttered, walking to the gate.

He laughed. "You're not doing this with me? You make it sound like you know what we're doing?"

Kate shook her head, feeling frustrated as she tried unsuccessfully to escape.

"Aren't you forgetting something?" he asked.

"What are you talking about?"

"I think it goes something like, *'Bring him to the towers. He's supposed to be part of it.'* "

"It obviously must have been talking about someone else. There's no way I can work with such an ignorant, self-centered jerk. I'm sure you can find your own way home." She tried to turn the gate's handle again, but it was locked. Grabbing hold of the bars, she shook the gate with all her force, but it didn't budge. "Can I have the key, please?" she finally said after recognizing her efforts were futile.

Charlie laughed. "You're serious?"

"Absolutely."

"Kate, you can't just leave."

"Oh, are you holding me hostage?"

"Don't be silly," he said, finally recognizing the extent of her irritation. "We just got here. I haven't even given you a tour yet."

"I've heard enough, thank you. Now, please, just open the gate so I can leave."

"You don't want to talk about this?"

"What's there to talk about? It's obvious that we're on opposite ends of the universe. I was hoping this relationship might be mutually beneficial, but it's clear that I was very wrong."

"What did I do?"

She shook her head in disbelief, glaring at him.

"What?" he responded defensively. "I'm not a mind reader."

"You're so ignorant you don't even know you're ignorant."

"Wow, thanks!" he responded sarcastically. "You obviously don't have any idea what you're talking about."

"Maybe not, but I've heard enough in the last few minutes to guess that you probably lost your way as soon as you started thinking this was all about you. I know next to nothing about the towers, but I've seen enough to guess that your lack of respect and reverence for this place is keeping you from understanding all that it has to offer."

"Oh, is that right? Well, thanks for the evaluation, Miss Social Worker. What do I owe you?"

"Charlie, don't you get it?"

"Get what?" he asked challengingly.

"That little exercise we had out there with Isaiah—watching the wind take Sammy's notes—the message on my bike yesterday—the reason we're here."

He stared at her, confused.

"Look, if I hadn't had the last couple of days to think about all of this, it might be easy to blow it all off, but don't you see there's something going on here that's bigger than me and you? Finding the notebook—figuring out Sammy's message—meeting you—the oracle. There's something big going on here. That kind of stuff might happen to you all the time, but I can't remember anything like this ever happening to me. I'm ready to figure out what it is and how I fit in, and it feels like you're just trying to figure out how to make a quick buck."

"What's wrong with that?"

"Have you ever considered that maybe there's a lot of things wrong with that? Isn't that what Isaiah was trying to tell us with that story about the guy who went searching for gold when he was sitting on top of something even more valuable?"

"Is that what that was all about?"

"You didn't get that?"

He rolled his eyes. "I don't know. Isaiah's always got some crazy story. I don't get half the crap he talks about."

"Okay, but don't you think it might help your project if you tried a little harder to understand what he's saying?"

Charlie shrugged.

"Charlie, from the sounds of it, the guy practically lives in that hut over there. He grew up in the neighborhood, right? His dad and Simon used to hang out. Don't you think he might have a pretty good understanding what this is all about?"

"I don't know," he responded impatiently. "It's like he's always talking in code and metaphors. I don't know if he's ever given me a straight answer."

"Why do you think that is?"

"Probably because he's just making it up as he goes."

She nodded thoughtfully, remembering their conversation with Isaiah. "Maybe, but didn't he say something about it meaning more if you find the answers yourself?"

"Yeah, he says crap like that all the time," he responded dismissively.

"And? What have you figured out?"

"Nothing to write home about."

"Nothing? Really? You've kept coming back here for the past five years because of nothing? No offense, but you're either a really slow learner or there's more to this than you're telling me. What was it that you said yesterday about people coming here and feeling…something?"

"Yeah, okay, but in case you didn't know, you can't take a picture or make a movie about a *feeling*. I've got to have something a lot more solid than some ethereal mumbo jumbo to base my movie on."

"How many pictures did you say you took of this place?"

"Easily a few thousand—plus I don't even know how many hours of video—dozens for sure. I know every square foot of this place. I've studied the pictures, even upside down and backwards, and I don't feel like I'm any closer to understanding the real reasons Simon built them."

"Are you sure he had a reason? What if he just got bored and decided to it would be a good way to recycle a bunch of junk?"

Charlie looked at her incredulously. "Have you ever known a bored person to spend thirty-three years doing anything constructive?"

"Good point. Okay, so maybe there's more to it than that. Tell me what Isaiah was suggesting when he talked about whatever it was that turned Sabato to Sam and later to Simon? It seems like whatever that was, it probably played a role in the creation of this place."

"It probably did, but I decided a while ago that that's not a road I want to go down."

"Why not?"

"Because it's a black hole with no end, and if you get too close to it, it will suck you in."

"What?" she asked, trying not to laugh. "Isaiah seemed to be pretty confident that that's what your movie's supposed to be about."

Charlie shook his head. "It's just more of the same ethereal crap I was talking about. I need proof. I need something tangible...solid... something *real*. There's nothing *real* about any of that stuff."

"So what is it, then?" she asked, feeling confused.

Charlie shook his head and was slow to answer. "It's basically a bunch of spiritual beliefs—craziness if you ask me."

"That's what changed him to Sam and Simon?"

"That's what they say." he responded dubiously.

"Who says?"

"A few of the old people I interviewed—and Isaiah."

"What did they say?"

Charlie hesitated. "Are you trying to push me into that black hole?"

"Are you afraid of the dark?" she teased.

He looked away, and Kate knew she had hit a nerve. After he didn't respond and the silence grew awkward, she spoke again. "So, where did you want to start?"

"What?"

"If you're going to keep me here, you better give me a tour. That's why we came, right?"

"I thought you said you didn't want to do this with me."

"Yeah, well, I don't feel like I have a lot of options."

"What does that mean?"

She sat down on the edge of a large planter and considered for a moment how to respond. "Charlie, I'm here because of a series of events that I can't explain. Those events have convinced me that there must be something here for me to do—or understand. I have no idea what the big picture is, but I feel compelled to find out. I came to California only because a door opened. I didn't know where it would lead me, but I came hoping to make a difference in the world. It's been one of the hardest things I've ever done—taking a step into the dark, not knowing how this would play out. Yesterday when I found that note on my bike, I knew what I needed to do—at least the next step. And to be honest, in spite of our rocky introduction, it felt a little bit better to know I wasn't going to be doing whatever I needed to do alone. I was hoping the information we individually had could be mutually beneficial, but if you're only in this for yourself—if you're only in it for the money, then I'm done."

"How do you know this isn't about money?"

"Because ..."

"Because isn't a reason. You gotta come up with something better than that."

She took a deep breath, wondering what to say, when an idea came to her. She pulled the notebook from her bag and flipped to a handwritten note on a scrap of purple paper that had been taped to a page about halfway through the book. She stared at it, questioning her idea, knowing his reaction to it could tip the conversation in a way she wanted to avoid.

"What's that?" Charlie asked.

"Oh, just another message—one that Dr. Hermansen received."

"What does it say?" he asked, sitting down next to her.

"I'm not sure if you'll like it," she responded, closing the notebook to hide it from him.

"Why not? Does it say anyone who makes money making movies is evil?"

"No."

"Can I see it?"

"I guess if you're supposed to be part of this, maybe you need to see it."

He slid closer, and she opened the notebook to the purple note. He looked at the words for a moment before shaking his head. "I can't read that."

"Try," Kate encouraged.

He shook his head and reluctantly looked at it again.

"How does that make any sense? Two of those aren't even words."

"They are if you try. Think about the message we got yesterday."

He shook his head and looked again, screwing up his face as he tried to find meaning in the scribbles.

"You...found ...wanting?" he muttered.

She smiled. "Exactly."

He looked at her incredulously. "And that means something to you?"

"It didn't at first, but what Dr. Hermansen wrote reminded me that it's from the Old Testament."

He rolled his eyes. "What does this have to do with me?"

"Probably a lot more than you would ever admit."

"Kate, maybe you should just go. This is ridiculous."

"That's exactly what Dr. Hermansen thought at first."

"What?"

"She found this note stuck to her office door one morning a few weeks after she started trying to figure all of this out."

"And this meant something to her?" he asked cynically.

"Not at first, but eventually, yes. It actually came to mean a lot to her. I think it kind of became a turning point. She understood the same message you did, but she had to have it interpreted."

"Who could interpret that? I mean, I know what it says now, and it still doesn't make any sense."

"Maybe not—until you really look for meaning. Dr. Hermansen ended up asking one of the nurses for a little help."

"And she was able to interpret *that* into something meaningful?"

"Yeah. Maybe I should just read it to you. It might make more sense."

"By all means," he said challengingly.

Kate flipped the page, looking through the entry she had read yesterday morning on the beach, trying to find the best place to begin.

...After trying to figure out what this means for the last several days, I took the note to Loretta this morning. I guess I shouldn't be surprised anymore that she knew what it meant, but I was. She answered my question by telling me the story of King Belshazzar in the Old Testament. As the story goes, the king was a having a rowdy party one night with all the important people in Babylon. They were drinking out of the goblets they had looted from the temple in Jerusalem and dancing around the idols they had made, when out of the blue, a mystical hand magically appeared and began writing on the plaster wall in a cryptic language no one could understand.

According to the story, everyone freaked out and left the party, and the king was left quaking in his golden slippers. He summoned all the kingdom's magicians and wise men to his court and offered them a generous portion of his kingdom if they could interpret the writing on the wall. But none of them could. Then the queen remembered the Jew who had interpreted the previous king's dreams and suggested maybe he could find meaning in this situation too.

Daniel was brought into the palace and shown the writing and, without hesitation, told the king what it meant —that the actions of his life had been witnessed and measured and that he had been "found wanting" —that he'd been put to the test and had failed and that because of this, his kingdom would be taken from him.

I must have looked as confused as I felt, wondering what that story could possibly have to do with me. She suggested that King Belshazzar had not learned to listen or exercise reverence, that he had gotten caught up in his own pride and put his trust and faith in himself, his wealth, and his idols rather than in the one true and living God who could help direct him and his kingdom.

I've been thinking about this all day. I even Googled the story and found the chapter this refers to, reading it directly from an online version of the Bible (Daniel 5). It's just about exactly as Loretta explained it. I was angry at first —feeling judged. But the writing was on the wall —my wall. It has caused me to take a deep look at myself and my life. King Belshazzar was a piece of work —multiple wives and concubines —a real party boy. I'm not any of those things, but I've found myself wondering throughout the day if all the time I spent in college, my degrees, and the last six years of practicing psychology might have made me cynical and proud. Of course the answer is yes. It seems to come with the territory. It probably describes the majority of my professors and colleagues, who have become jaded and cynical of nearly everything but especially of the existence of a higher power.

A month ago, I would have dismissed this as a stupid prank —if I had understood it at all. I am either going mad, or I am beginning to believe in a mystical element to life that I have completely overlooked. Part of me wants to run from this, but if I'm honest, I see that another part —a growing part —wants to run toward it. If I have indeed been "found wanting", it seems to suggest my life could benefit from a serious shift in where I place my trust and hopes. It's been difficult trying to be patient as I've waited for more answers, but I realized today that I can see enough to take the next step —maybe even two or three. I'm still at a loss for words to describe what all of this means to me, but it appears undeniable from this latest message that a close examination of my own life and attitudes is the place to start.

Kate looked up from the notebook to find Charlie looking contemplative.

"So what does this have to do with me and my movie?"

"Maybe nothing. But maybe there's meaning in it for everyone. Maybe we all need to take a look at our lives from time to time and see how and what we might change or improve. My dad used to always tell me that most of us are our own worst enemies—that we form our own roadblocks to progression and understanding. I'm not trying to judge you, Charlie. I'm just trying to suggest that maybe taking a look at the roadblock you've had with your movie might open some new ideas and help you get past it."

"You don't think I've been doing that for the last five years?"

"I'm not your judge. But maybe your roadblock is your drive for money. Have you ever considered that?"

"Have you ever considered that you should mind your own business?"

She laughed, trying to defuse the anger she felt coming back at her. "My dad used to say that the truth will make us free but first it usually ticks us off."

"You have no idea what you're talking about."

"You don't think so?"

"Kate, the film industry is all about making money."

"Okay, but isn't it first about telling stories? Isn't it also about inspiring people? You're right, I don't really know anything about the film industry, but I do know that of all the movies I've seen over the years, the ones I remember are the ones that have made me think or feel something bigger. It seems like film's one of most powerful forms of communication. I'm sure money is tied to a lot of that—maybe all of it. But I really want to believe that it's not the main driving force behind every film."

"I used to think the same thing."

"But?"

"But I learned that I was wildly naive. Money is the driving force behind all entertainment. It's just plain stupid to think otherwise."

She nodded, chewing on his words as she turned and looked up at the towers. "Do you think that's why Simon built all of this?"

He turned and looked then turned away without giving her an answer.

"Did he hope to build something that people would want to see so he could charge admission?"

Charlie looked like he wanted to respond, but he didn't.

"Was he showing off? Did he have some kind of little-man complex?"

He stood and began walking down the long inner corridor. Kate followed a few steps behind, giving Charlie plenty of space and silence.

CHAPTER 12

CHARLIE'S MESSAGE

*No one is discontented at not being a king except a discrowned
king...unhappiness almost invariably indicates the existence of a road not
taken, a talent undeveloped, a self not recognized.*
—Blaise Pascal

Charlie led the way without even a word of explanation, almost as if
he were trying to run away to avoid Kate's questions. They walked past
a wide adobe door frame where two green, sun-bleached doors hung on
hinges. The space between these doors offered a sliver of morning light,
leaving Kate confused that nothing stood behind them. They next passed
under a highly decorated portico that gave way to a narrower doorway
with nothing more than daylight behind it. An official sign that read
Authorized Personnel Only was suspended by a yellow chain, blocking
the doorway. Kate slowed to look at the details—so many tiles, pieces
of glass, shells, mirrors, even old Chinese plates were embedded in the

wall, the floor, even the ceiling of the portico. Every inch was covered with details.

When she looked up, she realized she was alone. Coming out from under the bedazzled portico, she looked down the Technicolored corridor, the towers looming overhead. They had looked impressive when she had seen them on Monday from outside the fence, but she could not have imagined the unique beauty that stood before her now—so close, so

strangely incredible. A freestanding, rounding structure caught her eye, drawing her to the right where it stood near the colorful wall. Tiered like a wedding cake and standing at least ten feet tall, this structure was also bedazzled with colorful, mismatched tiles and shells. As she examined it more closely, she saw that each tier formed a shallow catch basin. Stepping back, she tried to imagine what this might look like with water cascading from level to level—a joyful fountain.

Opposite the fountain, she found Charlie sitting on a bench under a spindly, spider web-like gazebo that domed well over his head. Similar to an umbrella, a central column supported at least two-dozen arms that sprawled from the center to the circular bench below. Like everything else here, these too were completely covered with mosaicked bits of all sorts.

She glanced at Charlie, who sat hunched over, his elbows on his knees, his eyes glued to the screen of his iPad. She decided not to disturb him, choosing instead to continue her exploration. It was not the tour she had expected, but in spite of the messy way it had begun, she decided she would try to make the best of whatever time she had left. She strolled around the gazebo, walking under the colorful flying buttresses that tied the outer wall to the gazebo and the looming towers. Having already looked down the south wall, she turned her attention to the north. The rising sun cast long shadows here, splashing the cement under her feet with a thousand dots of light. As she approached the north wall, sunlight reflected off a piece of glass, causing Kate to squint, though drawing her ever closer.

Centered in the middle of the arch-shaped wall, glass, sun-bleached seashells, tiles, and lava rock framed a sculptural cement relief of what looked like a bundle of wheat stalks and grapes. Compared to the eclectic assemblage that covered everything as far as the eye could see—seemingly without pattern or intentional design—this refined motif seemed quite unique and out of place. She wondered about its placement, if it had any meaning or if it were simply a way of taking up a larger space, perhaps when its creator had run out of tile. Intrigued, she continued looking for any clues, when she felt her kneecap connect with something big and unyielding.

Fearing she had damaged either herself or the artwork, she immediately looked down to see, jutting out onto the colored cement patio, a basin like a deep bathtub that formed a pocket at the base of the wall. The waist-high walls of this bathtub were embedded with tiny bits of colored glass. Kate rubbed her knee, grateful she hadn't hit it hard enough to cause damage to the structure but knowing the blunt contact would surely leave a bruise.

Her eyes followed the tall arms attached to the front side of the tub as they rose high above her head, tying into the flying buttresses that spanned the open space above, linking the tub to the largest tower. With every surface covered in mosaic, her eyes didn't know where to stop, and she felt drawn to explore the wonderland before her. She walked to the base of the largest tower and looked up through the skeletal

middle, somehow reminded of a kaleidoscope with its colors and structures reaching out into infinity.

"Pretty wild, huh?" Charlie asked from behind her, startling her.

"Yeah!"

"Hey, umm, I'm sorry. I…uh…I didn't expect it to go this way."

"That's a relief," she responded sarcastically. "How did you expect it to go?"

He shook his head. "Maybe you should tell me."

"Excuse me?"

"Are you in some kind of cahoots with Isaiah or something?"

"What are you talking about?"

He handed her a wrinkled piece of lined paper covered in dark handwriting. Recognizing the now-familiar scrawls, she lifted it closer to her face and read it over a couple of times before handing it back to him. "I should be asking you the same question."

"So this isn't some kind of insane game, trying to freak me out?"

"Why would I do that?"

Charlie looked at the paper again. "It's from him, right? It's the same handwriting. It's gotta be from him?"

She nodded, acknowledging he was probably right. "Where did this come from?"

"It was on the bench in the gazebo when I walked in—just sitting there—like it was waiting for me."

"Are you sure it was meant for you?"

He looked surprised by the question, almost as if he hadn't considered that it could be for anyone else. He sat down on the stairs at the base of the tower, staring down at the note, reading over it once more. After a moment, he looked up at her. "This is completely nuts, right? Yeah, this is totally freakin' crazy. I feel like my head's going to explode."

She smiled, remembering her own reaction to the first message she had received. "It sounds like you're convinced this one's for you."

He didn't answer, just continued to stare at the note.

"Is this the first one—I mean the first message that's been specifically for you?"

He grimaced almost painfully. "I think there've probably been others."

"What do you mean?" she asked, sitting down on the stair next to him.

He pulled his iPad from his backpack and opened it to the same photo of the notes hanging in Isaiah's office that he had shown her earlier. "I'm pretty sure I've seen at least three or four of these over the last couple of years, stuck to my windshield, or that bench out there under the tree. Do you know what the heck's going on?"

"Not exact...Wait, did you just say heck?" she teased.

"You're a bad influence," he responded, cracking a smile. "I would have said hell, but Isaiah made it pretty clear hell has nothing to do with any of this. But you do have some idea of what's going on, right?"

"I might."

"Then for the sake of my sanity, you gotta tell me!"

"I don't really know how to say it without sounding crazy."

"It can't possibly be any crazier than what I'm already feeling."

"I'm pretty sure you wouldn't understand."

"Why not?"

"Just judging from everything you've said about your aversion to this sort of thing."

He grimaced, looking down and reading the message again.

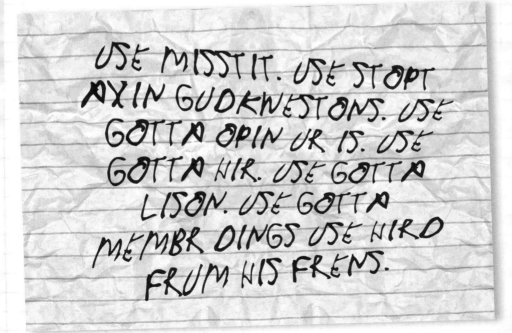

"It sounds like the universe is trying to get your attention," Kate suggested, looking over his shoulder.

"By sending me a cryptic message?" he asked dubiously.

"It's really only cryptic until you slow down long enough to try and understand it, right?"

He nodded reluctantly after a moment, realizing she was right and that arguing with such a direct, personal message felt pointless.

"Did you hang onto the other messages?"

"I had no idea they were..." He shook his head. "I'm sure I threw them away."

"It probably makes you wonder, right? What you might have missed, I mean?"

"Apparently I missed a lot," he replied, pointing to the note.

"Well, it doesn't look like the universe has given up on you yet."

He nodded thoughtfully, looking almost humble. "Do you think things would be different now if I'd understood them before?"

"Probably, but I don't think you'll ever know how. I also don't think it would be very productive to spend too much time worrying about that."

"Why not?"

"Is there anything we can do about the choices we've made in the past—messages we've ignored or never tried to understand? It seems like the only real solution is to try to listen now and in the future," she suggested, pointing back to the note.

"So, what am I supposed to do? Just sit around and wait for another message to fall out of the sky and tell me what to do?"

"Umm, no, I'm pretty sure that's exactly what you're not supposed to do," she responded with a little laugh. "You've got your instructions right there, don't you?"

He looked down at the message before letting out a long sigh, shaking his head. "It can't be *that* easy."

"You think that's easy?" she asked, surprised.

"You don't?"

She shook her head. "Most of those things seem pretty hard to do. Learning to hear—and actually listen—that's not something most people can learn to do overnight, especially after a lifetime of not listening."

Charlie looked confused.

"My junior year, I look a class on interpersonal communication. I thought it would help me overcome some of my social phobias. I was surprised when it turned out to be mostly about empathy—about learning how to listen with not only your ears but also your heart. It was a small class—only ten of us—and we spent most of the time listening to each other, both the things the others were saying and the things they didn't say but communicated nonverbally."

"You mean like body language?"

"That was part of it, but really only a small part. Most of it was just learning how to feel our way through things—how to understand people and situations by the aura and energy that came out of them."

He smirked. "Sounds like some kind of hippie lovefest. You got credit for that class?"

She smiled and nodded. "It was actually one of my favorite classes. But it was also one of the most challenging. The only textbooks were the other members of the class. My professor began each class with mindfulness meditation to help us learn how to set aside our egos and selfish desires and open our ears and our hearts so we could communicate with each other on a higher, more spiritual level."

Charlie looked away without a verbal response, but Kate knew what he was thinking.

"You're terrified of that, aren't you?"

He laughed. "You got that?"

"It wasn't hard, especially after what you said yesterday. Fear is one of the most powerful forces in the universe."

"Yeah, well…" he replied, getting to his feet.

She looked up at him, watched how he threw his backpack over his shoulder and brushed the hair away from his forehead before reaching for his camera.

As she watched him, she knew she was right to talk about fear. Through the practical applications she'd been taught in her class, she'd learned to recognize fear in the faces of people as she walked around campus. She had often found herself quietly observing people, identifying fear and other emotions in the way they walked, their facial expressions, and the energy that buzzed about them. Of all the emotions humankind had defined, she had learned that fear was the most debilitating, the most controlling, the most damning and was so often connected to other negative emotions. As she watched Charlie raising his camera to his eye, she could see some of the physical identifiers of fear. But more importantly, she could feel it.

"Why are you hiding behind your camera?" she asked.

"What are you talking about?" he responded, keeping his back toward her as he focused in on a distant target.

"Charlie, I know you're afraid of this conversation. You're hiding behind your camera."

He shook his head but didn't speak.

"The first step to overcoming fear is getting past denial. Why are you afraid of this?"

He didn't answer, continuing his departure, his camera leading the way.

As she watched him from behind, a thought came to her. A powerful thought. She knew what his fear was.

"You're afraid of the mystical parts of this place, aren't you?" she said, getting to her feet and following him.

He slowed but didn't stop.

"That's what you said, isn't it? You're afraid that if you can't see it—if you can't capture it with your camera—it's not real. You've felt the spiritual draw this place has, but you don't understand what it is. And you're afraid of asking—afraid of talking about it—afraid that people will think you're crazy."

He stopped walking but didn't turn around.

"Charlie, you know the power of the mysticism that this place has—

you talked about it yesterday, about the people you interviewed, about the change it made in Andy's life. You started to talk about it yesterday on the beach, but you stopped. What are you afraid of?"

"I'm afraid you'll think I'm a lunatic," he responded, his back still toward her.

She laughed. "It's way too late for that."

He shook his head but didn't turn around.

"This is the story you're supposed to tell, isn't it? And you know what's crazy? It's crazy that you've spent the last five years trying to avoid telling this story. That's what Isaiah was talking about, isn't it? You're afraid that if you go down that rabbit hole, you don't know where you'll come up or maybe even *if* you'll come up. You're afraid of getting laughed at. You're afraid that you and your career will be defined by this film alone and you'll be pigeonholed as a whacked-out fanatic. Am I right?"

He stared straight ahead, his back still toward her, but his body language told her she had hit the nail squarely on the head.

"You said something earlier—something about how people are reluctant to talk about their spiritual beliefs even though most of us admit a desire for some kind of spiritual connection."

He didn't respond.

Closing the distance between them, she felt the energy of fear all around him. Silently she moved until she stood in front of him, not more than twelve inches away. She was not surprised to see that his eyes were closed. She could feel the fear dancing about him and found that she could easily imagine the confusion he must be feeling. She wondered what she could say that could change things for him—that could offer hope—that could give light to the darkness that surrounded him. And as quickly as she asked, an answer popped into her head. They were in Watts—a place whose name itself seemed to incite fear—and yet she was not fearful.

She recalled the feeling of peace she felt when she first discovered these towers almost a week ago. This was an oasis—a refuge—a sanctuary. There was no fear that came from these spires, only warmth. And yet here was a kid who knew all about them and was somehow afraid to tell their real story. She remembered in their conversation with Isaiah that he had suggested to Charlie that he tell her what turned Sabato into Simon. She wondered if the message he had just received— to remember the things he had heard from his friends—might help to put off his fear.

Retire into yourself as much as possible. Associate with people who are likely to improve you. Welcome those whom you are capable of improving. The process is a mutual one. People learn as they teach.

Seneca the Younger

CHAPTER 13

THE QUANTUM LEAP

Truth is by nature self-evident.
As soon as you remove the cobwebs of ignorance
that surround it, it shines clear.
—*Mahatma Gandhi*

"Tell me what changed Sabato into Simon," Kate said softly.

Charlie opened his eyes, looking startled to see Kate standing so close. "Why do you want to know about that?" he responded, looking down at his camera that hung around his neck.

"Isaiah seemed to think you know the story, right?"

He nodded nearly imperceptibly but looked reluctant to answer verbally.

"So?"

He paused for a moment, his face registering discomfort as if he were trying to find a way out of answering her question.

"So?" she repeated.

"As far as I know, Simon almost never talked about the exact details, but somewhere around 1921, something happened that changed everything for him."

"What kind of something?"

Charlie looked uncomfortable, shifting his eyes from his camera to the wall and back again.

Kate rested her hand on his arm and waited for him to look at her. "I'm not going to laugh. I want to know. Something tells me this might be why we're here today."

His look of surprise was obvious, but her words seem to encourage him. "I'm not really sure where to begin."

"Well, why don't you tell me who he was?"

"Okay, that's pretty easy. He was just a humble guy with a desire to do something big."

"Well, I think he nailed it," she responded, smiling as she looked up at the towers looming overhead. "But there's a lot more to it than that, isn't there?"

Charlie raised his eyebrows.

"Okay, come on. People don't spend thirty-three years building something like this without a purpose beyond just making something big. Why don't you pretend you're a tour guide, and I'll pretend you're giving me a tour? Good?"

He smiled sideways and rolled his eyes.

"So," Kate began, clasping her hands in front of her, "Who was Sabato Rodia?"

Charlie laughed. "We're really doing this?"

"Yeah. Just pretend I'm a cute, interested tourist from somewhere exotic, maybe...Wyoming, and you're trying to impress me with the knowledge you gained from five years of research."

"Wyoming?" He laughed again. "That's the most exotic place you could come up with?"

"Off the top of my head. It's just pretend." she teased. "If you don't like it, you can choose somewhere else."

His smile remained. "No, we can stick with Wyoming. That's by Montana, right?"

She shook her head. "Close enough. Are you ready to get started, or are you in need of a geography lesson first?"

"Are you qualified?"

"If you're asking if I know where Wyoming is, then yes, I'm fully qualified. But you're avoiding my questions, and I can see right through you. Are you ready to answer my questions, or do I need to find a real tour guide?"

"Okay, okay," he said, holding back a laugh.

"So tell me, who was Sabato Rodia *really*?"

"From the beginning?"

"Sure. If you want you can tell me like you do in your documentary."

"Okay, Sabato Rodia was born into a large family in Northern Italy in about 1880. We don't know much about his early life other than the fact that his family was poor and so his education and opportunities were limited. Circumstances like that are fertile ground for seeds of discontent. And so, because of his lack of opportunity, he and his brother decided to emigrate to America in 1895, where they found jobs in the Pennsylvania coal mines."

"Wait, so did he get any training in sculpting while he was in Italy?"

"No. So far as I know, he never got any training in sculpting. He was completely self-taught."

"Wow! I also wondered about his job in the coal mines. I've never been to Italy, or in a coal mine for that matter, but it's hard to believe that working in dark and dirty mines could be a better life than what he left behind."

Charlie smiled. "Says the girl who left the presumably beautiful wilds of Idaho for the slums of the inner city."

She pursed her lips and nodded. "Okay, you're right. I hadn't considered that. It's not exactly the same thing, but I guess the promise of fourteen dollars an hour—seven hundred miles away—was more attractive to me than a job at the local cheese factory. But compared to crossing the ocean...it just seems like a very long way to come, especially at fifteen."

"Yeah, but when you don't even have the potential of a job at a cheese factory—or anywhere else for that matter? I've thought a lot about it—the lack of opportunity at home—the poverty of his family. Sometimes the unknown potential is better than the reality you're surrounded with, even if that potential is on the other side of the world. The promise of America must have seemed at least as charming back then as it does to immigrants today. I'm sure he probably had no idea what he was getting himself into."

"How did he end up in California?"

"His brother was killed in a mining accident just a few months after they arrived."

"Whoa!"

"Yeah, right? I think he was still only fifteen, he hardly spoke any English, and he was alone in a big new world."

"What did he do?"

"Well, I'm pretty sure he looked at what happened to his brother and had the brains to realize that spending all his waking hours underground was not attractive enough to bet his life on it. From what I've been able to piece together, I guess he gathered up his things and jumped a series of freight trains, picking up a few different trades as he headed West—eventually to Seattle. I'm not sure what he was looking for, but I don't know if his life was a whole lot easier on the West Coast. He worked a lot of odd jobs, mostly in construction, and eventually became skilled in the tile-setting trade.

"When he was about twenty-three years old, he married a woman by the name of Lucia Ucci. Somewhere between the births of their three children—who came in fairly rapid succession—the family moved to Oakland around 1903, probably looking for work. About that time, for some reason—possibly marital stress—Simon started drinking a lot. He had a couple of run-ins with the law, which only made matters worse. And then one day—April 18, 1906, to be exact—his whole world started shaking."

Kate looked confused. "Are you talking about an earthquake?"

"Impressive! Yeah, it happened a little after five o'clock in the morning, which leads me to believe he may have been sleeping at a job site or possibly at a bar because it took him a couple of days to find his way home and track down his family. Of course their house was heavily damaged by both the quake and the fires that followed. I'd guess that most of the construction projects he'd worked on were either damaged or destroyed. The whole region was a disaster zone. I can only imagine that his world was totally rocked. Unfortunately, that turned him to even more drinking, which only added to the marital stress, which could only have caused bigger problems with the rest of the family.

"Then, in the middle of all this, his daughter, only a toddler, got sick and died. Which led him to drink more, which led to more marital problems, which led him into a very dark place where he basically abandoned his family and spent the next ten years in and out of sobriety, roaming North and South America by hopping freight trains."

"Wow! So he was a hobo?"

Charlie nodded. "Yeah, he later told many people in his congregation that he was a very bad man during that time."

"Sounds like a really tragic life."

"It must have been. The neighbors said he never really recovered emotionally—that he was quick to tear up around children and spent a lot of time trying to help other people give up alcohol."

She nodded, listening to Charlie's story but at the same time distracted by her surroundings. "So how did he end up here? Why did he build all of this?"

"Those have been two of my biggest questions."

"And...what answers have you come up with?"

"If he ever shared the nitty gritty details, the secrets died before I started asking questions. But several people I've talked to said he

sometimes spoke about some kind of…mystical experience that seems to have rocked his world more powerfully than the earthquake."

"What was it?"

He took a moment to respond, and when he did, his voice was different, less confident. "It sounds crazy, but from what I've been able to stitch together, that experience—whatever it was— set him on a completely different path. He changed his name. He stopped drinking. He scraped together enough money for a down payment on a vacant lot that nobody wanted because of its strange shape. And he started building. After spending a whole decade without a place to call home— or even a reason to live—he spent the next thirty-three years putting down deep roots and building towers to the sky."

Kate smiled. "That sounded like you've gone over that a few times before."

"Yeah, well, without any budget, I do my own voice-overs in my film. I've been laying that out, asking myself that same stinkin' question for the past four years."

"And what question is that exactly?" she asked.

"What happened to him? Why, after living a life of freedom with nothing to hold him down for more than ten years, why did he come here and build all of this?"

"I think that was actually two questions. Couldn't he have just gotten tired of roaming?"

"Sure, but it's a big leap between roaming fatigue and going to all the trouble of building hundred-foot towers. This takes drive. It takes superhuman strength and endurance. And it takes something… something else to infuse it all with…well, with whatever it is that still draws people to it more than sixty years after he left it. I don't know what that experience was, but it seems it changed everything."

"He didn't leave any clues behind?"

"No, he did—plenty of clues. At least that's what Isaiah and a bunch of the other people I interviewed told me. I'm just not sure how to figure out what they mean."

"What have you got so far?"

"Well, to begin with, before he even started building, he changed his name to Sam."

Kate looked at Charlie for a long moment. "I don't understand what that has to do with anything."

"It sounds like you know at least a little bit about the Bible, right?"

She nodded. "Why?"

"Have you heard the story of Samuel? I think it's in the Old Testament."

"I'm sure I have. I grew up in a very Christian home, but refresh my memory."

"I don't fully understand Bible language, but I think the story goes that Samuel—he was just kid at the time—he was living in the temple as an assistant to some old priest or prophet or something. And during the middle of the night, he heard a voice call his name. He got up and went to the priest, thinking he was being summoned. But the priest was asleep and said he hadn't called him and told him to go back to bed. Three times this happened in the same night, and finally the old priest told Samuel that it was probably God who was calling his name and that if it happened again, he should answer..."

"Speak, your servant is listening," Kate said, finishing the narrative.

"Exactly! You know the story?"

"I remember it from Sunday School. So, Sabato, Sam, Simon— whatever his name is—you think he heard a voice? Couldn't he have just liked the name Sam? You know, thought it sounded a lot more American that Sabato?"

Charlie nodded. "Yeah, believe me, I've tried to explain it at least a hundred different ways, too. He never gave any one person the whole story, but from the many different bits and pieces I've been able to cobble together, it's pretty clear that something big happened that took his train wreck of a life off one track and set it on a completely different course."

"I don't mean to play devil's advocate here, but I'm sure—a cynical guy like you—you've probably examined every possibility that this could all just be a series of coincidences, right? I mean, couldn't those changes be attributed to at least hundreds of other possible reasons?"

He laughed. "Is my cynicism that obvious?"

She smiled and nodded.

"Yeah, well, believe me, I've spent the last four and a half years trying to find any other way to have all of this make sense—to have all the pieces fit together. But after exhausting every other possibility I could think of, I'm very reluctantly recognizing that nothing else could have triggered the colossal changes that Simon made over his last forty-plus years of his life. No, I've...I've really tried to find another way, but ..."

"You sound defeated."

He took a deep breath and let it out slowly, pensively, almost like he was brooding.

"There's still more, though, isn't there?"

"What do you mean?"

"You told me about how he changed from Sabato to Sam, but what about Simon? Why did he change his name again?"

"Isaiah and some of the others say that name was probably given to him by his congregation."

"Congregation? Why?"

Charlie shook his head. "Do you know what the name Simon means?"

"No." She paused for a moment, thinking. "It's an old name, right? I know it's at least as old as the New Testament. If I remember right from Sunday school, Simon was one of Jesus's original Twelve Apostles, right? He was a fisherman, I think," she said, screwing up her face as she sorted through the files of her memory for anything related to the subject. "Wasn't he the one who Jesus renamed Peter? Yeah, he was the senior apostle, right? The one Jesus put in charge of the church after he was crucified?"

Charlie stifled a laugh. "Really? You just happened to have all of that on the tip of your tongue?"

She smiled, blushing. "I grew up in a very religious home. We went to church every Sunday and studied the Bible. You pick stuff up over twenty-two years."

"Yeah, well, you don't have to make excuses. I was just impressed. But you don't know what the name means?"

"No. Do you?"

"Well, I can't remember if the name Simon is Greek or Hebrew, but apparently it means "he has heard.""

"No way!" Kate responded incredulously.

"Yep. Crazy coincidence, right? And the thing that's making me wonder what your Sammy has to do with all of this is that at least four different people told me Simon had some kind of a relationship with the wind—that he built all of this as a monument to the wind."

"A monument to the wind?" she asked, hiding no surprise. "Do you think that's true?"

"I don't know, but that's what some people say."

Kate looked around at the looming towers and the colorful, detailed walls. "Wouldn't it have been easier just to build a giant windsock?"

Charlie laughed. "You've got a problem with the monument-to-the-wind theory?"

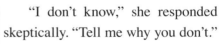

"I don't know," she responded skeptically. "Tell me why you don't."

He turned his head toward the tallest tower. "See that?" he said, pointing. "That nub on the leg of the tower there?"

Kate squinted, looking skyward, her eyes finally resting on a small cement outcropping at least seventy feet off the ground on one of the tower's many legs. It wasn't much to see—just a cement bump that could be easily missed. "What's that?"

"That was Simon's perch—what I was telling you about yesterday."

"Perch?"

"Yeah, the neighbors said he'd go up there in the evenings when the wind was blowing and just hang out, sometimes for hours."

"Did they say why?"

"They said it's where he went to sort through his ideas and figure things out. Whenever he was asked, he'd tell people he was listening to the wind. Not many people know about it—you'll never find it on any of the official websites or printed information, but Simon was kind of a...street preacher, for lack of a better word. This was his church. Some of the old timers around here told me they were actually baptized in Simon's birdbath, and he performed marriages in here somewhere."

"Really? What was his church called?"

"He called it *Cry for Christian Liberty.*"

"Do you know anything about it?"

"No, other than it was a Christian church—Protestant of some sort. It's really hard to find out anything anymore. Almost all of the folks who attended are dead now. One of the old guys I interviewed told me that by the time the Los Angeles Cultural Affairs Department took over, the history had been scrubbed so they couldn't be accused of preserving a religious structure with government funds. You know—the whole separation of church and state stuff."

Kate nodded. "It seems like it would be easy to hide. I don't think I'd ever guess this was any kind of a church."

"Maybe not, as long as you don't look too close."

"What do you mean?"

"The few things I know make me think there has to be a lot more here than I've been able to understand. I've never been to Europe, but I've seen a lot of pictures of cathedrals in Spain and Italy that look a lot like Simon's towers. I think he must have been influenced by the churches he would have seen in his childhood. There aren't any crucifixes or crosses, but in the right light, the towers look a lot like the profile of a cathedral."

Kate nodded thoughtfully as she looked around for a moment, wondering what meaning she might have missed in her casual glances. "So, I'm still trying to figure out what would possess him to go to all the trouble to build something like this in the middle of this neighborhood."

"Oh, I think it was a very deliberate choice to build the towers here."

"You do?"

"According to one lady I interviewed, Simon looked at a couple of other properties before he bought this one. Those other properties are in much better neighborhoods now."

"Wouldn't that be a good thing?"

"I don't think so. That same woman figured that if he had built them anywhere else, they probably would have been torn down to make way for other things. This property was so strangely shaped and so close to the train tracks that no one wanted it. She told me she thought the towers were a metaphor for life and the world—something about the value of hope that's found in dark places—that the darker the world is around you, the more valuable hope becomes."

Kate nodded thoughtfully. "So, do you think that was the visual sermon he was trying to preach by building all of this?"

"I think it might have been, at least in part. But I've been told there's a lot more."

"Like what?"

Charlie shrugged. "I didn't ask all the questions I probably should have."

"According to Isaiah, you seem to make a habit of that."

"Yeah, well, I'm just not comfortable stepping off the solid path and into the unknown."

"I noticed, but I'm not sure if that makes a lot of sense to me."

"Why not?"

"Because you say that out of one side of your mouth but with the other side, you're not afraid of having conversations with near strangers about personal beliefs."

"Yeah, well, faith—personal beliefs—it's intriguing, right? I've always been interested in how and why people believe what they do—or don't."

"I get that."

"You too?"

"Yeah. I even took a couple of comparative religion classes in college. It was fascinating to see that all people around the world seem to have some kind of inherent drive to connect with the supernatural or at least the transcendental."

"Do you really think that's true?"

"Yeah, I do," she responded after a moment's thought. "We may not admit it sometimes; and maybe when we're in the middle of a crisis or we're angry with the hand we've been dealt or when our head's grown too big for our hat…maybe when that's the case, we don't need or want a connection to God. But I think for most of us, at least by the end of our lives if not at some point before, we find ourselves thinking about the purpose of life and what happens to us when we die. I think most of us at some time or another consider our relationships with people we love and hope for them to continue beyond the grave."

"Right, so people invent myths to try to make sense of all this junk, and over centuries, myths turn into scripture and religion and fill people's heads with baseless hope and lies."

Kate forced a smile. She felt like he was baiting her, and she knew that her own fragile patchwork of faith was not in any position to fight a battle she knew she couldn't win without getting bruised or damaged. "I take it you didn't grow up in a religious home?"

He laughed. "No, not really. My mom was—maybe still is—a born-again Buddhist, and Dad is an atheist."

"I've never heard of a born-again Buddhist."

"Yeah, she grew up being a Christian but liked to dabble in all sorts of trendy religions. Dad called her a buffet believer."

"What's that?"

"She basically just picks the stuff she likes out of whatever religion she's exploring and leaves the rest behind. For a while, she found comfort in the idea that she might come back as a dog or a horse or maybe another human." He shook his head. "I remember trying to imagine what it would feel like to be stuck inside the body of a dog. That sounded scarier to me than facing nothing at all."

"And your dad's an atheist?"

"Yeah, my dad basically told me that I should just forget about the future and live for the moment. I decided a long time ago I'd just try to live the best life I could without religion or dogma to complicate things."

"How's that worked out for you?"

"Well, compared to some of my friends who are driven by guilt or fear or both, my life's been pretty good. I guess I figured that if I was fair and honest, karma would be on my side."

"I thought you said karma's for chumps."

He smiled. "Yeah, well, I don't know. I felt like I had things pretty well figured out until a few years ago. I was in school, following my dreams, having a lot of fun, and then BAM!"

"What happened?"

"I made my first trip here to Watts."

Kate nodded, encouraging him to continue.

"I had never felt that way before."

"What way?"

He let out a long breath. "I still don't have the right words to describe it, but it was like…a connection, definitely a connection—a feeling that something was connecting to me. But it was a strange kind of connection, almost like…like the fear you get when you walk through a spider web and you get all squeemy, like a spider's going to suck your brains out or something."

"Wait, what?" she said, trying to figure out if he was serious. "It was like that for you?"

"Well, no, I mean, same intensity but like on the opposite end of the spectrum. Like instead of sucking out my brain, it was like…an intense whoosh that blew through me and made all the hair on my body stand up, like I was plugged into some source of pure, intense energy."

"That's a whole lot of intense," she teased.

"I don't know how else to describe it."

"It didn't scare you?"

"It probably should've, but it was like I was immediately addicted. But in the good kinda way. It somehow felt elevating…almost like a transfusion of energy. In the beginning, I used to think it was some kind of magic; like I'd stumbled into some kind of enchanted forest."

"You make it sound like you changed your mind."

"Only because I realized the feeling went with me when I left."

"What do you mean?"

"It was almost like…whenever I came here, I'd go away with… it sounds silly, but it was like…it filled my pockets full of sunshine. Sometimes it felt like that sunshine would last for days."

"Pockets full of sunshine, huh?"

"I don't know. I probably sound like a lunatic."

"Only a little bit. I'm pretty sure that what I experienced was nowhere near the same intensity of having spiders suck my brains out," she teased, smiling at him. "But I get the sunshine thing. It made me want to come back. It made me curious about what's going on here."

"I hear that from people all the time," he responded.

"Did you ever figure out what it is?"

He shook his head. "I could see it headed off in a direction I didn't want to go, and I decided I didn't want to know. It felt like a waste of time—you know—trying to capture or even describe it for a movie."

"Maybe you should just interview people who come here. Let them do the talking."

"I considered that, but it just didn't feel right. I probably interviewed twenty people after they'd been here for a tour, and each one was different. They were all positive, but they were all over the board. Most of them were way different than anything I'd experienced."

"Were there any commonalities?"

"Yeah, everyone I talked to said in one way or another that the towers left them with a feeling of peace and joy. Several even mentioned feeling a strange sense of love."

"That's something!"

"Yeah, many of them told me they wanted to stay inside the fence long after the tour was over. I interviewed one lady a few of times because I kept bumping into her while I was here. She said she came to visit the towers at least once a week. If I could find a way to bottle that feeling and market it to the world, I'm pretty sure I could retire early."

"Maybe that's why you can't figure it out."

"Why?"

"Maybe you're not supposed to retire. Maybe you've got more work to do here than you know."

"Like what?"

"I want to go back to those pockets full of sunshine for a minute."

"What about 'em?"

"It reminded me of part of a behavioral science class I took a while back about how light and color are critical ingredients to a happy, well-balanced life."

Charlie nodded.

"My professor brought a really big prism into the class with her one day and set it on a sunny windowsill. I remember her fiddling with it until the prism cast a rainbow across the counter. Then she pulled out a disco ball and set it on the counter, right in the middle of the rainbow." Kate smiled as she remembered it. "There were rainbows everywhere—all over the room. She asked us to turn to each other and look at the smiles that had spontaneously erupted on all of our faces. She said she'd been doing that same exercise for years and she'd never had anyone not smile when the rainbows appeared."

Charlie nodded, smiling as he imagined it himself. "So, what does that have to do with my pockets full of sunshine?"

"Well, I'm sure you probably know that a prism can take regular light and divide it into the full spectrum of color. And from those seven colors that we can see with the naked eye, all the colors you could ever imagine can be created."

He nodded again. "Okay, but I still don't see what you're getting at."

"What's your favorite color?"

"Uh, red. Why?"

"I like red too, but yellow's my favorite color. Maybe it's a stretch, but I guess what I'm suggesting is that maybe the reason why the people you interviewed each experienced something different but each shared the common elements of peace, joy, and love is because they each experienced mystical light but each of them experienced it in the color they best connect with. Maybe there are elements of joy and peace in every possible color preference so that the light, whether it's physical or spiritual light—it can touch each person in a way that is as unique as they are."

Charlie nodded slowly. "But if I buy what you just said, then I have to accept the reality of the mystical."

"Haven't you already accepted that? Isn't that what we've been talking about?"

"Well, yeah, but I guess I'm still not completely ready to believe there is such a thing."

She looked at him incredulously. "What else could that feeling you just described be?"

He shrugged. "Wishful thinking. Emotional instability. Even indigestion. What did Dr. Hermansen call it...hallucinations? I don't know. I think most of us could probably talk ourselves into or out of just about anything."

"I don't doubt that's true, but what's the point of talking yourself out of stuff that you know you've felt?"

"You wouldn't understand."

"You're right. I don't understand. What are you doing?"

"I'm trying to be objective. I figured I can't really make an unbiased documentary if I'm thinking in any kind of a prejudiced way."

"So...instead you're just devaluing everything you've felt?"

"It's the price of being objective."

"I don't think that's the only price."

"What do you mean?"

She shook her head, looking frustrated.

"What's wrong?"

"I'm just trying to figure out how thick your head is."

He laughed. "Isaiah used to ask me the same thing?"

"Why did he stop?"

"I'm not sure. Maybe because he thinks I'm a lost cause."

"There's no such thing as a lost cause, just people who refuse to listen and end up turning into their own roadblocks. Charlie, you can't expect to get all the answers if you're not willing to do something positive with the answers you've already got. Isn't that the point of faith—to believe enough to take the next step even when you can't see the big picture?"

"I guess I'm still trying to figure out the whole faith thing. I mean, if this life is as important as you Christians say it is, why is so much of it left up to chance? There are so many ways life could be better if there were more road signs giving you a little direction along the way: which fork to take, which road has the best scenery, where's the shortcut to the highway to happiness."

"Do you really believe there's a shortcut to happiness?"

"I don't know. Wouldn't it be great if there was?"

"Well, sure, but isn't happiness a little more complicated than that? I mean, if there was a shortcut, wouldn't we all be there by now? I guess I've always believed that the journey is at least as important as the destination. Not only that, but it seems like everyone's definition of happiness is a little bit different. I can't imagine it being something that's a one-size-fits-all. And your point about the road signs along the way, I guess that's where faith works for me."

"How so?"

"Being a Christian—or maybe any person of faith—obviously doesn't give you all the answers either. I obviously can't speak for all believers, but my faith leads me to believe there are answers—answers that I can find through taking a step into the dark sometimes. I'd been praying for weeks before I came here, hoping that something would open up for me, that I could start paying off my student loans, and that I would end up where I was supposed to be. I wanted to use my education and talents to help people, but I never would have guessed I'd end up here on the opposite end of the universe."

Charlie nodded thoughtfully. "So, how much does that note you got from Sammy play into your belief that you're supposed to be here?"

"A lot, I guess. But the thing is, if I hadn't been praying—if I hadn't been asking for answers, I don't think that note would have meant much. My first week on the job would probably have been a lot different if I'd known this is really where I'm supposed to be—if I could have understood what the note said when I first found it."

"What kept you from understanding it?"

"You've seen Sammy's handwriting. I'm not sure it's clear to anyone at first glance."

"I guess that's really part of my question—what's the value of a message you can't understand?"

Kate paused thoughtfully. "I had several roommates over the past four years whose parents were paying for school. Without exception, they were much different students than me or any of my other roommates who had to pay our own way."

"And there's a connection there somewhere?" he asked, looking confused.

"The connection is that when you have to work for something, you do things differently. While my roommates who were living on Daddy's dime were sleeping in and staying up late, the rest of us were working hard. We went to class. We did our homework. We treated our education like it was our only hope to succeed in life. In four years, I think I only missed a handful of classes, and those were just because of an emergency appendectomy. My point is, when you have to work for something, you usually value it more."

"Are you telling me you wouldn't have valued Sammy's note if it had been easy to understand—if you could have just read it straight the first time?"

"I don't know. I don't think we get to choose the way the universe speaks to us."

"Sorry, but that sounds like a cop-out."

"Look, I don't know why things work out the way they do. I can't say I know how it would've been different if I'd understood his note the first time I read it. I've definitely had answers that are clearer, but I've also had others that weren't as clear as this one."

"So you really believe this was an answer from...the universe?"

She shook her head solemnly. "Charlie, I never prayed to the universe for answers. I prayed to God. I feel like that answer came from him."

"Really? You're ready to pull out all the stops and say that, without question?"

"Do you have a problem with that?"

"No, I just would have expected a college graduate to exercise a little more critical thinking."

"Wow! Are you questioning my intelligence or just my judgment?"

"Neither. I'm just wondering how you can take a couple of random notes and plan the next year or more of your life around them. What if that first note had told you that you were in the wrong place—that you should get a job on a shrimp boat or move to Canada? Would you have done it?"

She responded with a smirk and shook her head.

"I'm just asking. What's the difference?"

"Charlie, you already know the difference."

"I don't think so."

"Yes, you do. It all comes back to that feeling, right? That feeling of peace and joy that you've just described. I don't think that can be counterfeited—not after you've experienced the real thing. I don't know how else to explain it. If you've really felt what you said you've felt, I shouldn't need to explain anything."

"Well, if you're gonna put it that way!" he responded with a smile.

"Charlie, tell me: why are you so afraid of accepting that this is real?"

"Because real things actually exist in the real, physical world. There's no mystical mumbo jumbo about it. You can see it. You can touch it. You can perceive it with your senses."

"You don't think we have a spiritual sense as well?"

He shrugged. "I've never seen it. I've never touched it."

"But you've felt it! What more are you hoping for?"

"I'm hoping to understand whatever it is I've felt."

"How do you hope to understand it if you refuse to believe it's real? You're wasting your time."

"Why do you say that?"

"Because you're just talking in circles. You felt something. The mystical world made its existence known to you. You know what it feels like. You even described it somewhere on the opposite end of the spectrum of having spiders suck out your brains. That's not nothing, Charlie. That's a really big something."

He shook his head and let out a really long breath.

"Charlie, is the wind real?"

"That's a dumb question."

"Is it? You can't see it."

"What do you mean? Of course you can see it. We just saw it out there."

"Did we?"

"Of course we did."

"Convince me."

"Don't be silly."

"I'm serious. Convince me."

"Kate, the wind picked up those notes and carried them away. We both saw it."

"Did you actually see the wind do that? I saw the notes flying, but I didn't see what it was that carried them away."

"Okay, reasonably speaking, what else could it have been?"

"It could have been exhaust from a jet plane or, more likely, air that got stirred up from that helicopter we heard. Or maybe it was just a rogue flock of invisible butterflies."

"Now you really are being silly."

"Oh, you want silly? Maybe it was a...an army of paperboys from the fifth dimension."

He laughed "Okay, what's your point?"

"My point is that you can't prove that was the wind any more than I can prove that what you've experienced is a gift from a mystical presence. My point is that it's probably at least as easy to prove the existence of paperboys from other dimensions who like to rearrange and steal paper than it is to prove the reality of there being a parallel, mystical world that reaches into our world from time to time and fills our hearts with peace and joy."

Charlie looked at her intensely for a long moment before bursting into laughter.

"What's so funny?"

"Paperboys from the fifth dimension! Really?"

"Hey, I've heard of crazier stuff."

"Crazier than the fifth dimension?"

"Okay, maybe not. But the sad thing is that anyone who buys into hardcore cynicism only keeps themselves from the possibility of feeling what you described earlier. Charlie, it sounds like you've tried to talk yourself out of this being real for at least a couple of years, and you haven't made any progress. Maybe if you actually allowed yourself to believe in the possibility of this being real, things would work out differently."

"I don't think you understand what you're asking me to do."

"Maybe I don't."

"You're not only asking me to set aside more than a decade's worth of skepticism, you're asking me to embrace the very thing I've spent that time pushing against."

She looked thoughtful before she spoke and when her words came out they were nearly a whisper. "What has that skepticism ever brought you in terms of peace?"

He looked upset with her question. "I've always figured it's better to be a skeptic than a schmuck."

"Has that ever brought you any peace?"

"It's way more complicated than that."

"Okay, so has complicating your life and your belief system, or lack thereof, ever brought you even a sliver of peace?"

He looked at her for a long moment before looking away. "I'm an atheist, Kate. You're wasting your time."

"Charlie, I've got no skin in this game. It makes no difference to me whether you're an atheist or a believer, but it sounds to me like atheism hasn't brought you any peace—like you've been stuck in the same place for at least a few years, trying to talk yourself out of everything you've ever felt here."

"I refuse to be a sucker."

She nodded thoughtfully. "I wonder if it's possible to run so far away from something that you can go to the opposite end of the spectrum and become exactly what you didn't want to become."

"What are you saying?" he asked defensively.

"I'm not saying anything. I'm just asking a question. Besides your fear of being a sucker, what's so bad about choosing to believe? What are you afraid of missing out on by opening yourself to possibility? I mean, you've already felt something, right? Maybe a whole lot of something that you can't explain by using any version of the scientific method. Just because you can't explain it doesn't keep it from being real. What did Isaiah just say out there? Just because you don't know how it works, that doesn't mean it's not working."

He shook his head.

"Now you're the one who's being silly. What have you got to lose by accepting the possibility of a spiritual world being real?"

"A lot, actually, but probably most importantly my independence.

I don't want to be controlled. I don't want to have to subscribe to any dogma that doesn't work for me."

"Who's saying you have to?"

"You can't tell me that as a Christian you don't feel inhibited from fully experiencing everything life has to offer. I don't know if you noticed, but it's Sunday. Shouldn't you be at church right now?"

"There's no one forcing me to go, and I'm not afraid of someone screaming at me because I chose to come here instead."

He raised his eyebrows. "There's not going to be any guilt that you didn't worship at church on your Sabbath?"

Kate shrugged. "I'm not going to lie and say that this is different than what I normally do, but this conversation has probably been at least as spiritually stimulating as my time in church would have been. External measures of faith are important, but I feel like God's more interested in what's in our hearts. I'm not trying to dishonor my faith today by not going to church. If anything, I'm trying to understand it better."

"It sounds like you're more of a works versus grace Christian."

"You know the difference?"

"Just because I'm a heathen doesn't mean I'm ignorant to the other side."

She nodded. "I believe in both grace and works. It seems to me that they require cooperation in order for faith to be sincere."

"I've probably met too many Christians who claim to be saved but who, in reality, act like pigs."

"Don't we all act like pigs sometimes?"

Charlie nodded, conceding.

"What I've learned from Christianity is that in our natural state, we usually are pigs, but if we turn our hearts to God, he can help us become saints."

"Okay, but you can't deny that you still have to give up your will in that process."

"Is that such a bad thing? To take a handful of broken scraps to God and ask Him to make you whole?"

"But what if you don't like the way he puts those scraps back together? It still comes back to choice for me."

"I like having choices as much as anyone else, but I don't feel like I need to travel down every possible road in order to figure out which road is going to lead me to the greatest happiness."

"Isn't that being closed-minded?"

"I don't think so. It seems like it's more of a combination of common sense and…"

"And?"

"And being able to use the feelings we've been talking about to discern which road is going to be most right for me. I guess that probably means that I don't get to see every single road, but I don't know if that's a bad thing, do you?"

He shrugged. "I don't know. I like adventures. I don't want anyone to tell me which way I have to go. That's not really freedom, is it?"

"Okay, maybe not, but I don't feel like I need to try crystal meth in order to know it's not for me. I could ignore common sense and go down that road. But from what I know about how drugs affect people's lives, I don't get the feeling addicts have any more freedom than I do—and, in most cases, far less. Maybe there is a shortcut to happiness after all. Maybe it's just knowing all the roads that don't have to be traveled. If that's being closed-minded, then I guess I am."

Charlie smiled and shook his head. "I've never known anyone like you, Kate."

"Like me? What does that mean?"

"I just don't know how to argue with you. There aren't many people who'll discuss stuff like this without getting upset and feeling like I'm threatening them."

"Was that your intent?"

He looked away, not offering an answer either way. He picked up his backpack and wandered farther into the complex of towers. His silence disturbed Kate as she considered the many potential possibilities of his intent. But as she watched him walk away, she quickly chose to decide that his intent was either half-baked or confused. The fact that he just walked away seemed to only support her hunch. And in the silence that followed, she found herself considering what might have possessed a broken, flawed man like Simon to build this and to build it here.

She knew her exposure to Southern California real estate was limited to the six trips she had made to work and back along the I-405 corridor, but she couldn't help but imagine that there had to be plenty of more suitable neighborhoods for a piece of artwork like this. As her eyes swept from the towers and buttresses overhead, however, she was overwhelmed with the feeling that everything within view had been created very deliberately. As she looked around in the quiet that surrounded her, she found herself thinking about what Charlie had said about hope being more valuable in dark and chaotic places. She considered what she already knew about Simon—the tragic death of his brother and daughter; the ruin of a marriage and family; the years of addiction and homelessness. And in that nourishing silence that surrounded her, she knew that this—this place he had created—was no accident, no meaningless attempt at showing off, no place of baseless hope and lies. It was quirky and unique in every possible way, but it radiated authenticity, honesty, sincerity. And at that realization, she knew without a doubt that there was much more here than Charlie had been able to surmise.

CHAPTER 14

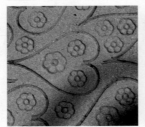

TRANSLUCENCY

There is enough light for those who only desire to see,
and enough obscurity for those who have a contrary disposition.
—*Blaise Pascal*

"There's something I can't figure out," Kate said when she caught up with Charlie.

"Only one thing?" he responded, laughing.

She smiled. "No, I'm sure there's probably a lot more, but I really can't figure out why you're such a chicken?"

"Excuse me?"

"Yeah, you've pretty much told me you know more about this place than anyone alive and that you know you're supposed to make a film about all of this and that you can't graduate until you finish your film, and yet you're basically doing everything but that. I don't get it."

"Kate, I'm not going to gamble my future away by doing something I can't believe in."

"Oh, you mean like spending all your free time making YouTube videos of people doing stupid things?"

He shook his head, looking angry.

"I'm serious. If you don't want to do this, why do you keep coming back? Why can't you just walk away and work on something else—maybe get a job with a big studio or something?"

He shook his head again. "Because I can't."

"What do you mean, you can't? It seems pretty easy to me. You drive away and never come back. Delete the photos from your hard drive and iPad. Move on. What's the big deal?"

"I'm afraid of missing out," he muttered.

"So instead, you're missing out because of what—indecision? Apathy? Procrastination? No offense, but you've spent the last five years working on a documentary that—what? Only a handful of people have ever seen?"

"Forty-three."

"What?"

"Forty-three. That's way more than a handful. That's almost nine handfuls. Of course, most of those were in my film class and have only seen an earlier cut."

She laughed. "So what's the main message of your film so far?"

"That there's more to Watts Towers than most people see."

She raised one eyebrow.

"What does that mean? That eyebrow thing?"

"Look, I obviously don't know anything about producing a documentary, but it doesn't seem like you'd have to spend five years doing research to tell that story. What aren't you telling me?"

"The same thing I've been unable to tell the rest of the world for fear of looking like a fool."

"Nothing risked, nothing gained, right?"

"Yeah, well, I'm not convinced it's true in this case. If I risk this and it totally bombs, people will never watch anything else I make."

"What's the alternative?"

"Excuse me?"

"Charlie, I'm not a film person, so feel free judge what I'm about to say as coming from someone who's ignorant on the matter. But it seems to me that if you don't make the film you know you're supposed to make, then you're cheating everyone."

"How do you figure?" he asked, looking confused.

"We talked about this yesterday. Haters will always be haters. You can't do anything to change that, so you might as well put it out there and let them hate it if they want to."

"That's an interesting philosophy—just handing the baby over to be eaten by wolves."

"Okay, so that sounds a little harsh, but as long as you're not making the film you're supposed to make, is it possible for you to be happy? Will you ever have the chance of your film being awesome if you never finish it? You're letting the haters win just by not letting your real voice be heard. And if you have passion for it, you'll definitely find people who'll love it."

"Look, there's been a handful of films made about Simon and his towers over the years. They've all given hints about a deeper meaning behind them, but they've all shied away from it—like it's poison or something vile. It scares me when filmmakers who are much bigger than me don't even want to touch it."

"Maybe they've just been waiting for someone with different sensitivities to tell that story."

He shook his head. "I don't know."

"Charlie, yesterday you said something about how this place is like an island in the middle of a troubled sea, right?"

"Yeah."

"I agreed with you then, but I feel even more that way today—and I still don't really know anything about what's going on here."

"So why are you so positive about this?"

"What do you mean?"

"I mean, you're running toward this, and I've been running away from it."

"Maybe I'm just running blind."

"I don't think so," Charlie said, shaking his head. "You're ready to jump in with both feet, and you don't even know what you're jumping into."

She shrugged. "I don't really have any idea what's going on here or what my role is in all of this. I have way more questions than answers, but…"

"But what?"

"But I feel compelled to throw whatever I can at this to try to understand whatever it is. I'm trying not to freak out, but it seems pretty clear that I'm here in Watts for a reason. And it's not just because I got offered a crappy job for fourteen dollars an hour." She looked around at the towers looming overhead, then back to Charlie. "I guess I'm beginning to feel like I'm part of some plan that's way bigger than me. And…"

"And?"

"And, well, maybe it's like that note said yesterday—maybe we're supposed to help each other."

Charlie's face registered confusion. "I don't remember it saying anything about helping each other."

"Okay, well, yeah, but it was kind of implied, right?"

"I'm not sure what it meant." He laughed, turning away. "To be honest, I feel more afraid of this than ever."

"Even after your message? Even after seeing Sammy's drawing and that whole…wind thing with the notes?"

"You're not at all freaked out about any of that?"

Kate paused for a long moment as she thought about his question. "I guess I'm not."

"Really? Do you usually take instruction from pieces of garbage you find stuck to your bike? Is it normal for you to have drawings randomly show up that paint some prophetic picture of future events? What did you call them? Oracles? Oh, and have you ever seen anything like what just happened out there with the wind and all those notes? This is full-on crazy, and you're acting like it happens all the time. Forgive me if I'm totally freakin' out. But I like to consider myself a fairly sane guy, and this seems to be going in a totally…weird direction."

She nodded. "But how does it feel?"

"What? Didn't you hear what I just said?"

"Yes. You basically said that nothing like this has ever happened to you before. I get that, but how does it *feel*?"

"You're kidding, right? You're trying to diagnose me right here, right now?"

"Don't be silly. Yesterday you talked about this place feeling somehow different, right?"

"Well, yeah, but that's a different kind of different."

"Okay, but how does this new stuff feel compared to what you've felt before?"

"Totally insane!"

"Really?"

"Are you suggesting that any of this is normal?"

"No, not at all. *Paranormal*, maybe, but…"

"So why aren't you freaking out at least a little bit?"

"I'm not sure. I've always been a pretty intuitive person. I really don't have much tolerance for things that are dark. Since Friday, I've been constantly checking the pulse of my intuition, and even though a lot of the things that have happened in the last few days are…strange and new, I've tried to pay close attention to how it all *feels*."

Charlie looked thoughtful for a long moment before nodding. "It doesn't feel dark, does it?"

"I wouldn't be here if it did."

"How can you be so calm about all of this?"

"I got a head start, remember?" she said, holding out the notebook. "Dr. Hermansen felt pretty much the same way you did. She freaked out when she first started taking a look at Sammy and wasn't able to use any of the tools she'd gathered through her education or work experience to appropriately define what was going on."

"Didn't you say that she thought he was delusional or something like that?"

"Yes, in the beginning."

"So, why did she change her mind?"

"Because she learned to feel."

Charlie shook his head as he turned away. "I'm not there yet," he muttered.

"Maybe I can help."

"I don't think there's anything you can do."

"You sound like you don't even want to try."

"I've been trying for five years. I'm burned out and frustrated."

"So what are you going to do about it?"

"I don't know."

"I could help you. We could figure this out together."

"Thanks, but...I really work best alone."

"You don't even want to try?"

He shook his head. "I'm sorry, but I think I just need to get out of here."

"Charlie, why are you doing this?"

"Doing what?"

"I don't even know how to answer that. Giving up? Blowing me off? Why are you so afraid of feeling?"

"I think I got a bad bagel," he responded, rubbing his belly. "Sorry, but we better go. I think I'm gonna be sick."

Kate watched him, trying to read him. The fear was still there—that was easy to see. But there was something else—something darker and more troubling that she couldn't pinpoint. He didn't wait for her to respond but started walking back to the front gate.

And so the tour was over before it had really even begun. As she walked through the shadows cast by the towers and buttresses, she was surprised by her feeling of disappointment. She couldn't remember what she had expected, but it certainly wasn't this. Instead of answers, there were only more questions. Her feet felt heavy, and she slowed her pace, feeling reluctant to leave. Discouraged, her eyes fell to the cement sidewalk at her feet, where she noticed something she had missed before. She looked around from side to side, even turning backward, recognizing she had missed it—everywhere. The pattern was different from section to section, but everywhere she looked she could see the simple, repeated motif ornamenting the colored concrete: hearts! Everywhere! Hundreds of them. The sidewalk seemed to be paved with them as far as the eye could see. She looked up to find more hearts on the walls. She turned to the gazebo and was surprised to find that its arched entryway was crowned with a heart. At every turn, she spotted hearts.

"I'm ready when you are." She heard his voice behind her, but she didn't want to leave—not now—not after finding this. In her mind, she remembered something Isaiah had said—something about how few people understood what the towers were all about even though the meaning was clear for those who wanted to see. Could it really be that simple? Could this really be about love? She didn't need to ask herself a second time. She knew by the way it felt.

Kate turned back around, feeling anxious to share what she had discovered with Charlie, but she immediately knew he was in no place to listen. She hurried to his side when she saw him leaning, his forehead pressed against the gate and his body looking weak, his face pale.

"What's wrong?" she asked, taking the key from his hand and unlocking the gate.

"I don't feel well," he responded as the gate opened and he staggered out onto the lawn.

"Can I help you?" she asked, grasping his arm to steady him.

He handed her his backpack before he spoke. "Wait for me. I've got to get to the bathroom."

She took the pack and swung it over her shoulder as he jogged awkwardly across the lawn to the art center. Unsure of what she should do, she decided she would wait for him on the bench near the guard shack. She had just sat down when she heard Isaiah's voice behind her.

"How'd it go?"

She turned to see him limping towards her. "Not very well," she admitted.

"I'm sorry to hear that."

"Yeah, so much for the oracle."

"Why do you say that?"

"Well, nothing really worked out, did it?"

"What was supposed to work out?

His question surprised her. "I guess it just didn't go the way I expected it to go," she said as she handed him the key.

"That hardly means it didn't work out the way it was supposed to. As far as I could tell the oracle never said stuff would work out the way you had it in your head. You were here together. That's what matters. The oracle couldn't have been true if you hadn't brought that boy with you today."

"Yeah, but we didn't even get to the tour."

"That's too bad. Where is ol' Charlie, anyway?"

"He got sick. He's in the bathroom."

Isaiah nodded, hobbling around the bench, where he sat down next to Charlie's backpack. "Sick again, huh?"

"This has happened before?"

He nodded again, looking out across the lawn. "I was hopin' it'd be diff'rent today."

"How so?"

"I told you I've been waitin' for this day for a long time."

"Yeah?"

"It's hard bein' patient when so much is ridin' on him figurin' things out. Did he get any closer today?"

"I'm not sure," Kate replied, feeling confused. "How would I know if he did?"

Isaiah smiled. "I s'pose you wouldn't." He nodded before turning to face her. "What'd ya think?"

"It's amazing," she responded. "I feel like I could spend a week in there."

"Hmmm." He smiled softly. "You felt it, didn't ya?"

"Yeah, I did."

"And you know what it is?"

"I think so," she admitted, unable to keep from smiling. "It's love, isn't it?"

Isaiah's smile only broadened. "You got that from just one visit?"

Kate nodded. "I didn't see it until just the end, but yeah, it's everywhere in there."

"That's good. Did Charlie feel it?"

"If he did, he's not admitting it. He seems to be trying hard not to feel anything at all."

Isaiah pursed his large lips and nodded slowly. "I've been watchin' that boy for mosta five years. He's got a big ol' chunk of greatness in 'im, but he don't like nobody to see it."

"Why do you think that is?"

Isaiah sat quiet for a moment, looking like he was slowly digesting her question. "You ever heard o' folks who're 'fraid of the dark?"

Kate smiled and nodded.

"There's some folks who're afraid of the light, too."

"You think that's his problem?"

"Without question. I'm guessin' the light musta got a little too bright in there this mornin'."

Kate nodded, not knowing how to respond.

"You're a woman o' faith, ain't ya, Kate?"

"I'm a woman who's tryin' to figure it out."

"That counts fo' somethin'."

"You think so?"

"Sure. You ain't given up, have ya?"

She shook her head.

"You're still fightin'. You're still lookin'. You still gots your sense o' wonder. It might not be all that you want it to be, but it's 'nough to keep the light on in your eyes."

"Thanks," she responded, surprised.

"You grew up with God in your life, or are ya just findin' 'im now?"

"Both, I guess. I...I got lost for a bit, but I'm trying to find my way back."

"I thought so."

"Am I that transparent?"

"No, you're that translucent."

She looked confused.

"It's the light. There's still plenty of it there for those who are lookin' for that sorta thing."

"And you're lookin' for that sort of thing?"

"Every day."

"Why?"

"We're all lookin' for somethin', ain't we? And there ain't no use in lookin' for darkness. Heaven knows there's plenty o' that to go 'round. The way I figure it, we might as well be lookin' for light. It ain't hard to find if you're always lookin' for it. And when you find it, it's like findin' a tall glass of iced tea on a summer day. The world needs more of it—more light—more love."

Kate nodded. "That's what this is about, isn't it? That's why Simon built these towers?"

Isaiah nodded. "I like to think of it as an invitation."

"An invitation?" she asked, looking confused.

"A real big one. It's invitin' folks to let their light shine—a city built on a hill. Only when you ain't got no hill, you gotta improvise."

Kate nodded thoughtfully. She was no stranger to the reference of a city built on a hill. Her parents and Sunday school teachers had taught that parable from the time she could talk, but never had she seen such a big and colorful interpretation of it. In her heart, though, she knew there was much more to this place than just an artistic interpretation of a

Matthew 5:14–16

classic parable. "Can I come back and talk to you about this sometime?" she asked before she could stop herself.

"Of course. You're welcome around my little campfire anytime."

"Even if I don't bring Charlie?" she asked, looking over Isaiah's shoulder to see Charlie gimping his way across the lawn.

"Yes. Bring 'im with you if he'll come. That boy could benefit from your open heart and mind. But if he don't want, come anyhow."

"Thank you," Kate replied as she looked deep into Isaiah's eyes, surprised by the brightness of the light that burned just beyond the darkness of his pupils. "I'll be back soon."

Live according to your highest light and more light will be given.
Peace Pilgrim

CHAPTER 15

SOLITUDE

All the unhappiness of men arises from one single fact,
that they cannot sit quietly in their own chamber.
—Blaise Pascal

The ride home was mostly quiet. Charlie's stomachache left him somehow even more irritable, and before they had even pulled away from the curb, he had put in his earbuds and turned on his music—the internationally recognizable sign that a person doesn't care to communicate. Kate was disappointed. She had so wanted more. More understanding. More time to look and take it all in. More time to figure things out. Her disappointment only grew as she realized that without Charlie, she would likely be unable to have the same access to the towers. But she knew there was nothing she could do about that now, so Kate chose instead to think about her conversation with Isaiah. The notion that he could see in her some portion of light was intriguing. The idea of people being carriers of light wasn't an entirely new concept.

She remembered several discussions from her class on interpersonal communication that had touched on similar ideas—that the eyes are the windows to the soul and, more than any other physical feature, give the most honest clues to a person's true character. She wondered if Isaiah might know the same thing.

Kate was surprised how this recollection triggered another distant memory. She remembered that it was while she was enrolled in this class that she had begun to open her heart again to the possibility of the reality of a God after having ditched the remnants of her faith during her sophomore year.

It felt juvenile now—abandoning the faith of her childhood when things didn't go the way she had hoped and prayed they would. But as she stared out on the busy LA freeway, she also remembered the heartache and darkness of that time. It had started with the death of Emma Hansen, Kate's lifelong friend, who was only a week younger and lived on the neighboring farm. In her nineteen short years, Emma had had a more profound influence on Kate than any of her own siblings. Born deaf and with extensive learning disabilities, Emma had plenty of challenges. None of those, however, kept Kate away, and she became Emma's spokesperson from a very early age after the two toddlers developed a crude sign language that was unique to the two of them. Having experienced the joys of finding ways to help Emma, Kate seemed to always know that she wanted to study social work when she grew up.

Their connection had ebbed slightly in high school when their differences in ability could no longer be ignored. But Kate and Emma maintained their close friendship even after Kate left for college. Though her health had never been great, Emma's slow but steady decline started shortly after the beginning of freshman year. Kate continued to stop in to visit whenever she was home, but her visits became more irregular and infrequent with each passing semester. Emma had already outlived her doctor's expectations by more than a decade, offering joy to all who knew her. And even though Kate had known that her early death was expected, the reality of it stung her deeply.

Still reeling from Emma's death, Kate had imagined that the pain in her gut was just a physical manifestation of her emotional pain. For several days she tried to ignore it, hoping and praying it would go away. The ambulance ride to the hospital, however, and the surgery that followed left Kate feeling like the universe was conspiring against her. She learned that poison from her ruptured appendix had likely diminished her ability to conceive, if not altogether squelched it. She was only twenty years old at the time. Children were a far-off dream, but they were still a dream.

In the weeks that followed, Kate had struggled to maintain her faith in a merciful God. It had seemed so easy to let it all go—easier than trying to make sense of a God and a plan that included death, pain, and suffering. Her struggle was only compounded when the medical bills began arriving—the result of a lapsed insurance policy. And in those emotionally, spiritually, and physically challenging months, doubt prevailed as cynicism rushed in.

Having watched her parents' heartache associated with the wayward advances of their youngest daughter, Jill, Kate decided not to burden her parents with her own doubts. Leonard Larsen was a man of integrity and deep faith. He and his dutiful wife, Shirley, had provided a firm foundation for all of their seven children to build their lives on. And all of their children had been grateful for their strength and commitment to God and humanity—all of them except Jill, who seemed to have been born with a contrary spirit.

Kate had watched closely as Jill and their parents learned to navigate around each other, frequently fumbling and clashing. Despite their many differences, the sisters had always been close. Their mother had frequently credited Kate's soft, receptive heart to her close friendship with Emma and had openly wished Jill could have similarly benefited. But no amount of wishing and praying had changed Jill into what her mother wanted, and Kate had been forced to serve for many years as a buffer between her rebellious sister and their befuddled parents, who had tamed the wilds out of five strong-willed boys only to be broken by their youngest teenaged daughter.

As Kate's struggle progressed, she found it difficult to attend church, engage in spiritual conversation, and eventually even to pray. In time, she found others who were dealing with their own faith crises. The coffee shops and mountain trails near campus slowly became the unconscious alternatives to the Sabbath day observances of her youth. Here, there were no expectations or judgment, and everyone was welcome.

For nearly a year, Kate enjoyed this freedom of thought and activity away from the ideology of religion and even faith in general. But something had changed during that class she took junior year. The last thing she had expected to find in a class about communication was an element of spirituality she didn't even know she was looking for. As she remembered it now, she realized that it was in that small, intimate setting that she felt something she hadn't felt for some time. She didn't know what it was at first. But she found herself looking forward to that class more than any other time in the week. She had learned that human nature required connection—physical, psychological, intimate connection. She discovered the power of that connection with every member of the class as they took turns pairing off to learn to communicate on a more intimate, personal level.

Now, more than a year later, she remembered the names and faces of each member of her class. They had become friends—all of them. Only six months earlier, Kate had attended the wedding of Joe Morrison and Jennie Albers, two of her classmates, whose friendship and love had developed as a result of the principles they had learned in their class together. Like her, Joe and Jennie had experienced faith crises of their own. And, like Kate, the lessons they had learned about communication had given them each individually and independently new desire to reconnect with something spiritual.

For Kate, that desire led to questions. They weren't new questions. Most of them, in fact, were the same questions she'd had for years. But armed with new insight and communication skills, Kate approached these questions with a sincerity and an intensity she'd never had before. She wanted answers—honest answers. And so she began asking the old questions with new, sincere desires. It wasn't exactly prayer, at least not in the formal way she'd been taught as a child. There were no rote sayings or trite phrases. Most times, there weren't even words—at least not uttered words. Rather it was a change in mindset from an unfocused stream of consciousness to a place of mindfulness.

It was while she was in such a place that she experienced that first *something*. She had thought back dozens of times, trying to remember the intensity of that event in December just six months earlier. She'd been driving home for Christmas, and in an effort to put away the stresses of finals, she'd turned off the radio and tried hard to be mindful. In the quiet of her car, she watched the sun setting across the valley where she'd grown up, bathing the world in a golden light and filling her whole body with a most indescribable sense of internal electrification. It was on that road home, as the sun's last rays illuminated the trees on top of the mountains like filaments in a light bulb, that she made her discovery.

It was such a simple idea that she second-guessed the discovery at first. But the more she considered it and the more she tried to recreate it, the more she realized that through it something about her whole mentality was profoundly different. Gratitude. It was far from an unknown concept. Her parents had taught her the basics from their very first lessons on prayer. But this was different. It was unlike those childhood prayers where she would quickly race through the same oft-repeated items on her habitual list so she could get on to the long list of things she wanted. Instead, she had realized on that winter's day that she had forgotten her wants. Overwhelmed by the beauty that surrounded her, she had simply and spontaneously begun to express thanks.

She was surprised how comforting it felt after more than a year of giving up on the possibility of God to begin again with a glimmer of hope that someone might care enough to be listening. On her walks around campus, on her drives, during hikes in the mountains, and even in quiet moments at work, she found herself opening her heart to hope.

And with that hope, peace had come into her life. She learned quickly that peace and hope were fragile and in need of constant nourishment. And so, with a conscious effort, her ventures into mindfulness took on new meaning as gratitude filled an ever-enlarging part of her journey. And with that gratitude had come something else: humility.

From the time she was a child, Kate had heard about humility. From Sunday school lessons and talk around the dinner table, she gathered it was considered a virtue worthy of emulation. She had witnessed its opposite—pride—in the lives and attitudes of athletes and professors alike, but it wasn't until this change of mindfulness occurred that she recognized it in her own attitudes as well. Over the next several months as she consciously tried to root pride out, she experienced a new and genuine sense of humility. Instead of her natural tendency to be impatient and anxious, she slowly became calm and even-tempered. When she began applying for jobs and was faced with rejections and dead ends, she tried to continue to express gratitude, feeling at peace that somehow, somewhere, a door would open for her. And when that place was Watts, she faced the opportunity with a much more open mind than she ever could have just six months earlier.

Her first week at the hospital had been completely anticlimactic. Not once in her over-the-phone interview had she been informed that she would be spending most of her days sorting through medical files, trying to determine which patients might be most eligible for early release. It wasn't until after she arrived that she learned that the state hospital, like all of California's state institutions, was facing budget cuts and reforms. She had since heard from the other interns that they had been hired to take the place of much-higher-paid doctors and social workers. She had even heard whisperings that the Watts Hospital, one of the oldest and most run-down in the system, was on the chopping block. Morale was low. The work was boring. And Kate had wondered several times each day if she had made a colossal mistake in coming all this way.

But that was last week. Things had taken an interesting turn late on Friday afternoon with the discovery of the notebook. She still had no idea how it hadn't fallen into the wrong hands in the eleven months since Dr. Hermansen had hidden it away in the bottom drawer of her desk. Eleven months it had sat there buried under old phonebooks, waiting for her to arrive. The idea of it was still mind-boggling, but Dr. Hermansen's note left little question that the notebook, like a baton, had been left for Kate to pick up and run with. After finding the second note, she had felt certain she was on the right track, especially when Charlie had agreed to accompany her to the towers.

Now on their way home, Kate felt entirely less certain. Nothing had gone the way she'd expected. Charlie, the guy whose character and judgment she had questioned previously had proven to be just about as valuable as she feared he would be. She glanced over at him, wondering if he was as disappointed as she felt. His eyes were closed, but she doubted that the volume of the music coming out of his earbuds would ever allow anyone to sleep.

"We're back," she said, shaking his arm as she pulled up in front of his house a few minutes later.

He opened his eyes, looking either tired or sick or maybe both. He blinked several times before reaching for the door handle. "I'm sorry," he mumbled.

"For what?" Kate responded.

"I'm sure it was a disappointment."

"Yeah, I'm not gonna lie. It pretty much was."

He nodded solemnly. "Sorry."

"So am I. I really hoped we could help each other with this... whatever it is."

"Yeah, well, it's probably a stupid idea to take direction from scraps of litter."

"Charlie, you know that's not what it was."

"Whatever," he said, opening the door. "If you change your mind about reliving that stunt on your cruiser, you know where to find me. I still think it could be worth a bucket of money."

Kate shook her head, laughing. "What about your documentary?"

"What about it?"

"How are you going to finish it?"

"I've been thinking about that all the way home."

"Really?"

"Yeah." He nodded several times before shaking his head. "You're right. I'm wasting my time. I've decided I'm just gonna shelve it. There's no point in pushing this any further."

"Whoa! I never suggested you should give up. I said you should…"

"It's never gonna happen," he said, cutting her off as he stepped out of the car.

"Really? After five years you're just gonna give up like that?"

"I've got better things to do with my time."

"What about your degree?"

"Screw it."

"Really?"

"I'm making good enough money to live. I'm tired of hitting my head against the wall and not making any progress. It's just not worth it."

"Wow! All right. Well, thanks for introducing me to Isaiah, anyway. He seems like a really great guy. I think he'll be a lot of help in figuring all of this out."

"Yeah, whatever. I'll see you around." Charlie said, closing the door.

Kate wasn't sure what she felt as she pulled away from the curb. Disappointment. Confusion. Anger. She'd pegged Charlie as a shallow-minded, womanizing beach bum when they'd met on Friday night at the convenience store. After spending several hours with him, she knew he was more complicated than that, but that was of little consolation. By the time she pulled onto the Pacific Coast Highway, she'd considered several potential spectrum disorders that could account for his unusual, irrational behavior. Whatever the case, something in him was definitely broken.

She drove south with no destination in mind, trying to make sense of the day's events. A sign for Balboa Island intrigued her, and she turned off the highway, curious. A narrow bridge led over the tranquil bay

and onto Marine Avenue, a picturesque, tree-lined street with quaint shops on either side. A dozen people were cued up outside a colorful sweetshop with a sign advertising Balboa Bars and chocolate-covered bananas, reminding Kate that she hadn't eaten in several hours. Distracted by the windows of art galleries and gift shops, she nearly rear-ended the slow-moving car in front of her and decided she'd be better off exploring the island on foot. After passing several streets named for gemstones, she found a parking space on a narrow street filled with charming and colorful vacation homes and their manicured, miniature yards.

Excited by the sight of her very first lemon tree, she got out of the car, feeling anxious to stretch her legs and fill her head with something other than Charlie George. She fell in behind an elderly couple enjoying a lazy afternoon stroll. Looking around, she recognized the strange juxtaposition of the two places she had been that day, deciding it would be hard to find two places that were more different than Watts and Balboa Island.

The couple in front of her turned onto a wider sidewalk that paralleled the water's edge. She walked to the thigh-high seawall that separated the island from the bay. Dozens of sailboats and expensive-looking yachts bobbed in the harbor, and across the water, the Newport Pavilion with its Ferris wheel sparkled like a temple of fun.

Kate followed the sidewalk until she came to a bench that offered a lovely view of the harbor. Feeling her lack of sleep finally catching up to her, she sat down to watch the boats lazily moving about in the calm

waters. With the sun shining and the warm coastal breezes blowing, Kate soon found herself wrestling with her sleepy body. But she couldn't sleep. Not now. Not with so much to think about. She stood, pushing sleep away, and started off again, walking around the island. As she walked, she couldn't help but think about how different this place was from where she'd spent the morning. Every yard was clean, pruned, and free of weeds. The houses were clean, neat, and tidy. New multilevel mansions stood next to older single-level homes, but all of them looked like they'd been built for a life of leisure. This was the California she'd imagined—sun and sea and beauty everywhere she looked.

She thought about what Charlie had told her about the towers—how he believed they would have been torn down to make room for other things if they'd been built in a more expensive neighborhood. Curious about prices on the island, Kate stopped at the next real estate sign. A glossy brochure showed beautiful pictures of a newish house with views of the harbor. It had six bathrooms and five bedrooms and boasted plenty of space for entertaining, both inside and out. She looked up to see that the house and patio all but swallowed the small lot, leaving only a small patch of land for palms and flowers. As she turned the brochure over, she nearly dropped it, counting the zeroes to make sure she had read it correctly. $9,700,000.00. She felt her face flush. Could that be possible? She put the brochure back and kept walking, anxious to find another real estate sign that might make her feel a little better about her hourly wage. But the next brochure did nothing to help. $8,975,000.00 for a slightly smaller, slightly older home. She tried to imagine what a monthly mortgage payment would be but quickly gave up and tried to forget about it when she realized it would be multiple factors more than what she made in an entire year.

As she walked away, she looked at the size of the lot and realized that Watts Towers sat on a lot at least five times as big. Granted, it was nowhere near the beach, but she knew Charlie was right about at least one thing: if the towers had been built here, they would have been torn down long ago to make way for multimillion-dollar homes. But several questions remained. Why would anyone spend thirty-three years building such a strange, complicated structure? If there was meaning behind the towers, as everything seemed to suggest, how could one learn to understand what Simon was trying to say? And, perhaps most importantly, what was her role in all of this?

By the time she got back to her car after circumnavigating the island on foot, she knew three things. One, that it was highly unlikely she would ever be able to afford to live on Balboa Island. Two, that fourteen dollars an hour was a pitiful wage for California. And three, that her mind would not be able to rest until she could figure out why she was here.

As she drove back to her sister's home, Kate's mind began to reel with the events of the past seven days and especially the last seventy-two hours. It felt good to feel like a part of something big. But those things also left her with so many questions. She knew she needed help. And the only person who seemed to have some answers and to have his head on straight was Isaiah. She knew she needed to go back.

CHAPTER 16

LOOKING UP

Life is short and we have never too much time for
gladdening the hearts of those who are traveling the dark journey with us.
Oh be swift to love, make haste to be kind.
—*Henri Frederic Amiel*

After spending the rest of Sunday afternoon rereading Dr. Hermansen's notebook, Kate was excited to get to work on Monday morning. Her disappointment with Charlie had faded away, and she was determined to not let his attitude and lack of ambition keep her from moving toward better understanding Sammy and his connection to the towers. Her excitement was dulled at staff meeting when she received three large boxes full of patient files to sort through in search of inconsistencies. But her excitement was renewed at the end of the meeting, when she was introduced to the hospital's head art therapist, Yolanda McKinley, a woman whose name Kate recognized from multiple entries in Dr. Hermansen's notebook.

Kate had difficulty trying not to seem overly excited to meet her but managed to ask if she might have time for a visit about a person of mutual interest—Sammy. Yolanda looked surprised but readily agreed to a meeting that afternoon when Kate showed her the same sign Isaiah had given her the day before. For the first time since she had started the new job, the hours sailed by quickly as she read through the patient files she had been given. But still she wondered when and if she would ever have contact with real patients, having grown tired of paperwork after a week of seeing little else.

Just before five o'clock, she left her office and made her way to the basement of Building 3, following the campus map she had been given on her first day. Kate knew she was headed in the right direction when she saw the brightly colored tile mosaic on the walls of the stairway. Words pieced together with bright bits of tile announced the subterranean art room, giving life and light to what Kate imagined would be an otherwise dark and gloomy basement.

She descended the stairs and was pleasantly surprised to see that the color and design of the mosaic not only continued into the hallway but also grew more vibrant the farther she walked. She smiled as she passed under the mirror mosaic that covered the ceiling around each of the nondescript fluorescent lights, multiplying the amount of light they offered to the passageway. Even the same industrial tiles that were used throughout the hospital campus looked brighter and somehow happier in this light.

The colorful hallway opened into a large room. Like the hallway, its walls were covered with mosaic interspersed with sections of corkboard hung with art in many different mediums. Several pillars that supported the tall ceiling were also decorated; one looked like it had been turned into a tree, with papier-mâché branches and leaves stretching out across the ceiling, making the basement feel anything but gloomy and oppressive.

Music was coming from one corner. Kate was drawn in by the lilting sound of the acoustic guitar that resonated across the large room. A woman with a colorful scarf wrapped around her head sat with her back toward Kate, singing softly to a group of patients who sat quietly on the folding chairs that encircled her. In another corner, several other patients played with clay on long tables, quietly working on various projects. In the center of the room under the shade of the tree-pillar, Yolanda McKinley was working with ten other patients, using brightly colored acrylic to paint pictures on repurposed strips of cardboard.

Kate walked to the middle of the room while the guitar serenade continued, muffling her own footsteps across the tiled floor. She was only a few feet away when Yolanda looked up.

"Is it five o'clock already?" she asked, looking a little stressed as she glanced at the clock on the far wall.

"Would it be better if I came back tomorrow?"

"No, no," she said, waving her hands, encouraging Kate to come closer.

"Who dat?" a male patient asked, obviously distracted from his painting.

"This is our new friend, Miss Kate," Yolanda announced.

Most of the patients looked up to see her.

"She pritty," another male patient announced to the amusement of rest of the group, who laughed at various degrees of volume.

"Yes, she is," Yolanda agreed. "Maybe she could be our model one day."

Several of the patients clapped their hands, one patient spilling a cup of paint water on the floor as she did so.

"Okay, maestros, that's enough for today. The nurses will be here to pick you up in the next few minutes. Will you please help me put our paints away? Jessie, will you please gather up the brushes and put them in the buckets? Arnold, will you please help Joe clean up the water on the floor?"

Kate watched as the patients responded, each of them helping out with one task or another. But she noticed that one woman was not helping—still sitting as she rocked back and forth, looking quite upset. Reading the woman's movements and facial expression as signs of distress, Kate came closer to her, resting her hand on the woman's shoulder. The woman turned to her and smiled. She was missing several teeth, making her look much older than her eyes suggested she was.

"What's your name?" Kate asked softly.

The woman's smile broadened, but she did not respond verbally.

"That's Patty," Yolanda responded from several feet away, where she was busy gathering up the cardboard canvases. "Be careful. She bites."

"Be careful, she bites," Albert repeated, making a face like he knew what he was talking about.

Kate nodded but wondered how a woman with so few teeth could do much damage. Patty continued to rock back and forth in front of her piece of cardboard, on which she had painted bright yellow stripes, bold and nearly straight.

"Good, huh?" Patty asked, beaming with pride.

"Yeah, really good," Kate responded. "Nice job."

Patty slapped her knees several times as if she were clapping for herself, and she produced an increasing flow of slobber from off the end of her already soggy chin.

"Maestros, it's time to head back to your rooms. We'll see you next Monday."

At this announcement, Patty's hands turned from slapping her knees to slapping her face.

"Patty, it's okay," Kate whispered. "You'll be back in seven days."

Patty's hands slowed at this announcement.

"You be here?" she asked, looking at Kate.

"I hope so," she responded, smiling with assurance but knowing it would not happen.

"New fren," Patty said, wrapping her arms around Kate's middle, smearing saliva on her shirt.

"Yes. New friend."

Kate looked up to see Yolanda smiling at her.

Patty released her grip around Kate and joined the others, who were lining up behind a nurse for the trip back to their rooms.

"Goodbye, maestros," Yolanda said, waving as they disappeared into the mosaicked hallway. She turned to face Kate, looking at her closely for a moment before she spoke.

"Who are you?"

"I'm Kate Larsen. I'm the new..."

"I know you're one of the new interns. I got that this morning. *But who are you?*"

"I'm not sure what you're asking."

"I've known Patty for at least twelve years, and I know for certain that no stranger has ever been able to talk to her without getting bit. You ended up with a hug. I'm just trying to figure out who you are."

Kate smiled and shrugged.

"Follow me," she said, walking toward the far end of the room, where several doors opened into small offices. Yolanda walked into one of the offices and waited for Kate to follow before closing the door. "Have a seat."

Kate nodded, sitting in the chair in front of the desk.

Yolanda walked to the other side of the desk and sat down, not taking her eyes off Kate. "You gave me a sign this morning."

Kate nodded.

"How do you know that sign?"

"Um...I...um, I read about it," she said, pulling the notebook from the bag around her shoulder. She laid it in front of her on the desk.

Yolanda looked relieved. "You're the one," she said, her eyes wild with excitement. "I thought you might be when you approached me this morning, but I've been afraid to hope too much."

"Uh, I don't what that means."

"Yes, we've been waiting for you. Sammy has been telling us that you were coming for at least two years. Some of us were getting ready to give up."

"Who's us?" she asked, looking very confused.

"You don't know?"

"I don't know anything. I just found this notebook in my new desk on Friday. After I read about Dr. Hermansen's interactions with you, I wanted to meet you."

Yolanda smiled. "You *are* the one."

"I really don't have any idea what that means."

"Does anyone else know you have this notebook?"

Kate nodded. "Yeah, uh, two people. Why?"

"What two people?"

"Well, this guy named Charlie, and Isaiah, one of the guards at Watts Towers."

"I know Isaiah. He's part of us. Who's Charlie?"

"He's just a guy I met this weekend...on the beach."

"You shared that book with a guy you met on the beach?" she asked, her eyebrow raised. "You do know that notebook is potentially damning to all of us, right?"

"Yes, I'm sorry, but it's not like that. I mean he knows I have it, but he doesn't know what's in it."

"That's good. Why does he even know you have it?"

"Long story. He actually tried to...It came out of the basket on my bike when I crashed. He found it buried in the sand. I had to get it back from him."

Yolanda smiled. "You make it sound like you had to hurt him."

"I wanted to, but..."

"But what?"

"But he let me have it back when he found out I had been to Watts Towers. He makes movies—kind of—and he's been working on a movie about the towers. Isaiah seems to know him pretty well."

"Yeah, I've heard about him," she said, looking intrigued. "Does he know about Sammy?"

"Kind of," Kate responded reluctantly.

"Explain."

"We kind of met him yesterday at the towers. I..." She opened the notebook and pulled out several pieces of paper. "I found this message on my bike on Saturday just after I met Charlie." She passed her the message written on the napkin. "And yesterday, Isaiah gave us this," she said, unfolding the oracle before sliding it across the desk.

"I see," Yolanda said after looking the picture over. "I can't say this is a total surprise, but it's not what I expected."

"What did you expect?"

"No one knew for sure. We knew someone was coming. Sammy told us that. But I didn't expect…no offense…for you to be so young—and an intern."

"I'm sorry. I probably should have left the notebook in the drawer. I didn't know what I was getting into."

"No, I expect you wouldn't. So now that you're into it, what do you think?"

"I'm not sure what to think, to be honest. It's compelling…I mean…I want to help. I'm not sure what that means, but I want to help wherever I can."

Yolanda nodded, "That's good. Do you have any experience with art?"

Kate laughed. "Uh, I took a couple of pottery classes in high school, and I used to dabble in watercolor when I was younger."

"Good enough. Has Dr. Singh assigned you to a department yet?"

"I don't think so, unless going over boring files is a department. Why?"

"We requested an intern to replace the therapist we had to let go last month because of budget cuts. Would you be willing to work with me as an art therapist intern?"

"Uh, do I have to do any file work?"

"Yes, but not like you've been doing. We have to be able to justify what we do by showing progress with our patients, but of all the therapies the hospital offers, art therapy has been proven to be one of the most universally beneficial."

"It looks like it could be fun."

"It can be, but I'll warn you that it may not be a long-term internship. I've been told that art therapy is probably on the short list for the chopping block."

Kate nodded. "All the interns have heard the same thing about basically every department. If I'm gonna be chopped, I guess I might as well have some fun while I'm here."

"When can you start?"

"Well, I suppose that's probably up to Dr. Singh, right?"

"Ultimately, yes. But if you're okay with it, I'll make the request tonight and we could probably get you started tomorrow or Wednesday at the latest."

"I think I'd like that. What do I need to do? I'm not sure if I have the skill set to be very helpful."

"If you got this far, you have the skills we need. You can pick up the rest of it by watching."

"But I'm not an artist."

Yolanda smiled. "But you once were. Every child is. The trick is learning how to reconnect with that child and learning to let go. You'll see. The biggest hurdle is fear. Once you get past that, you can do anything. Most of these patients are still kids, even though they may have reached the age of adulthood long ago. I learn more from them than they ever learn from me."

Kate nodded thoughtfully. "Is that why you call them maestros?"

"Yes. Most of them don't have years' worth of fear to keep them from creating like the rest of us do. So much of their art is free from the trappings of the world." She handed Kate the stack of cardboard paintings.

Kate flipped through the first several. Each one was different, playful, but they seemed to have no common thread. "What are you teaching them?"

Yolanda shook her head. "This isn't a painting class where everyone paints the same picture. It's a safe place where people can learn to express themselves in a positive, individual way."

"What about this one from Patty?" Kate asked, holding up the artist's picture.

"What about it?"

"Stripes? What do you think she's expressing?"

"She told me it was sunbeams coming out of the sky."

Kate looked at the simple painting much differently than she had before.

"The first time Patty came to painting, she cried most of the time. It's taken a few years, but she's gone from regularly ripping the cardboard up with her teeth and spitting it on the other patients to finally seeing some sunshine."

"Sounds like progress."

"We like to think so."

"What do you attribute the change to?" Kate asked, trying to imagine how she would handle attempting to lead a group with someone who was so distracting to the rest of the patients.

"We tried a lot of different things, but I think the biggest difference was the introduction of music to the art room. That and the addition of color to the walls."

Kate looked confused. "The color—the mosaics—that's a new thing?"

"Yes."

"It's beautiful," she replied, remembering her first reaction to it. "It feels inviting."

"Thank you. That's what we were going for."

"What did it look like down here before?"

"Dark and depressing—pretty much like the rest of the hospital, only worse. Because, if you haven't noticed, there are no windows down here. I think all of us were in a funk and we didn't even know it until the colors started to change and it began feeling like we were coming out of long winter."

"Did you get the idea from the towers?" Kate asked, looking past Yolanda to a large jar full of bright bits of pottery and glass.

"I've come to learn that all good ideas—ideas full of truth and light—they all come from the same source. I've learned to recognize that if an idea's got any bit of real hope in it at all, it must have been inspired by that same source of goodness. I got into art therapy because I wanted to help people find a positive way to express their emotions. I did six years of college and practiced for close to twenty years before I discovered that there's a lot that I missed—that I'd been ignoring."

"So what changed?"

Yolanda turned in her chair, taking hold of the jar behind her. She lifted it from its place and set it down on the desk between them. Closer now, Kate could see some of the objects in the jar—pieces of glass, a bottle cap, a couple of rusty nuts and bolts, lots of broken pieces of colorful tiles, a gold cross, and what looked like a rolled-up piece of paper.

"My life went to pieces," she said with a somber smile. "My baby boy was shot and killed almost six years ago. He was only seventeen years old. Caught a stray bullet from a gang fight just outside a house where he was working. A piece of me died with him that day. My heart felt like it was broken into a hundred million pieces. I was in such a bad way that I was forced to take a leave of absence until I could put myself back together. After a couple of weeks of feeling hopeless, I couldn't think of any reason to keep living in a world filled with so much hate and darkness."

She stood and removed the lid of the jar. Reaching in, she fished out the rolled-up piece of paper and handed it to Kate.

Kate unrolled the paper carefully and read it before looking up.

USE CAN PUTSIT BAK TOGETTA. GOD WIL HEP USE

"This came from Sammy?" Kate asked.

Yolanda pursed her large lips and shook her head.

"But you know these notes come from Sammy, right?"

Yolanda nodded. "I know that's Sammy's handwriting, but I hadn't been praying to Sammy for an answer to my troubles."

Kate nodded slowly, remembering the first message she had received and the prayers she'd prayed beforehand.

"That note was on my back step one morning after a long night of tears and pleading to God to just take me home so I wouldn't have to keep on hurting." She reached into the jar again and pulled out a small bright yellow tile that was chipped on three of its edges. "This was sitting on top of that note." She handed the tile to Kate.

Kate looked at it for a moment, recognizing that it was the same color as some of the tiles in the mosaic on the stairway.

"The same day I got that message, I drove past the house where Tyrone was killed. He'd been working with a contractor, remodeling old houses. There was a pile of garbage out in front of the house waiting to be tossed into the dumpster, and on top of it all was a bucket full of yellow tiles just like that one. When I saw them, I felt like God was looking down on me, giving me some hope. I knew I had to have those tiles even though I had no idea what I was gonna do with them. But it didn't take long to find out. On my way home, I found myself driving past the towers. I'd been around those towers all of my life, but until that day, I don't think I ever really saw them. Walking around the fence, looking up at those big, beautiful towers—I felt like my son was next to me, opening my eyes, helping me see."

"It seems like it's a place of hope for a lot of people," Kate suggested.

Yolanda nodded. "I try to drop by to visit whenever I'm feeling down and need a boost. They inspire me. Before I lost my son, this was just my job, but after—now that we made the changes we made— this has become my passion. It's strange how just a little color changes your whole environment—changes your whole disposition. I've tried to re-create the same feeling I get when I'm at the towers. It's changed everything down here."

Kate nodded. "Dr. Hermansen's notebook says that Sammy spends time here."

"Yes, he does. He helped us with the mosaic. We couldn't have done what we did—what we're still doing—without his help."

"Still doing?"

"Sure. We're not finished yet. There's still plenty of room for joy. The word got out that we were working on something big over here, and contractors from all over bring us their scraps to recycle into happiness. Some of them even bring us mortar and grout to keep us goin'. We probably have enough material right now to cover the rest of the basement and half the first floor in mosaic, but we've had to pace ourselves."

"What do you mean?"

Yolanda looked at Kate for a moment before responding. "Did Dr. Hermansen say anything about her relationship with Dr. Singh in that notebook?"

"No," Kate responded. "What kind of relationship?"

"Oh, not that kind of relationship," she said with a smile. "But I'm sure she left a note in there about keeping the notebook out of the hands of Dr. Singh, right?"

"Yes, but she didn't say why. I actually wanted to ask you about that."

"What can I tell you?"

"I obviously don't know him very well, but he seems like a bit of a killjoy. How did you get away with decorating the basement?"

Yolanda laughed. "Sometimes it's easier to ask forgiveness than to get permission."

"He doesn't know?"

Yolanda shook her head. "He's been so concerned about cutting budgets that he hasn't really made it this far yet. He's only been here for just over two years. The last director was so tied up in legal problems that he never got around to visiting either."

"Wait, so the past and current directors of the hospital don't know what goes on down here?" she asked with a mischievous smile.

"I show up to staff meeting every Monday. We do our work, and we're producing positive results. We don't ask for any additional funds, and we try to keep our heads down. Why would a busy guy like Dr. Singh be concerned about a few art therapists like us?"

"This sounds like the right place for me. What do you need me to do?"

"What you did with Patty—I want to see more of that. I could probably teach any of the interns how to teach art. It's way more difficult to teach a person compassion and love if it's not already part of who they are. You impress me, Kate."

"Thanks," she responded shyly.

"Now, please, you best keep that notebook tucked away. I'm afraid of the potential problems it could bring to all of us."

"Okay, but..."

"Yes?"

"I've been trying to figure this out since I found the notebook on Friday. If it has the potential of falling into the wrong hands and doing damage, why would Dr. Hermansen leave it in her old desk?"

Yolanda looked surprised by the question. "You don't know?"

"No."

"Because she wanted you to find it."

"Me?"

"Yes. I told you we've been waiting for you." She passed Sammy's oracle back across the desk. "He told us you were coming. We didn't know when or how it would work out, but all of us have learned to listen when Sammy passes a message on to us. I know it was a difficult thing for Leslie to learn how to let go, but it's worked out well for her."

"Wait, you still have contact with her?"

"Yes, she calls every few months to check in, you know, to see if anything has happened. It's been a test of faith for all of us, but I'm sure it's been especially hard for her."

"Why?"

"Leslie wasn't raised with faith in a God of any kind. She put her faith in education and science and her own hard work. It was difficult for her to let go of that, to take a step into something without having a diagnosis or hypothesis to comfort her and give definition to her path forward. I never really considered it until I met her, but not having faith, not having a relationship with God—your world has to work by a whole different set of rules than I'm used to. Those rules—the rules of the unbelievers—they can be both loveless and hopeless. You might be able to still be a good doctor without hope and love, but I'm not sure it's possible to be a true physician without hope in a Creator who has the ultimate understanding of his creations."

"But she came to believe, right? That's what I've read in her notebook."

"Yes, she did. But faith is a fragile seed, especially before it puts down roots deep enough to soak up nutrients on its own. I believe Leslie's conversion was significant enough to get her started on faith's long and dusty road, but we all need friends to support us along the way—and regular reminders of the reasons we have departed one path for a different, often steeper, one. She put a lot of hope in the answers she got, but all faith, especially young faith—it can feel lonely sometimes. Faith, as I'm sure you know—if it's for real—it requires us to leave neutral ground and commit ourselves to serve a higher cause—a higher king. And once you've been enlisted in His service, I don't believe there's any way of going back to neutral ground."

Kate nodded thoughtfully.

"I'll give her a call tonight," continued Yolanda. "It's been almost a year since she left. That's a long time to wait on faith. I'm sure she'll be excited to hear her notebook is finally in the hands of the yellow-haired white girl she hoped would come."

CHAPTER 17

LEARNING TO FLY

God became man to turn creatures into sons:
not simply to produce better men of the old kind,
but to produce a new kind of man.
It is not like teaching a horse to jump better and better,
but like turning a horse into a winged creature.
                    —*C.S. Lewis*

A memo was taped to Kate's office door when she arrived at work on Wednesday morning, asking her to report immediately to Dr. Singh's office. She quickly and nervously walked to the administration building and rode the elevator to the top floor, where she was greeted by Dr. Singh's secretary and asked to take a seat in the waiting area. Her nervousness only grew in the minutes that followed, and so she tried to busy herself by organizing the magazines on the coffee table. After gathering them together, she proceeded to lay them out according to publication date. She had made her way through nearly half the stack when something on the cover of one journal caused her to pause. There staring back at her was a familiar name printed in the lower right-hand corner: *Dr. Leslie Hermansen: Reimagining the Reality of the Spiritual-Self, page 43.*

Kate was familiar with the publication, *Journal of Personal and Social Psychology.* She had referenced it many times in the papers she had written in the last two years. She knew it was one of the most respected journals in the field of psychology. Immediately she flipped it open, turned to the article, and began to read the abstract.

Dr. Leslie Hermansen, Psy.D, and her colleague Dr. Craig P. Monaghan, PhD/Psychologist, report their findings on the advancing research into the promising yet somewhat controversial Watts Hypothesis, introduced to the world by Dr. Hermansen nearly a year ago. This developing hypothesis examines the possible links between expedited psychological healing and a personal spiritual awareness in patients of all ages, races, and socioeconomic levels. This unique marriage of science and mysticism is turning..."

"Miss Larsen," the secretary called out, putting an end to Kate's reading.

She looked up.

"Dr. Singh will see you now."

"Oh, right. Thanks." She got up quickly and set the journal down on the table, wishing she had more time to continue reading. She opened the door and wandered into the office. The doctor sat behind his desk, which was stacked high with papers.

"Ahh, Miss Larsen," Dr. Singh said, getting to his feet. "I'm glad to see you got my note. I'm also glad to see your punctuality problem seems to have resolved itself. I trust you have acquired an adequate GPS."

"Yes," she replied, forcing a smile. "It was good advice. I'm sorry I didn't take it seriously before."

"Yes, well, I hope you have come to appreciate the reality that you're not in Kansas anymore, or Wyoming, or...where are you from again?"

"Idaho."

"Yes, of course. Right next to North Dakota, right?"

"Uh...it's close," Kate responded, not wanting to correct him.

"Very well. Please, have a seat," he motioned to the chair in front of his desk.

She sat down and waited patiently while he sorted through a stack of papers.

"Yes," he said, looking up when he found what he was looking for. "As you may have noticed, we have been a little short staffed lately. We appreciate you accepting this opportunity to intern with us. It has been a week now, and after a review of your work and careful consideration of the budget issues we're facing, we have decided to let you go."

"What?" Kate responded, feeling shocked.

"Yes, I'm sorry it didn't work out. As I mentioned in our initial interview, attendance and cooperation are imperative. Calling in sick three days in the first week and completing only a fraction of the work assigned you offers us little hope that you're a good fit for our team. I'm sorry. You will be paid for the days you worked. Please clean out your desk of any personal items and hand in your ID badge at the guard station when you leave the parking lot."

"Uh," Kate uttered, feeling like she had just been kicked in the stomach. "Uh, I think maybe there's been a mistake."

"Excuse me?"

"I'm Kate Larsen. I haven't missed any work, and I can't imagine sorting through files any more efficiently than I've been doing for the last seven days. If I need to do more, I..." She stopped as she watched Dr. Singh shuffling through the papers.

"Is that right?" he replied, looking suddenly very nervous as he set half of his papers aside and sorted through the rest of them.

Kate looked on, wondering if she should laugh or cry but not feeling as if either one was appropriate. Looking on Dr. Singh's desk, she noticed a manila folder with her name on it at the top of a pile. She watched Dr. Singh continue to shuffle the paper for a bit longer, wondering if she should say anything. "Are you maybe looking for this?" she asked, pointing to the file.

He looked up, taking the file in his hands. He opened it quickly, hiding his face behind it as he read. "I'm sorry," he said after a moment. "My secretary seems to have made a mistake. I wasn't supposed to let you go. I...I was actually hoping to invite you to take a more permanent and designated position."

"Really?"

"Yes. You've been requested to be assigned as an intern to Dr. Yolanda McKinley."

"Really?" Kate repeated, feeling relieved but trying not to act like she knew this might be coming.

"Yes," he said, looking back at the file as if to make sure he wasn't making another mistake.

"Wow, that would be great. When do I start?"

"Uh," he replied, looking down at the file. "HR would normally handle this, but with budget cuts, we've had to eliminate most of that department. It looks like they won't need you until the twenty-ninth."

Kate nodded. "Wasn't that yesterday?"

He looked at his watch. "Yes it was. I'll have my secretary fix this immediately," he said, closing the folder. "Well, thank you very much for coming in. You can clean out your desk and make the move immediately to the...just report to Dr. McKinley's office. Can you handle it yourself, or would you like one of the maintenance folks to lend you a hand?"

"I think I got it."

"Very well, then. Sorry about the mix-up there. I hope I didn't cause any undue stress. I'll let you get on your way."

Kate left quickly after Dr. Singh excused her, and she was all the way back to her office when she remembered the journal she had meant to grab on her way out. She hoped she could find the article online.

By nine o'clock, Kate had transferred her things into her new office.

Since she had admitted to some experience with pottery, Dr. McKinley assigned her to work with clay. Her first group of patients arrived at ten, and Kate soon acknowledged that she was in way over her head. The previous therapist had been working on masks with the patients, but after she was let go, the masks had been wrapped in plastic bags and stored on a shelf. The patients were excited when Dr. McKinley told them they would be working in clay again, but the excitement proved to be too much for two patients, who very quickly started arguing over the ownership of one mask. While the rest of the patients quietly worked on their masks, the twins, as Kate soon learned they were called, continued to fight over the single mask, cussing and spitting at each other and threatening to poke each other's eyes out.

Kate hoped Dr. McKinley would come to her rescue, but, busy with her own patients, she did not appear to be in any hurry to intervene. When the twins' behavior escalated to throwing punches, she knew she needed to do something. Having never had any training in controlling such behavior, Kate did the only thing that came to mind—she approached them with a spray bottle filled with water and sprayed both of the men in the face. The sudden addition of water into the situation made them pause long enough for one to look down at the disputed art and recognize that the mask in question was not good enough to be his. He left the mask with his brother and went to look on the shelves for his own, which he soon found under a pile of plastic bags.

"I was impressed with the way you handed the twins," Yolanda said after the patients had left for lunch.

"Oh, thanks."

"You've worked with hostile patients before?"

"Patients, no. Brothers, yes." She laughed. "My mom used to say that hot heads can't think until they cool down. I hope I didn't go too far with the water."

"I couldn't have handled it better myself. I might have normally called for security, but the officer who was assigned to our building is now over three buildings and is often difficult to reach. I will warn you, though, that it's better not to get between the twins. They've sent far bigger people than you to the hospital."

"Aren't we at the hospital?" she asked with a smile.

"You know what I mean. I think those boys musta been born without even a shadow of a conscience. You don't want to find yourself on their list. The last doctor who did left with a broken jaw and several stitches. Got it?" Yolanda asked, one of her painted eyebrows raised high above the other.

Kate nodded.

"Good. Do you know how to use these?" she asked, turning to the six mismatched potter's wheels.

"I used to, but it's been close to five years. Why?"

"Well, if you think you can use 'em, we'll keep 'em. Otherwise they're just taking up space down here. I've been considering getting rid of them for several months."

"It would be fun to try to do it again," Kate said, remembering the fun she'd had on the wheel in high school.

"Okay, I'll give you a couple of weeks to see if you can figure it out. I know some of our patients would enjoy working on the wheel again. I love art, but I've never been willing to sacrifice my nails for it."

Kate looked down at Dr. McKinley's long, brightly manicured nails and smiled.

Over the course of the next several workdays, Kate practiced on the wheel whenever the time between patients allowed. She also spent time painting, remembering how to crochet, hand-building with clay, and honing her finger-painting skills. Dr. McKinley also assigned her the task of recycling the cardboard boxes that had been donated by a local grocery store, turning the largest pieces into canvases for painting projects. The work was far different from what she had expected when she left Idaho, but she was learning and working with real patients. And she recognized she was even having fun.

It was just after quitting time on the Friday of her third week of work when Kate remembered what had brought her to the art basement in the first place. As she struggled once again to center a stubborn piece of clay on the potter's wheel, she found herself thinking about Sammy, Dr. Hermansen's notebook, the oracle, and the message she had found in her car. She even found herself wondering about Charlie.

Kate had considered stopping by to talk to Isaiah several times in the past two weeks but each time had chosen instead to turn her car to the fastest route to the freeway and face the inevitable traffic jams. But something was different today, and she not only felt compelled to visit but to hurry. She quickly cleaned up and was just leaving her office when a strong impression came to her: take the notebook. She turned around and retrieved it from her desk drawer, where she had been stowing it for safekeeping.

Unlike the first time she discovered the towers, Kate now knew her way around Watts, at least this corner of it, and she drove there with much more confidence and deliberateness than she had weeks earlier, when she was lost and confused. The barred windows and shuttered buildings that she passed along the way reminded her that she was still deep in the hood, but she recognized that she no longer feared the desperate sight of it all. She spotted the tops of the towers when she was still a couple of blocks away, and she smiled to herself as she drew nearer. She parked her car and was just getting out when she noticed Isaiah standing in the doorframe of the guard shack, staring out across the lawn, looking a little tired. She waved to him, and he waved back, smiling.

"What took you so long?" he asked when she was still twenty feet away.

"Pardon?"

"I've been waitin' for you for more than a week."

"I'm not sure what you're talking about," she said, feeling confused.

"The wind told me you were comin'. I've been waitin'. It's good to see you," he said, extending his big hand to take hers. "I was hopin' to see you back sooner."

"Yeah, well, I would have come, but…it's been busy at work. I'm working with …"

"Yolanda McKinley," Isaiah said, cutting her off. "I know."

"She told you?"

"Yes, but I heard it first from Sammy."

"What? How did he know?"

"He's seen you down there in that dungeon."

"Seriously? I haven't seen him."

"Maybe you're not lookin' hard enough."

"I guess not. What did he say?"

"He said you've been tryin' to make pots on a potter's wheel."

"Tryin' is a good word for it," she said, surprised. "It's been a mess. I was never really good at it, but I remembered being better than I am. It's kickin' my butt."

Isaiah chuckled. "That's what I heard. Maybe you should ask him for help."

"Sammy?"

"Sure."

"He knows how to make pottery?"

Isaiah nodded, turning to the short vase filled with pens and pencils on the desk behind him. "He made that one several years ago, back when they had a full-time pottery therapist over there. He's no expert, but he'd know enough to give you some pointers."

"I will ask, if I ever see him. Dr. Hermansen's notebook said he spent a lot of time in the art basement, but I've been wondering if maybe he isn't a patient there anymore."

Isaiah smiled. "He hasn't been a patient there for close to a decade."

"What?" Kate asked, looking surprised. "But what about this notebook?" she asked, pulling it from her bag.

"What about it?"

"If Dr. Hermansen…and Yolanda know him…I guess I just thought he must have been one of their patients."

Isaiah shook his head.

"So, wait, if he's not a patient, how did Dr. Hermansen get to know him? How does he know I've been struggling with pottery? If he's not a patient, why does he hang out there?"

Isaiah smiled, pointing to the bench in the shadow of the eucalyptus tree. "Let's have a seat."

She followed him to the bench, her mind filled with so many questions that she had trouble finding the words for even one.

"He has friends at the hospital," Isaiah offered when he read the confusion on her face. "There are many of the staff who care about him and do what they can to protect him."

"But how does he get in and out? I get checked every time I come and go. Most of the buildings are on lockdown...and the fence...how does he navigate his way through that?"

"You don't know his story, do you?"

"No. I have no idea, other than the few things you told me last time and the stuff I've read in this notebook."

"I've been hoping you'd come and ask for more," Isaiah said, smiling.

"What do you mean?"

"There's an order to all things. And with things like this, a question's gotta be asked 'fore an answer can be given. I could tell that your head was filled with questions when you were here last. It ain't easy sometimes to be patient and wait when you got somethin' to share—things you know'll be gifts to those who chose to receive 'em."

Kate nodded thoughtfully. "I'm sorry I didn't come back sooner. Dr. Hermansen's notes have answered some of my questions, but I feel like there are lots of things I'm still confused about."

"I'm willin' to help if I can."

"That's actually one of my questions."

"What's that?"

"Why? Why are you willing to help? Don't get me wrong, I really appreciate it, but I'm just curious what your motivations are."

Isaiah nodded, taking a deep breath before he responded. "You and I live in different worlds. I'm from an old-school generation where people still chat with their neighbors face to face. We look out for each other. We recognize we need each other—that we're stronger together than we are alone. Folks o' your generation don't seem to have the same 'preciation for community. You kids think you can learn all you need to learn by sittin' in front of a computer, surfin' the net. A friend of mine once said, *"Where is the life we have lost in living? Where is the wisdom we have lost in knowledge? Where is the knowledge we have lost in information?"'*

Kate smiled. "You were friends with T.S. Eliot?"

"Ahh, you know the quote?"

"My father wrote that in a letter he gave me when I left for college. I found out later he gave the same quote to each of my brothers when they went away too."

Isaiah nodded. "My father did the same when I left for college. He was a big Eliot fan. It took me four years and a big helping of humble pie to begin to understand what he was tryin' to tell me. He never went to college. I'm ashamed to admit there was a time when I thought he was just an ignorant fool. Thing is, each generation believes their world is so much more advanced and enlightened than the one before it, but humanity is still faced with the same issues that boggled our first parents. The details are gonna be different, but we're still faced with the same inabilities our granddaddies faced as we try to wade our way through our foolish pride. Wisdom always comes too late, and the next generation rarely learns from the folly of those who went before them. You asked what motivates me to help you kids: that's the answer—to see the risin' generations be able to avoid our pitfalls and to somehow slow down our collision course with sorrow and destruction."

Kate nodded thoughtfully. "So...that's why you came home after college—why you work here?"

He nodded his head. "I was just foolish enough to believe I could do somethin' to make the world a better place."

"Do you feel like you've accomplished what you wanted to do?"

"Some days yes, some days no. But I'm tryin'. Sometimes it's hard to see any progress in a neighborhood like this one. And there are plenty o' days when I feel like the battle's lost. But the sun keeps risin', and each new day holds the potential of undiscovered beauty and grace. That's the hope I hold onto."

"But why here? I mean the towers are amazing, but it's such a rough neighborhood. Why did you come back?"

Isaiah took a deep breath, exhaling slowly as he looked blankly across the lawn. "I'll give you the same answer I once heard my daddy give when a man asked him why he stayed and tried to change the neighborhood into somethin' better 'stead of livin' a comfortable life of ease in the suburbs, away from all the trouble and darkness. Daddy told the man that the whole loaf don't rise if all the leaven's concentrated in one place. He instilled in all of us kids a responsibility to make our surroundins a better place day by day—to be the leaven. I coulda done anthropology in some faraway place. I coulda seen the world. But in a way I never coulda 'magined, I've seen the world. It comes parading past my door every day, almost twenty-four seven."

"You found the gold," Kate mused, remembering Isaiah's story from her visit with Charlie.

He pursed his big lips and nodded.

Truth is ever to be found in the simplicity, and not in the multiplicity and confusion of things.
Isaac Newton

CHAPTER 18

NAKED TRUTH

God is not looking for extraordinary characters as His instruments,
but He is looking for humble instruments through whom
He can be honored throughout the ages.
—*A. B. Simpson*

"So, I've been curious about your relationship with Sammy," Kate said.

"What do you want to know?" Isaiah asked.

"I got the impression from something Dr. Hermansen wrote in her notebook that you've known him most of his life."

Isaiah nodded. "Since he was about three years old."

"What? How?"

"He's my brother. Foster brother, technically. But we stopped bein' technical a long time ago."

"Tell me about that, about his background, I mean—how that all happened."

"We don't know anything about his father, but his mother musta had a rough life. She got into some heavy stuff and ended up overdosing one night on the train platform over across the way. The police found him in his momma's arms, nearly starved to death. The best I know, he bounced around the foster system for 'bout a year 'fore he ended up in the hospital. When he came to our family, his little head was still wrapped in bandages. I think he was Momma's favorite, and that's sayin' somethin' as she had more than twenty to choose from."

"Wait, your parents had twenty kids?" Kate asked incredulously.

"Give or take. We were all foster kids. Some of us stayed for a few months. Some of us musta stayed for close to two decades."

"Wow! How long did you stay?"

"Almost fifteen years. Daddy was a preacher, and Momma figured he shouldn't try to preach anything on Sunday that he wasn't livin' the rest the week. They saved all of us with their love. Somehow they always had 'nough of it to go around. It made for a chaotic home life and a whole lotta bunk beds, but there ain't nothin' I'd trade it for."

"I thought I had a big family, but that's sounds crazy."

"Crazy ain't even the beginning of it," he said with a smile. "But we always had someone to play with, and it gave us all roots. I've now got family from coast to coast—people who grew up knowing the same kinda love I learned—people who are teachin' their kids that same kinda love. Was it crazy? Heck yes, but it was the most beautiful kinda crazy."

Kate couldn't help but grin as she looked at the smile that filled Isaiah's whole face. "And your folks—are they still alive?"

"Nope, both gone—died within two months of each other back in '07."

"I'm sorry."

"Ain't nothin' to be sorry 'bout. They lived good, long lives and left a legacy of kindness for all of us to follow. I don't know if you can live a better life than that."

"They sound like they were amazing people."

"The very best. If it weren't for them, half of us woulda been dead a long time ago. As you mighta heard, Watts has had more than its share of trouble. But love kept us all flyin' straight. Love gives folks the power to overcome their past, and their genetics."

"Charlie said something about your parents knowing Simon."

"Yes ma'am. We were neighbors. Everyone knew Simon."

"You knew him too?"

"Not well enough to claim it, unfortunately. I was only three when he left Watts, but my older siblings called him Uncle. Daddy grew up just over across the way, and Simon used to pay him a nickel for every gunnysack of old bottles he'd bring him. He spent most of his childhood watchin' him build all of this."

Kate nodded. "I've been wondering about that. Last time I was here, we talked about Simon—Sam—how he built these towers to be a city set on a hill."

Isaiah nodded.

"There's a lot more to it than that, isn't there?"

The big man smiled. "What has Charlie told you?"

"Nothing. I haven't seen him since the day I was here last."

"Is that right?"

"Yeah. I don't know what's up with him. If I didn't know better, I'd guess he was probably borderline schizophrenic."

Isaiah sat quiet for a moment, looking thoughtful, and Kate wondered if she might have said too much. "I understand what you're sayin'," he finally said, putting her mind at ease. "But there's more to Charlie's hesitation than just his fear of doin' what he's sposta be doin'."

"Do you know what it is?"

"Not exactly. Ain't that your job—figurin' out what makes folks like him tick?"

Kate laughed. "Some folks don't wanna be figured out."

"Oh, I dunno. I think all folks wanna be figured out."

"You do?"

He nodded slowly. "Ain't that part of who we are as humans? Ain't we all lookin' to be understood?"

"Yeah, I guess so, but Charlie…he's…I don't have any idea how to understand him."

"That's 'cause he don't understand himself. There's a whole lotta hurt in there somewhere. I've caught little glimpses of it from time to time over the years. He's a tough nut—a thicker shell than most for sure. But most folks with shells that thick are protectin' a very soft heart that's been hurt by somethin' big."

"So, how can I help him if he won't let me in?"

"You can't."

Kate grinned. "That's not what I expected to hear."

Isaiah nodded. "Change ain't never easy, 'specially when that change has got anything to do with a heart."

"So what am I supposed to do? That note that came from Sammy—Charlie's supposed to be a part of this, whatever *this* is. But if he doesn't want help, what am I supposed to do?"

"That's the trick, ain't it? Tryin' to figure out how to help, when to help, and when to just sit back and wait. A man's gotta wanna change 'fore anything can happen. He's gotta be willin' to sacrifice what he is for what he can be. That's a scary thing sometimes, and fear only makes it harder."

Kate felt confused.

"Just wait till you have kids," Isaiah continued. "You'll want the best for 'em, but there'll be times you watch 'em doin' stupid stuff you know's only gonna bring 'em pain and trouble."

She nodded knowingly. "I watched my parents go through several years of that with my baby sister. It still eats 'em up."

"It hurts to see anybody makin' choices you know'll lead them into dark and lonely places, but it's a whole lot worse when they're your own flesh and blood. The greatest blessing of mortality comes from havin' choices. But just havin' choices to make don't make nobody happy. Sometimes it feels like some folks missed the memo that you gotta choose smart—good—right, and you gotta keep choosin' 'em and not be afraid of turnin' back when you see you chose the wrong one.

"But most of us don't turn back—not right away. We might see the error in our ways, but it's like we think that if we just keep goin', if we just keep movin', that things'll get better. And we don't see that we're only just gettin' further from where we're wantin' to be. I had a buddy once who dated a girl everyone knew was trouble. When she ditched him after helpin' him blow his money, 'stead of turnin' 'round and headin' back to the safe harbor, he started datin' her sister. That boy'll be payin' for those choices for the rest of his life, or at least till he has the sense to change. Jesus's parable of the prodigal son is just as real today as it was two thousand years ago, and men are just as foolish as they ever were."

"I didn't peg you as a cynic," Kate teased.

"On my best days, I'm an optimist. On most days, I'm a realist. And unfortunately, no matter how hard I try to push it out, there's always at least a sliver of cynicism. And like all slivers, it festers from time to time. I like to consider myself a work in progress."

"I like that."

He nodded. "We're all a work in progress. Hopefully we will be till the day we die. And even then, I got hopes that we can keep movin' forward as we make our way through whatever comes next. You wanna help ol' Charlie, I'll tell you what you can do. You can help him open his eyes to the reality of God's love. Love's the only thing that has any hope of bringin' 'bout real change in anyone. That's the secret the prodigal son had to learn for himself. And that's the secret we all gotta hear in our own heart if we ever hope to change."

Kate nodded. This wasn't what she'd expected. It was better. "That's the secret that turned Sabato to Simon, isn't it?"

Isaiah nodded. "Charlie got close to seein' that once, a long while back."

"What happened?"

"He got scared of the light."

"You mentioned that last time. You really think it's true?"

He nodded. "When you don't feel worthy of the love that surrounds you, love can be one of the scariest things there is."

Kate nodded, looking out across the lawn, reminded of the bees from their first visit. The lesson had been clear to Kate, but it had admittedly been lost on Charlie. "Tell me something, Isaiah."

"Shoot."

"Do you think Charlie isn't hearing it because he doesn't understand, or do you think he doesn't understand because he's not hearing it?"

Isaiah smiled. "You noticed he's not a great listener?"

"Yeah. He put in his earbuds as soon as we got in the car last time. It just felt like he wanted to avoid it altogether."

He nodded. "That's a big problem."

"Are you talking about Charlie or in general?"

"Both. It seems sometimes like all the world is afraid of the whispers of the wind. I often feel sad for the kids of your generation and the babies growin' up today."

"Why?"

"'Cause most of you don't know what it is to be still. It seems as though all the world is in motion, makin' noise, avoidin' silence. On the rare occasion that life gives you a moment of quiet, you reach for your phones or turn up the tunes and blast away the stillness. You're livin' your lives at a hundred miles an hour, and it seems you've all forgotten how to slow down and just be—if you ever knew how. It used to be that families would sit down to dinner together and talk around the dinner table. That ain't enough anymore. Most families don't even sit down together. I've heard of kids eatin' Pop-Tarts three meals a day. On the rare occasion momma cooks a meal, it's more important that it gets posted to social media than it that it nourishes her family. And if and when the family sits down together, there ain't much talkin' goin' on. They don't even look at each other—too busy runnin' their thumbs over their phones. It ain't right, but it's the way it is. Sometimes I think Simon musta known what was comin."

"What do you mean?"

"His message coulda been said in a thousand easier ways. Instead, he built hundred-foot towers so what he had to say wouldn't be ignored. I think he musta known his message would have plenty o' competition. But if he could just get people to slow down long enough to stop and smell the roses, maybe do a little bit of thinkin', they'd hear what he hoped they'd hear. People've forgotten how to listen. They've forgotten how to see. They want to be entertained, but they also want their entertainment prechewed so they don't have to feel or think for themselves. And my biggest fear is that if we forget how to feel—how to listen—humanity's gonna be lost in a whirlwind of apathy and neglect.

"Too many times I've watched Charlie go through those gates, hopin' today's the day that he gets it. Too many times I've seen him come out of there with his camera around his neck and ears full of headphones. I ask myself what he's hopin' to experience if two of his best senses are already occupied. I can't tell you how many times I've wished I could send him in there in his underwear with no distractions and see if he wouldn't come out knowin' somethin' new."

Kate smiled but shook her head, trying to forget the image Isaiah's words had conjured in her mind.

"You wanna give it a try?"

"What do you mean?"

"Goin' in there—all by yourself."

She looked shocked.

"Keep your clothes on, of course," Isaiah said with a wink. "The last tour'll be comin' out any minute now. I could give you a half hour of alone time if you promised not to climb on anything."

"You're serious?"

"Yes."

"Why would you do that for me? You hardly know me."

"That's why you're here, isn't it? You came looking for answers."

"Well, yes, but how did you know?"

"Through a little whisper that told me a week ago that I should be lookin' for you."

It is by teaching that we learn; by knowing that we discover; by reading that we think, by writing that we draw water into the well. Henri Frederic Amiel

CHAPTER 19

LOVE

Love is life.
All, everything that I understand,
I understand only because I love. Everything is, everything exists,
only because I love. Everything is united by it alone.
Love is God, and to die means that I, a particle of love,
shall return to the general and eternal source.
—*Leo Tolstoy*

Kate was surprised by the feelings of excitement and nervousness she felt as the gate closed behind her. "Do you have any advice for me?" she asked Isaiah through the wire fence.

"I was hoping you might ask," he responded with a grin. "Yes. I want you to remember how you felt when you 'scovered the hearts last time. Take yourself back to that point. That's where you should begin."

"Okay," she responded, remembering that day. "Anything else?"

"Open your heart, and let yourself feel."

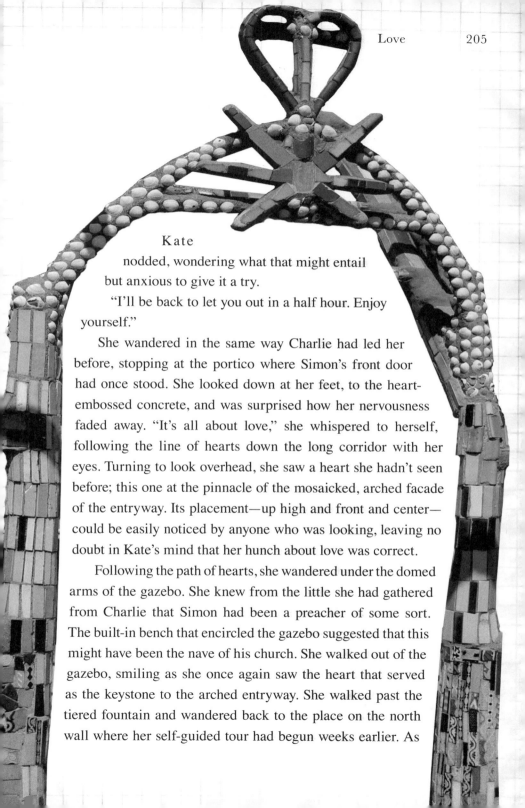

K ate
nodded, wondering what that might entail
but anxious to give it a try.

"I'll be back to let you out in a half hour. Enjoy
yourself."

She wandered in the same way Charlie had led her
before, stopping at the portico where Simon's front door
had once stood. She looked down at her feet, to the heart-
embossed concrete, and was surprised how her nervousness
faded away. "It's all about love," she whispered to herself,
following the line of hearts down the long corridor with her
eyes. Turning to look overhead, she saw a heart she hadn't seen
before; this one at the pinnacle of the mosaicked, arched facade
of the entryway. Its placement—up high and front and center—
could be easily noticed by anyone who was looking, leaving no
doubt in Kate's mind that her hunch about love was correct.

Following the path of hearts, she wandered under the domed
arms of the gazebo. She knew from the little she had gathered
from Charlie that Simon had been a preacher of some sort.
The built-in bench that encircled the gazebo suggested that this
might have been the nave of his church. She walked out of the
gazebo, smiling as she once again saw the heart that served
as the keystone to the arched entryway. She walked past the
tiered fountain and wandered back to the place on the north
wall where her self-guided tour had begun weeks earlier. As

she approached the relief sculpture of the wheat and grapes on the wall, she once again wondered about its placement. It was so different, so much more refined and detailed than all that surrounded it, that she had to believe it was meaningful. She looked at it for a long moment, first with her head, then with her heart. "Wheat and grapes. Wheat and grapes. Wheat and grapes," she whispered to herself.

The answer came peacefully, a gentle calm falling over her as she saw an image in her mind. It was a story she remembered from her youth—an upper room, twelve apostles, and a final supper. Bread and wine were made of wheat and grapes! She smiled at the realization. Of course it was bread and wine. He was a Christian. He would have taught the story to his congregation, perhaps even administered the symbols of Christ's sacrifice during services. Bread and wine. So simple that she had missed it before. And if this was a symbol of His sacrifice, the deep basin just below it could only be one thing. A baptismal basin. Most Christian churches had one. It only made sense for there to be one here.

Two unadorned pillars rose from the middle of the basin, joining together to form an arch about six feet high. Two other pillars tied into the wall of the basin. These were much more decorated and rose higher,

tying into the flying buttresses. Realizing she'd missed a detail before, she took a closer look at the top of the left pillar and found what looked like two unadorned cement work boots melded into the pillar. She couldn't think of what this could mean, but she knew it had to mean something. Concerned about the time, she shelved the question and moved on.

Following the overhead buttresses led her across the heart-covered pavement to the first

of the great towers. Kate walked around the entire thing, taking in as many details as she could before trying to make sense of it. On the north side, the stairs that climbed to the brightly colored central platform were divided by one of the tower's legs, but on the other side, a narrower set of brightly colored stairs descended to meet the heart-embossed cement again. An idea occurred to her; she walked around the tower once again, trying out her theory. Before she had made it all the way back around, she knew her theory had to be right. The placement of the brightly adorned tiered fountain just feet away from the narrower staircase only confirmed her suspicions. This was a place for weddings—a place where two people entered and then symbolically left as one.

Again worried she would run out of time, Kate continued on. The second tower was different from the first. Its base was made of rocks embedded in the cement. She stood at the base and looked up at the structure of this central tower. Thirty feet up, the tower seemed to be wearing a wide, highly decorated hoop. From this angle, it was difficult to see the details of the hoop, and Kate made a mental note to look again from a vantage point outside of the fence. Though this tower was not as wide as the first, it appeared to be just as

tall, its intricate structure rising high above her. Moving farther around to the east side, a number of buttresses attached this second tower to the third. Mosaicked hearts centered in the middle of these buttresses seemed to prove once again that Simon's message was all about love.

She moved on. This third tower was not as tall as the other two, and Kate noticed another difference that was readily apparent. Unlike the structures of the first two towers, whose inner workings looked similar to spokes on a wheel, this one looked more like a linear tower within another linear tower. The decorations covering this tower were also different. Instead of the random, conglomerated bits that adorned the other two towers, this one incorporated almost exclusively only two different elements. The covering of the outer tower was composed solely of glass, mostly old 7-Up bottles with labels  that could still be read. The inner tower was covered almost entirely with sun-bleached seashells. Again, she was struck with the idea that Simon's choices of materials were no accident. But with time running out, she knew she needed to move on. She wished she could take pictures, but she realized that not having her iPhone with her forced her to really look at the details; she knew much of this would be missed if she were viewing it all through the screen of her phone.

The next structure was the most different one yet. Looking much like a boat with tall masts, this sculpture was covered with hundreds of sun-bleached seashells and bright tiles. Some of the shells were missing, leaving behind only the convex shape of the cement that once held them in place. Lower to the ground, Kate imagined these would have likely been easy pickings for vandals and souvenir hunters. Looking up, she noticed that a mosaicked heart sat atop the foremost mast of the ship as it sailed off into the confluence where the north and south walls met at a rather sharp angle. And there at the end of this point, two thinner poles rose from the tops of the walls. On top of one sat another mosaicked heart, and on the top of the taller one was a detail she couldn't quite make out—it almost looked like a small lantern.

She heard the sound of the gate opening, and she knew her time was up. But as she walked away, she kept her eye on that small lantern—if that's what it was.

"How'd it go?" Isaiah asked, holding the gate open for her.

Kate smiled in response, unable to find adequate words. "I need to come back here."

"You do?"

"Yeah. And I need to find a way to get Charlie back here. I think he's missed a lot of really good stuff."

"And how are you going to do that?" Isaiah asked, handing her her bag as he locked the gate.

"I don't know yet. Do you have any suggestions?"

He smiled broadly. "I was hoping you'd ask. Help him feel the love you've felt."

She looked disappointed. "That might be a little awkward. Do you have any other suggestions?"

"I ain't suggestin' that that love needs to come from you. Maybe just through you."

"What do you mean?"

"There ain't no one alive who can't carry the message of God's love if they're willin' to share whatever light they have."

Kate chewed on his words for a moment, trying to decide if she could swallow them. She looked into Isaiah's eyes and saw it, sparkling beneath the surface—the same bright light she had seen at the end of her last visit. And in that moment, the flash of an idea came to her. She turned and looked through the gate to the far end of complex, where the walls converged and the spindly pole rose to a small, simple, lantern-like top. Taking a deep breath, she looked away.

"Are you afraid?" Isaiah asked softly.

She shrugged. "I just don't know where to start."

Isaiah nodded, knowingly. "When I was back at Penn State a hundred years ago, I became friends with an old Quaker man who taught me somethin' I've never been able to forget."

She looked up, waiting.

"He told me it's a Quaker proverb, as old as the hills—'Proceed as the way opens.'"

Kate thought about it for a minute. "I don't understand."

"You're familiar with John 14:6?"

"I'm not sure."

He smiled kindly. "'I am the way, the truth, and the life. No man comes to the father 'cept through me.'"

"Yeah, I remember that."

Isaiah nodded. "So if Jesus is the way, and the whole purpose of his life's mission is to help folks like you and me come back to the presence of God, we gotta be willin' to move our feet when he opens the way for us. We gotta proceed as the way opens."

Kate nodded thoughtfully. "There's gotta be an easier way," she suggested, breaking a smile.

Isaiah pursed his lips and shook his head. "There are always other ways, but believe me, they ain't easy. Not after you've left neutral ground. When you became a Christian, you signed up to be a bearer o' light. And Jesus promised you that if you take his yoke on your shoulders and open your heart to learning, he'd make your burdens lighter."

Kate nodded as she felt a gentle calm wash over her, offering peace to her heart.

"Answers will come," Isaiah spoke softly, resting his big hand on her shoulder, "but never until you ask for them. And it seems we only hear 'em when our hearts are open and we're willin' to listen."

Matthew 11:29

CHAPTER 20

CONNECTIONS

The chief purpose of life, for any of us,
is to increase according to our capacity our knowledge of God
by all means we have, and to be moved by it to praise and thanks.
—J. R. R. Tolkien

The road home was mostly a blur to Kate, who was deep in thought, her mind consumed with the things she had just seen and heard. She felt as if she had taken a bite of a delicious chocolate cake that left her wanting more. But something in that bite also left her feeling unsettled. It was not until she was nearly home that she discovered what it was: how to somehow convey the truths she had been given to someone who didn't—and maybe couldn't—understand. Still, she knew she needed to find him and figure out a way to get him back to Watts. Remembering the first time they'd met, she drove to the convenience store, knowing her need for quarters could offer an easy excuse for bumping into him again.

But Charlie wasn't at the convenience store, the register being staffed by an annoyingly beautiful blonde girl instead. Disappointed, Kate exchanged a few dollars and retreated back to her house to get started on her laundry. The house was empty when she got home, and Kate remembered the plans she'd heard her roommates making the night before about the Jack Johnson concert in Long Beach. Jill had invited Kate to come along, but the ticket price of $75 and the coinciding arrival of her first student loan bill made the decision easy. It had been hard not to feel sorry for herself and her financial situation since her arrival. Kate was the only one of the five roommates with a college degree, but it was obvious from the way they spent their time and money that they were all earning more than she was—waiting tables or cutting hair.

After starting a load of wash, she made herself a peanut butter sandwich and went to the deck to try to remember why she had come here. A sliver of light between the beach houses in front of hers offered a tiny glimpse of the sunset on the ocean. Kate fell into a chair, exhausted.

As she finished her sandwich, she was reminded of the things she had just seen in Watts. Isaiah's gift of a half hour with the towers had filled her eyes and head with new ideas. But his suggestion that she might help Charlie feel the love the towers had to offer was still hard to swallow. She wondered what she could possibly do to change his heart. After all, he knew the towers far better than she ever would. But she knew he had missed at least a few things. The wheat and grapes motif had certainly suggested there was something more to see and understand. As she thought about what she had just seen, she knew there would certainly be even more to understand than the little she had been able to glean in a half hour. She knew she needed to go back.

Curious what the internet might offer by way of pictures and explanation, Kate pulled out her iPhone. A search for "Watts Towers symbolism" yielded mostly dead ends. The unofficial website of the towers—a site that looked like it was pieced together by an amateur—offered a few photos of Simon. He was a scrappy-looking fellow, small in stature, who looked to be most comfortable in a pair of overalls and

a sleeveless shirt. She flipped through all the photos she could find, not sure what she was looking for, until she came to a black-and-white photo of Simon standing behind a large, white slab. Kate zoomed in as much as she could on the small screen and recognized the pattern carved in the slab's surface. Wheat and grapes! She also noticed something she hadn't before—flowers. From the fuzzy photograph, she could tell there were at least two different kinds—a four-petaled flower on either side of the wheat and, in the center just above the grapes, another flower with several petals.

Kate stared at the photo for a full minute, intrigued by Simon's posture. He was pointing with two fingers to the wheat stalks, his mouth turned up, almost a smile. She wondered if this might have been the mold or model from which he created the relief sculpture on the wall. Curious if there might be meaning in the flowers, she took a screen shot of the photo before Googling "Christian symbolic flowers." She clicked on the first page that popped up—a website devoted to Easter symbolism. She scrolled down to a few basic drawings, including two flowers—the four-petaled dogwood and the Easter lily. She flipped back to the photo of Simon to compare the pictures and immediately knew she was on to something.

Flipping back to the website, Kate read about each of the flowers. The dogwood with its four petals was symbolic of the cross. Small notches with a reddish hue at the tips of the white petals suggested nail marks while, at the flower's center, a cluster of yellow texture symbolized a crown of thorns. The site also suggested that the dogwood's red berries were symbolic of Christ's blood. She also learned that the Easter lily, with its white, trumpet-like flowers that bloom in early spring, was a symbolic proclamation of the good news of the resurrection. Kate took another screen shot, adding to the evidence she already had.

As she considered the deeper meaning behind these symbols, her mind returned to the hearts that were scattered everywhere across Simon's creation. She remembered that Charlie had suggested that the towers in silhouette looked a lot like the profile of a cathedral. She was no stranger to churches, and though she'd only ever been to one cathedral, she was quite certain she'd never been in any religious building where hearts were used as a primary decoration motif. Flipping back to the picture of Simon, she knew one thing for certain—with the wheat and the grapes, the dogwood and the lily, and the hearts he had embossed into many of the walls and all the cement underfoot, the towers could symbolize only one thing: the love of God!

She sat back in her chair, taking in the beauty of the red and orange sunset that cast a golden light all around her. And in that moment, sitting alone by herself on the weathered deck of a dated beach house far from the comforts of home, she felt that love engulf her with an electrifying warmth. She sat still, basking in the memory and beauty of that warmth long after the feeling began to fade away. And as the golden light faded into twilight, she knew one more thing for certain—she needed to find a way to get Charlie back to Watts so he could experience this beautiful feeling of connection and love.

For the first time since she had arrived in California, Kate opened her journal to record the unique events of the previous weeks. In the quiet of the abandoned beach house, she laughed and she cried as she wrote, recognizing for the first time in several years how the hand of Providence had been shaping and influencing her life. And as this recognition came and she began counting her blessings, she was once again overwhelmed with gratitude. The flood of warmth she felt before stayed with her until long after she had closed her journal and lay down on her makeshift bed. She knew then that despite her discomforts and financial concerns, she was indeed where she was supposed to be.

We have to be continually reminded of what we believe. No belief will automatically remain alive in the mind. It must be fed. C. S. Lewis

And in that feeling of comfort and belonging, she knew that everything would work out somehow. The love she felt streaming from an unseen source was more real than anything she had ever known. With gratitude in her heart, she fell asleep. And with gratitude in her heart, she woke the next morning knowing she had to go back to the towers.

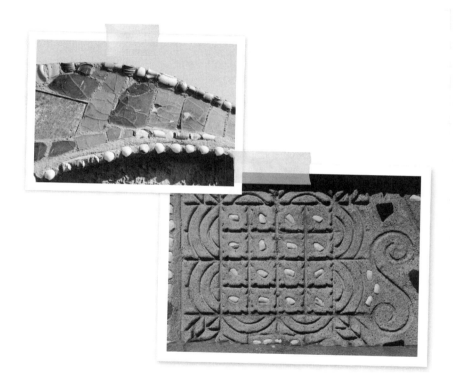

Those who thank God much are the truly wealthy. So our inner happiness depends not on what we experience but on the degree of our gratitude to God, whatever the experience. —Albert Schweitzer

CHAPTER 21

OISCOVERY

If you can't fly then run, if you can't run then walk,
if you can't walk then crawl,
but whatever you do you have to keep moving forward.
—Martin Luther King, Jr.

"You're up early," Isaiah said, standing in the doorway of the guard shack.

"Is that why the freeway was so empty?" Kate responded, handing him a brown paper bag.

"What's this?"

"It's a breakfast bribe."

"Hmmm. Is that somethin' like a breakfast burrito?"

Kate smiled. "I need to get back in there," she said, nodding to the towers.

"Sounds serious. You got a bee in your bonnet?"

"More like a hunch."

"What kinda hunch?"

"I saw something in there yesterday—the wheat and the grapes."

Isaiah raised one eyebrow. "And that gotchew outta bed early on a Saturday mornin'?"

"Do you think I'm crazy?"

"No. Not at all."

"Can you give me more than thirty minutes in there this time?"

"It depends."

"On what?"

"On what you brought me for my breakfast bribe."

Kate smiled, feeling relieved. "It's a muffin—blueberry. I hope you're not allergic."

Isaiah grinned, looking down at his wristwatch. "A bribe like this oughta be good for about an hour."

"I think that's more than I'll need."

"We'll see how it goes," he responded, reaching into his pocket for the keys.

"I also wanted to ask if you have any advice for me."

He looked up, appearing both surprised and pleased by her question. "I'd say keep your eyes and heart open, but it's obvious you've already been doin' that. Ain't many folks ever take notice of the things you've already seen and figured out. So I s'pose my advice would be to look at these towers through the lens of your faith."

Kate nodded. "Anything else?"

"Yes. Remember how you expressed yourself before you could read or write." "Okay," she responded slowly, looking confused.

"Charlie mighta told you Simon was illiterate."

Kate nodded.

"You also gotta remember that he was born in Italy. Every man's gotta learn to communicate, and when you don't read or write, you gotta figure out how express yourself in different ways. Simon was driven to communicate some complex ideas, but all of those ideas—as you've already found out—revolve around one theme."

"Love?"

"That's right. You could forget almost everything else, but keep love in mind as you look and learn." He handed her the key. "And if you please, resist the temptation to climb the towers."

Kate thanked him and quickly walked across the lawn. A chill of excitement washed over her as she approached the gate, knowing she was doing something few people would ever be allowed to do without a guide.

She walked past the portico and stopped at an adjacent area she had missed before. At first glance, she was confused at what it was, but looking closer she realized it looked like an outdoor kitchen, complete with a domed, mosaic-covered bread oven with a tall chimney. She set her bag down on the bench next to the opening of the old oven and removed her phone and a notebook. Kate was just about to walk away when she looked up and saw them—seven ears of corn, made of cement, melded to the wall just above the oven. She smiled as she leaned in to take a closer look, reminded of the cornbread sticks she had grown up with, her mother making them in an old cast-iron mold. She was about to walk away when the first questions of the day arose: Why? What's up with the corn? Why here? Why seven?

She stood back, recognizing that their placement so near the oven could simply mean that this is where Simon baked his cornbread. But her gut told her there had to be more. Remembering Isaiah's advice to apply the lens of her faith, she looked at the wall with new eyes. It took only a second for her to remember the story: Joseph's interpretation of Pharaoh's dream of the seven ears of corn, followed by his seven years of work and preparation that saved an entire nation from the seven years of famine that came after the plenty. Could this be a nod to the Old Testament story? She had never worked with cement before but couldn't imagine it being easy to simply attach cement ears of corn to walls willy-nilly without a fair amount of effort and thought. She wondered

what Sam might have meant by it. She noticed that the corn was surrounded by dozens of embossed flowers. She had noticed similar flowers embossed in the cement of other features in the complex but had not paid much attention to them. She wondered if they might have any meaning or if they were perhaps just a way of decorating that didn't require the tedious effort of mosaic.

Kate opened her notebook and quickly sketched the six-petaled flower. There was something familiar about the design—she'd seen the impressions in other parts of the work, but she couldn't place it. She was about to move on to other things when she noticed the colorful mosaic on the adjacent wall. Though similar to its arch-topped neighbor, this wall was considerably more colorful. Chunks of old crockery, bottles, and colored glass dishes were embedded in the walls, but there was also another familiar feature—boots. There were four of them, and as she looked at them closely, it appeared they had been petrified in the action of stomping and crushing the bottles and crockery underneath them.

Immediately an idea came into her mind. She remembered hearing about a Jewish wedding tradition in her comparative religion class—that of stomping on a glass as a symbol of…something she couldn't remember. She took a picture of the frieze to help her remember to look up the details of the tradition when she had more time to consider whether this had anything to offer in building her understanding of what Sam was trying to say.

As she walked around the corner, another thought came to her. It was what Isaiah had given her by way of advice—to remember how she expressed herself before she could read or write. The answer was easy. Like most children, Kate had grown up drawing and coloring with crayons. Looking up at the colors and creative architecture all around her, she thought she understood what Isaiah was trying to say. This was more than just art. This was expression. And based on the things she had already seen and been able to surmise, this was also narrative. With that in mind, she looked at the creations all around her as objects with meaning and stories to tell.

Everywhere she looked, her eyes were rewarded with the playful conglomeration of color, texture, and whimsy. Walking between the back wall of the outdoor kitchen and the gazebo, she noticed the telltale signs of vandalism. Like the missing shells on the boat that she noticed the day before, the shells and pottery in this area  had been damaged and looted, leaving many imprints where the missing items had once been embedded in the cement. She wondered if Sam had witnessed this destruction or if it had all happened in the sixty years since he'd left.

Saddened by the evidence of destruction, she turned her back to the wall to face the gazebo. She walked along the circular structure, stopping at the sight of a ticket stub resting atop the waist-high wall. It was an admission ticket similar to the one she had found in Dr. Hermansen's notebook—the one that had started all of this.

She picked up the ticket, smiling to herself as she remembered her interaction with Charlie on the beach. He had been such a jerk. She wondered where he was now—probably sleeping in after a night of harassing innocent bystanders with promises of stardom in his YouTube videos. She was just sliding the ticket into her pocket when she noticed it next to the iconic cobalt blue Chinese pottery shard: it was a bright yellow shard, but it wasn't the just the color that stopped her. Sandwiched between red and blue shards, this yellow piece of ceramic was ornamented with an unmistakable bumblebee. Looking closer, she saw the texture of honeycomb and imagined this bee had once been part of a honey jar.

She stepped back when she again remembered Isaiah's advice—looking at the towers through the lens of her faith. She didn't think that bees were commonly associated with faith, but she did remember something about bees from her childhood. For many years, her father had allowed a local beekeeper to keep a few dozen hives on their farm in exchange for a couple of gallons of honey each year. And it was her father who had once told her, as she sat sucking the honey from a piece of freshly harvested honeycomb, how the settlers who had first come to their valley had formed a farmer's cooperative and had chosen the beehive to symbolize their united efforts. It was a symbol of industry, hard work, and unity. As Kate remembered that interaction with her father, her eyes rose from the bee to the structure it was attached to.

She remembered her first interaction with the gazebo—how she had chosen to leave quickly after finding a grumpy Charlie there distracted by his iPad. But as she looked at it now, she could hardly believe she could miss something so big—simply not seeing it for what it was. The large, domed structure was a beehive! She was sure of it. She quickly walked to the front and entered again under the mosaicked heart at the top of the arched portal. As she circled the gazebo, walking through the spider web-like shadows cast by the overhead dome, she noticed that the vertical surface of the encircling bench was covered with the

same flower impressions she had seen before—hundreds of them. She took a photo of this, believing there must be a meaning behind them.

At the center of the gazebo, an ornate pillar flared out to form a

round table before thinning out again and
rising to the top of the dome and continuing
on into the sky. She could tell that something
was on top of the pillar, but she couldn't tell
what it was. Curious, she walked out of the
gazebo, hoping a different vantage point
could offer a more discernible view. With her naked eye, she couldn't tell
what the object on top was. An idea came to her as she stood wondering.
She set down her notebook on the fountain and aimed her phone to the

top of the pillar, zooming in with the
camera as far as she could. The image
was a bit blurry, but she took a picture
anyway. Taking a closer look at the
small screen, she thought the sculpture
looked like the body of a woman or
maybe an angel, its wings—or maybe
its dress—flowing behind. But its head
was missing. Kate couldn't imagine
Sam putting a decapitated figurine on
top of his church, and she immediately
began wondering if maybe its head
had fallen into the same hands as
some of the shells and pottery shards.
She snapped a few more photos before
continuing her exploration.

The wheat and grapes called
out to her once more. Sunlight bathed the wall, giving the relief more
definition than before, and as she approached it, she saw something she
hadn't seen before. Mirroring the wheat and filling in the background
were several clearly defined palm fronds.

A chill ran through her at the recognition of what this meant.
Through the lens of her faith, this highly symbolic frieze captured the
essence of the Christian Holy Week. From the palm fronds laid out on the

ground for Jesus to walk on during His Triumphal Entry into Jerusalem, to the symbols He made holy at the Last Supper, to the cross and nails symbolized by the dogwood flower, and finally to the lily—heralding the miracle of the Resurrection. It was so simple, and yet she knew she

would have missed it had she not taken a closer look—had she not seen it through eyes of faith. She wondered if Charlie knew anything about this. She took a couple of photos and had already walked away when she looked back, realizing she'd missed something else.

Returning quickly to the wall, she stood back a few feet, taking in the whole of it. She looked around at the other walls, realizing that the wheat-and-grapes motif in the center of this wall was not the only thing that set it apart. Unlike its neighbors, covered with colorful tiles and pottery shards, this wall was much less colorful and included only rocks and glass.

Kate looked around, looking for other walls or places where rocks were used. She didn't have to look far. Behind her, running along the opposite wall, rocks were embedded in the cement of a sculptural outcropping where green glass covered the surfaces of several conical pillars rising from the rocky base. After taking

several photos, she turned around, remembering the other rocks she had seen on her last visit. She nearly ran when she saw them, forming the base of the middle tower. Smaller rocks of all shapes and colors were embedded in the vertical surface, while larger rocks—some as big as small boulders—were cemented in place, forming a domed and bumpy foundation.

She had noticed the day before that the foundation of this tower was very different from the others'. There were no steps that might enable a person to climb into the center of this one. And with rocks making up the majority of its decorative ornamentation, it was easily the most simple of the three. But as Kate set her hand on top of one of the foundation rocks, she once again remembered Isaiah's advice. And that's when it happened. Looking at this again through the lens of faith, the mystery began to crack wide open and reveal itself.

She hurried back to the wheat and grapes, running her hand gently over the rocks that surrounded the relief before she rushed to the rocky foundation on the opposite wall, where the green glass cones rose above the height of the walls. From here she looked up, her eyes resting on the wide band that encircled the middle of the center tower. And what she saw there only confirmed her hunch. She lifted her phone and took several pictures. Filled with an electrifying energy and excitement, she rushed past the middle tower to the third tower, where she sat down, feeling overwhelmed by the beauty of the simple yet profound symbolism all around her. She felt like her chest was filled with warm chocolate pudding. As she looked up through the middle of the third tower, she reviewed in her mind the things she had just seen. Could this really be what she thought it was? It felt so true, but she had to know. She had to talk to Isaiah.

There was still more to see, though. She knew there had to be meaning in the boat sculpture too, but she couldn't think about that now—not with everything she'd just discovered. She quickly circled the boat, taking photos as she walked so she could examine it later when her heart wasn't racing and she could think about something else.

She hurried back to the gate and had just inserted the key into the lock when she remembered her bag. She ran back, realizing she had also forgotten her notebook. By the time she entered the shadows of the eucalyptus, she was winded and sweating. She rushed to the open door of the guard shack and peered inside.

"Can I help you?" a young black man asked, getting up from a chair behind the desk.

"Oh, uh...I was looking for Isaiah," she managed, feeling flustered and disappointed.

"You just missed him."

"What do you mean?"

"He just left three minutes ago. Are you Kate?"

"Yeah," she said, feeling confused. "Who are you?"

"I'm Jeremiah. Isaiah told me you were in there; said he was sorry to miss ya and told me to thank you for the muffin and tell you he hoped to see you soon."

Kate felt like the wind had been knocked out of her. "When will he be back?"

"Monday. He's got the weekend off."

"Dang! I was really hoping to talk to him."

"Yeah, sorry. Is there anything I can help you with?"

She shook her head, distracted. "Did he say anything else?"

"Only that I should get the key back from you."

"Oh, right," she responded, fumbling with her notebook and nearly dropping her phone before freeing the keychain from her fingers. As she handed it to Jeremiah, she saw something on the leather key fob she hadn't noticed before. It was so quick as it passed from her hand to his that she wasn't certain what she had seen, but as she walked across the lawn, she tried to recall its simple design. Somehow it was familiar, but she couldn't place it. She sat down in her car, and before she pulled away from the curb, she quickly sketched what she could remember of the small design that looked as though it might have been branded into the fob's dark leather. She looked at the sketch when she was done and realized it looked like a rocket blasting off into a black hole.

CHAPTER 22

ANDY

There is force in the universe, which, if we permit it,
will flow through us and produce miraculous results.
—*Mahatma Gandhi*

Kate was glad she had come, but not having someone to share her discoveries with was completely anticlimactic. She considered going back to the guard shack and asking Jeremiah if she could at least get Isaiah's phone number. It only took a second for her to recognize that that was probably a bad idea. Even though he had seemed pleased with her interest in the towers, she knew Isaiah would probably not feel the same way if she were pestering him at home, especially after what she guessed was a long shift.

As she drove home, she reviewed in her mind all the things she had seen that supported her hunches. She wondered what Charlie might think, if he would accept the things she had discovered—or if he would even listen. He had been so reluctant to talk about the possibility of the towers being endowed with anything of a mystical nature that she doubted he would be willing to hear anything about it. In the weeks since their visit, Kate had considered his sensibilities several times, wondering what had brought him to his state of denial and avoidance.

On a whim, she decided to drive past his house and see if he was around. She parked outside the stenciled garage door and was happy to hear music coming from the other side. Feeling anxious, she knocked on the big door, worrying that she'd made a mistake in coming here. She wondered what she'd say, trying to imagine a scenario in which a conversation might not be awkward. And so she was relieved when her knock went unanswered. She had just gotten back into her car when a shadow passed her window.

"Can I help you?" the man asked, his voice sounding winded.

Kate jumped at hearing his voice. "Oh, hey. It's Andy, right?"

"Yeah," he responded, looking a little confused, like he was trying to figure out who she was.

"I'm Kate—a friend of Charlie's. We met a few weeks ago."

"Oh, right. The farm girl who knows her tools. How's it goin'?"

"Good. I was just dropping by to see if Charlie was around."

"No. He got up early to go surfing or something. He'll probably be back before too long. Is there something I can help you with?"

She looked at him for a minute, considering his question. "So, this might sound weird, but are you busy right now?"

"Uh, I was just coming down to get started on some bikes. Why? What's up?"

"I don't want to keep you from your work. Could I maybe talk to you for a minute while you're doing whatever it is you're doing?"

"Uh, okay," he replied. "Come on in."

Kate got out of her car again and followed Andy through the tall gate on the side of the garage. Dozens of bikes in all colors and styles were leaned against each other, clogging up the walkway. He flipped on the light as he opened the garage door, and Kate noticed that the garage was nearly overflowing with bikes.

"It looks like business is good," she said.

"A little too good right now. You want a job?"

She laughed. "Are you serious?"

"Yeah. I'm at least a week behind. Charlie's been busy with his photography lately, and I haven't been able to keep up with the demand."

"What needs to be done?"

"All sorts of stuff. You said you've worked on bikes before, right?"

"Yeah. I mean, just a little bit. If it's straightforward, I can probably handle it."

"Good enough for me. Do you think you could replace some tubes?"

"I'm sure I could figure it out."

"Great. A lady brought in those eight cruisers over there almost two weeks ago. She's been leaving nasty messages for the last few days, saying her grandkids are arriving sometime today and she wants her bikes."

"What needs to be done?"

"I ordered new whitewall tires and tubes for all of them, and the chains need to be lubed. I don't think any of those bikes have seen the light of day in at least thirty years."

"Sounds easy enough. You have tools I can use?"

He pointed over her shoulder. "You can use Charlie's tools and bike stand. There are some rags over there, and here's a bucket of grease."

Kate responded quickly, throwing on the cleanest of the shop aprons before lifting the first dusty cruiser into the jaws of the bike stand. Andy watched for a minute, but when he saw that she was capable, he got to work on his own pile of bikes. The old tires were easy to take off. Rotten and cracked, they nearly fell from the rims by themselves. Installing the new tires proved to be much more difficult. Andy helped with the first one, showing her how a little grease and leverage helped the tire slide into place without the need of too much muscle.

"You wanted to talk to me about somethin'?" he asked as she finished dusting off the first bike.

"Yeah, I did—I do," she replied, moving on to the next bike. "I...

Charlie told me you've been to Watts Towers."

"Yeah. I've gone up there with Charlie a bunch of times. Why?"

"He also said something about it...changing you?"

"He did?"

"Yeah, something about how you used to be a big partier but how something changed after you went to the towers a few times."

Andy nodded sheepishly.

"So, what happened?"

He set down his wrench and wiped his hands on his apron. "Why do you want to know?"

"I know this is probably really personal, but I just came from there, and, well...I was curious about your experience. You know—what happened up there to make you...I don't know...change your ways?"

Andy picked up a red rag and began polishing the bike in front of him. "It's kinda hard to talk about my life back then. It's pretty painful."

"Sorry, I don't mean to be nosey."

"That's all right. It's good to remember how far I've come. My life was a lot different back then." He laughed. "That sounds like it was a million years ago. I guess in a lot of ways it was. I've been sober two years, four months, and...sixteen days."

"Congratulations."

"Thanks. It's been a really good change. I'm happier now than I ever remember being. And the cool thing is, I can remember the good times."

"Did you drink for a long time?"

"Almost eight years."

"You must have started when you were just a kid."

"Yeah, I was thirteen—seventh grade. I found a stash of beer in my dad's garage when I was visiting one weekend and was just dumb enough to sneak a few cans. I liked the way it made me feel, but before I even knew what I was doing, I felt like I needed to be buzzed just to be me—whoever that was." He laughed before going silent, and Kate wondered if she'd asked too much. He swapped out the bike for another one before he spoke again.

"I did some really stupid stuff back then. I ended up in juvie for three months when I was sixteen after gettin' caught stealing beer from Sev. And before I even turned eighteen, I became a father with a random girl I met at a party."

"Wow! That's a lot to take on when you're still a kid yourself."

"Yeah, well, neither of us were mature enough to know what we were doing, and fortunately for our baby, the girl's parents had enough sense to talk us into placing her for adoption—thank God. You'd think that somethin' like that would cause a person to grow up and get real, but I pretty much just stayed the course, bein' stupid, raging with even more anger and self-hate, tryin' to find a way to medicate myself so I didn't have to think about anything or anyone. I lost a few good years in there somewhere."

"So, how'd you meet Charlie?"

"He was down in San Diego—where I'm from—running a camera for the X Games, and I got teamed up with him through a temp agency, draggin' around his power cords and microphones. You've probably noticed the title *key grip* in the credits of movies?"

"I think so."

"Yeah, I was one of those. Anyway, we started talkin', and I found out he and his buddies were lookin' for another roommate, so I moved up here. That was almost two and a half years ago."

"Were you working on bikes back then?"

Andy shook his head. "I was just doin' the temp job thing, workin' whatever I could find. The bikes musta started about…well, about the time I started goin' to Watts with Charlie, I guess."

"Was there a correlation?" Kate asked, feeling confused.

"Kind of. I assume you know Simon's story, right?"

"A little bit."

"The dude was an alcoholic too. Lost his wife and kids because of it."

Kate nodded.

"But somethin' happened—musta been somethin' big 'cause he gave up the drink and built all that instead. After seein' what one dude could do in his spare time, I decided…well, I decided to stop wasting my life and my health. Instead of buyin' booze I started buyin' tools and lettin' people know I was takin' care of bikes. I guess I've been busy ever since."

"That's a really cool story."

"Thanks. Sobriety has plenty of disadvantages, but the perks for sure outweigh the stupid stuff I miss."

"So, do you know what happened to Simon to make him give up drinking?"

He shook his head. "I don't know if anyone does for sure. But I think he musta found God—or God found him."

"Why do you say that?"

Andy looked surprised by her question. "You've been there. You've seen all that, right? I felt somethin' up there on that first visit that I'd never felt before."

Kate nodded, encouraging him to continue.

"It was the craziest thing. I wondered if someone was cuttin' onions 'cause my eyes just kept waterin', and it felt like my chest was gonna pop. It was like this crazy mix of feelings—excitement and peace and love—all comin' at me at once. I'm not a crier, but I just sat there under that gazebo and cried like a baby."

"Huh. And how did Charlie respond to your reaction?"

Andy chuckled. "He called me a big freakin' baby."

"Really?"

"Yep. At first he wanted to talk about it, but when I told him what I was feeling, he basically walked away and wouldn't talk to me for the rest of the day."

"Interesting."

"What is?"

"He pretty much did the same thing to me. It was almost like he ran into an invisible wall and turned around and ran the other direction— like a switch turned off."

Andy nodded. "I take it you don't know his story?"

"Charlie's? No. But I can tell there's something broken in him—something that won't allow him to even think about anything that's gonna let him feel what you just described."

He looked at her, surprised. "That's a pretty amazing observation for not really knowing him."

"So, you're his roommate. You've been around him for at least a couple of years, right? What happened? What's he so afraid of?"

"You're askin' for my opinion?"

"Sure."

Andy stood silent for a moment, looking thoughtful. "Charlie's an artist. Everything in his whole world is visual and physical. If you ask me, I think he's afraid of admitting there's something out there in the universe that he can feel as it taps him on the shoulder from time to time; when he turns and can't see anything there, he basically freaks out. I guess we all do that sometimes. I know I did."

"Tell me about that."

"I've been workin' my way through understanding this with my sponsor in AA. Basically I didn't want to feel the pain of my reality, so I drank until it all disappeared. But in the process of chasin' away the darkness, I realize now I was also chasin' away the light. Charlie almost never talks about it, but from the little bits of stuff I've heard over the last couple of years, there's a whole bunch of sadness in that hard-shelled heart of his."

"Do you know what it is?"

"Maybe, but I'm pretty sure he has no idea that I know. And I doubt he'd be happy if he knew I told you."

"Okay. Fair enough," she said, turning back to the bike in front of her.

"That's it? You're just gonna give up that easy?" he asked with a teasing smile.

Kate laughed. "Well, you know I'm a social worker, right? I might be able to help him."

"Yeah, well, you might not have noticed, but Charlie doesn't want to be helped."

"Actually, yeah, I did notice. But lots of people act that way involuntarily. It's almost like it's their way of silently screaming for help."

Andy raised an eyebrow, looking dubious. "So you think Charlie's screaming for help?"

"Okay, so maybe not *screaming*," she responded with a grin. "I don't know why he acts the way he does. I barely know him. But I've been around him enough to know something's going on up there in Watts that scares him. I get the feeling he's been struggling with whatever it is for a long time. Honestly, I only want to help—if I can."

He looked at her, bemusedly. "You're not anything like the girls he's hung out with before."

"Uh, thanks…I think?"

"No, that's a compliment for sure. It's not like he has a bunch of ladies—he's actually pretty awkward when it comes to women. He's a really great guy, but most girls don't hang around long enough to find that out. He's been so distracted by the towers for the past several years that I think he's kind of forgotten how to communicate with people on a social level. You're actually the first one I ever seen twice since I've been here—other than the girls who come for their bikes, and none of them have ever had much patience with him."

"I can understand why," Kate said, remembering her first interaction with Charlie on the beach.

"Yeah. Well, he's broken. I mean we all are, right? But his brokenness is harder than most."

"Tell me about that—I mean if you want to."

Andy looked sideways, pausing like he was wondering what he should do. "Okay, but I'd appreciate it if he never finds out you heard this from me."

"Sure."

Andy didn't respond for nearly a full minute, and when he did, his words came quickly. "Charlie had a sister…"

She waited for more, but nothing came. *"Had* a sister?"

"Yeah. I heard a little about it from Brian—one of our other roommates. He's known Charlie since they were kids. I think her name was Sarah. She was only two years younger than Charlie, and Brian said they were really close."

"You make it sound like she died."

Andy nodded. "She drowned."

"Wow! How?"

"Charlie's family—back when his parents were together—they were at the beach one day, and his mom put Charlie in charge of watching his sister while they were boogie boarding. I guess his sister lost her board, and some older kids grabbed it. So, being the protective big brother, he went to get it back. By the time he turned back to the water, Sarah had been swept out in a freak riptide. I think she was only nine and wasn't strong enough to swim out of it."

Kate shook her head as she imagined the tragedy. "Riptides—I think I've heard about that. That's like a real thing, right?"

Andy smiled. "That's the main reason we have lifeguards. Riptides form on pretty much every beach around here every day. Kids and tourists are always getting caught up in them. Most people make it out, but it didn't work out that way for her. Brian said she swallowed a ton of water, and the lifeguards that went after her just barely made it back themselves. They did CPR for like an hour—even brought in a defibrillator—but it was too late.

"Wow!"

"Yeah. Brian said Charlie's always blamed himself for her death—and everything else."

"Everything else?"

"Yeah, well, his parents divorced less than a year later. His dad has always been a real jerk about it."

"Wait, he blames Charlie?"

Andy nodded. "I don't know if he's ever come right out and said it, but I guess there's always been an underlying tension between him and his dad—like Charlie's the cause of all his problems. He once told me he's never felt like anything more than a disappointment to his dad."

Kate looked shocked. "That can't be healthy. This actually makes a lot more sense now."

"It does?"

"Sure. I don't know anyone whose belief system wouldn't be negatively affected by a tragedy like that." She shook her head as the reality of what she just heard settled into her mind. "If I'd known what he's gone through, I think I would have tried to be more sympathetic."

"In what way?"

She stood still for a moment, remembering the day they'd gone to Watts and the disappointment she'd felt when they'd left before they really even had a chance to talk. Since that day, she had reviewed the visit in her mind several times, trying to recall the beginning of Charlie's apparent discomfort. But despite her efforts, she'd had trouble pinpointing any obvious moment. The note he'd found in the gazebo was the only thing that stood out to her as potentially upsetting. But she had nothing to do with that. Still, she wondered what she might have done had she known this tragic story of his past.

"I don't know what I would have done differently," she managed as she peeled another tire from a rusty rim. "But I didn't stop to even wonder if he might be protecting himself."

"Protecting himself?"

"Yeah. Between his sister's death and the way I imagine he's been treated by his dad—and then the fact that he hasn't been able to finish his film and graduate—when you get emotionally beat up like that, most people tend to protect themselves from any further damage or rejection. I should have seen it."

"Why, 'cause you're a social worker?" he chided.

"Well, yeah."

"Kate, I've been Charlie's friend for going on three years, and I don't think I've ever even thought about tying all those things together and blaming it for the mess that he is."

"Okay, but that's basic stuff for a social worker. I totally missed it."

"Don't beat yourself up. I'm sure he considers me one of his best friends, but he's never opened up to me about any of this. He's never been an open book. He's the kind of book that's wrapped up with chains and a big padlock and a laser security system. I love the guy, but he's kind of a porcupine."

"Uh, yeah, that sounds like a guy who's trying to protect himself."

"Against what?"

"Against more of the same—pain, disappointment, sadness."

Andy nodded slowly as he pumped up the tires of the bike he was working on. "So what's the answer?"

"I wish I knew."

"Wait, so your training is supposed to help you identify a problem, but once you do, you don't know how to solve it?"

Kate shook her head. "It's usually not that easy. There's no such thing as one-therapy-fits-all. It would be nice if there was a magical book we could open to look up people's troubles and find out how to solve them in three painless steps, but every problem a person encounters is internalized totally uniquely. In my line of work, there's mostly just several different types of talk therapy and advocacy and, in some cases, medication. But every treatment has plenty of limitations, and there's always the potential of making the problem even worse."

"That sounds promising," he responded sarcastically. "Why'd you go to school for that?"

"Because I wanted help people. I felt like it was my calling in life. I recognize now that I was super naive. I still want to believe that sharing a little light with someone who's in the dark can offer hope. The reality is that the most people are afraid of change, even when they can see that change leading off in a positive direction. And part of the problem is that unpredictable things like hormones, mental illness, environment, and personal tragedy can flip things for any of us in the blink of an eye."

"You make it sound like we're all doomed to misery!"

Kate smiled, shaking her head. "I didn't mean to. Your life was headed in a negative direction, but it's better now, right? And Simon— it sounds like he was in a pretty miserable place for at least a decade before he found himself and created something beautiful. How does that happen?"

Andy looked thoughtful for a moment as he continued to work. "It's probably different for everyone, right?"

She nodded.

"But thinking about it from my perspective and maybe Simon's too, the common thread—if there is one—maybe it's...love?"

She smiled at his answer.

"Can it really be that simple?" he asked

"I think it can be," Kate replied after a moment's thought.

"Really?"

"If anything can change a life for the better, it seems like love has what it takes. It's gotta be at least one of the most powerful motivators in the world, right?"

"You think so?"

"What else is there?"

"You mean besides money...and fear...and praise? And maybe power and greed? Those seem to be pretty big, too.

She nodded, acknowledging he was right. "But love seems to trump all of those, doesn't it? It seems like it's probably an even bigger motivator than faith."

He looked thoughtful. "Hey, have you ever heard that Ziggy Marley song, "Love Is My Religion?"

"I don't know, but I like the title. It actually reminds me of the towers."

"How so?"

"Andy, I was up there this morning. There are hearts everywhere. You walk on them, they're embossed on the walls, and they're flying on the towers. After seeing all of them, it seems pretty clear to me what

Simon was trying to express in his creations."

"You think it's all about love?"

"I do. Specifically, I think it's all about the love of God."

Andy smiled. "I think you're right."

"You do?"

"Yeah. I didn't understand it at first—what I was feeling on my first visit. It was such a new and different sensation than anything I was used to. It wasn't until I started going to AA meetings—until I started to believe in a power bigger than myself—that I felt like I really understood what Simon was trying to tell me."

"Through the lens of your faith," Kate mused, almost in a whisper.

"What's that?"

"It was something Isaiah told me this morning. I asked him if he had any advice about understanding the towers, and that's what he told me—look at them through the lens of your faith."

Andy smiled but shook his head, tossing a wrench onto his workbench and picking up a pair of pliers.

"What are you thinking?"

He took a moment to answer, as if he were still processing Isaiah's advice. "I was just thinking that maybe that's the problem Charlie's had—maybe that's the trouble he keeps running into."

"What do you mean?"

"The only faith Charlie's ever talked about is Pastafarianism."

"Do you mean Rastafarianism?"

Andy laughed. "No, it really is *Pastafarianism*. You've might have heard of it by its other name—The Church of the Flying Spaghetti Monster?"

"You're kidding, right?"

"No. I think it's basically just a spoof on faith. I looked it up a while ago. If I remember right, it's a church founded by a group of agnostics who got upset about intelligent design being taught in public schools. I'd never heard of it before I met Charlie. He has one of the decals on his bumper."

"I guess that explains a lot."

"What do you mean?"

"It's hard to see anything through the lens of faith if you don't have any faith to begin with. I guess I'm just confused because of his questions. They seem to conflict with someone who claims to be agnostic."

"Yeah, I know what you mean. I think he's confused about what he believes—or doesn't believe. Sometimes he asks me questions when we're working together or just hanging out. It almost feels like he's bating me, like he wants to know what I believe—up to a point. But when he doesn't like my answers, he just pulls the plug—kind of gives up on the conversation and changes the subject."

"What do you think about that?"

Andy smiled mischievously. "Honestly, I think it's kinda funny."

"Hmm. In what way?"

"It just seems like if he spent even half the time trying to understand instead of trying to avoid or mock, his life would be in a much different place. It's almost like he's angry at a God he won't even admit exists. I mean, I get it—kind of."

"You do?"

"Yeah. If mystical stuff isn't part of your belief—or nonbelief—system, how are you supposed to process it when you experience it?"

Kate shook her head—stumped. "I can't say I've ever thought about it that way before."

"But you've got to admit that experiencing the spiritual could be potentially disturbing, at least the first time, right? It's probably even more disturbing—or at least confusing—if you've spent several years denying the existence of anything spiritual."

"Okay...I could see that."

"And what if you stumble upon it when you're not even looking for it?"

Kate didn't respond, thinking about Andy's words. What *if* this were all new to her? How would her response to it be different? As she tried to answer these questions in her mind, she realized how different her life experience was from Charlie's—or Andy's. Having attended church every Sunday for most of her twenty-two years, she had believed in the spiritual realm most of her life and had often encountered it. Prayer had generally been a habitual, if not important, part of her life. She had wandered from the proverbial straight and narrow path of the Christian gospel from time to time but never for long, always returning to the safety and familiarity of the sure foundation her parents had given her from her youth. She had experienced loss, but not like Charlie. Even in her darkest moments, she had always maintained at least a sliver of hope in the truthfulness of the things she'd been taught. She knew if she was ever going to help Charlie, she would need to find a way to empathize.

Don't shine so that others can see you. Shine so that through you, others can see HIM.

C. S. Lewis

CHAPTER 23

CONSPIRATORS

There is a loftier ambition than merely to stand high in the world.
It is to stoop down and lift mankind a little higher.
—*Henry Van Dyke*

"So, I'm wondering...if I were going to try to help Charlie work his way through this...would you have any suggestions for me?" Kate inquired.

Andy looked up from his work. "Patience."

She blinked her eyes a few times, waiting for more. "Really? That's all you got?"

"Are you saying that's too easy?"

"Don't get me wrong; I'm sure patience is important, but I was looking for something maybe a little less...apathetic."

"Oh, I get it. You're looking for something that can completely change a man's life in six quick visits?"

"Well, no, not exactly," she responded, backpedaling. "I was just hoping to be able to do something a little more proactive than sitting around waiting."

"I don't know how things'll play out for Charlie—or if they ever will, but I think most of us have to come to ourselves in our own time and place. It seems like it's human nature to question the purpose of life, right? To try to figure out where we belong in the universe. He'll get there eventually."

Kate nodded but felt discouraged.

"I remember lots of mornings—and afternoons—waking up after a night of partying, thinking there had to be something more, something better than that. I wish I could have figured it out earlier and not wasted so much time. But the timing and the circumstances had to be right, and it was something I had to come to on my own. I had to want to change bad enough to be willing give up what I was. I couldn't have done that without the help of a higher power—or the help from my sponsor and the lessons I'm still learning in AA. I guess what I'm saying is—I had to want it. I don't think Charlie's there yet. He's still got too much fight in him—too much independence—too much pride. Looking back, I think I was probably in a similar place for at least three years."

"Do you mind me asking how and why things changed for you?"

He shook his head, but didn't answer right away, looking like he was searching for the right words. "I think you might be right."

Kate laughed. "Remind me what I'm right about."

"What you said about love. I can't say I've thought about it until just now, not really. But maybe love really *is* the world's greatest motivator."

"Tell me why you say that now."

"I was just remembering that day in the gazebo. That overwhelming sense of love I felt…that was the first time—that was the tipping point for me—that made me want to change or at least start things moving in a different, better direction."

She nodded slowly. "So if you felt it and I felt it, I'm sure others have felt it too. Charlie's spent who knows how many hours up there. He's had to have felt something, right?"

"It would be hard to believe he hasn't. But the thing is, when you're not ready for it, when you don't feel worthy of it, when you can't understand how or why anyone or anything could love you—and then it's unexplainably there, showering you with something that feels both totally foreign but also strangely familiar, it can be completely... unnerving...intimidating...even frightening."

She knew he was right, and yet she also knew from her limited experience that love has the unique ability to push out all fear if people could only give it a chance. "So...how'd things change so you aren't afraid of love anymore?"

He laughed. "I never said *that* changed."

"Love still scares you?" she asked, surprised.

"Only every time."

"Really?"

"Yeah. I'm slowly learning to accept it—even embrace it, but it's taken me way out of my comfort zone. I've tried to live a better life, but I still think about how my past and my stupid choices made so much trouble for so many people. For these last two years, I feel like the light is constantly trying to chase away the darkness, but I still wrestle with feeling worthy of it."

"I remember reading that those kinds of feelings are fairly common for recovering addicts."

Andy nodded. "My sponsor told me he went through the same thing for years, feeling like he'd gotten so used to living his life by dim candlelight that when the sunlight came in, it was overwhelmingly frightening. He warned me that when light chases out the darkness, you have to learn how to navigate through everything differently. I guess that's where I am now—figuring out how to navigate through a world of light for the first time in my life. It's like learning how to walk all over again."

"That's a beautiful idea—learning to walk in the light," Kate mused. "Honestly, I feel like I'm learning the same thing."

"You?" He looked at her incredulously. "You strike me as a good girl who's always known where she's going."

She shook her head. "I think the only people who aren't regularly questioning the purpose of their existence, or at least the direction they're traveling, are the ones we don't know very well."

"You just dashed all my hopes," he said, looking deflated

"I'm sorry," she teased. "What were your hopes?"

"It probably sounds stupid, but I've always had this idea that there are gurus out there somewhere—you know, people who have reached nirvana or whatever and are anxious to share their wisdom and knowledge with anyone who'll listen."

"I remember thinking something similar."

"But not anymore?"

She shook her head. "It's a really nice idea, and I'm sure there are lots of people who are way closer than we are, but I've been working on a theory for the last couple of years. It's still only half-baked, but it just seems like all of us are somewhere in the process of stubbing our toes as we grope around in the darkness, desperately searching—whether we admit it or not—for the light and hope that comes from love."

"I didn't know social workers dealt with things like love and spirituality."

Kate shrugged. "We all need love and light, right? And it seems like everyone at least dabbles in some version of spiritual awareness at some point in their lives, if at no other times than the beginning and the end."

"You think even atheists dabble in the spiritual?"

"I can't say for sure, but it seems like everyone, when we're confronted with death or hard times—we all try to find a way to make sense of life's big questions. Before I moved down here, I used to work at a nursing home. I found you can learn a lot about human nature by spending time at a place like that. I discovered that most of the patients, as they got closer to dying—they were all concerned with what was on the other side of life. Some looked forward to it like a kid waiting for Christmas, but others were doing everything to stay as far away from the edge as they could. I don't know if it was always the case, and maybe it's too big of a generalization, but I noticed that the only patients who had any peace as they approached the end were the ones whose faith openly played a role in their lives."

Andy nodded slowly as he considered what she said. "This is definitely not the conversation I expected to be having this morning."

"Sorry. I swear I'm not usually like this. It must be what I saw this morning…"

"I'm not saying I mind it. It's actually given me a lot to think about."

"You made it sound like you don't ever talk to Charlie about stuff like this."

"Yeah, no," he said with a laugh. "Never actually. It's not that I'd mind, it's just…it's hard to have a meaningful conversation about this kind of stuff with someone who's totally not into it. I stopped going with him to the towers a while back because I was tired of watching him wasting his time and avoiding the stuff that matters. He knows there's something there, but I don't know if he's ever going to let himself feel it. It's a hard thing when your head's so thick that it kills your ability to see and hear—and even think."

"So what's the answer?" she asked, feeling a little hopeless.

"Someone's gotta stop taking his crap."

She cracked a smile. "I nominate you."

"I've already tried. The problem is I've got to live and work with him. If things get messy, it would be better if it was someone else— someone who didn't have anything to lose," he said, raising one eyebrow.

She smiled, shaking her head. "I hardly know him."

"You know him well enough to know he's full of crap."

"That's not hard to see."

"Maybe not. But you've got the expertise, right? You can obviously see through it. He's basically just a good bluffer, playing it cool and sometimes impulsively saying and doing reckless stuff that he really doesn't mean."

"Yeah, that's really comforting. You make him sound like an unpredictable maniac."

Andy laughed. "Don't get me wrong. I love the dude. He's like a brother to me. But I worry about him."

"Why?"

"I think this film project has been really hard on him. I've watched it drive him to the edge more than a few times. Two weeks ago, I went to take out the garbage and found a bunch of his photos and notebooks—all of his research—just dumped in the trash."

"What?! Did he say anything to you about it?"

"No. He wasn't in any mood to talk, so I left him alone. He's been pretty quiet since then."

"Wait. Two weeks ago?"

"Yeah, why?"

"I was there with him two weeks ago."

"Yeah, I know. He dumped his stuff as soon as he got home from being with you."

She shook her head. "Great, so now I'm the cause of him ditching his passion."

"Oh, I wouldn't give yourself so much credit. You were probably just the final straw. I think he's been looking for an excuse to ditch it all for a long time."

"Andy, we can't let him do that, right? He's gotta get back there. He's gotta figure this out. I'm guessing there was probably a lot of good stuff that he threw away."

Andy smiled coyly. "Five years' worth of research. It seemed like such a waste."

"Wow!"

"Yeah. I couldn't let him do it."

"What do you mean?"

He smiled impishly. "I fished it all out of the garbage."

Kate laughed. "Why?"

"It just felt so…stupid—like he was just reacting like an idiot kid who got his feelings hurt and didn't know how else to respond. I pulled it all out and put it in that box up there," Andy said, pointing to a cardboard box on the shelf over his tool bench.

"What are you going to do with it?"

"I don't know yet. Save it, I guess, until he comes to his senses."

Kate smiled and turned back to the bike she was working on. "This almost feels like an unplanned conspiracy," she said after a few moments.

"How so?"

"Neither of us knew what the other has been doing, but it seems like we're both trying to find a way to get Charlie back to the towers."

Andy nodded. "So what should we do?"

"I don't know. Maybe we just have to be...patient, dang it!"

Andy didn't have any answers, and they worked in silence for several minutes, each of them lost in their own thoughts.

"I think I might have an idea," Andy said, breaking the long silence, "but I'm not sure if you'll like it."

"Why not?"

"I think it might require more of that P word you don't seem to like very much."

She let out a long, exaggerated breath. "Bring it on."

"One of the turning points for me, when I really started to want to change—it was inspired by something Isaiah told me on one of those early visits. I still think about it all the time. He told me it's a Quaker proverb or something like that. "Proceed ...""

"As the way opens." Kate said, unable to stop herself.

"You know it?" he asked, looking surprised.

"Yeah. Isaiah just told me about it yesterday. Crazy timing, huh?"

Andy smiled. "Maybe it's not so crazy at all. Maybe he's part of the conspiracy."

"You think so?" she asked, smiling back.

"If anyone could be, it would be him. That dude has a better read on people than anyone I've ever met. And it seems like he's been willing to bend over backwards to help Charlie get his movie made."

"I noticed that too. Why do you think that is?"

"I never asked him, but I got the feeling several times that he's been waiting for years for someone like Charlie to come around. It seems super important to him."

Kate nodded thoughtfully. "If it's so important, why wouldn't he just come right out and tell Charlie what he needs to do?"

"I get the impression that it's one of those chicken-and-the-egg sort of things."

"Huh?"

"Do you ever watch professional wrestling?"

"Uh, no," she responded, looking confused.

"Oh, then this might not make much sense, but in tag team wrestling, you have to tag your partner—kinda ask for his help before he's able to jump into the ring and help you."

Kate's look of confusion only deepened. "And the connection is…"

"It just feels like Isaiah's been waiting for Charlie to ask for advice and direction."

She laughed. "Andy, you could have just said *that* and not messed up my head with chickens and eggs and sweaty wrestlers."

"Oh, sorry."

"That's actually an interesting idea."

"Wait, what is?"

"Well, when we were there together, I was surprised that Charlie didn't know that Isaiah graduated from Penn State. He didn't even know that he went to college. It just seemed weird that he's known him for five years and never asked about his background. It's like he enjoys the perks of having someone who can let him through the gate, but he's missed out on really getting to know Isaiah and all the wisdom he has to offer. The more I'm around Isaiah, the more I recognize how anxious he is to share what he knows with anyone who's curious enough to ask."

If a thing is free to be good it is also free to be bad. And free will is what has made evil possible. Why, then, did God give them free will? Because free will, though it makes evil possible, is also the only thing that makes possible any love or goodness or joy worth having. C. S. Lewis

"Yeah, I got exactly the same vibe from him. I've even suggested to Charlie that maybe the old guy might be smarter than he looks, but Charlie's never listened."

"Do you think he's afraid of finding out more?"

"Definitely. If what someone has to say doesn't fit into his agenda and predetermined ideas—especially if there's any kind of a spiritual component—he drops them."

Kate nodded thoughtfully. "Maybe we all do that."

"You think?"

"Yeah, I mean, isn't that part of human nature? Most of us hate being wrong. I know I do. Most of us try to defend our opinion tooth and nail, especially when we're faced with opinions that push against our long-held ideas and beliefs. It happens all the time in politics. Even with stuff like global warming. No matter what side of the fence you're on, people don't usually like to change their minds."

Andy chuckled. "It doesn't sound like you have much hope that Charlie can change."

"Everyone can change. But you know—change is hard. It usually requires us to admit that we've been hanging onto false ideas. It requires that we open our heart and mind to other possibilities of truth. It's like when we were teenagers. I don't know about you, but I thought my parents were pretty dumb when I was fifteen. My little sister thought they were complete imbeciles. But somewhere about the time I was getting ready to leave home, I started seeing that maybe they weren't as dumb as I thought—that maybe some of their experience in life could be worth something to me. But getting to that point is tough, right? I don't think my sister's there yet. It requires humility, and humility doesn't seem to be a virtue that comes naturally to anyone."

"So how did it change for you?"

Kate shook her head. "Humility is a tough thing for me—always has been. A couple of years ago, I woke up one night with a terrible pain in my gut. I tried to ignore it, thinking it was just something I ate. I'd overscheduled my life and didn't have the time to go to a doctor. So, long story short, my appendix burst and probably ruined my chances of ever having kids."

"I'm sorry. That sucks."

"Yeah, it does," Kate responded, looking away. "But I learned something from that."

"That life isn't fair?"

"No, I already knew that. But while I was in the hospital after my surgery, I started to recognize that humility is a funny thing. We really can't learn anything of value until we have it. But getting it can be tricky. The way I see it, we can either choose to be humble or try to avoid it and just take our chances while we wait for the natural forces of the universe to bring us to our knees as a consequence for the choices we make. I'm sure there are plenty of exceptions, but for most of us, it seems like we either choose to be humble or we get compelled to become humble."

Andy nodded in agreement. "Go on."

"Well, I'm still working my way through this, but it seems like the humility to bend our will to meet the will of God requires effort—either internal or external."

He laughed. "Easier said than done, don't you think?"

"Absolutely! It requires that we put our trust in a God we can't see—that He'll lead us ultimately to a better life than what we've got now. I don't know if that's ever easy, but especially not without humility."

"And if you don't believe in God...or if you're mad at him...that would for sure stand in your way of making much progress, right?"

"It seems like it would have to."

"No, that makes sense," Andy said, nodding. "That's kinda like what my sponsor told me just last week—he was a river guide for a decade and has some cool analogies about life. He told me that our attitudes and choices have the potential of basically damming us by blocking up the river of God's love and creating stagnant backwater full of stuff like resentment and apathy and bitterness. He said that one of the keys to happiness is to keep the river open—to stop building dams even when the river seems full of rapids and goosenecks—and learn instead to trust that God knows where the river will take us, that His love will bring us safely to a better place."

"I like that. It sounds like your sponsor's figured it out. Is he a guru?"

Andy laughed. "Maybe. He's just...Tony."

She nodded thoughtfully. "Maybe that's the way real gurus are."

"What do you mean?"

"I don't know. I have this idea of a guru being hidden away in some remote hermitage in the Himalayas or something. But maybe gurus are just the people around us who are willing to share the wisdom they've gathered as they've bumped down the same road. Have you ever talked to Charlie about any of that stuff Tony told you?"

"I try to drop stuff into our conversations every now and then, but he usually shuts me down before I can say much."

"He's playing the rebel," she mused, as she moved on to another bike.

"What do you mean?"

"Oh, it's just an idea I've been thinking about for the last few months as I've been consciously trying to understand God's will for me. I'm beginning to recognize that pride turns us all into something like a rebellious, headstrong teenager who's asking to borrow the car. I imagine God being the patient parent who's anxious for us to go and explore our world and is willing to hand over the keys. But before he does, he says something like, "I know a bit about this road. You might want to be careful of the falling rocks at milepost 18 and maybe slow down before the curves at milepost 22 or you'll end up at the bottom of a cliff." And the teenager says something like, "Yeah, whatever. I know what I'm doing and where I'm going. Just shut up and get out of my face." I'm still working my way through it, but for the first time in my life, I feel like I'm starting to understand my relationship to God. I see Him as someone who wants to help me make sense of my life. Sorry, I... this is deeper than...I'm probably boring you."

"No, you're not," Andy replied. "I used to imagine God—not that I thought of Him much—as an angry and spiteful being who waits for us to screw up so he can thump us when we're not looking."

Kate tried not to laugh as she imagined Andy's scenario. "And now?"

Andy looked thoughtful for a moment before he responded. "I had it all wrong."

She nodded, waiting for him to continue.

"Tony has finally convinced me that God is way more about mercy than he is about justice. For the first time in my life, I'm beginning to feel like God's really more about love."

"Andy, I think you're right. And I really believe that's what Simon was trying to tell people. It doesn't surprise me that you had such an emotional experience—even a mystical experience—that first time you went there. I think that's what it's for."

"What do you mean?"

"My gut tells me that he built those towers as a monument to the God who saved him from himself. It's seems crazy that in a place like Watts someone can find such a strong sense of hope and love, but the more time I spend there, the more I recognize that Simon must have experienced something so profound that it took him thirty-three years to express it. I know Charlie appreciates the unique beauty of the towers, but without a lens of faith to look through, he's missed all the best parts of that beauty. He's missed out on what it really means."

While they continued to work, Kate told Andy more about the things she had discovered that morning. Feeling like she could trust him, she also told him about Sammy and the things she had learned about him from the notebook.

"So, where do we go from here?" Andy asked as Kate finished up the final tire of the eighth bike.

"I don't know," she said, shaking her head. "But I gotta do something. I don't know why or how, but I like to think this is part of why I'm here. I gotta help Charlie see what he's been missing."

"Did you ever watch his movie?"

"No. We never got that far. Why?"

"Do you want a copy?"

"You have one?" she asked, her eyebrows raised in surprise.

"Yeah. I have, like, ten copies," he said, nodding to the box.

"Sure. I'll take one."

Andy turned to the high shelf. With the help of a long screwdriver, he pulled the box to the edge, where it fell into his outstretched arms. "Actually, maybe you should just take the whole box."

"Really?" She tried not to be excited as she imagined what was inside.

"I didn't know what I was supposed to do with this stuff when I found it in the garbage, but I knew I couldn't let it go to the dump." He hesitated for a moment before looking her directly in the eye. "I don't like being patient either, Kate. But the last two years have given me plenty of time to think and remember that my impatience never brought me any closer to finding real happiness. Sometimes it feels like I'm moving slower than I ever have before, but the difference is that I have confidence in knowing that I'm goin' the right way this time. I used to call stuff like this coincidences, but Tony—he calls it serendipity. He says it's a good name for stuff we can't explain that leads us to a better place. It's happened a lot more in the last two years than it ever did before. It's almost feels like it's a sign and it's tellin' me I'm on the right path. I know I've spent too much of my life second-guessing things, and I'm still trying to understand what the big picture's supposed to look like. But this sure feels like a way is opening."

Kate smiled, feeling the same thing. "Then I guess we shouldn't hesitate to proceed."

Unbelievers think they have made great efforts to get at the truth when they have spent a few hours in reading some book out of Holy Scripture, and have questioned some cleric about the truths of the faith. After that, they boast that they have searched in books and among men in vain. Blaise Pascal

CHAPTER 24

THE BOX

"There is a vitality, a life force, an energy, a quickening that is translated through you into action, and because there is only one of you in all of time, this expression is unique. And if you block it, it will never exist through any other medium and it will be lost. The world will not have it. It is not your business to determine how good it is nor how valuable nor how it compares with other expressions. It is your business to keep it yours clearly and directly, to keep the channel open."
—*Martha Graham*

"I'm sure Charlie will be back soon," Andy said, looking up at the clock on the wall with the slightest hint of worry in his eyes. "If he finds this box—and you and me together—he's gonna think there really is a conspiracy going on."

"Yeah, I need to get going anyway." Kate responded, wiping her hands on the apron.

Andy carried the box to her car before handing her a fifty-dollar bill for her work. They exchanged phone numbers quickly, and Andy promised he would help if she could find a way for him to be involved without compromising his friendship with Charlie.

Kate found her sister and her other housemates sunbathing on the deck when she returned home. Knowing she wouldn't be able to spread out the contents of the box on the kitchen table without drawing attention, she decided to join the girls on the deck and try to make up for her early-morning jaunt with a nap. But with her mind being constantly drawn to the unknown contents of the box, sleep never came. She considered telling her sister about her morning and the box in the back of her car, but she worried that word might somehow get back to Charlie. She stewed on this for the next couple of hours, and by the time her housemates got up to get ready for work, Kate was feeling anxious and stir-crazy. With a desire to find a quiet place to dive into the box, she made herself a sandwich and headed out for an exploratory drive in search of place that could offer some peace and inspiration.

The Pacific Coast Highway was clogged with Saturday afternoon traffic, and after just a few slow miles, she turned right onto a residential street and headed west. The road ended at Ocean Boulevard, running parallel to cliffs that looked like they dropped into the sea. Swanky houses in a broad range of styles and colors proudly lined the east side of the street. She turned left and drove slowly, trying hard not to guess how many lifetimes at fourteen dollars an hour would be required to afford a house like these. Hoping to find a parking space so she could get out and walk, she continued driving and was just about to give up when a big, white convertible pulled away from the curb just in front of her.

A coral-colored bench on the edge of the cliff offered a commanding view of the coastline while she ate her sandwich, tempting her to stay. But a narrow blacktop path leading down to a small, secluded beach appealed to her sense of curiosity. Summoned by the sounds of the sea, she awkwardly followed the path with the box in her hands and a blanket draped over her shoulders. She found a quiet patch of sand where she laid out the blanket and sat down to watch the waves roll over the rocks, flood the tide pools again and again, and splash over a small, rocky arch that rose from the water's surface. With a feeling of contentment in her heart, she closed her eyes and turned her face to the sun. As the wind tousled her hair, she tuned her ears to what she imagined was the faint sound of distant church bells.

Opening her eyes, she followed the sound to the cliffs and farther down the beach, where three large pipes—a wind chime of epic proportions—hung from the outstretched branch of an evergreen, its gnarled roots growing over the edge of the rocky cliff. Again, she closed her eyes, remembering the lessons of silence Isaiah had shared with her and Charlie. The silence here was much different than it had been in Watts. The non-stop hum of the waves. The cry of the gulls. The sounds of children playing.

Kate concentrated, trying to forget the box at her side and just listen without distractions. Five minutes passed, then ten, as the wind tied her hair into increasingly snarly knots. But she didn't notice, too caught up in the glorious richness of her surroundings to be distracted by less important things. As she focused all her attention on the sounds around her, keeping her eyes closed, she tried to remember a quote she had heard in her comparative religions class. It had so struck her when she had first heard it that she had written it down on the palm of her hand and even talked to her father about it later that week. "*I like the silent church before service begins, better than any teaching.*" It was her first real introduction to the poet and Transcendentalist writer Ralph Waldo Emerson. But that quote and several others had catapulted her through a unique time of reflection and seeking.

As she listened to the waves, she remembered a special visit with her father, sharing with him the things she was learning at college as they sat on the front porch of the family home, looking out at the freshly harvested grain fields glowing gold in the waning autumn light. It was during that visit that she came to appreciate her father in a new way. She had always known him as a simple, hardworking, gentleman. But listening to him talk about the joy he often felt as he quietly contemplated the workings and the wonders of nature under the creative hand of God opened a door to her father's soul that she had never before entered. It was a tender evening, just the two of them watching as the lights in the heavens turned on one at a time over the farm their people had worked for more than a hundred and fifty years. Stillness, he admitted that evening, had been a critical part of his spiritual well-being. Prayer, he had told her hundreds of times, was the only thing that had kept the farm going for as long as it had. But she learned that night that it was the stillness the farm offered him that meant more to him than almost anything else. It was in that stillness, he'd told her, that he experienced the most profound feelings of love he had ever known.

Kate had remembered that magical evening many times, but something was different about it tonight. Her cheeks turned cold, chilled by the wind as it mingled with her tears. It had been four years since she had left for college, but still she felt a longing for the familiar and safe. With her eyes still closed, she listened as the chimes on the cliff played the same three tones, reminding Kate of an ancient hymn her father often whistled. She was six years old before she learned the tune had words when she wandered into the barn one evening before dinner and overheard her father singing to himself. He had told her that night that it was a song his grandfather had taught him. Over the years, she had asked him to sing it to her as he tucked her into bed at night. The words worked their way into her memory, and the thought of them now, here, only made her miss home more. She wrapped her arms around her knees as she opened her eyes and looked out at the ocean waves. Without warning, her mouth began to hum the tune involuntarily as the words paraded through her mind.

Through all the world below, God is seen all around;
Search hills and valleys through, There he's found.
The growing of the corn, The lily and the thorn,
The pleasant and forlorn, All declare God is there.
In the meadows dressed in green, There he's seen.

See springs and water rise, fountains flow, rivers run;
The mist below the skies hides the sun;
Then down the rain doth pour, the ocean it doth roar,
And dash against the shore, all to praise, in their lays,
That God that ne'er declines His designs.

The sun, to my surprise speaks of God as he flies:
The comets in their blaze give him praise;
The shining of the stars, the moon as it appears,
His sacred name declares; see them shine, all divine!
The shades in silence prove God's above.

Then let my station be here on earth, as I see
The sacred One in Three All agree;
Through all the world is made, The forest and the glade;
Nor let me be afraid. Though I dwell on the hill
Since nature's works declare God is there.

by Jeremiah Ingalls

It was memories like this that had remained with Kate to strengthen her over the past four years as she had struggled to find herself and define the borders of her faith. Like a beacon of hope, this hymn had often brought her comfort in times of self-doubt and darkness. She had witnessed for herself the hand of God in the wonders and miracles of nature. But what had become even more important to her were the simple feelings of comfort and peace she had come to recognize as God's personal expressions of love. Those feelings had kept her going through many difficult times. They had given her an anchor when she needed security and buoyed her up through doubts and challenges.

As she considered some of these small miracles, she became aware of the box at her side and remembered why she had come. She lifted the flaps of the box and stared into the jumbled contents. Photos, compact disks, and notebooks were piled on top of each other as if they had been dumped there haphazardly. She imagined Andy discovering these items in the garbage and pulling them from the can as quickly as he could, finding a quick, safe place to hide them.

Kate reached in with both hands and gathered up a shuffled bunch of photos, eight inches thick. Laying them in her lap, she attempted to straighten them. Some of them had writing on the back, and others had small holes punched along the top edges, where she imagined they had once been pinned to a wall. Photos of several older individuals, men and women, were bunched together, with names like Pedro Martinez, Ruby Black, and Josephine Gonzalez scrawled on the back. Kate imagined these might be the individuals Charlie had interviewed. She set these aside and sorted through the rest of the stack, mostly photos of the towers themselves. Some looked like they must have been taken with a fish-eye lens, producing round pictures and distorted, curved lines. There were many close-ups showing details as well as dozens of photos taken from a vantage point that took in the whole of the complex. Some even looked like they may have been taken from a drone flown overhead.

She began sorting them into piles, and as she did, she gained an even stronger appreciation for Simon's work. As she sorted through the photos, she also caught details she had missed in her visits to the towers. These only confirmed her theory that the towers were built as a monument to the God who had saved Simon. This theory became even more pertinent as she isolated the photos of the middle tower. Many of these looked like they had been taken from outside the fence, perhaps across the street. From this vantage point, the colorful band that circled this tower was clearer than it had been from where she had seen it that morning. One photo focused in on the band itself, and Kate paused, taking in the powerful yet simple symbolism. Alternating hearts and circles with crosses in the middle of them circled the top of what she now could see was a crown. Several other photos focused on the flying buttresses that tied the middle tower to the first. Hearts, circles, and crosses were built into the central column that tied all of the buttresses together.

Kate paused at one photo of these buttresses. The image showed the sunlight reflecting off the glass and tiles that adorned them, and she was just about to move on to the next photo when another thought came to her. With her finger she carefully counted the buttresses. Twelve. Of course there were twelve, she thought. For her theory to be correct, there would have to be twelve. But as she set this photo aside, she knew that only those who looked at this number through the lens of faith would find a deeper meaning in the structure. She stacked the now nicely straightened photos and placed them back in a corner of the box to keep the wind from carrying them away.

Just as Andy had suggested, there were several DVDs in clear plastic cases. Most of these had the same label on them: *Simon's Towers*, and Kate guessed these were copies of the documentary that Charlie had created for his class. She would have to check it out when she got home to her laptop. Several other CDs were labeled with things like *Interviews, Photos*, and *Miscellaneous Watts*. She straightened these, stacking them neatly in another corner of the box before moving on to a stack of books, notebooks, and a commercial DVD case entitled *I Build the Towers*.

Kate turned to the books. A couple of them looked like they had been written for kids, while others offered a general glance at the towers and their creator. She looked for any reference to anything spiritual, but she couldn't find anything to support her hunches. She set these books aside on the blanket and turned to the stack of six spiral notebooks, each one different from the other in color and size. Charlie George's name and phone number were printed on the covers of each of these; each also had a number on the bottom right-hand corner—#1 through #6. She set aside all but the first one before opening its cover.

Written in journal format with dates scrawled across the top of the page, Charlie documented his first visit to the towers, written a week after the fact. Just as he had told her on that first day at the beach, he had visited the towers on a whim, having heard about them from a friend and his humanities textbook. He wrote of immediately feeling a connection to the place and experiencing "...a strange but peaceful feeling," as he put it, after driving through the sad, neglected streets of Watts. Like Kate, he hadn't been able to take a tour that first day—a Wednesday, when no tours were given. But even from the outside of the fence, he had experienced something "magical, mind-boggling, even incredible."

Other entries spoke of meeting Isaiah and other members of the Art Center staff. He wrote about Isaiah suggesting to him that maybe there was a documentary to be made. In another entry, he wrote about his professor shooting down his first choice of intended documentary subjects—Frank Salisbury, Orange County's oldest surfer, and his many encounters with sharks—and wrote about homing in instead on his second choice: Simon Rodia and the Watts Towers. The entries that followed related mostly to discussions with Isaiah as Charlie picked up several suggestions of people he might interview.

Kate was impressed that Charlie didn't dither, recognizing that he was having interviews with people sometimes only hours after a suggestion had been made. Turning to one page where Charlie's handwriting was darker and less neat, she paused to read what he had written.

    I went back to talk to Margaret Smith today. She told me last week that Simon had been a preacher. I realized over the weekend that I should have asked more questions. Today she told me that he taught his small congregation a unique interpretation of the trinity—that there was a god the father, god the son, and god the holy spirit. That they were three separate gods but somehow united in purpose. I asked her what that purpose was and she told me it centered around a gospel of love. She even quoted some passage from the bible that says "god is love." As a young girl she attended services in the gazebo and remembered most of Simon's sermons focusing on the message of the patient, kind, and endless love god has for all the people of the world.
    I'm not sure what to do with any of this information. She suggested it was important to understanding Simon's ideas and purpose for building the towers, but I'm having a hard time wrapping my head around it. Growing up in a mostly secular home—god, Santa Claus, and the tooth fairy all fell into the same category of "grand illusions," as dad used to call them. My

conversation with Margaret triggered lots of old memories—things I've tried to forget. I remember feeling like there was a fight going on in my head after Sarah died—wondering what life was about—wondering how anyone could believe in god and even wondering if her death was some kind of curse for not believing. I remember feeling like it made the most sense to just try to forget all of those dark, painful feelings. I thought I had. But Margaret seems completely convinced that god does exist, that he created the earth and all mankind, and even that he loves us. Part of me wishes I could have stayed and asked more questions, but the rest of me had to get out of there before my head exploded.

I'm sure she didn't have an agenda. I was the one asking the questions. And her answers seemed honest and sincere. But it's hard for me to understand how people can still be so naive. She is 89 years old, has seen her share of sadness and trouble, and somehow she still has faith. Part of me admires her for it, but the cynic in me can't understand how people can still believe in a god in the 21st century when science and reason have debunked so many of the superstitions and myths about religion. But Margaret seemed convinced that Simon had it right, and it felt pointless and disrespectful to argue with a woman who's almost 7 decades older than I am. I tried to stay neutral throughout the interview, but there was a joy in her eyes that was undeniable. I've been thinking about that all day. To be honest, I'm not even sure if I know what joy is. Her convictions are almost enough to make me take a critical look at my cynicism.

But a god who lets innocent children die? What kind of a god is that? Just thinking about it makes me angry.

Kate set the notebook down in her lap, recognizing that she had missed a lot of important things in understanding Charlie. But reading this very personal account in his own words and pen also left her feeling like an interloper. She looked at the box of Charlie's stuff, feeling a little bit guilty. But this was stuff he had thrown away—stuff he didn't care about. This was stuff that would be sitting in the landfill by now, offering no one any insight or help. Was it right for her to hold onto it? It seemed like such a waste to toss it. Staring down at the other notebooks, she quickly set aside her hesitation and continued sleuthing. She looked for other references to Charlie's struggle with God and wasn't totally surprised when she couldn't find anything.

The first notebook ended about halfway through the pages. She moved on to the book marked #2. It too was filled with more interviews and entries documenting Charlie's exploration. He spoke of visits with Isaiah, often calling him a "cool old dude," but mentioned in several other entries that he wondered if the old man might be "losing his mind," speaking in what Charlie called "weird codes and incomprehensible metaphors." Kate guessed that many of these codes and metaphors might have been understood through a lens of faith in ways that appeared only abstract and convoluted without one.

In each of the notebooks that followed, she found herself wondering where Charlie would be today if he could have opened his head and heart to the bits of wisdom and guidance Isaiah and others attempted to give him. In all cases, that wisdom and guidance seemed to have fallen on deaf, unyielding ears. She was surprised to read that for a while, Charlie followed a hunch of his own, trying to figure out if the many occurrences of the letters SR that were embedded in the concrete and tile work throughout the complex might have been something more than simply Simon's initials. Charlie had wondered through the pages of two notebooks if they might also be associated with the Scottish Rite, a branch of Freemasonry. The idea was intriguing, and Charlie had offered several possible connections that supported his hunch. The number thirty-three, for example, was a sacred number to the Masons and, coincidentally or otherwise, was the number of years Simon had worked on the towers. Thirty-three multiplied three times was ninety-nine, the height of the two tallest towers. But even though the idea was intriguing, Charlie had been unable to find any truly plausible connections and had given up on the idea when Isaiah suggested he'd been reading too much Dan Brown.

Kate enjoyed reading passages of Charlie's writing that recorded portions of interviews with several different people as they outlined Simon's life through personal observations. It became apparent that he was a man driven by a superhuman inner strength to create something that would long outlast him. In the thirty-three years it took for him to finish his masterpiece, Simon grew old as he dedicated his time, his meager income, and even his health to the construction of the project he so earnestly believed in.

Charlie also recorded his thoughts about a difficult interview with Xiomara Maria Campos, the daughter of Luis Sauceda, the neighbor to whom Simon had deeded his property on his way out of town, never to return. It was Xiomara's older sister who had found Simon in a pile at the bottom of a tower the morning after his neighbors noticed his lights had been left on all night. Bruised and broken and with what she guessed was a considerable concussion, she had helped Simon into his house and tried to clean the dried cement from his hands. It was unclear to the woman what happened next, but she said Simon never fully recovered, at least not before he left town. Kate knew that the serious symptoms Xiomara mentioned—vomiting, slurred speech, and lack of coordination—were all indicators of a traumatic brain injury. This seemed to be consistent with a couple of other interviewees who mentioned a major change in Simon's personality following what everyone seemed to agree must have been a harrowing fall from the towers. Many suggested that his quiet departure in 1955 and subsequent absence from Watts marked a noticeable change in the prevailing spirit and feel of a neighborhood already in flux with racial and economic transitions.

Kate might have entirely missed the passage of time except for the orange hues that washed the pages of Charlie's notebooks like watercolors. She looked up just as the sun sank below the horizon. It had been a good day, full of serendipity and answers. But in spite of all that, there was an unmistakable feeling of emptiness in her gut that she knew was more than just hunger. She tried to define the emotion, settling on a plate of frustration, a bowl of disappointment, a cup of sorrow, and a sprinkling of uncertainty. Or maybe it was a plate of uncertainty and bowl of sorrow. Either way, there was certainly frustration, and she knew most of it was directed toward Charlie George. The rest of it came from not knowing where to go from here.

She sat silent on the nearly abandoned beach, feeling the damp chill of evening settling in. She was grateful for the additional information but was left wondering what to do with it. When no answers came, she gathered up the notebooks and was just about to put them back in the box when she noticed a scrap of paper at the bottom of the box. Her heart skipped a beat when, even in the waning light, she recognized the nearly illegible script. She quickly pulled the paper from the box, surprised by its weight. Before she could even attempt to read it, she noticed that a coin had been taped to the bottom of the paper with several pieces of Scotch tape.

She examined the coin the best she could in the growing darkness. A woman in a flowing dress seemed to be walking toward the sun, but she couldn't tell for sure. Nor could she read the rough writing on the paper. With excitement racing through her, she quickly gathered up her blanket and the box and hiked back to her car. Stepping into the circle of light cast by the streetlamp at the top of the hill, she read the words of the note.

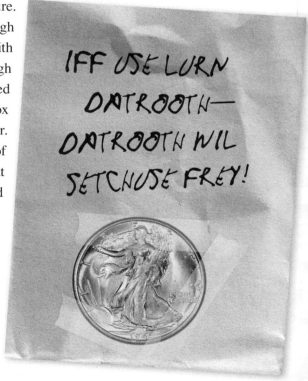

Realizing what she had just read, Kate sat down on the adjacent bench. "If you learn the truth, the truth will set you free," she whispered to herself. She knew this note had been intended for Charlie, but she couldn't help but feel like it had been intended for her as well.

In this better light, she looked closer at the coin. She knew it was not entirely unfamiliar, but neither was it common, at least not anymore. What little she knew about old coins she had learned from her grandfather. She had only seen his collection a few times, and she guessed it had been more than a decade since she had last stumbled upon the shoebox under his bed while playing hide-and-seek with her cousins. He had taken the time that night to show all of the grandchildren his small collection of coins. Kate remembered wheat-back pennies and the nickels with Indian heads and buffalos. There were also a handful of silver dollars that seemed enormous, filling up most of her palm. And as she looked at this coin now, she knew there must have also been a few of these in the collection.

Judging from its size, she guessed it was a fifty-cent piece, but she knew Google would know for sure. She pulled out her phone and did a search for "walking lady fifty-cent piece." Several images of the coin quickly popped up, identifying it as the Walking Liberty half dollar. The clear image of the coin backlit on her phone screen gave her pause as she examined its unique characteristics and became immediately curious about the meaning behind the symbolism. Narrowing her search, she added the word "symbolism" and was happy when several options popped up. She picked the first one and learned that the coin was minted between 1916 and 1947 and is widely thought of as America's most beautiful coin. The site went on to list the value ranging from five dollars to several hundred depending on the condition, date, and mint. She visited the next site and the next, piecing together the symbolism endowed by the sculptor, Adolph A. Weinman. She learned that he designed Liberty to be walking toward the rising sun, welcoming the dawn of the new day. In her hand, she held laurel and oak branches symbolizing military and civic victory, while her outstretched arm served to impart the spirit of liberty to all.

Kate sat back against the bench as she stared down at the scrawled note. The meaning of the note was clear, but the apparently deliberate inclusion of the coin seemed less clear. Liberty and freedom obviously held similar meanings. A quick Google search of both words showed they were similar enough to often be replaced with each other. Words like independence, privilege, and self-determination were found in the definitions of each word. But she felt like there had to be something more. Looking down at the coin again, she was reminded of something she had seen somewhere ...

In a flash of memory, she opened her phone again, this time to her photos. And there it was— the sculpture from on top of the gazebo. A chill ran through her as she looked at the four photos she had taken earlier that morning. Looking down at the coin for comparison, she knew without any hesitation that the headless sculpture of the woman on top of the gazebo was none other than Lady Liberty.

Kate clicked off her phone and stared out over the cliff into the darkened ocean and night sky, her head full of wonder. Why? Why this? Why her? Why now? What was she supposed to do with this? It was exciting to find these connections, but without knowing what she was supposed to do with it, it was all beginning to feel a little overwhelming. She wondered if Isaiah knew anything about this, and she immediately decided he had to. Perhaps this was what he was hoping for Charlie to discover. But why? She needed to know. She considered driving back to Watts in the morning but remembered Jeremiah saying Isaiah had the weekend off. It would have to wait. And maybe it was better that way. It would give her some time to formulate the right questions. She walked to the car feeling grateful for a handful of answers but knowing her list of questions was only growing longer.

CHAPTER 25

PARABLES

Our God has boundless resources. The only limit is in us.
Our asking, our thinking, our praying are too small.
Our expectations are too limited.
—*A. B. Simpson*

For the first time since her arrival in California, Kate got up early Sunday morning, put on a dress, and headed out to church before any of her housemates had even stirred. It felt like home to be surrounded by a congregation of believers, even though all of them were strangers. She left feeling more at peace than she had in a long time, and she spent the afternoon resting, thinking about the box of Charlie's stuff, and considering the questions she would like to ask Isaiah.

Monday passed quickly, and she recognized that she was beginning to feel more comfortable in the windowless basement, creating art with the patients she was learning to work with. With a half-hour left before quitting time, Kate tried to make herself useful by cutting up a pile of donated cardboard boxes into manageable sizes to use for paintings. She was nearly done when Dr. McKinley approached her on the way to a staff meeting. She quickly handed her a set of keys, asking Kate to put the box cutter back in her office and lock the doors to the basement on her way out. She would get the keys back from her in the morning.

Kate was happy to oblige and was just locking up on her way out when she noticed the logo branded into the dark leather fob on the keychain. She recognized that it was the same design as the key fob on Isaiah's keychain that he had left with her on Saturday. She took a closer look at the logo, wondering what it represented—this rocket blasting off into a circular hole. It seemed like a strange coincidence to see the same logo twice in such a short period of time, but she quickly dismissed it, deciding it was probably for a clothing brand or something she was not familiar with.

She made her way quickly to the towers and was glad to see Isaiah leaning against the doorway of the guard shack as if he were waiting for her.

"I had a feeling you'd come today," he said when she was still a ways off.

Kate smiled. "Did Jeremiah tell you I wanted to talk to you?"

Isaiah nodded. "Sorry to miss you the other day. I forgot when I let you in that I'd arranged for Jeremiah to take my place while I ran to an appointment."

"It's okay. Not having you here to talk to gave me a chance to think things over. Do you have some time to talk?"

He nodded. "My wife tells me that's what I do best."

"I didn't know you were married."

"You didn't ask," he responded with a smile. "It'll be thirty-seven years in August."

"Cool. Do you have kids?"

"Yes ma'am. Three girls and boy. Me and the misses, we also got five grandkids."

"That's great!"

"Better'n I ever thought it could be," he said with a generous grin. "What brings you here today?"

"I...I was hoping to talk to you about some of the stuff I saw in there on Saturday."

"Sounds serious. Let's have a seat." He led her to the bench where they had sat before. "What can I do for you?"

"I've just been thinking a lot over the weekend," she said, pulling a notepad from her bag. "I'm trying to put all of this together, and I was hoping you could tell me if I'm headed the right direction."

"Sure."

She looked down at the notepad, trying to decide where to begin, turning through several pages of notes before looking up. "My first question I guess is about you."

"Oh, good. A subject I know well."

"Yeah. Um, you said something about your dad being a preacher, right?"

"That's right."

"And I think you said that he and Simon were friends, right?"

"Good friends. Daddy always said he spent more time with Simon than he did his own father. I think that musta had a big impact on him."

"In what way?"

"Well, you mighta heard that Simon didn't read."

"Yeah, I did. But that was actually one of my questions."

"What's that?"

"There's just so much stuff in there that's right out of the Bible. How, if he couldn't read, did he know so much?"

"Have you ever known anybody who didn't read?"

Kate shook her head. "I don't think so. Do you?"

"Sure. Literacy is a privilege and a blessing that don't come equally to all people. Schools these days do their best to help most folks out, but it wasn't always so. I've found though that lotsa folks who don't read are some of the scrappiest, most resourceful people around. It's like they're constantly trying to make up for that missing piece that's different from other folks. Some of them folks who don't read end up gettin' into trouble. But a whole lot of 'em end up figurin' out a way to make a life for themselves without readin' or writin'."

"I noticed that some of the letters Simon put in the tile and cement are reversed."

Isaiah nodded.

"Do you think he might have been dyslexic?"

"I'm sure you ain't the first person to wonder that. There's no tellin' for sure. But Simon was one of those scrappy guys who figured out a way to bypass the need for readin'. I think Daddy musta played a role in that."

"How?"

"Daddy didn't just sell Simon old bottles and shards of china. Daddy said he used to read to Simon. Simon would pay him a nickel a week to read the Bible to him. He did that for more than ten years, workin' his way up to a quarter a week."

"Wow!"

"And when you read through the Bible that many times when you're a kid, somethin's gotta stick, right? Daddy said Simon had a way of seein' the pictures even though he couldn't read the words. And when he'd talk about the Bible stories in his sermons, he'd always paint a brighter, more vivid picture than Daddy had been able to put together in his own head. Simon found his own way to make those stories real."

"I like that," Kate said, smiling as she imagined a young boy reading the Bible to a man who filled his world with the stories that came to life through its pages. "That must've had an influence on your father becoming a preacher too."

"No question. He felt the love early on, and it never left him."

"And your father — he decided to stay in Watts?"

"That's right. He taught school during the week and taught the word of God on Sundays and whenever else he could. When you grow up in a community and learn to love the people, ain't no other place that feels quite like home. He actually married Momma right over there," he said, nodding to the towers.

Kate looked excited. "Did they get married at the bottom of the first tower?"

"Yeah, how'd you know that?"

"When I was in there with Charlie, he told me Simon used to perform marriages. With the two sets of stairs heading up and only one set coming down the other side—and then all the hearts on the stairs—it just made sense to think that's where marriages might have happened."

"I thought you might have also seen the wedding cake."

"Yeah, you're talking about that colorful sculpture with all the layers? The one that looks like it might have been a fountain?"

"You didn't miss much, did you?"

"Are you kidding? I'm sure I missed a ton. There's so much to see in there. Did both of your parents attend services here?"

"Yes, for close to twenty years. Daddy was actually baptized there."

"I knew it! That pocket on the side of the north wall, that held water for baptisms, didn't it?"

"Now how would you know that?"

"Because of that frieze on the wall above it—the wheat and the grapes. That represents the last supper, right?"

"Yes," he responded, looking at Kate a little closer.

"And the rocks on the wall above the baptismal basin…there seems to be a tie to the rocks that form the foundation of the second tower."

Isaiah shook his head incredulously. "Where are you getting all your information?"

"Am I right?"

"Yes. The towers are kinda like a visual parable."

Kate looked confused.

"Jesus, when he taught the people, he often spoke in parables, didn't he? That way people could learn different lessons from the same story, depending on where they were in life and faith."

"But it seems like there's a potential of leading people into a lot of confusion."

He nodded affirmatively.

"So why do it? What's the point?"

"A whole lotta artists' work can be considered visual parables. Artists often replace words with images. Words have their limits, but pictures and images—as they say, they can paint a thousand words. I've seen paintings that could be understood at least a million different ways."

"Yeah, but that's kinda my point. One of my professors used to talk about how we live in a time of what he called symbolic illiteracy—how people don't understand the meaning of anything anymore. Sometimes it seems like people don't even try or care."

"How true it is!"

"So why, if his message is so important, why would Simon put it out there in a way that could be so easily misunderstood?"

Isaiah smiled mischievously. "How do you know that's not part of his genius?"

"Huh?"

"Questions," Isaiah, said, raising his index finger as he shifted on the bench. "Questions are the beginning of all understanding. We all learn that, whether we remember it or not. Any fool can read a book and gather bits o' knowledge, but wisdom don't really come till he starts askin' questions and lookin' for the answers. It means you gotta slow down, recognize your own ignorance, and be willin' to do somethin' to change that. Some folks are easily pacified with an easy answer, but that kinda answer don't have the same value as one you gotta sweat for. Sometimes it's better to give a man a question, or better yet, a reason to ask one of his own. And with any luck, if the man is humble, he'll keep askin' questions, lookin' for better answers and better sources and teachers till he gets the real wisdom he's after. There've been people who have spent a lot of time in there tryin' to understand Simon's symbolism, but few of them have been able to see the meaning you've been able to decipher. Where are you getting your information?"

Kate shrugged. "I've just been thinking about it, trying to make sense of it all. Your suggestion to look at it though a lens of faith was really helpful, and Charlie pointed out a few things. But I've been thinking there's a lot more in there than he knows about."

Isaiah laughed. "You think so?"

"Am I right?"

He nodded. "You won't find any written record of it, but anybody who's got any background in Christianity, whose eyes and mind are even half open—they see it too. It usually starts with the hearts, but it only blossoms from there if you're lookin' for it."

She turned and looked at the towers. "It's a boat, isn't it? A boat sailing due east, into the rising sun."

"Yes," he said, smiling.

"And the three main towers—the sails—they represent the trinity—the Godhead, right?"

"You got all that out of just a couple of visits?"

She blushed and shrugged again. "I want to say it's all symbolic of the love of God, right?"

He nodded. "You know, it's all there—like a giant Technicolor billboard—but most people don't see it. They might feel somethin', 'specially the young kids and those with open hearts. Some see a boat. Others see a cathedral. Not many see it as the trinity that Simon planned it to be. What else do you know?"

"Charlie said that his names also had meaning—Sam and Simon."

"Yes. You know the meaning behind those names?"

"Yeah, Charlie told me, but he didn't go into it much. Do you know why he changed his name?"

"Not for sure, but it ain't an uncommon thing to do. Most every pope for the last fifteen hundred years has changed his name to a hero he wanted to emulate. There's a history of name changin' in the Bible. God often changed people's names or gave them a new one when he called them to live a better, higher life. Abram became Abraham, right? And his wife, Sarai had her name changed Sarah. Names are powerful, and people often live up to the names they're given, for both good and bad. My neighbor once had a cat named Lucifer, and I'm tellin' you, he lived up to his name," he said with a smile. "There're a couple of interesting ties to the name Simon in the Bible. One of them was the Simon who carried the cross for Jesus; another was the Simon that Jesus put in charge of the church before he was crucified."

"Simon Peter," Kate whispered.

"That's the one.

"And Saul became Paul and...Jacob became Israel," Kate mused, recognizing the pattern.

"That's right. Daddy used to say that people's names were often changed when they came to a place in their life when they started listening to God. In nearly every case, there was some big event that changed everything. Saul, for example, was an enemy to the Christians till he saw and heard the voice of Jesus while he was walkin' the road to Damascus. That event changed everything for him. God changed his name to Paul, and instead of fightin' 'gainst the Christians, he became one of their most dedicated champions."

Kate nodded. "Didn't he end up writing almost a third of the New Testament?"

"Yup. It seems crazy that a former enemy of the Christian faith would be allowed to record and write so much of its doctrine—so much that would shape the way millions of people around the world would believe for thousands of years."

"I've never thought of it way."

"It was always one of Daddy's favorite sermons—that God isn't afraid of using broken, ignorant people to share his message and help in his work of savin' souls."

Kate nodded thoughtfully. "What else does he have to work with?"

"Exactly. There's hope of redemption when you choose Jesus. Simon learned that for himself. Just 'cause he had a past and he couldn't read or write, that never stopped 'im from hearin' the voice of the wind—the voice of God. Simon, in Greek, means "He has heard." My daddy used to say that God often speaks to his children through their weaknesses—if they're humble 'nough to hear His voice. He said Simon knew God better 'an any man he'd ever met and that even though he was still rough around the edges, God still chose to use 'im to share a message of love and light. You know that story?"

"Only a little bit. But Charlie made it sound like the first part was pretty rough."

Isaiah pursed his lips and nodded. "After his wife left 'im and his daughter died, he fell into a deep, dark hole. For almost a decade he was a drifter—a drunk. He rode freight trains from town to town, bummin' his life away."

"Charlie said something about that, but he didn't say what happened to change him."

"No, I 'spect he wouldn't. That's where Charlie's doubts and closed mind stand in the way of findin' any understandin'. The story don't make much sense if you've got a hard head and a stiff neck. He's been stunted by his inability to believe in anything he can't see."

Kate nodded, looking back to the towers. "Do you think that's what this is? Do you think Simon was trying to offer a physical definition to something otherwise intangible?"

"Yes, I do."

"Do you know what happened to change him into Simon?"

Isaiah nodded. "I've gathered up bits and pieces from people who knew him over the years, and the stories are all mostly consistent. He was hoppin' freight trains one minute, and the next, he was shoppin' for a lot to build his home. There doesn't seem to be much of a transition period. It's like he was a washed-up drunk one day and the next he's movin' as far away from his rootless life as he could."

"But why? I mean there are people who join AA every day, but most of them don't spend the rest of their lives building a...this," she said, gesturing to the towers.

"Nope."

"So what's the difference? There's still something you're not saying. Why did he do this?"

"You've seen some of the symbolism—you already know more 'an Charlie figured out in five years. You tell me why he built them."

She looked at him intensely for a moment before turning her head to the towers. As she asked herself once again why someone would do this, an idea came to her. She had known there was something different about this place since the first time she saw it. Of course there was! Who builds hundred-foot towers in their backyard and covers them with mosaic? Of course there was something different about this place. Anybody could see that. But there was also something much bigger than the towers. She realized that *something* was something she couldn't see. But it was something she could feel. She remembered her visit with Charlie—the first time she met Isaiah. She remembered sitting right here, discovering the honeybees before she could even see them by narrowing her senses. Closing her eyes again, she attempted to do the same thing now.

With her eyes closed, she tried to remember everything she had already learned about Simon and his towers. She tried to remember what she had seen as she had walked through the promenade with Charlie. And most importantly, she tried to remember what she had felt during each of her interactions with this place. As she did, a curious thing happened. A memory came to mind. It was Sammy sitting on the cement steps of the amphitheater, the wind circling about him, carrying away his notes like a flock of doves. The memory intrigued her, leaving her wondering why it had returned at this time. But as soon as she could ask the question, the answer came.

"Simon was a listener like Sammy, wasn't he?" she asked, her eyes still closed.

"Yes," Isaiah responded.

"And it's the same wind that inspires both of them?"

"Yes."

"And the towers," Kate said, pressing her eyes tightly closed, "Simon built them to honor the Gods who saved him from himself."

Isaiah laughed.

She opened her eyes and turned to see him shaking his head, a broad smile on his face.

"You're a listener too."

"I am?"

"Well, aren't you?"

"I'm not even sure what that means."

"Oh, I think you do."

"Uh, I'm pretty sure I don't," she responded, feeling confused.

"That's not uncommon, and it's not a bad thing. We all got the potential to be a listener. But most of us fill our lives…and the space between our ears…with everything else. Most of us tend to fear the voice of the wind, so we tune it out. We go inside and close the doors and windows and fill our heads and hearts with somethin' else—somethin' louder. 'Stead of seekin' out quiet places where the voices of the wind can nourish us, we surround ourselves with noise. We turn on the TV or the radio. We surf the internet. We block out the wind's subtle whispers with headphones and then busy ourselves so we don't have to hear any of it. And when the wind still gets in, too many folks run from it, medicating themselves with all sorts of nonsense so they don't have to hear, or feel, or believe.

"But the wind keeps blowin', movin' the clouds and the waves, findin' its way up and over the fences we build to hold it back. In rare moments of humility, some folks learn to listen, learn to hear, learn to accept the nourishment. But for most, those moments are given no credence, and they come and go without much notice."

Kate nodded slowly. "That's why Simon built his perch on the tower, isn't it?" Kate asked, all of this suddenly making sense.

"Charlie told you about that?"

"Yeah, kind of. He said Simon used to go up there in the evening to listen to the wind. I wasn't sure what that meant, but maybe it makes sense now."

Isaiah nodded, looking at the small cement outcropping on the tallest tower. "He used to go up there every night. He told Daddy that sometimes that was the only supper he ate—sittin' up there, fillin' himself with the nourishment he needed most."

"My father does something similar—but usually after dinner. He'll often just disappear—wander off into the fields. He calls it 'being still'."

"Sounds like he might be a listener too."

"Uh, if I am, he definitely is."

"Can I ask you a personal question?"

"Uh, sure," she responded, not sure what to expect.

"I wanted to ask you about this when you were here with Charlie, but it didn't feel like the right time. Sammy's been tellin' us that you were comin' for a couple years now. Sometimes it's hard to understand all the nuances of his communication, but we've been lookin' for the person who would come, knowin' she would have unique sensitivities and abilities to communicate. I've wondered about this a hundred times—what this means, how it will work. I heard from Yolanda that you can communicate with even the toughest patients and I..."

"Wait, you've heard from Yolanda? What's going on here?"

He smiled and shook his head. "This is probably soundin' pretty freaky, isn't it?"

"Yeah, it is."

"Yolanda is a good friend. We look after Sammy. There are a bunch of us around here who are guardians."

"Guardians? As in the sign from Dr. Hermansen's notebook?"

"Yes. I'm sure it all sounds overwhelming right now. It seems a little crazy to everyone in the beginning, but I promise it will all make sense at some point soon. This is all uncharted territory for me too."

"Then how do you know it will ever make sense?"

"I've learned to trust my heart and the feelings that surround things."

Kate nodded slowly. "I've been trying to do the same."

"That's good. If ever things don't feel right, I hope you'll walk away."

"I already have once."

Isaiah raised one eyebrow. "Are you talkin' 'bout Charlie?"

She nodded.

"I've had to do the same thing with him many times."

"So why do you keep encouraging him?"

"Because I believe the boy can change. I believe we all can. He felt somethin' once—prob'ly a whole buncha times—but he let his head get in the way of his heart. Still, I'm encouraged that he keeps comin' back. He knows there's somethin' more here than he's been able to figure out. I got hope he'll get it someday, and soon. I was hopeful when you showed up together and that oracle was realized, and I was saddened when you left so quickly—but not totally surprised either. He's a tough nut, that one. But seein' you here and hearin' from Yolanda what's been happenin' at the hospital—I'm hopeful. I still ain't got any idea what the big picture is, but I can see enough of it to be grateful that I'm a small part of it and grateful for the little gifts of hope that have come along the way."

Truth, like gold, is to be obtained not by its growth, but by washing away from it all that is not gold.
Leo Tolstoy

CHAPTER 26

GIFTS

I believe that the first test of a great man is his humility.
I don't mean by humility, doubt of his power.
But really great men have a curious feeling that the greatness
is not of them, but through them.
And they see something divine in every other man
and are endlessly, foolishly, incredibly merciful.
—John Ruskin

Kate smiled at Isaiah, considering her own little gifts of hope she had recognized over the course of the last few weeks. But looking down at her notepad, she remembered the many questions that remained unanswered. "So, there's another thing I'm still struggling to understand."

"Okay."

"Charlie seemed to think Simon had other reasons besides just the high cost of property downtown or close to the beach for choosing Watts to build all of this. I was just wondering if you might have a take on it."

Isaiah nodded slowly. "I think his reasons for choosin' this place are as much a metaphor and parable as are the towers themselves."

"Tell me about that."

He turned and looked at them. "There's meaning in everything Simon did here, from the materials he used to the subtle symbolism he built into his work. It's all a message for those who choose to hear and see it."

Kate nodded, staring at the towers for a long, quiet moment before responding. "I haven't thought about it until just now, but maybe this place is kind of like a relationship with God—you have to seek it out," she mused. "And sometimes you have to go through a rough patch before you really want to find it. And you usually have to take a step into the dark before you can reach the light of better understanding."

Isaiah smiled as she made the connections. "The metaphors are as many and as varied as the people who look for 'em. I believe Simon was inspired to plant seeds all over in there—hopin', I'm sure, that they'd grow in thoughtful hearts and turn people to the same source that inspired him."

"That actually leads to another one of my questions."

"Yes?"

"You make it sound like there's no question he was inspired by God to build all of this."

Isaiah shrugged. "I don't know what else could inspire a man to spend more than a third of his long life buildin' a monument like this. There've been others who have spent parts of their lives building monuments—architects and artists like Antonio Gaudi and Niki de Saint Phalle, but they worked with huge crews and had others payin' the bills. Simon worked alone and paid for every bag of cement and piece of rebar he used. You can't do somethin' like this without somethin' special. You can't stick with somethin' as long he did without believin' in what you're doin'. Unlike those other artists, he didn't build this in hopes of gettin' rich. He never got a dime for what he did here. He did this 'cause he believed in what he was doin'. Some say he did this to try to stay sober.

I'm not doubtin' that's true, but it could never be the whole story. His heart and his faith were a part of every square inch of this place."

"It feels like they still are," Kate mused.

Isaiah nodded. "I feel it too."

"And you really think Charlie has also felt it?"

"I got no doubts about that. You don't keep comin' back over and over again for five years if you don't feel somethin'."

"So, in your opinion, why hasn't he been able to finish his movie?"

"That's easy—he's doesn't want to admit his own feelings. And the fear of going in too deep has kept him from askin' the bigger questions. You can't get answers if you don't ask questions. And only askin' easy ones don't getcha very far."

Kate nodded.

"Fear's an awful curse. It keeps so many folks from knowin' all they could know. He's a good kid. I still got lotsa hope that he'll come around. I'd hate to see him struggle for another five years or give up all together outta frustration."

"Isn't there something you can do to help him?" she asked, knowing that the box in the back of her car was a clear indicator that he may have given up already.

"Sure, there's lotsa things I can help him with after he gets over that roadblock, but the roadblock's his own. It's got Charlie *Thickhead* George written all over it. He's got to decide if he wants it to be different."

"You don't think he wants it to be different?"

"Sure I do. But wantin' ain't much different than wishin'. There ain't nobody who can make that change for him. The timing's all his, like it is with every one of us."

Kate nodded. His words triggered a memory, and she pulled Dr. Hermansen's notebook from her bag and flipped through several pages, stopping where a small strip of paper was taped to the page. Kate turned the book so Isaiah could read it:

> There is time enough, but none to spare.

We arrive at the truth, not by the reason only, but also by the heart. Blaise Pascal

He nodded. "Old Mr. Chesnutt."

"Excuse me?"

"That there's the wisdom of Charles W. Chesnutt. He's one of my heroes. He had it right, didn't he?"

Kate looked at it again before nodding.

"Doors can only stay open for so long, Kate. Then the wind blows 'em shut and life moves on."

"That's exactly what Dr. Hermansen said," Kate reported, pointing to the handwritten passage below.

"Yep, I remember that day—musta been close to two years ago. She sat here on this same bench and tried to talk herself outta listenin' to an old black man with a gimpy leg."

"That's actually exactly what she said. Why did she decide to listen?"

"The same reason you did."

"I'm not sure what you mean," she responded, looking confused.

"I'm talkin' 'bout before you came to Watts. There was a time, probably not so long ago, when you was stumblin' around, lookin' for your own faith and direction in life, right?"

Her face changed from confused to shocked. "How did you know that?"

"It takes one to know one," he said with a wink. "Most of us go through a time in our lives when the ground beneath us falls away, and we either learn to fly or we fall with it. I knew when I met you that you were learnin' to fly. I was glad to see you hangin' out with Charlie— hopin' you could keep that boy from fallin'."

"Yeah, well, if I've got wings at all, they're definitely not big enough to support both of us."

"They never could be, no matter how big your wings."

"What do you mean?"

"At some point in our lives, the ground drops away from all of us. If we're lucky enough, we'll see there's more to this life than just a quick joyride in the wrong direction. If we're open enough, we'll look around and realize not everyone's fallin'. If we're wise enough, we'll seek out help. And if we're persistent enough, we'll find the answers that'll keep us from splattin' face-first on the rocks at the bottom."

Kate nodded thoughtfully. "And if we're not enough of any of those things?"

"Then we get to spend the rest of our lives wishin' it was all different—graspin' at straws—chasin' after the light of every tiny firefly in hopes of redemption."

She chewed on his words for a moment. "So, how did *you* learn to fly?"

"The same way you did. The same way Simon did. The same way everyone does who ever learns to fly."

She nodded, remembering. "You're talking about love?"

He smiled. "You know it!"

"On my best days, I do. But I still wonder sometimes."

"Course you do. We all do."

"But if that love's so important—if it's such a huge part of figuring out who we are—of finding happiness—why does it take us so long to get to the place where we can see it?"

"Because we gotta be hungry before we want food. We gotta know we're broken before we seek a physician. We gotta ask the questions before there's room in our hearts for the answers."

Kate nodded, swallowing hard to control her emotions as she remembered her own journey to discovering God's love. "That's what all of this is about, isn't it?"

Isaiah grinned as he nodded. "Folks come and go here, all hours of the day and night, but not all of 'em get that. Somethin' draws 'em in like a bee to a flower. They come from all over the world to ooh and ahh over the colors and the creativity. Most get inspired by the story of one man doin' all of this in his spare time. But some—usually those folks who are learnin' to fly—they *feel* there's somethin' more. I knew you felt that the first time I saw you—saw that look on your face as you walked around the fence, lookin' in, wantin' to be closer."

"You saw me that first day?"

"Sure did."

"Why didn't you say something?"

"That's not my job."

"Well, yeah, but couldn't you have said *something*?"

He shook his head.

"Wait, what's the point of knowing how to fly if you don't try to inspire others to learn how to do the same?"

"Oh, I try to do my share of that too, but I've also learned I gotta feel my way around things. Sometimes I feel inspired to open my big fat mouth, and sometimes I feel inspired to shut it."

"But you could have saved me some time."

"Maybe, but there was obviously a bigger plan in the works."

She thought for a moment. "Are you talking about Charlie?"

He shrugged. "Could be. I told you a few weeks ago that I don't know what the plan is."

"Then how do you know there is one? How do you know this isn't just a series of coincidences?"

"The same way you know it ain't. You're here for a reason, aren't you?"

She looked away and didn't answer right away. "It feels like it." He watched her as she looked up at the towers, and silence fell between them. "Do you think I might be here to interpret for Charlie?" she asked after a long minute.

"That's what you are, right? That's your gift?"

"Are you talking about sign language?"

"That could be part of it, but that ain't your only gift. We all have at least one gift to share with the world. I like to 'magine God handin' out gifts and talents to each of his kids, hopin' they'll use 'em to make the world a better place. But I don't think he ever sets a limit on the number of gifts he'll give us. I feel like he's anxious to give us more if we ask for 'em or if we ask for instructions on how to use 'em better. I guess I feel like we set our own limitations on how we use 'em. It seems like things get better if we put our candles on a candlestick and help illuminate the world rather than hidin' 'em away out of fear they'll get blown out."

Kate smiled. "You're talking about the Sermon on the Mount! I told Charlie about that when we were here."

Isaiah nodded. "That there's the gift I'm talkin' about."

"What do you mean?"

"Charlie's been comin' here for five years and hasn't made the connections you've made in just a couple of visits. That's a gift."

"That's just from going to Sunday school—from reading the Bible with my family when I was a kid."

"Are you sayin' that knowledge ain't a gift?"

"Well...I don't know. I guess I've never really thought about it like that."

"All knowledge that brings a person truth and light is a gift. Your parents, besides givin' you life itself, they also gave you light for your path. That's a fortunate kinda love—a gift that's only becomin' more rare in a world that's growin' ever darker. If that ain't a gift, I don't know what is."

She nodded slowly. "That's the light, isn't it? That's the candle the parable's talking about."

"Kate, knowledge is always light. When the knowledge of truth is taken from the world, the world becomes a dark and hopeless place. It's happened many times over the history of the world—when men love darkness more than light. I know of no truth or light that burns brighter than the love of God. It's the only truth that shatters all darkness. It heals and comforts and scatters hope in every direction. Simon gained that knowledge for himself at a time when darkness had nearly snuffed out all hope. His work here became a work of enlightenment. His candle became a torch, and then a lighthouse, inviting people from near and far to come to the safe harbor and feel the hope and safety and grace of God's boundless love."

Kate nodded slowly, thoughtfully, feeling the truth of what she'd just been told echoing through the deepest canyons of her soul. She knew it was true. But still, as the echoes drove deeper, spreading the warmth of

true light, there was a piece of her that remained restless. Turning back
to the towers, she knew what it was. The understanding brought little in
the way of either comfort or hope. She realized it felt heavy, difficult,
even weighty. There was no question in her mind what it was, and it had
Charlie *Thickhead* George written all over it.

She turned back to find Isaiah with a smile on his face, his eyes
closed as if in a state of peaceful meditation. She sat silent for a moment,
enveloped in a unique feeling of both warmth and hope despite the
uncomfortable sliver of restlessness. Looking down at her notepad filled
with questions, she realized that most of them didn't matter anymore.
After a weekend of thought and searching, love was the only answer that
mattered. A peculiar awareness settled around her as she closed her eyes.
For a moment, she wrestled with a feeling of discomfort, wondering how
she could possibly help a guy who didn't seem to want any help. But
she let the question go as another wave of love and peace washed over.
Again, a silent voice of doubt arose but quickly gave way to another
wave of love and hope. This continued for several minutes until it felt as
though all doubt had been washed away. She opened her eyes to a new
hope, a new direction, a new reality.

Suddenly aware that Isaiah was still sitting next to her, she turned to
find him looking out across the lawn, his face filled with a remarkable
calm. Neither of them spoke for another minute or two, and Kate
continued to feel the waves of love and peace moving through her like
a gentle breeze.

"Did you find what you were looking for?" Isaiah asked in a low,
mild voice.

Kate nodded. "I thought I was looking for something else, but I
found something better."

"Strange how that works, ain't it."

She nodded again. "Did you feel it too?"

"Yes," he whispered. "Thank you."

"Wait, what do you mean? Why are you thanking me?"

"You brought the question that allowed the answer to come."

She nodded thoughtfully. "Is that always the way it works?"

He shook his head and turned to look at her. "I think it must be different for everyone. Uncle Ralph used to say that God enters by a private door into every individual."

"Uncle Ralph? As in Ralph Waldo Emerson?"

"You know another Uncle Ralph?" he asked with a playful smile.

"You like him too?"

"What's there not to like? Every seeker who stumbles across his writings finds a kindred spirit." He reached into the hip pocket of his cargo pants and withdrew a small, tattered leather book that looked like it had been well loved. He handed the book to Kate. She opened the cover to reveal the title: *The Conduct of Life*, by Ralph Waldo Emerson. A yellowed bookplate—from the library of Isaac Bingham—was glued on with even yellower paste.

"Who's Isaac?" she asked, pointing to the bookplate.

"He was my friend back when I was a lost and impetuous kid and had a thick head of my own."

"You?"

He laughed. "I told you, it takes one to know one. I discovered that summer that all men have it in them to be both saints and sinners, angels and demons, lambs and lions—and all shades of critters in between. The details are different, but at some point, all men and women come to a place where the plot twists and the hero becomes the fool."

She nodded, encouraging him to continue.

"I think I told you I went to Penn State on a football scholarship."

"Yeah. That must have been a great opportunity."

"It was," he said, looking a little distracted as if he were wondering how much he wanted to say.

"That was actually one of my questions," she said, pointing to the notepad.

"What's that?"

"I guess my question is…why did you come back here? You mentioned something the other day, but I got the sense you had something more to say about coming home to Watts. What didn't you tell me?"

"Not a lot gets past you, does it?"

She shrugged. "I know it's none of my business, but I've been curious."

"Well, you're right, there's more, but it's a long story."

"The best ones always are."

"This one was kinda like the Dickens novel—*A Tale of Two Cities*."

"It was the best of times, it was the worst of times," Kate said in a melodramatic voice. "That one?"

"You know the rest of the quote?"

"Uh, I'm sure I used to back in junior high."

He nodded. "It was the best of times, it was the worst of times, it was the age of wisdom, it was the age of foolishness, it was the epoch of belief, it was the epoch of incredulity, it was the season of Light, it was the season of Darkness, it was the spring of hope, it was the winter of despair, we had everything before us, we had nothing before us, we were all going direct to heaven, we were all going direct the other way…"

"Wow! That's good. I should have paid better attention. I'm sure I was just trying to get through the book."

"Yeah, I should have paid better attention too," he mused.

"But wait. How was that like your time at Penn State?"

"I look back on that time as some of the best, most rewardin' times of my life. But all things got their opposites, and sometimes the brightest days are followed by the darkest nights. I told you I played for Penn State. But I had bigger plans. My stats as a linebacker drew the attention of scouts from almost every NFL team, but I only had eyes for one— Miami. After watchin' their undefeated season and them winnin' the Super Bowl, I was mo' than ready to accept their offer."

"Wait, you played in the NFL?"

He shook his head. "I was this close," he said, showing the tiny space between his thumb and forefinger. "That was one of the best days of my life—shaking hands with Coach Don Shula and accepting the Dolphins' offer. But life sometimes has a brutal sense of humor, and my darkest night wasn't far behind. A couple of my buddies who'd also been drafted—we drove up to Erie to celebrate one Saturday before we all split up for the summer. We'd just graduated, and we were on top of the world. My girlfriend came along. We'd been together for more than a year and had just started talkin' 'bout havin' her join me in Miami." He faded off, staring blankly at the grass at his feet.

"So, what happened?" Kate asked after at least a minute had passed.

Isaiah took a deep breath and let go of it all at once. "We decided Nancy should drive home—made sense, she'd had the fewest beers. Long story short, the car rolled more than a couple times. Nancy was killed. I shattered my femur and shoulder. And my buddies each ended up with broken bones and bruises. They healed up quick enough to make it to summer workouts. Both of 'em went on to successful careers. I ended up spending close to three months in the hospital, tryin' to get better while I faced a whole lotta tough realities. If it hadn't been for Isaac," he said, pointing to the old book, "I doubt I coulda made it."

Kate looked down at the bookplate and ran her finger over his name.

"We all ended up at the nearest hospital in this strange little town called Niederbipp. After 'bout a week of lyin' there on my back, half my body tied up in casts and slings, getting more and more depressed with my reality, I looked up one evening to see this dude in overalls standin' at the foot of my bed. He told me my doctor was a friend of his and he'd come for a visit to see if there was anything he could do. I was just so desperate and broken—and probably drugged—that I couldn't think of a reason not to chat. If it hadn't been for him, I'm quite sure I'd still be hurtin'."

"Was he a therapist?"

Isaiah laughed. "No, he was a just a potter—a potter with a big heart. He got me talkin'—got me to believe that my life wasn't over—that I still had a reason to live—that I still had somethin' to give. He helped me see that I'd put myself in a box—that I'd defined myself as a football player, a linebacker, an athlete. He helped me see that box was way too small— that I had more to discover and be and give. He helped me see there was so much more to life than I'd been able to see for myself. But the best medicine he gave me was helpin' me to feel God's love. Isaac used to say that love is the only medicine we need—that if we could see ourselves as God sees us, we'd never have any reason to fear or to doubt ourselves or to have anything to be sad about. I found myself lookin' forward to his visits more than I looked forward to eatin', and that's sayin' somethin'. He helped me get out of my own head and to want a relationship with God—a real relationship with God."

"But your dad was a preacher. You didn't feel like you had a relationship with God before?"

Isaiah shook his head. "It sounds crazy that you can grow up with faith and grace all around you and still not know of God's love for you. The sad truth is that some of us have to be swallowed by a whale and get coughed up on the shores of a faraway land 'fore we come to a place where we'll finally let God's love in. It was there all along, knockin' at my door, but I had to let it in. I had to be broken before I could feel the healing love that'd always been there.

"Before I was strong enough to walk, Isaac helped the nurses put me in a wheelchair, and he took me for a walk. He rolled me under the canopy of this giant weeping willow tree that grew on the banks of the river, and he told me his story. The guy had lost everything that he loved—his wife and unborn child to illness, his parents to a house fire, his swanky job in New York. I remember feelin' confused, wonderin' how anyone who'd been through that was not only happy but was findin' ways to make other people happy too. He told me that he'd found the secret of his happiness under that tree, where God had revealed himself in the form of love that had washed over him and comforted his broken heart. He pointed to a limb where he'd carved the words, 'Be still, and know that I am God.' He told me he'd brought me there to see if maybe God wanted to talk me, too."

"Did he?"

Isaiah nodded. "I was afraid he wouldn't at first. Isaac left me alone for an hour and told me the only instructions I needed were written on the limb of that tree. I didn't know what to think at first. I didn't know what it meant to be still. But somethin' happened as the sunlight danced on the water and sent reflections flyin' all around me. It was like everything in the world slowed down and all the clouds of heaven showered—more like dumped—their love on me. It felt like the air was electrified, pulsin' with life and peace. That was the day I gave up the fight."

"Which fight?"

"Growin' up in a preacher's house is a beautiful experience that ain't ever easy. I don't remember a time when Daddy didn't have us out doin' service projects, takin' care of the widows, pickin' up garbage— eatin' up most of my Saturdays and lotsa evenin's too. They were all good things, and I know his heart was pure. But I don't know many kids who'd freely trade a mornin' of sleepin' in for a five-hour service project. I grew up knowin' Sunday was made for worship. That was all good, lookin' back. It was good for me to have expectations. It was good to have a solid foundation to build my life on. But at the time, tryin' to think with a head that was growin' thicker every year, it felt like I was dyin' a slow and painful death. Lookin' back, the love was always there, knockin' at my door, wantin' to be let in."

"You didn't feel it then?"

"I didn't want to feel it."

"Why not?"

"Because I knew what came with it. I knew I'd have to do somethin'. I knew I'd have to think about someone besides me. After watchin' Daddy givin' up all his time to help other people, I figured I knew what strings were attached to doin' God's will. And then one Sunday morning when I was about sixteen, I was lyin' in bed, and I made a decision I'd never made before. I decided I was done with church and Bible study and choir. I was gonna do my own thing and be my own man."

"How'd that go over with your parents?"

Isaiah shook his head. "Lookin' back, they tried to love me the best they could. But I didn't make it easy for 'em. That's always been one of my biggest regrets."

"Leaving your faith?"

"No, I needed to leave my faith in order to find it—in order for me to come to a place where it really meant somethin'. But I regret the pain I caused my folks. I know they spent years prayin' for me. I know they had nothin' but good intentions and hopes for me. I regret that after all they'd done for me, I gave 'em so much hell. It used to make me so mad, seein' my folks in the stands at my football games, still supportin' me after I'd pushed 'em away. They never gave up on me—tried to love me through it—but I wouldn't take it. I pushed it back in their faces and was happy to get as far away from 'em as I could when I went to college."

"Was it really so bad?"

"No," he said without hesitation. "I was blinded by my own pride and foolishness. It still hurts when I think about it—hurts me to know all the pain and sorrow I caused my momma—all the tears she musta shed for me. I was the seventh child they adopted and the first one to push away. I regret the bad example I was to my siblings."

"Did they stay in the faith?"

He nodded. "A few of us wandered crooked paths for a while, but we all came back."

"My sister's story is pretty similar to yours, and I know my parents are heartbroken."

"Course they are. Wherever there is great love, there is the potential for great sorrow. Every parent learns that the hard way regardless of the choices their children make."

Kate nodded solemnly.

"But on the flip side, wherever there's great love, there's the potential for unbounded joy. I don't know if you can understand either the depths or heights of love until you marry and have children of your own. But all of us, regardless of our station and circumstances, we all got the potential to love deeply. And with it, each of us can come to know the power and meaning behind a God who holds the whole world in his hands and his heart. It was his love that I felt on

If you would be a real seeker after truth, it is necessary that at least once in your life you doubt, as far as possible, all things. Rene Descartes

that magical evening under the shelter of that tree. It was his love that brought me home. It was his love that took the fight out of me. But I had to want it before I could fully experience it.

"Kate, I've learned a couple of things as my skull has thinned out a bit over the past four decades. Like with any good parent, God's love is always there, but the kids have gotta be open to it—we gotta want it. We gotta open our hearts and heads and be ready to receive it. Sometimes that love feels more like a kick in the pants than a warm embrace. But if we'll open our hearts and feel the goodness, the patience, the gentleness, and the tolerance behind it, we'll come to know that God is love. And when we accept that love and learn to love others, the world becomes brighter, kinder, and fulla hope.

"You might think that workin' at a place like this, where there's so much love—that this would be easy. But I've come to recognize that love don't come naturally to nobody. It's a gift. I regularly have to remind myself what Jesus said when the crooked lawyers asked him what the most important commandment was. To love God and to love your neighbor as you love yourself. As far as I can tell, there ain't no better answer for the question of what this life is all about. Two thousand years later, the answer's still love. Anything else is a counterfeit. Anything else, as far as I've been able to tell, is the wrong answer. And I've learned that if we can keep our love in order—that if we always love God first— our priorities will never lead us off the path to true joy."

We are not merely imperfect creatures who must be improved; we are rebels who must lay down our arms.   C. S. Lewis

CHAPTER 27

FINDING CENTER

Most people, including ourselves, live in a world of relative ignorance.
We are even comfortable with that ignorance, because it is all we know.
When we first start facing truth, the process may be frightening,
and many people run back to their old lives.
But if you continue to seek truth, you will eventually be able to handle it better.
In fact, you want more! It's true that many people around you now may think you
are weird or even a danger to society, but you don't care.
Once you've tasted the truth,
you won't ever want to go back to being ignorant.
—Socrates

Kate had a lot to think about on her ride home. Before she left, she had asked Isaiah if he had any additional advice for her. "Proceed as the way opens," he had told her once again, "And take some time to be still. If you do those two things, you'll get all the answers you'll ever need." But the idea of approaching Charlie about any of this felt intimidating.

He had, after all, made it clear that he was done with Watts. How could she convince him to come back?

After worrying about it all day Tuesday, imagining dozens of scenarios in her head—none of which produced a pleasant outcome, she found herself sitting once again at a potter's wheel in the art basement. Yolanda had been patient with her, giving her plenty of time to try to remember how this worked, but she was still struggling to make anything bigger than a dog bowl, and even then they were all skiwampy and asymmetrical. She was just about to give up for the day and head home when she had the uneasy feeling that someone was watching her.

As Kate looked up, she felt a rush of excitement as the hooded figure moved closer. He picked up a stool and sat down in front of her. She had only seen him a couple of times over the course of the last month, but with all she had read about him, she felt like she knew him. He signed "hello," offering her a generous smile. She returned both the gesture and the smile.

Sammy reached out his hand to make a proper introduction.

"I'm dirty," she signed with clay-covered fingers.

He shook his head, putting his hand forward.

She smiled and shrugged as she stuck her muddy hand in his. Looking into his dark eyes, she was surprised and disarmed by the warmth and kindness she found there. She couldn't remember exactly how she had imagined him after reading through Dr. Hermansen's notebook, and even after their brief, distant encounter weeks earlier, she knew she had been way off. As they attempted to communicate using sign language, she could see he was older than she had imagined. Illuminated like the filaments in a light bulb by the overhead fluorescents, short graying hairs framed his face, sticking out from under his hoody. Reading the lines in his face, she guessed he was in his mid-fifties.

Watching carefully as Sammy's hands worked, she recognized some of the nuances Dr. Hermansen had written about. He knew the alphabet signs, but he was slow at stringing the letters together and didn't seem to understand many of most basic ASL signs. When it was clear that he didn't understand the sign for bowl, she slowly spelled it out for him, pointing to the small, muddy bowl in front of her.

"I'm glad to see you're finally getting acquainted," Yolanda said from behind. She stood next to Kate and passed a sign to Sammy that Kate didn't recognize. Sammy nodded vigorously, exaggerated, in an almost childlike way. Kate had expected this. In her notebook, Dr. Hermansen had suggested that Sammy had cognitive deficits, but she had offered little by way of detail. As Kate watched Sammy playfully interacting with Yolanda, she was reminded of her moon sister, Emma. There was an innocence and purity about him that was endearing. But as she watched them communicate, she could see that many of the signs they shared were not typical ASL signs. It was almost as if they had their own language, one that only the two of them understood.

"He wonders if you want any help," Yolanda said after Sammy had displayed a long string of signs.

"Help?" Kate responded bemusedly.

"I think he means with the clay. He said he's been watching you—that you keep making the same mistakes."

Kate laughed. Turning to Sammy, she signed, "Please."

He pushed up the sleeves of his hoody and scooted his stool closer to her. After moving aside the bowl she had been working on, Kate handed him a round ball of clay, which he threw onto the center of the wheel. With a gentle touch, he took her hands in his, cupping them around the clay. Kate pushed down on the pedal, and the wheel began to spin. Without using words, he firmly moved and pressed her hands with his, massaging the clay until it was perfectly centered in the middle of the wheel. He let go of her hands and sat up, encouraging her to continue.

She went on as she had before, plunging her thumbs into the spinning mass, opening it slowly to form a flat bottom. He stopped her for a moment, crudely indicating, with attempts at words, to keep her elbows down. She did as he instructed, continuing with the process, pinching, pulling, and supporting the spinning clay as it rose higher and higher. For the first time since her high school days, the clay rose higher than four inches, then six, then eight. He clapped like a child, nodding his head with exaggeration. She shaped the cylinder with her hands, giving it form and volume before bringing the wheel to a stop.

"What did you do?" she both spoke and signed.

He pointed at her, smiling broadly.

"It looks like maybe we'll be keeping the wheels after all," Yolanda said.

"I don't know. I'm not sure what I did different. It's like he has a magic touch."

"What did you do?" Yolanda asked Sammy, both speaking and signing with their unique signs.

Kate watched closely as Sammy communicated back. He moved his lips, but the sounds that came out were indiscernible, and the signs he gave seemed to be a funky conglomerate of ASL and signs that were unfamiliar to Kate.

"I'm not sure what he's talkin' about, but he said that you *haven't been in the middle*," Yolanda reported.

She thought for a moment. "Does he mean centered?"

Yolanda signed back, spelling out c-e-n-t-e-r-e-d.

Sammy nodded and clapped. He signed again, looking from Yolanda to Kate and back again as if he were hoping one of them would understand him as his hands and lips moved quickly. He touched his elbows with his muddy fingers, then, as if he were playing a game of charades, he repeated many of the movements Kate had just done as she created the vase. Kate watched closely, trying to make sense of his movements.

"Did you get that?" Yolanda asked when he finished.

"Actually, I think maybe I did," Kate responded, feeling a little surprised. She cut the vase off the wheel with a wire and grabbed another round ball of clay. She threw it onto the wheel and started again, pushing and holding the clay as it spun through her fingers. She looked up to find Sammy nodding encouragingly. She kept pushing, harder than ever. Soon she recognized that the clay was no longer unevenly gyrating but had come together in a smooth and polished dome. As she had before, she began driving her thumbs into the middle of the dome. She heard a grunt and looked up to see Sammy pointing from this elbow to his knee. She realized her elbows were up, unsupported, and she responded quickly, putting her elbows back on her knees. She smiled at Sammy as she finished this second vase. It was even better than the first one, and leaps and bounds beyond the dozens of dog bowls she had made over the past weeks.

He pointed to the center of the wheel and made signs that Kate didn't know. She turned to Yolanda, looking for help. Kate was impressed by the patience Yolanda had, signing back and forth as she tried to discern what he was trying to say. As Kate watched this interaction, she was surprised by the feeling of inadequacy that swept over her. She knew how to use sign language to communicate effectively. She had used it every day since she had started working in the art basement. But this was different. In many ways it felt more like communicating with her nieces and nephews rather than with an adult. If communicating with Sammy was one of the reasons she had come—as she had wondered— she knew she had a long way to go.

"I think he's trying to say that you've been struggling because you haven't been centered."

Kate laughed. "Yeah, I got that part. The clay has really been ..."

"I don't think he was talking about the clay," Yolanda responded, cutting her off.

Kate was thoughtful for a moment before she nodded, flashing Sammy the "thank you" sign.

"Maybe I misunderstood him," Yolanda said as Sammy broke into a frenzy, his hands moving quickly, paired with grunts and squeaks. Kate watched his facial expressions change dramatically and rapidly, displaying a huge range of emotions. She could tell these had to be at least half of what Yolanda was reading, and she wondered how long it had taken her to come to an understanding of what all of this meant.

"I think what he's actually saying is that..." She paused as Sammy continued his attempts at communication through his physical expressions. "He says you need to help other people find...the center. Does that make sense?" Yolanda asked, looking doubtful.

"Kind of," Kate responded, uncertain. "Can you ask him how I'm supposed to help someone who may not want any help?"

Yolanda nodded.

Kate watched her closely as she signed, but despite her best efforts to understand, she felt increasingly ignorant and helpless.

Sammy grunted as he listened, and when she was done, he stood, cut the vase off the wheel with a wire, and moved it carefully to the board next to Kate's other pieces. Staring down at the thin circle of clay left in the middle of the wheel, he reached out his index finger and poked at the very center of it. Then he sat back down in front of her, pointed to Kate's head and chest, then pointed to the place where he had poked the clay. He repeated this motion several times, looking to both Yolanda and Kate.

"Do you have any idea what he's saying?" Yolanda asked.

"No, I..." she began, but she stopped herself as an idea came to her. Getting Sammy's attention, she touched her head and heart at the same time with her index fingers and then pointed them to the center of the wheel. To her relief, he nodded.

He reached across the wheel, poking his finger into the clay circle again, this time about an inch away from the center. He pinched a small piece of clay off the block next to Kate and rolled it into a round ball before placing it on top of the second dot. He moved his foot to the pedal, depressing it slightly, and the wheel began to spin. The ball of clay made several rotations before the centrifugal forces sent it flying off the wheel. He caught the ball and stopped the wheel before placing it on top of the dot he had made at the center of the clay circle. As Sammy depressed the pedal again, the wheel sprang into action, but unlike in the first example, the ball of clay stayed put. He put his foot down hard on the pedal, taking the wheel to top speed, and still the ball stayed steady. Again, he pointed to Kate's head and chest, then pointed to the ball at the very center of the wheel.

"Do you understand what he's trying to say?" Yolanda asked.

Kate nodded, smiling at Sammy. She looked back down at the wheel as she slowed the rotation to just a creep. She watched the second dot rotate around the center like a satellite. And though it was close to the center, the lesson was clear: close to center was not close enough to allow her work to progress and grow without being wonky or becoming a casualty to centrifugal forces.

She looked up to see Sammy sliding the sleeves of his hoody back down his arms. He quickly sponged off his hands before smiling at Kate and giving Yolanda an awkward hug; then he left without another word.

"Where's he going?" Kate asked, watching him disappear through a door in a distant wall.

"Where does the wind go?" Yolanda replied, smiling as she watched the door close behind him.

"Is that a riddle?"

"Maybe it is." She sat down on the stool in front of Kate. "Sammy's never been one to be tied down. He comes and goes like the wind, gently rearranging things in his path. He's been that way for as long as I've known him."

Kate watched her as she spoke, and as she did, a thought came to her. It seemed incredible at first, but in her heart she knew it was true. "He's your brother, isn't he?"

Yolanda looked surprised. "How do you know that?"

"Those signs you were using—those aren't ASL signs. Are they something you two created together?"

"We taught each other, I suppose. I was five years old when our parents brought him home, all bandaged up, lookin' like he needed a whole lotta love. We figured out how to talk by making up signs." She laughed. "It drove our family crazy. Some of our siblings learned some of our signs, but we're still the only ones who can carry on a conversation. He's always been my favorite sibling. Our connection runs deeper than any of the others."

"So, wait. That means Isaiah's your brother too?"

"Yep. He was there almost ten years before I was, so we only had a few years together between the time I came to the family and he left for college. We didn't really get to know each other until he came home."

Kate shook her head, smiling as she started putting the pieces together. "Isaiah said there are something like twenty kids who came through your family."

"That's right. Twenty-two, actually. We were all lucky enough to find a happy home to grow up in. I'm sure it changed the course for all of us. I know my life would have taken a much different route if it weren't for our folks takin' me in after my father died and my mother went to jail."

"I'm sorry," Kate said, recognizing the sorrow in her eyes. "What happened?"

"My father was at the wrong place at the wrong time. Of course, back in the summer of '65, this was all the wrong place to be. He was killed in a fire that was set during the riots."

"I'm sorry," Kate repeated.

"So am I. I didn't know my father well. He and my mother never married. I remember him droppin' in for birthdays and holidays, but the daddy I share with Isaiah and Sammy is the only daddy I ever really knew."

"And your mother?"

"She was arrested during the riots. Looting. She went to jail for a month, and I was put in state custody. She never came to get me."

"Wow! I'm really sorry," Kate said sincerely.

"You know, we get to choose a lot of things in life, but there aren't many of us who get to choose the consequences of either our actions or the actions of others. My foster parents, Joshua and Patsy Jones, taught us that in spite of all of that, we still gotta make our own choices. They taught all us kids the importance of choosin' right from wrong, light from darkness, and hard work over slothfulness. They made each of us feel like we were a necessary part of their family, that we each had gifts that could help all of us be better and stronger collectively."

"Your gift was art?"

"Yes. I wasn't the only one. My brother Ruben is an artist too. Momma taught us that it was our job to share the light that comes from creativity and make the world a more beautiful place."

"And Isaiah—what was his gift?"

Yolanda smiled. "Daddy said it was his gift to share light by playin' football, but Momma saw things different. She believed God made Isaiah big and strong so he could protect people who were smaller than himself and stand up for the rights of others. When Isaiah came back home after an accident that made it impossible for him to play football anymore, Daddy had to admit that Momma saw the bigger picture. I think Momma's vision kept us all out of trouble—kept us thinkin' about who we were and where we belong in the world. It kept all of us from thinkin' that the world owed us somethin' and instead kept us askin' what we can do or give to make it better."

"I noticed you mentioned light in both your choice and Isaiah's. I like the idea that our gifts come with light."

Yolanda nodded. "Every sermon Daddy ever gave was centered around that truth: God plants a seed of light in the hearts of all his children, and that light grows bigger and brighter only in the sharin' of it with others. He taught us all that it was up to us to help illuminate the world and chase away the darkness."

Kate nodded slowly as Yolanda's words swirled around the memory of Simon's small lamp that stood on the far end of the towers, as well as the memory of the towers themselves. "That idea—that light—do you think your father might have gotten that from Simon?"

Yolanda raised one of her sculpted eyebrows, looking surprised. "Have you been talking to Isaiah?"

"Yes. It sounds like Simon had many of the same ideas."

"I think you're right. I never knew Simon. He left Watts before I was born. But his influence in my life is probably far bigger than I'll ever know. Daddy always felt a sense of responsibility—like a man with a mission—to help other people understand and nurture the light inside them. Both he and Momma had the ability to identify the light and beauty in other people, even the most difficult people. They had the kind of love that let them see through thick heads and hard hearts and find even the smallest bits of light in dark places. They believed that light engenders light—that seeing it awakes in all of us the desire for more light, igniting the potential for light as it spreads out in every direction like a sea of candles."

"It sounds like your parents were visionaries."

Yolanda nodded. "They believed there was goodness to be found in all people. The trick was nourishing it. The influence Simon had on Daddy was huge. And the same light Simon shared with him has been shared with thousands of others. And who knows how many have been affected indirectly? Daddy's dying wish for all of us was to continue that legacy—to find the light in others and do what we can to help it burn brighter."

"That's a beautiful legacy," Kate responded thoughtfully.

"I can't think of a better way spend a life."

"Isaiah feels the same way, doesn't he?"

Yolanda nodded. "We all have to come to this in our own way and in our own timing. Daddy taught me that timing was an especially critical part of the recipe for igniting a sustainable light. He used to teach us that God waits patiently for each of us to turn to him and accept the light he's anxious to give us. For some of us, that timing happens naturally, even spontaneously. But for most of us, our heart has to crack open before the light can come in—before we can feel his love. I think that was the reason Momma did all she could to help us discover our gifts."

Kate nodded as she considered this. It seemed to jibe with the little she knew about Simon. But she also recognized it jibed with her own personal experience of finding light and the direction that light gave her. But the idea that her gifts and talents could somehow be connected to that light was also intriguing. "Can you tell me more about the connection your mother made between gifts and light?"

Yolanda smiled. "I think you already see the connection, don't you?"

"I think so, but I'm still trying to wrap my head around it."

Yolanda nodded, reached into her pocket, and withdrew a set of keys, setting them down on the wheel in front of Kate.

Kate looked down to see the now-familiar logo branded into the leather key fob. She had only seen the logo in passing, but staring at it now, oriented in this way, she realized she had entirely missed it. It wasn't a rocket blasting off into a black hole as she had thought. It was a candle on a candlestick, its flame burning bright! "Hey, Isaiah has one of these too," she said, looking up to find Yolanda smiling.

"I know. We all have one—all of our siblings."

"I had it upside down," she said, turning the key fob to show Yolanda. "I thought it was just a weird coincidence that you both had one."

"There are probably far more connections and far fewer coincidences in life than you might imagine. When Isaiah came home after his accident, we all worried he would be a broken man. The disappointment of having the world at your fingertips and then having it all jerked away so quickly would be tragic for anyone. But the way he described it, the time he spent in the hospital gave him time to think and pray and figure things out. I'm sure he'll always have some disappointment and longing for what might have been, but he came home with his light burning brighter than any of us had ever seen.

"The truths our folks taught us, and the talents they championed in each of us gave Isaiah the courage and knowledge that he had more to give. Momma taught us all that there is a very real light that comes to life, burning bright with hope and beauty as we share our gifts with the world. She taught that all beauty was art and that the more of our heads, hearts, and hands we could put into our art, the more light it could shine into dark places. We always had a garden and musical instruments and paper to write and draw. We each had our own library card and were encouraged to spend time readin' good books. She and Daddy read to us from the Bible and hundreds of other books that offered light from their pages. And so when Isaiah came home with stories of a man he'd met who'd told him about an ancient order of Candle Lighters, it all rang true to us."

"Candle Lighters?"

Yolanda nodded, pointing to the key fob. "The way he described them, there is a group of people, young and old, scattered throughout the world who are committed to seeking out the great and eternal truths of God. When they find them, they are committed to sharing them with anyone who's inclined to ask or listen. Isaiah came back from Pennsylvania believing that our Daddy and Momma musta had the same training as the man who visited him in the hospital. He even thought they may have sent the man to find him. When he told us about the Candle Lighters, we all decided we wanted in."

"So this group—these Candle Lighters—how do you become one?" Kate asked, pointing to the key fob.

"Oh, there's nothing formal. It's not like joining a church. In fact, I've heard there are Candle Lighters in every religion across the world. It's more of a commitment you make to God and yourself to be willing to stand as a witness of his love and the light of truth wherever you go."

"And the key chain?"

Yolanda picked up the keys, stroking her thumb over the indentation left in the soft leather. "Isaiah made these key chains for every member of the family the Christmas after our parents died to help us remember the promise we made to live what we believe is true, to remember that love is the key to this work."

"Do you know Candle Lighters outside your family?"

"Yes. We cross paths from time to time."

"How do you know one when you see them?"

Yolanda smiled. "It's probably different for everyone. I usually feel it before I see it. They're almost always the kind of people whose love hovers around them like auras of goodness. They've almost always got a sparkle in their eye and are quick to smile."

"You pretty much just described yourself...and Isaiah...and Sammy. I felt your goodness the first time I met you."

"Thank you. I felt that goodness in you as well. I wouldn't have asked you to join me here if I hadn't felt that. You can't work in a windowless room without having a strong inner light."

Kate shook her head. "Thank you. I...I don't know what to say."

"You don't need to say anything. Some of the best Candle Lighters I've ever met are the ones who don't even know that they are, who have come to their understanding in their own time and place as God has worked His light and love in their lives. He always leaves His fingerprints on the people whose lives He's touched. When you know what you're looking for, they're easy to recognize."

Kate nodded thoughtfully. "I think that would describe my father... and my grandmother...and one of my favorite professors...and..." Kate faded off before looking up to see Yolanda smiling at her.

"That's one of your gifts, Kate. You've felt God's love. That's one of the greatest gifts you can receive in this life—to know His unconditional love. I was fortunate to have the Joneses to teach me over time what that unconditional love is, but no one has taught me that more than Sammy. I thank God every day that I had a brother like him to help me discover the joy and love that comes from people who have the gifts he has. He's taught me to look for beauty in everyone I meet regardless of their physical and mental abilities."

Kate nodded, wanting to ask more about Sammy but not sure if she should. After a moment, she realized she had nothing to lose. "I don't know how to ask this without sounding offensive, so I'm just gonna ask and hope you'll know I'm only hoping to understand."

"Okay. Shoot."

"What *are* his abilities?"

Yolanda smiled. "Sammy is...he has some of the most unique abilities I've ever seen. Momma called him the "The Disciple of the Wind." Except for his sense of hearing, he has all the senses you and I have, but he has a couple of extra ones, too."

Kate nodded. "I saw what the wind does with his notes. There's obviously some kind of connection there, but I won't pretend to understand it."

"Girl, I've been around it for close to fifty years, and I still don't understand it. I don't even know if there are words in any language to explain that."

She nodded. "Those messages he writes—where do they come from?"

Yolanda looked surprised. "You've received at least a couple of those messages. You tell me."

Kate took a deep breath, smiling nervously. "I feel like they can only come from God. He's the only one who would know those things."

She nodded. "But you weren't listening, were you?"

"Excuse me?"

"God had probably been tryin' to get your attention for days, maybe months, but you weren't listening, were you?"

Kate thought about the first note she received, then the second. Compared side by side, the notes and the circumstances around which she had found them were quite different. One had felt like a long-awaited answer after an agonizing time of questioning the direction of her future. The second had come quickly, after just a moment of wondering how to move forward. But in both cases, the notes were tied to a question, an uncertainty. And in both cases they offered her clarity, if not direction. "Is that what my problem was?" she asked. "Was I not listening?"

"You tell me."

Kate shook her head slowly as she asked herself the question, already knowing the answer.

"Communicating with God is different for everyone. But many of us are impatient when we need an answer. Some of us throw out questions to the Creator of the universe only when we're in trouble and have nowhere else to turn. And it's been my observation that few of us are patient when it comes to answers. I know it's been that way for me. It ain't ever easy to trade in the control we think we need for something as uncertain as hope and faith. And if we ever make it to a place of wisdom, most of us have to suffer and stumble our way down that path. Daddy used to quote C.S. Lewis all the time, and one of his thoughts I've never forgotten is the cold truth that our own reiterated cries often deafen us to the voice we hope to hear."

Kate nodded solemnly.

"I don't believe it has to be that way," continued Yolanda. "It's taken me fifty-four years to figure it out—and the constant nudges from my little brother to help me learn that there's better ways to wisdom and understanding. Wisdom always comes at a cost, but there are far better, less painful ways to get there than most of the world is pursuing, if they're pursuing it at all."

"Tell me about that. It sounds like something I read in Dr. Hermansen's notebook."

Yolanda nodded. "Leslie and I talked about this many times. I feel like we helped each other come to a better understanding of what Sammy was tryin' to share with each of us—tryin' to share with everyone. I don't believe that life is as complicated as we make it—filling it up with all the stuff and noise that we think's gonna make us happy but instead only clutters up our hearts and heads, makin' it tough for us to see and hear and feel.

"I'm convinced that we're our own worst antagonists in these stories we knit together and call life. We create our own monsters and feed them on the lies we tell ourselves and the hopes we're way too willing to give up. People spend all sorts of time and money trying to find inner peace, when all they really need is to give it all up, to sit and be still, to learn to listen to the wind blow or hear their own heart beating out the rhythm of the dance. Instead, we've become afraid of silence. The universe continues to invite us to recognize the subtle patterns and fingerprints of our Creator by offering us small feasts in the form of nourishing silence. But I've watched how most of us, when such moments present themselves, we reach for our phones, turn up the radio or TV, or switch on a device that deafens us to the peace and calm that's trying to reach out to us. In the process, we haven't even noticed how we have glorified busy-ness and filled our lives with all forms of digital clutter, separating ourselves from so much that can offer us nourishment and direction."

Kate nodded thoughtfully, considering how her own path had felt burdened, even encumbered, by her worries and concerns. She had spent plenty of time wrestling with her decision to come here, but she acknowledged that taking the time to be still had not been part of that process. "Tell me something," she said, turning back to Yolanda. "Do you believe it's possible to live in a place where inspiration from God can flow freely?"

"Yes," she answered immediately. "I'm not sure about a lot of things, but I've come to a place in my life where I don't question the love God has for us anymore. Losing my son was the worst hell I've ever been through, but the love I've felt reaching out to me—that love has extinguished the fires of hell. I could've missed all of that. It would be easy to curse God and spend my life ranting about the injustice of it all. But there's no hope in that. There's no life. Anger is a bitter pill that only proves to further separate us from the only balm that can bring peace. I was consumed with a lust for justice for way too long. I've resigned myself to the fact that justice will probably never be served in this life. But I made a very conscious decision to not concern myself with that. There's too much good that requires my heart and soul—I can't give any more thought or effort to the insatiable vices that I know can only bring misery. Sammy's note helped me see that. I knew I needed God's help to put things back together. And sometimes faith requires us to drop the obstacles that clog up our path back to him."

"But how do you do that? I mean, what if the obstacles aren't even ours? What if they're just there? How do we work our way through that maze?"

"Daddy used to always say that faith gives us wings to be able to lift ourselves above the fray. It enables anyone to fly over many of the challenges and roadblocks that try to hold us back. It offers believers and seekers a bird's-eye view with answers and direction to a brighter path."

"Do you think Simon might have felt the same way about faith as your father?"

"Absolutely. Kate, most of my father's sermons and the way he and Momma lived their lives were a result of the same influence that changed Simon's life forever. He learned to listen. He learned to recognize God's love for him. And once he learned that, he could never go back to the man he was before. Daddy said that the fingerprints of God were as easy to find in the man as they are in Simon's creations. His faith enabled him to look past the pain and trouble of his first forty years and give hope and direction to his last forty years. It encouraged him and gave him hope that things could be different, better, more meaningful. It gave him passion to live out loud, to share what he knew, and to invite others to embrace the joy and light that had found him as he called out in the darkness of his self-inflicted despair."

"And that's the greatest message of the towers, isn't it?" Kate said with a smile. "That everyone can experience the same joy he did."

Yolanda nodded. "Simon's story has always inspired me—how a bruised and broken man can change through the love of God. Daddy told me many times that Simon never intended to get rich or famous. He created what he did as a beacon of hope and love. It wasn't just a candle; it was a lighthouse through which the light of God's love could shine into the hearts of all sincere seekers."

Kate smiled.

"The symbolism inside that fence is as vast as the viewer's heart is open to discover it. Daddy told me many times that Simon's favorite hymn was a song about a grand lighthouse and the lower lights we can lift to help guide the weary travelers to the safe harbor. You may have heard of it—'Brightly Beams Our Father's Mercy.'"

"I'm not sure."

"Daddy asked that it be sung at his funeral. Of course all of us knew it by heart. It was his favorite hymn too. Hearing all of my siblings sing it together on that sad day of goodbyes, it became my favorite hymn too." Yolanda lifted her head and closed her eyes as the words flowed from her mouth, echoing off the walls of the art room like a choir of angels.

Brightly beams our Father's mercy
From His lighthouse evermore,
But to us He gives the keeping
Of the lights along the shore.

Dark the night of sin has settled,
Loud the angry billows roar;
Eager eyes are watching, longing,
For the lights along the shore.

Trim your feeble lamp, my brother;
Some poor sailor, tempest-tossed,

Trying now to make the harbor,
In the darkness may be lost.

Let the lower lights be burning!
Send a gleam across the wave!
Some poor fainting, struggling seaman
You may rescue, you may save.

The echo continued long after Yolanda had stopped singing. Kate was aware of the tears on her cheeks, but she did nothing to brush them away, basking instead in the warmth and glow of the light she felt all around her. "Why didn't Simon find a way to make a record of the purpose of his work?"

"He did."

"Where?"

Yolanda touched her heart. "I've known what his purpose was for as long as I've been aware of the towers. Daddy and Momma filled our hearts with stories of Simon's generosity and spirit."

"Yes, and that's beautiful, but those stories are limited to those you meet and know. Who will tell the story? Who will make sure the story never dies?"

"You will," Yolanda said with a smile, her eyes brimming with tears. "You will make sure the story never dies, won't you? And everyone you tell will tell another."

Kate felt the burden of the assignment. "There's gotta be a more effective way."

Yolanda nodded. "Daddy used to say that Simon always believed there would come a time when the darkness of the world would cause seekers to search out all the light they could find. His bedtime stories often gave us glimpses into that time when men and women throughout the world would be starved of love and light. Daddy's sermons and Bible readings often centered on these sad days when men's hearts would grow cold with apathy and indifference and chaos would be the rule of the day. He always believed that people would come to the towers, drawn by the words of poets and musicians who would write and sing words of hope and grace and mercy. He believed that writers, filmmakers, and artists would open the eyes and hearts of the hungry and weary and tell the stories of the light and love and faith that built the towers. It's happening, Kate. The darkness and apathy is strong but will never be strong enough to keep the people from coming. They come and feel their heavy burdens lightened. The most sincere will continue to ask the questions that will bring the light and answers they seek."

Kate looked down, feeling the truth settle on her soul like a warm blanket, but it wasn't entirely comforting. "So, what's my role in all of this?"

"That answer isn't mine to give."

"Why not?" she asked, looking disappointed.

"Because it's your decision. You have to decide how much you're willing to give. You have to decide if and how you'll lift your lamp. You have to decide what's real. No matter what you decide or where you go, you'll find there will be others who'll stand with you. And there'll be others—sometimes many others—who'll do all they can to blow out your lamp and silence your words. But every time you choose to lift your lamp, the whole o' heaven'll stand beside you. You may not see 'em, but if your heart's open, you'll feel them lifting you up and showering you with the light of God's love."

Kate nodded slowly. "I feel like I've been swimming in that light since I got here."

"I've noticed."

"You have?"

"Yes, of course. It's been fun to watch."

"Why haven't you said anything?"

"Because...you never asked until now."

Kate shook her head. "You sound like Isaiah."

"Thank you. We had the same teacher, you know."

"Your father?"

"Well, yes, him too, but I was actually thinking about Sammy."

"What has he taught you?"

"More than anything, that the connection between heaven and mankind is real. Because of Sammy, I realize that God is anxious to speak to all of us. I believe He wants a connection, He wants to communicate, but finding the time to listen to His whisperings can be tricky in a world filled with so much noise and commotion.

"Being deaf has given Sammy an advantage over those of us who are easily distracted by the auditory stimulation that bombards us. The rest of us have to make a conscious effort to seek out quiet places where we can be still. Those places are becoming increasingly difficult to find as our devices draw our attention away with their empty promises of immediate gratification."

Kate nodded. "So what do we do to combat that?"

"You can only control yourself. You want to know what God wants you to do? You need answers? Leave your phone at home. Go for a walk. Put yourself in a place where heaven can reach down and touch you. It's far easier than you can imagine. And if it doesn't work the first time, go back. Try again. And again. Take a notebook with you, and write down the truths that come into your heart after you've asked your questions. You will find there are answers that grow out of every sincere question as you tune your heart to listen to those whispers that float on the gentle breezes of grace."

Kate took a deep breath, nodding slowly. There were still so many questions, but most of them, she knew, could only be answered by someone who knew even more than Yolanda. "Thank you," she said, pushing away the desire to ask her for advice about helping Charlie understand the things they had been talking about.

"You are always welcome," she replied, standing to go. She was all the way back to her office door when she turned back. "Love is always the answer, Kate—whatever the question. Don't ever forget that."

CHAPTER 28

THE WEDGE

*If only you could see the whole picture, if you knew the whole story, you would
realize that no problem ever comes to you that does not have a purpose in your
life, that cannot contribute to your inner growth. When you perceive this, you will
recognize that problems are opportunities in disguise. If you did not face problems,
you would just drift through life. It is through solving problems in accordance with
the highest light we have that inner growth is attained.*

—Peace Pilgrim

Despite her best efforts to find answers to her questions surrounding
how to help Charlie, Kate felt stuck. For the rest of the week, thoughts
of him continued to pester her. It didn't help that she spent her evenings
going through the box of his things. She watched several iterations of his
film and recognized the tangle he had slowly created for himself over
five years by not allowing himself the ability to observe the connections
to anything spiritual. His notebooks expressed frustration with the

clues Isaiah had given him, but he seemed repeatedly unwilling to even consider the possibility that the answers could be deeper than what he had been able to see with his natural eyes. But Charlie's research and the pictures he had taken continued to be helpful in Kate's understanding of Simon's towers as she worked her way through the box.

The drive home on Friday night was longer and slower than she had experienced before, and as she sat in the parking lot that was I-405, she found herself wishing she had stayed in Watts and visited with Isaiah. But his last words to her continued to cycle through her mind as they had all week: "Proceed as the way opens." It had been good advice, inching her closer, she felt, to a better understanding not only of Simon's purpose for building the towers but also of Charlie's hesitations and roadblocks. But she wanted more. More clarity. More answers. More than anything, she wanted to see the big picture, to understand how she fit into this. It was difficult for her to accept the slow, sometimes imperceptible progress as she did her part to ask God for patience, understanding, and even love.

While going through the box of Charlie's things again after she finally got home, Kate realized she was missing something. She hadn't been still—not really. She'd had a couple of quiet evenings with the house to herself, but she had filled the time with Charlie's pictures, movies, and notebooks. She wasn't entirely sure what constituted the act of being still, but she doubted those activities—with all their tangents and distractions—would qualify.

Kate awoke the next morning with her pillow bathed in soft light. She stared up at the wood-paneled ceiling for several minutes, feeling a deep sense of serenity. She didn't have any more answers than she'd had when she went to bed, but there was a calm in her heart that had not been there the night before. She looked at her phone, curious of the time. Six twenty-three. She rose from her bed and walked to the sliding glass doors, looking out onto the quiet street below, still swimming in a thin morning fog. In spite of the early hour, she was drawn out by the downy light and the coolness of the air.

Without hesitation or delay, Kate changed into a pair of shorts, a sweatshirt, and a ball cap to hide to her crazy hair. She was just about to leave when she decided she might need Dr. Hermansen's notebook. She hastily emptied her bag on her bed and repacked it with only the notebook and her wallet. But as she turned to leave, another idea came to her. She quickly returned to the side of her bed and picked up the small travel Bible her parents had given her when she left home, adding it to the bag before heading to the garage for the rusty beach cruiser.

With no destination in mind, she pedaled south through the quiet streets until she got to the boardwalk. The foggy marine layer was thick and low, making the tranquil morning feel damp and dreamlike as she continued south. As she pedaled, her mind reviewed the past month, turning each day like pages in a book. So much had changed in one short month. Her confidence had grown with each passing day. She had made new friends at work and found joy in making art with the patients. Her visits with Yolanda and Isaiah and her time with the towers had deepened her faith and her understanding of her connection to God. As she visited these memories, her thoughts turned into prayer. But unlike so many of her recent prayers, she asked for nothing. Instead, her prayer was filled with only gratitude and thanksgiving.

When the boardwalk ended, she wove her way onto the quiet backstreet that ran parallel to the beach. But before long, the street ended at a roundabout, and Kate found herself sitting on a bench overlooking the inlet to Newport harbor. It was still early and quiet, but the marine layer was already beginning to burn off as the sun crested the hills, paving the water with pure gold. Watching the glittering amber, she was overwhelmed by the beauty of this place, and her prayer of gratitude continued to pour from her heart.

In the solace of the morning air, Kate remembered why she had come. She pulled the Bible from her bag and held it closed in her hands for a moment, staring down at it. She knew she needed some direction, but she realized she wasn't entirely sure if she would want to accept the direction she might receive. Deciding to leave it up to chance, she let the book fall open on her lap. To her surprise, it opened to where a piece of paper had been stuffed into the book's gutter. When she recognized her father's handwriting, she immediately pulled the note from the pages.

Dear Kate,

It's difficult to admit that you're leaving home tomorrow. I have spent the last several days wishing I could give you something that might help you in this next chapter of your life. Your mother reminded me tonight that we have spent the last 22 years trying to do just that—to give you a solid foundation to build your life on. If you have found this note, it is probably because you are feeling a bit lost. I wish I could be there to offer you some help, but I know the direction you receive from God will be worth far more than anything I could give you.

Kate, I promise you that the answers you seek are never far away if you will listen and be patient in humility. I believe God has an individual plan for each of his children. I have known for many years that God's plan for you would take you far from home. Because of this, we have tried to prepare you for bigger things. I don't know what will come your way. But I do know that God will lead you through your life and all your trials if you let him—if you will ask in faith—if you are humble enough to listen.

Your mother and I are proud of you and all your efforts to improve your life. We will be praying for you, and we know God will bless you. If you want His help, you must decide to open the door and let Him in.

I'll love you forever!

Dad

Kate wiped a tear from her eye as she slid the paper back between the Bible's pages. She was about to close the book when she noticed that several verses had been highlighted. She wiped her eyes again and lifted the book closer to her face as she began to read the highlighted passage:

James 1:5–8

If any of you lacks wisdom, let him ask God, who gives generously to all without reproach, and it will be given him. But let him ask in faith, with no doubting, for the one who doubts is like a wave of the sea that is driven and tossed by the wind. For that person must not suppose that he will receive anything from the Lord; he is a double-minded man, unstable in all his ways.

Kate read the passage again, letting it into her heart. As she finished, she was distracted by the voices of three teenaged boys who parked their bikes next to hers and ran barefoot across the sand, their boogie boards under their arms. She watched them go, aware for the first time of the sound of waves crashing. She had never been to this part of the beach, but looking around she could see that a long, narrow jetty stretched out into the sea, sheltering the mouth of the harbor. Watching the boys run, she nearly missed the fishing boat motoring its way through the calm waters of the harbor, its decks filled with smiling fishermen, seemingly oblivious to the roar of the waves just a few dozen yards away on the other side of the jetty.

As she watched the boat grow smaller and smaller as it moved farther away, she remembered the verses she had read. Staring down the length of the jetty, it was difficult to imagine a more contrasting juxtaposition—frothy, roaring waves on one side, crashing and throwing water high against the rocks, and on the other side, calm, tranquil waters. It was the same sea—the same blue water on both sides of the jetty—but the difference couldn't have been more profound.

She set the Bible on the bench next to her and closed her eyes, focusing her senses on the singular purpose of prayer. Thinking of her father's note, she thoughtfully remembered how her parents had taught her to pray as a child; to express gratitude to God along with the true, sincere desires of her heart. She needed to ask—sincerely ask for help, for direction, for an answer.

As her supplication for direction began her chest was filled with the familiar warmth she had known so many times before. An image flashed in her mind. She could see herself in her car, driving through the unremarkable California desert, wondering to herself what she was doing, if she had made the right decision, if she would find any happiness in this decision to come here. Immediately, another image appeared in her mind. Sitting in the same car, this time in the passenger seat as she searched the car for quarters so she could do her laundry. She saw herself finding the note, opening the crumpled paper, reading the words, and finally understanding them. "You are where you're supposed to be," she heard herself say. The words were clear, their meaning unmistakable.

As she continued to pray, another image came to mind. It was the note she had found on her bicycle. "Bring him to the towers with you. He's supposed to be part of it." Again, the words were clear—their meaning without question. But what did that mean for her now? She had done what she was supposed to do. She had gone to the towers and taken Charlie with her. What more was she supposed to do?

And even as she asked, she felt a pang of fear creeping in. What if she didn't like the answer? She pushed that notion away, trying replace it with the faith she had that God would make it possible, maybe even endurable. But as she thought this, another image popped into her head. It was the Sunday she had gone to the towers with Charlie. Almost as if she were in a drone hovering overhead, she could see Charlie sitting down on the bench in the gazebo, sorting through pictures on his iPad. But she also saw herself standing a little ways off, examining the north wall of the complex. Looking closer, Kate remembered being at that exact spot when she suddenly knew what the towers were all about.

With her eyes still closed, the image in her mind went back to Charlie sitting there on the bench, hunkered down in the shadows of the towers, looking frustrated and confused. What she saw next caused her some anxiety. It was Isaiah, and the words he uttered were simple and unmistakable: "You're the interpreter."

Kate opened her eyes, feeling a little sick. She had asked for direction, but this was not exactly what she had in mind. She closed her eyes again, hoping to see something else, something more, something different. But there was nothing else. Nothing came. After a minute, she recognized she was clenching her teeth. Again the passage of scripture her father had highlighted came into her memory.

But let him ask in faith, with no doubting, for the one who doubts is like a wave of the sea that is driven and tossed by the wind. For that person must not suppose that he will receive anything from the Lord; he is a double-minded man, unstable in all his ways.

Kate opened her eyes again. She was frustrated, and her frustration only grew when she realized she was frustrated. She had, after all, come looking for direction. But what if she didn't like the direction she got?

Feeling uncomfortable and hungry, she got up from the bench and walked to her bike. Trying to separate it from the boys' bikes, she quickly noticed that the lock they had secured around their wheels had also snagged a couple of her spokes, tying her bike to theirs. She couldn't leave. She looked out at the beach, where now several dozen boogie boarders bobbed on the angry surf. She knew she couldn't call them all in to ask if they were the idiots who trapped her bike with theirs. She would have to wait, but for how long? She looked down again at her bike, wondering how much difference a couple of spokes would make if she were able to just break them off. She decided she didn't want to find out. She would have to wait for the boys to leave.

She grabbed her bag and walked toward the jetty, figuring she could blow some time exploring while she waited. From a distance, the waves appeared to be rolling in steadily in even sets. But as Kate neared the wet sand, she quickly noticed something different about the waves here. Deflecting off the jetty, they rolled backward, smashing into incoming waves with massive force, shooting water high into the air. She took a seat on the soft sand and watched boogie boarders rally for turns to ride these unpredictable collisions. Kate was quickly drawn in by the excitement of it, finding it difficult not to participate with the gathering crowd, who were oohing and ahhing as young daredevils rode the waves, often being slammed into the sand with stunning force.

"Great morning, huh?" a middle-aged woman asked, sitting down in the sand next to Kate.

She nodded. "Is it like this every day?"

"No, it's usually pretty wild out here, but this is huge. My son's been tracking this swell from the tropical storm down in Mexico since last week. He said it's supposed to get *gnarly* by high tide, around eleven. The lifeguards will probably have to close the beach by then."

"You're son's out there?"

"Yeah, he's the one with the blue boogie board," she said, pointing to the pod of surfers, at least three of whom had blue boards. "We drove down this morning from Riverside, trying to beat the crowds, but it looks like everyone and their dog has been watching the surf reports too. It's a bummer. Rory's been trying to get sponsored by Quicksilver, so we hired a local photographer to take some video. I hope he gets something good with all those people out there. It will cost us either way."

Kate closed her eyes and shook her head. "Let me guess, Charlie George?"

"You know him? That's so cool. Apparently he's kind of the *dude* for local surf videos. My son's been *totally stoked* on his YouTube channel for months. I was glad we could get him. I couldn't believe that a guy who charges five hundred bucks for a half day actually answers his own phone."

Kate tried to keep a straight face as she looked out at the water, searching for a photographer. She quickly spotted him bobbing up and down, only his ratty hair and the black shoulders of his wetsuit visible above the surface as he pointed his finger toward one of the boys. Forgetting her hunger and frustration, Kate watched as Charlie skillfully maneuvered himself over and over again into the right position to capture his subject riding the waves.

As she watched, she noticed something she had missed in Charlie. He appeared patient and kind as he coached the boy. Even at this distance, she could see the boy's enthusiasm as he rode the increasingly large waves. After at least an hour, Kate noticed a flash of red out of the corner of her eye. A lifeguard ran from his perch on the stand to assist a floundering surfer who had washed up on shore after being beaten down by a rogue wave. Coughing and spitting, he struggled to get to his feet just in time to be beaten down again by another wave and dragged back into the surf. The lifeguard struggled to find his own footing and finally reached the surfer again, handing him the swim buoy just as another wave crashed over their heads. When they surfaced again, the young surfer looked dazed and exhausted. Kate watched as several men and women rushed from the beach and rallied to their aid. With the waves pounding in unrelenting, unpredictable sets, the pair somehow made their way to the shallows, narrowly escaping the force of the sea with the help of the several strong men and women who stood with them.

A voice called out from a loudspeaker atop the lifeguard stand just as a white pickup truck rolled to a stop and two more burly lifeguards stepped out. "This beach is now closed for surfing due to extreme surf. Please return to the beach! Please return to the beach immediately!"

Kate watched as the yellow flag with a black dot in the middle, which had been hanging on the lifeguard stand, was replaced with two red flags. The lifeguards moved quickly and collectively toward the water, motioning for everyone to come in. Kate watched as many of the surfers looked disappointed and reluctant to follow direction.

"Well, there goes five hundred bucks," the woman next to Kate said, getting to her feet and walking to the top of the steep, sandy bank. Waves were now crashing up and over the jetty, and Kate watched as three surfers struggled hard to keep themselves from being thrown against the rocks. All of the lifeguards were now in the water, pulling and pushing the remaining surfers onto the sand. Kate was just wondering if she should help when the biggest wave yet smacked the beach with a deafening roar, pulling several people back into the surf as it retreated.

She hurried to the edge as another wave hit, its waters coming up and over the top of the bank. The crowd collectively fell back while a couple of men rushed to the aid of those who were still struggling. Kate had never seen such display of natural power before. She found it stunningly beautiful yet frightening. Scanning the water for those who were still out, she noticed a boy with a blue boogie board being pushed along by a man in a wetsuit swimming parallel to the beach. Even from a distance, she could see it was Charlie. Several hands pointed to the pair, who were much farther out than when they had started. A whisper of "riptide" was on the lips of many of the spectators. Kate remembered the word. Anxiety rose in her when she remembered why. It was a riptide that had taken Charlie's sister. She watched intently, observing how a path of lighter-colored water seemed to be retreating away from the beach, carrying the two stragglers farther out to sea. They continued swimming hard, parallel to the beach and away from the jetty.

The crowd watched on with shared anticipation. Soon after they reached beyond the edge of the riptide, a yellow lifeguard boat appeared out of nowhere, picking them up. It moved them quickly a hundred yards up the beach, dropping them off in calmer, shallower waters where they could stand. The boy looked exhausted, and Kate watched as his mother broke free of the crowd, running to the edge of the surf.

"That was close," Kate heard a woman say from behind her. "They were lucky," a man responded.

Kate watched as the lifeguards retreated from the raging sea, scanning the water for any additional surfers until they seemed satisfied that everyone was safe. Moving together toward the crowd, they announced that this section of the beach would be closed until at least seven o'clock that evening.

"This is stupid," one surfer said to his buddy. "Biggest waves of the year and they shut us down. We should sue."

"Yeah, freakin' bas...."

She saw his mouth move, but his words were drowned out by the roar of another crashing wave that sent water rushing high over the dry sand. People scrambled, jumping back or running to retrieve their things that were being dragged into the sea. Kate rushed to grab her own bag, reaching it just in time to lift it above the surging water. But the woman's blanket and purse were not so lucky. She wrung out the blanket the best she could and waited for the woman to return.

"Thank you," the woman said, taking her things back from Kate when she and her son finally returned. "That was way more excitement than I expected this morning."

Kate nodded and looked at the woman's son, who was shivering uncontrollably. "You looked pretty sick out there," she said, realizing this was the first time she had ever used "sick" in this way, hoping she had used it correctly. "Did you get what you wanted?"

"I hope so. I'm not going back out there today," he managed.

"Are you folks okay?" a lifeguard asked from behind.

The boy nodded.

"Good. That was probably the biggest riptide I've seen in a couple of years. You're lucky that guy was with you. It coulda been bad out there."

The boy nodded, looking cold and humble.

Kate noticed that Charlie was approaching just behind the lifeguard, and she quickly lowered the brim of her hat, not wanting to be seen.

"I'll try to get that editing done and be in touch within a week or so," Charlie reported.

"Oh, thank you, and thanks for saving my son," the woman said. "I'm glad you were out there with Rory."

"Yeah, sure. You're welcome," he responded, smiling. "I'm glad I could help."

"Can I buy you lunch or something?"

Kate watched out of the corner of her eye as the woman reached for her purse and quickly withdrew a folded green bill.

"No, no, that's fine," he said, waving it off.

"I insist," she said, reaching out her hand.

"Well, if you insist."

"Maybe you could find a date or something," she said, nodding to Kate, whose face was still hidden by the brim of her hat.

Charlie laughed nervously. "Thanks."

"You'll email us the movie then?" she asked.

"Yeah, look for it in about a week. If you don't mind, I'll post it to my YouTube channel too."

The boy smiled and nodded.

"Oh, and thanks for saving my stuff," the woman said, extending her hand to Kate. "I'm sorry I didn't catch your name."

"Oh, I'm...Kate," she replied awkwardly. "Good luck with getting sponsored."

"Thanks," the woman replied as they walked away.

"Not Kate as in the laundry girl from Idaho?" she heard Charlie ask in a playful voice.

She reluctantly looked up to face him. "What's up, Charlie?"

"Just workin'." He smiled an annoyingly charming smile.

"That's what I heard. Five hundred bucks for a couple hours of work, huh? Not bad."

"Right? Pretty sweet. Plus tip!" he said, holding up the green bill. He unzipped the back of his wetsuit and stripped it off down to his waist, exposing his tanned, toned chest. "What's new with you?"

"Oh, just hangin' out. That was pretty crazy out there, huh?"

"Yeah. That kid was *freaked out*!"

Kate nodded, remembering what she had seen. "I'm glad you were there to help him. That kid's mom was pretty freaked out too."

He nodded, looking distracted. "Hey, uh, I don't mean to be rude, but I'm starving. I need to go."

"Oh...sure."

"I guess I'll see you around," he said, stooping to gather up his stuff.

"Yeah, okay, see you later." She turned and began walking to her bike, but her legs felt heavy. The last person she had expected to see this morning was Charlie George, but here he was. "Proceed as the way opens," she heard a voice say somewhere deep inside her. She looked around for Charlie, finding him next to his bike, stripping off the rest of his wetsuit until he stood in only his board shorts. He was better looking than she remembered, but she pushed that thought away, knowing she didn't need any more distractions.

"Hey, I think I owe you a meal, don't I?" she asked before she could think of a reason not to.

"You do?"

"Yeah, you bought me that Reuben sandwich, remember?"

He nodded. "It seems like there was a bet involved, wasn't there? Or I was trying to make up for being a jerk?"

"Oh, yeah, that's right. I could buy you breakfast anyway. Then you'd owe me a meal."

Charlie smiled. "I don't know if that's a good idea."

"Oh, okay," she said, looking away. "I guess I'll see you…"

"It's actually a really bad idea," he said, cutting her off.

She looked at him, surprised by the rudeness of his response. "Sorry I asked."

"Actually, I was gonna say it's a really bad idea because I've got this fifty-dollar bill that lady gave me, and that buys way more pancakes than I can possibly eat by myself."

"So…what does that even mean?" she asked, feeling confused.

He ran his fingers through his wet hair, pushing it back, away from his face. "I guess it's my lame way of saying it would be nice to hang out, and I'm sorry I didn't ask you first."

Kate laughed. "I don't get you."

He looked away, but quickly turned back. "Kate, I'm sure you've figured this out by now, but I'm pretty clueless about…any of this kind of stuff, and you intimidate the he…ck out of me."

She laughed again. "Okay, first of all, yeah, you're clueless. And second, you're full of crap."

"So…are you saying you don't want pancakes?"

She closed her eyes and shook her head. "Sure," she responded with exasperation.

"So, wait, does that mean you *do* want pancakes, then?"

"If you're really offering, then yeah, I want pancakes."

"Cool," he replied. "Uh, do you...want them now?"

"What? As opposed to...tomorrow?" she asked, trying to not to be as sarcastic as she felt.

"No, I just...yeah. Let's go get some pancakes."

"So, let me just get this straight," she responded. "You're offering to buy me pancakes right now?"

"Or...we could go out to Ruby's on the pier," he said, looking up at the sun. "It's probably almost lunchtime, right?"

Kate couldn't help but smile. "I'll tell you what. Why don't you get on your bike and lead off. I'm hungry enough that I think I'd probably eat day-old pancakes with ketchup."

"Whoa! You like that too?"

She closed her eyes and shook her head, wondering what she was getting herself into.

"I'll just go...to Ruby's, I mean. You should come. I mean, if you want to. I mean, if you don't want to I'll understand, but ..."

"Charlie, just shut up and ride."

He nodded, stuffing his wetsuit and fins into his backpack and unlocking his bike from the trunk of the palm tree. He headed out, smiling a crooked smile as he drove past her shirtless and barefoot. Kate followed close behind until she could see there was room enough on the road for her to ride next to him.

"So how's it been?" she asked.

"Really good, actually. I got a job on a film crew."

"Congratulations. What are you doing?"

"Nothing yet. I actually won't start for another couple of weeks. A friend of a friend is working on some kind of dystopian apocalyptic surf movie with mechanical sharks from outer space."

"Oh, that's...cool, I guess. Will you be behind the camera?"

"Not on this one, but it's like a foot in the door, right? You gotta start somewhere."

"So what are you doing?"

"Uh, I'll be a grip. You know, running cables and taking care of things behind the scenes."

"Oh."

"What? You look underwhelmed."

"Sorry. I just thought that you wanted more than that."

"I do, but I don't know."

"The Charlie I met a month ago seemed pretty bent on changing the world with his films. What happened?"

"I just...I...So you can't be excited for me?"

"Are you excited for you?"

"Yeah, I'm stoked. This is my first real movie. I'll have my name in the credits and everything."

"Okay, so it's a dystopian movie about surfing and sharks from outer space?" she asked, trying to wrap her head around it.

"Yeah. I haven't seen the script yet. They're just polishing it up. Probably next week."

"Is that common for grips to see a script?"

"Uh, I don't know. Maybe not."

"Have you made any progress on your film about the towers?" she asked, knowing full well he hadn't.

"No. I decided to move on. I've wasted enough time with it."

"I'm sorry you feel that way."

"You are?" he asked, obvious surprise on his face.

"Sure. I've been spending some time with Isaiah and some of the members of his family. It's a compelling story."

"Which part?"

"Simon's story. How one man could create something like that and give it so much life and meaning. I've gone back several times. Isaiah's let me in. It's a special place, Charlie. A real-life utopia."

"You think so?"

"Yeah. It's amazing that a man who couldn't read could find such colorful and creative ways to preach the sermons that mattered most to him. And then leave it all behind. He's changed a lot of lives with his work, including mine."

"You think so?" he repeated dubiously.

She nodded. "I'm convinced he couldn't have created what he did without some kind of supernatural powers and an understanding of his relationship with things that are deeply spiritual."

"Yeah, that was kind of the nail in the coffin for me."

"What do you mean?"

"Kate, I don't believe in God. And I for sure don't want to spend any more time with this. There's nothing there for me. Not anymore."

"How do you know that?"

"Because I've spent five freakin' years going up there. That's plenty of time for me to know there's nothing there for me."

"So why did you keep going?"

He shook his head.

"I'm serious. Why didn't you give up three or four years ago? You could have saved yourself a lot of time and trouble."

"That's for sure."

"So why'd you keep going?"

He shook his head but didn't answer. "Follow me," he said, leading off the main road and onto a perpendicular street.

She followed him up the ramp where the beach sand edged the cement boardwalk. The marine layer was all but burned off now, and the beach was alive with activity. The scent of food wafted out of the open beach house windows and across their path, making her stomach growl. He pedaled harder than before, staying a couple of bicycle lengths in front of her, making it feel that he was trying to avoid any more questions. Kate didn't know how to respond. As she followed close behind, she also felt like she couldn't let it go. Not now. Not yet. She knew it might be the last time she ever talked to him, but she knew she had to try.

After several blocks, the beach houses gave way to restaurants and surf shops, and Charlie turned sharply left where a side street intersected the boardwalk. He rode through the huge parking lot, avoiding cars that were searching out the last of the available parking spaces, and up onto a colorful sidewalk. The ramp of the Balboa Pier was right in front of them, and Kate wondered how she'd missed this in her explorations.

They parked their bikes at a bike rack, and Kate held onto Charlie's backpack while he washed the saltwater off his body under the public shower. He put on a damp T-shirt and a pair of sandy flip flops before taking the bag back.

"Thanks," he said, throwing the pack over one shoulder. "Ruby's is at the end of the pier."

He led out, but he waited for her. The wooden pier rose before leveling off at what felt like fifty feet above the water. Fishing poles lined the sides of the pier, where anxious fishermen tended them. An Asian woman wearing a straw hat in the shape of a lamp shade flopped a small green fish on the planks in front of them and ran to unhook it, dropping it into a water-filled bucket.

"Mackerel," Charlie offered.

"Are they good to eat?"

"I don't know," he responded as he looked down into another bucket where a handful of mackerel were splashing about.

"You've never tried them?"

"I can't say that I have." He stopped and took a closer look as another fisherman pulled a fresh mackerel from the sea. "Do you like fish?"

"Sure. My dad used to take us fishing when I was a kid. Mostly trout. I'm pretty sure I've never seen a mackerel before. How about you?"

He nodded, looking down into yet another bucket, this one nearly filled with dark-colored fish. "This is the only place I've ever fished. My dad brought us out here when I was eight or nine."

"Did you catch any?"

"I don't remember," he said, staring into a bucket like he was lost in a memory.

They kept walking, but Charlie didn't say anything more. Kate found herself wondering if memories of his sister and family had given him pause. Walking to the edge of the pier, she said a silent prayer in her heart that she would have the nerve and the heart to be able to proceed as the way opened.

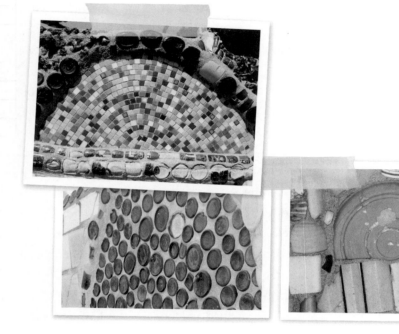

Faithless is he that says farewell when the road darkens.   J. R. R. Tolkien

CHAPTER 29

COLLATERAL

It is not because things are difficult that we do not dare;
it is because we do not dare that things are difficult.
—*Seneca the Younger*

The Forties-style diner stood at the end of the pier like a boxy white bunker, and Kate began salivating the moment she caught the scent of burgers and fries. The striped umbrella-covered tables on the roof were mostly unoccupied, and she imagined herself sitting up there, taking in the surrounding beauty.

"On a clear day you can see Catalina Island," Charlie said, pointing off to the right, where the fog still clung to the distant horizon.

They walked around to the back side of the restaurant, where a pretty hostess greeted them in a red-and-white-striped dress and an exaggerated retro hairstyle.

"Table for two, please. Upstairs, maybe?" he asked, looking to Kate for approval. She nodded, and they were soon seated at a table that had a grand three-hundred-sixty-degree view of all things Californian. Kate couldn't help but smile and had a hard time concentrating on the menu.

"So tell me more about your new job," Kate said after the waiter had taken their order.

"What do you want to know?"

"I want to know why you're excited about it."

"It's kind of a big deal. These guys have produced some of the best horror films in the industry, and this is their first real jaunt into the pure dystopian movies."

"Do you like those kind of movies?"

Charlie shrugged. "Not really, but it's a paycheck in the right direction. My buddy who got me the job started out gripping for these guys and is now working for a big studio up in LA."

"And that's the direction you want to go?"

"Do you have a problem with that?" he asked, sounding a little defensive.

"No, not at all. It just seemed like you had...different aspirations, that's all."

"Yeah, well, I guess I've just come to the realization that maybe there's more to life than unrealistic aspirations."

"You really think they were unrealistic?"

"Don't you? Making films no one wants to see and hoping to make a decent living doing it?"

Kate forced a smile, not knowing how to respond.

"No, I finally came to my senses," he said. "I hate to admit it, but my dad was right. I've wasted too much time trying to create something nobody wants or needs."

"You think people need or want dystopian movies?"

Charlie smiled. "You haven't been paying attention to the movies lately, have you?"

"No, I've been in school for the last four years and never had extra money for movies. I think the last movie I saw was probably *42*.

He laughed. "I don't know if that even made a hundred million dollars."

A sign of a culture that has lost its faith—Moral collapse follows upon spiritual collapse. C.S. Lewis

"That sounds like a lot of money to me."

"Well, it's not." He pulled out his iPhone and ran his fingers over the screen. "Ninety-seven million dollars," he replied. "Pitiful."

"I thought it was a really good film. It had a great story. A strong moral message."

"Nobody cares about any of that anymore, if they ever did. It's time to grow up, Kate."

"Ouch," she responded.

"It's the truth." He poked his screen and looked closer. "There were at least ten dystopian blockbuster hits that came out the same year as *42*. Every one of them made at least twice as much."

"So I guess it really *is* all about money."

"Of course it's all about money. Most films that make a ton of money start out with budgets in the tens of millions. It's an investment. You can't make a movie without a lot of money, and you can't get your hands on a lot of money unless you can promise your investors a handsome return. Everybody has to be paid, from the actors to the caterers. Everybody wants a piece of the pie. The only genres that have a decent return on investments are action, horror, and dystopian. This film's gonna be a hybrid of all three. It's what people want."

Kate nodded, feeling both defeated and disappointed.

"You're not excited for me?"

She shrugged. "It sounds like a good opportunity."

"But?"

"But I'm still wondering what happened to the idealism you had just a month ago."

"Look, I've tried bucking the system. I've tried making it work other ways. I guess I've just come to the realization that nobody cares. People want to be entertained. They want escapism, not reality."

"But if all they're escaping to is dystopian…? How can that be good for society?"

Charlie shrugged. "People vote for what they want with their wallets. When a dystopian or horror movie makes three hundred million and a drama or documentary struggles to bring in a hundred million, investors pay attention."

"So what about idealism?"

He shook his head. "That's all a fantasy, Kate. There's nothing real about any of it."

"Okay, but isn't that kind of the point with idealism—that you have to work to make it real? That you work hard for a hope and a dream of what things can be?"

"Yeah, well, as far as I can tell, idealism started dying out at least twenty years ago."

"You really think that?"

"Absolutely. In order for idealism to have any power, people have to have hope that things can get better. Otherwise, what's the point? I don't know if you've noticed, but there isn't a lot of hope out there. It's a dog-eat-dog world. No one's looking out for the other guy. No one even cares. With news stations feeding us from the fire hoses of greed and war and societal cancers, movies are just a reflection of the crap that's all around us. That's what people want. They prove it every day by the movies they choose. There are probably only a thousand people on earth who choose what movies get made and what books get printed. And I don't think any of them care about spreading hope or goodwill. It's all about how many tickets and books they can sell. It's all about the money. Idealism is dead."

"So if you can't beat 'em, join 'em?" she asked sarcastically, feeling depressed.

"Pretty much," he responded, either not noticing her sarcasm or not caring. "What's the point of fighting a war you can never win? It's about as pointless as fighting against the rising tide, trying to save the sandcastle you built too close to the water's edge. The entertainment industry is just trying to stay ahead of the rising tide that swallows every sandcastle in its path."

Kate looked away, her disappointment growing. When she looked back, she found that Charlie was on his phone. She waited for him to look up, but he didn't. She looked around at the other tables and noticed that many of the customers were also distracted by their phones, not engaging with the people right in front of them. Struck by the cold feelings of loneliness, she looked down to the pier and noticed that even many of the fisherman standing shoulder to shoulder with other fishermen were more engaged with their phones than they were with their neighbors. Maybe Charlie was right. Maybe it was true that no one really cared. The very notion of it felt contrary to everything she believed in, but the reality all around her seemed to mock her own idealism about the hopes and the goodness of humanity.

Her thoughts were distracted by a line of huge birds flying north. Pelicans. Six, seven, eight of them lined up and soaring almost effortlessly against the southbound breeze that kept their giant wings aloft, just out of reach of the table umbrellas. She looked around, recognizing that nobody else saw the majestic birds. No one, that was, except a young girl who looked up from her crayons just in time to see them. Kate watched as the girl pointed and spoke excitedly. But her parents were slow to respond—distracted by their phones—and so they missed them.

She looked back at Charlie, his eyes and hands engaged in a parallel world she could not see. This was far from the first time Kate had felt like she was playing second fiddle to a digital distraction. Ever since phones began appearing in the halls and lunchroom of her high school, Kate had watched attention spans being challenged by the devices. She remembered how one of her friends, Kimberly Paulsen, had broken her nose their sophomore year when she had walked into an open locker door while attempting to text as she walked to her next class. Over the next six years, Kate had struggled not to feel like an outcast—first when she was one of the last people in her class to get a phone, and later, in college, when she realized she was last person to still be using her dated flip phone.

Her attention was drawn to a pod of dolphins frolicking in the water beneath them. She looked around and noticed that she was the only one who saw them. And as she watched them, for the first time she recognized that the financial challenges that had kept her from enjoying more digital distractions might have been a blessing in disguise.

Their food arrived before Charlie looked up from his phone. Shakes, burgers, and fries.

"Checking emails?" Kate asked, nodding to Charlie's phone.

"Oh, no, just checking the tide schedule and posting some pictures from this morning on Twitter and Facebook."

Kate nodded, taking a big bite of her burger before she could say anything that might come out sounding negative or judgmental. The food was delicious, and they both ate like they hadn't eaten in days. She was working on her shake when she heard the buzz of a low-flying airplane. She looked out from under the umbrella to see a single-engine plane leaving puffs of white smoke in the air as it dipped and dived, writing across the sky as if with clouds. It took less than two minutes to write the message WILL YOU MARRY ME?

"That's kind of romantic," she said, turning back to Charlie who had returned to his phone and wasn't paying any attention.

He looked up and smiled. "I suppose it could be, if the guy or girl it was intended for was watching. Otherwise that's a waste of at least five hundred bones." He laughed. "It's more likely that the pilot got the wrong beach or the woman it was intended for is asleep in the sand and missed it all. Or there are six random women on the beach down there wondering if this is the message from their boyfriend that they've been waiting for for years."

"Is there no end to your cynicism?" she responded, trying to forget the image his words created in her mind of six girls making phone calls to their boyfriends to find out if they'd just been proposed to. She turned and looked at the dotted message, already beginning to shift in the breeze. "It's not exactly my style, but it's still romantic."

He grunted and shrugged, but as he did, Kate noticed a parallel. She took another draw of shake from her straw, working out the idea in her head. She knew she had nothing to lose, but the idea would require more boldness than she had ever had before.

"Charlie," she said, waiting for him to look up from his phone before she said anything else.

"Yeah?" he said, after a moment, looking annoyed.

"What would you say if I told you that message was for you?"

He laughed. "Who would send me a message like that?"

"What if I told you I did?"

He looked confused. "Then I'd probably say you're even crazier than your sister."

She smiled. "Okay, but what would you do if you were trying to get someone's attention but they weren't listening? Would you make the message even bigger—maybe spell it out in the sky?"

"I can't think of any message I'd want to give anyone that would be worth fifty bucks a letter."

"But what if it was really important? Like the most important message ever?"

He shrugged. "Where are you going with this?

"I'm trying to figure out why someone who believes in changing the world would give up on something he loved so much that he spent five years working on it."

"Are we seriously going back to this?"

"Yeah."

"Why? Why do you care?"

"Because I got a message—a couple of them actually." She pulled the notebook from her bag and opened it, pulling out the note she'd found on her bicycle, as well as Sammy's drawing that Isaiah had given them. She set them down on the table between them. "I don't know what you think about this, but stuff like this doesn't happen to me all the time. Just like that message up there in the clouds; I'm sure it could be interpreted several different ways, but I'm guessing there's someone sitting on the beach right now in a wild state of joy because someone they love has just invited them to share the rest of their lives together."

She pointed to the note and the drawing. "For anyone else, these messages would just be meaningless scraps of madness. But they're not to me. And if I remember your reaction when you first understood what this one says, you also knew this wasn't meaningless."

He looked away.

"Charlie, I'm sure the universe communicates with people in billions of different ways, but this is the way it's chosen to communicate with us right now. And like it or not, that communication has brought us together. I've tried to ignore it. I even tried to figure it out on my own when you made it clear that you didn't want to cooperate. But I can't do this by myself. I'm only a piece of the puzzle. But you're obviously a piece too," she said pointing to Sammy's drawing. "I understand your skepticism. It's not easy putting your trust in something as intangible and obscure as all of this, but there's something we have to do—together. I get that you've made other plans. That you're moving on. But I'm asking you to reconsider."

Charlie shook his head. "I've been waiting for this door to open up for me ever since I was seventeen. This is what I've always wanted to do. I'm not going to pass this up for something as uncertain and maddening as spending any more time on a documentary that no one will ever care about."

"But you care about it. You've felt something up there, Charlie. You can't deny that."

He shook his head again, looking disgusted. "Kate, this is crazy. I've gone over that whole complex up there with a fine-tooth comb. I know the details better than anybody I know. I took thousands of pictures and close to a hundred hours of video and interviewed dozens of people. I know that place like the back of my own hand."

"I'm not doubting that, Charlie."

"So what are you saying?"

"I'm saying you missed it. You missed the big picture."

He rolled his eyes and turned his head.

"Why did Simon build those towers?"

"Because he wanted to do something big. He had a little man complex, and he wanted to prove that he was someone."

Kate laughed.

"You think that's funny?"

"You spent five years up there, and that's the best you can come up with?"

"You've got something better?"

"Absolutely. And it didn't take me anywhere near five years to figure it out. You've just gotta open your eyes, Charlie. But you've also gotta open your heart. His meaning is right there for anyone who cares to see and feel."

"Oh, I get it. You've spent an hour there and suddenly you're an expert!"

"I never said that. And for your information, I've spent a lot more than an hour up there. Isaiah and I have become good friends. He's been anxious to share what he knows."

"I'm sure he has," he responded, shaking his head.

"Charlie, I only want to help you. I feel like you missed seeing the big picture. I'm here for a reason," she said, pointing to Sammy's picture. "I only want to help."

"Thanks," he said with a saccharine smile, "but I'm done. After that last visit, I came home and threw it all away. Even if I wanted to start over, which I don't, it would be impossible. All my research—all my interviews—it's all rotting in the landfill under the rest of the county's garbage. I'm done."

Kate nodded slowly, feeling disappointed. "I'm sorry you feel that way," she said as she picked up the note and drawing, sliding them back into Dr. Hermansen's notebook. She looked up to see Charlie staring down at the notebook out of the corner of his eye. As she watched his eye quickly shift away, an idea passed through her head—a frightening, reckless idea. Before she could talk herself out of it, she opened her mouth and spoke.

"Would you like to borrow this notebook?"

"What? Why?"

She took a deep breath, trying to decide if this idea was totally nuts. She knew the information written on the pages had the potential of being damaging to many people she had learned to respect. But it felt like the decision had already been made by someone else. "I wouldn't have this notebook if it weren't for you." She reached into her bag and pulled out her wallet before sliding the notebook back into her bag and handing the whole thing to Charlie.

"Why are you doing this?" he said, looking reluctant to take it.

"You wanted it, right? A month ago you tried to take it from me."

"You left it in the sand!" he protested.

She smiled calmly, leaning closer to him so the bag hung over his lap. "You asked me if it was map to buried treasure."

"Yeah?"

"I might have lied to you that day. It actually is."

"A map to buried treasure?" he asked incredulously, with more than a hint of sarcasm.

"That's right," she said calmly.

"So why are you giving it to me?"

"Because the map is in a code I don't completely understand," she responded, trying to think on her feet.

"And you think I'll understand it?" he asked, one eyebrow raised.

"I don't know. If you're supposed to be part of it like the note says, then I'll meet you tomorrow morning out in front of your house at seven. If you want in, we'll be heading to Watts, so bring some breakfast. If you're out, you can hand me the notebook and you'll never have to see me again."

He looked at her as if he were waiting for her to crack. "You're serious?" he asked after a moment.

"Of course I'm serious."

He took the bag from her. "Why are you doing this?"

"Because there's way more treasure than I need. There's plenty to share."

"And you're just gonna trust me with this—without collateral or anything?"

"That's a good idea, actually. I should have some security. What have you got?"

He looked down at his backpack. "I've got my wetsuit and...my cameras."

"How about that?" she asked, pointing to his phone.

"You're serious?"

"Yeah."

"What are you going to do with my phone?"

"Nothing. Just hang onto it until I get my notebook back. Isn't that how collateral works?"

He looked confused. "Wait, for how long?"

"Till seven a.m. Tomorrow. What's that...just over nineteen hours?"

"And you're not going to throw it into the ocean or anything like that?"

She rolled her eyes. "Look, if your phone isn't in the same shape tomorrow as it is right now, you get to keep the notebook—and the treasure. You've got nothing to lose."

"So, if there really is a treasure at the end of this—which I am totally doubting—what's gonna keep me from running off with it?"

"You don't think I planned for that? I've got this figured out," she lied. "I have the last pages of that book stored in a safe place just in case you get any crazy ideas. Both pieces are necessary to make the map work."

"But..."

"I actually don't have any more time for questions right now," she said, cutting him off as she pushed the home button on his phone to reveal the time. "Do we have a deal or not?"

"You're serious?"

"Yeah. I'm serious. You've got just over nineteen hours to decide if you're in or out." She stood, picking up her wallet and sliding his phone into her pocket. She turned to depart before her nerves cracked. "I'll see you at seven," she said, leaving him holding the bag.

Live your beliefs and you can turn the world around.
Henry David Thoreau

CHAPTER 30

PROGRESS

In order to help usher in the golden age we must see the good in people.
We must know it is there, no matter how deeply it may be buried.
Yes, apathy is there and selfishness is there—but good is there also.
It is not through judgment that the good can be reached,
but through love and faith.
—Peace Pilgrim

Kate was shaking by the time she had descended the restaurant's stairs. She walked back the length of the pier, expecting Charlie to catch up with her at any moment, but he didn't. She unlocked her bike and began pedaling home, being careful with the phone she had taken as collateral, knowing that any damage to it would make it difficult for her to reclaim Dr. Hermansen's notebook.

As she pedaled, she raced through the memories of the notebook. She had seen each page at least a couple dozen times. She wondered if

Dr. Hermansen's words might influence Charlie the same way they had influenced her. Would he understand them? Would he even care? Would he be able to see the promised treasure? As she got closer to home, she wondered if she was foolish to have let the notebook go with such relatively small collateral. But by the time she parked the cruiser in the garage, her heart had returned to a reasonable rate and she was filled with an unexpected calm. She didn't know if she would be driving to Watts by herself in the morning, but she didn't doubt that she would get the notebook back.

Kate found her roommates lying out on the deck, and she lay down on the lounge chair beside them, feeling more content than she had in weeks. She found herself wondering if Dr. Hermansen had felt the same way when she had hidden the notebook in the bottom drawer of the desk she would soon abandon. Surely she would have experienced some level of anxiety. Surely it would have felt reckless. But she had done what Sammy had told her to do. He had seen a bigger picture—a picture that included Kate—many months before Kate even knew how she would be spending this summer.

With the perspective she had now, it wasn't hard to recognize that something much bigger than herself had orchestrated the details and timing to fall into place just as they had. She dozed off, knowing she was undoubtedly where she was supposed to be to recognize the hand of Providence shaping the path before her. She still couldn't see where the path ended, but her faith had been strengthened as she had put her trust in God, believing—even knowing—there was a plan.

When her roommates left for work, Kate got back to work as well. From the stacks of Charlie's printed photos, she selected a much smaller collection of pictures that supported the ideas and theories she had been developing over the last month.

As she reviewed this smaller stack, looking closely at the imagery and symbolism, she was once again convinced that her theories were correct. And with this came an increase of admiration for the man who had spent thirty-three years of his life putting his mark on the world so that others might come to see and understand the grace and love that had changed his life forever.

Sorting through the photos one last time to make sure she hadn't missed anything, Kate stopped at a picture she didn't remember having seen before. It was a photo of a slightly younger Charlie, his arm resting on the shoulder of a black-and-white cardboard cutout of Simon. Though the cutout was pixilated and blurry, it was easy to recognize this small, simple man dressed in overalls, not quite coming to Charlie's shoulder. Wiry and with a receding hairline, he smiled directly into the camera, looking a little goofy but nonetheless warm and welcoming. She stared at the picture for a long time, feeling grateful for this man who had inspired her with his art and his passion. She pulled this photo from the pile, setting it on top of the smaller stack before gathering up the rest of Charlie's things and placing them back into the box.

She put in a load of laundry and straightened up her space in the house, but she was restless. Her restlessness only grew as she thought about Charlie and the notebook. What was he thinking? Was he getting it? Was anything penetrating his thick skull?

When the restlessness overcame her, she went back out for a bike ride to clear her head. The sun was just setting as she turned onto the boardwalk for the second time that day. With the wind at her back and the scent of salty brine on the air, she rode on, wishing she had someone to talk to, someone to listen to her as she sorted out the things in her head.

Kate parked her bike at a rack in front of a long row of beach shops and restaurants. The lights on Newport Pier had just turned on, casting light out into the darkening sea. After she

did some window-shopping, the scent of seafood drew her across Newport Boulevard, where a line of people stood outside the boxy red Crab Cooker restaurant. She got in line, unsure of what to expect. Signs advertising the World's Best Clam Chowder persuaded her to give it a try. She bought a small loaf of sourdough bread and a cup of chowder to go, deciding to enjoy it with a view of the ocean. But a good meal and beautiful surroundings did little to calm her restlessness. As she walked out to the end of the pier and back again, her thoughts turned once again to prayer. And by the time she made it back to her bike, she was feeling much better. She still had no idea how things would work out, but she was once again left with a calm in her heart that work out they would. She was just about to mount her bike when some small picture albums in a bin outside a souvenir shop prompted an idea. A minute later, she was pedaling home with one of the small albums in her basket.

Kate was awake long before she needed to be the next morning. She got up and showered before trying on several different outfits, finally settling on a long lightweight skirt and a blue top that she hoped would not offer Charlie any distractions. Four minutes early, she pulled up just outside of Charlie's garage. There was still some anxiety, but she pushed it away, replacing it with the memory of the calm she had experienced the day before. She closed her eyes prayerfully, inviting that peace to stay and rub off on Charlie, giving him direction that might shed light and dispel any confusion.

"I hope you have my phone," she heard him say through the open car window. "I've been going through withdrawals."

"It's right here," she said, lifting it up for him to see. "I hope you have my notebook."

He lifted her bag through the window, setting it on the passenger seat and extending his hand for the phone.

"Are you coming with me?"

He squatted so their eyes were on the same level. "Why are you doing this, Kate?"

"Why am I doing what?"

"Why are you here? Why do you care?"

Kate looked at him for a long moment, not knowing what to say. Her mind raced though many possible answers, but she wasn't sure how he would respond to any of them. She wanted to say something that would make him get in the car—something that would make him listen. But nothing came to mind that didn't sound either desperate or manipulative. She wished she would have thought about this before and had a quicker answer. "I just want to help," she finally said.

He looked at her closely as if he were searching her face for any hints of insincerity. "That's good enough for me," he said, opening the door and stepping inside.

"You're coming?" she asked, feeling both relief and excitement.

He closed his eyes and nodded.

"Why did you change your mind?"

"Because of that stupid notebook."

Kate tried not to smile, grateful she had listened. "You read the whole thing?"

"Twice. I didn't sleep much."

"I'm sorry. You must be tired."

"No," he replied, shaking his head. He turned to look at her. "The weird thing is, I'm just the opposite. Why didn't you tell me all of this before?"

"I tried. You didn't want to hear it," she said, starting the car and pulling away from the curb just in case he decided to change his mind and bail.

He nodded. "I'm sorry."

"For what?"

"Part of the reason I couldn't sleep was because it felt like I was being crushed under a load of all the crap I've given people who've tried to help me. I've been a jerk—a big, fat, blind jerk. I'm sorry."

She nodded slowly, deciding it wasn't a good idea to be too quick to agree with him. "So what changed?"

"Kate, I've spent the last nineteen hours trying to figure this out, wondering how I could have misunderstood so many things. I feel like I've missed something that's made it impossible for me to see clearly."

"What's that?"

"I've been thinking this whole time that if I can just learn all there is to know about the towers—interview all the people who knew Simon, spend boatloads of time up there—that I'd understand why Simon went to all the trouble to build them. But I missed it. I feel like I've been trying to break through this by using my head as a battering ram. But after five years, I've only given myself a massive headache."

"So what's different now?"

He pulled out the notebook, opening it to Dr. Hermansen's note. "I never opened my heart and mind to possibility," he said, pointing to her handwriting. "Last night, I remembered Isaiah giving me the same advice on one of my earliest visits. It's been right there from the very beginning, but I didn't listen. I didn't want to. I was too full of my own ideas and too distracted by the color and texture of it all to think there was something more than skin-deep. And...I was afraid."

"Of what?"

"Of admitting that I felt something—maybe a lot of things. Like I told you in the beginning, you can't capture that on film. You can't make a movie about some feeling you don't even have words to explain. It felt like a waste of time to try to understand something that seemed like it was going the wrong direction. Almost two years ago, I tried explaining some of this to Isaiah, hoping he might be able to help me. I told him I felt like a beached whale—like I couldn't get back in the water and swim again."

"What did he say?'

"Oh, he basically told me that when the tide comes in, I need to be ready to swim and trust the people and the forces that were trying to help me back into the water. It sounded better than that, I'm sure, but that was the basic idea. And there was something cryptic about proceeding as the way opens and not letting my pride get in the way."

Kate smiled. "Charlie, what if we started from the beginning? What if we went up there today and forgot that you spent five years taking thousands of photographs? What if we looked at it through new eyes, without any biases? What if you let me interpret some of the symbolism I've discovered there?"

"I don't know."

"Have you got a better idea?"

"I thought I did."

"But?"

He shook his head. "I thought if I could just get rid of all my research and forget how much time I spent up there that I'd be able to forget it and move on with my life."

"It didn't work?"

"Nope. Not even a little bit."

"Do you know why?"

"I've been trying to figure that out all month. And then you handed me this notebook yesterday, and I'm feeling like...like maybe I missed something. Maybe a lot of things."

"I don't mean to sound too eager to agree with you, but I think maybe you missed some of the most important things."

He took a deep breath and nodded. "So, what is it that you have that I don't?"

"What do you mean?"

"I thought you might have some kind of secret decoder ring or something when we were up at the towers last time. It felt like you saw stuff that I couldn't see even though I'd been looking at it a hundred times longer. What's your secret?"

"I don't really have any secrets. I don't think it's rocket science.

Maybe it's not even science at all. My dad was always quick to remind me that genuine humility is the only shortcut to all the wisdom the universe has to offer. Maybe it's just asking questions and learning how to listen for the answers."

"So you think Isaiah was right? You think it comes down to pride?"

"I can't say that. I'm not judging you. We all have roadblocks that keep us from learning—I mean, it seems like we're all stumbling around lost, but there aren't too many of us who stop and ask for directions."

"Pfff, who do you ask? I mean if we're all lost, who do you ask?"

"I guess there's always God, right?"

"Does everything in your life come back around to your faith?"

She nodded thoughtfully. "I guess it does—everything that's important anyway."

He forced a smile. "Sometimes I wish it was that easy for me."

"Who said anything about faith being easy?"

"So...it's *not* for you then?" He asked, looking surprised.

She looked at him incredulously. "Hey, I've had to earn every ounce of faith I have. I don't know any believer who would say their life's been easy. If anything, I would think that you atheists are the ones who have it easy."

"Why do you say that?"

"What do you have to defend? If there's nothing out there, as you claim, then I imagine you're life's got to be pretty easy—not worrying about your actions, not worrying about the future. I can see why it would be an attractive ideology."

"You can?" he asked, looking surprised. "I've never known a believer to admit that."

"I think that every believer has probably at least wondered what it would be like to live life on the other side of the fence—to run wild and free, not caring about tomorrow, doing whatever feels good. But I'd guess that most believers can see far enough down that road to recognize that that line of thinking has never really ended well for anyone. It seems like most people who live that lifestyle either end up looking a lot like a car wreck themselves or leaving a wake of carnage and heartache in their path."

"That's a pretty big generalization."

"Maybe it is, but tell me I'm wrong."

Charlie just shook his head.

"Listen," Kate continued. "I get that we're on opposite ends of a long stick, but maybe we could meet somewhere in the middle."

"What are you suggesting?"

"I guess I'm suggesting that there's probably an ideological place where we could find peace."

"You sound like Isaiah."

"Thanks. I'll take that as a compliment."

"He's crazy, you know."

"Some of the very best and wisest people I've ever known are a little crazy."

"Isn't that a contradiction?"

"I don't think so. Sometimes crazy is just…different from the status quo. Was Simon crazy?"

"That's debatable. I've heard it argued both ways."

"But in the end, does it really matter either way?"

Charlie shrugged.

They pulled onto the freeway, creating a pause long enough for Kate to consider the direction she hoped this conversation would go. "So, can I go back to a question Isaiah asked the last time we were up there?"

"Uh, I guess."

"He seemed to think you were headed in the right direction, at least for a while. But he said you stopped asking questions. How come?"

Charlie didn't answer, but his facial expression made him look very uncomfortable.

"Do you think that maybe there was something about the answers you were getting that made you feel vulnerable?"

He turned his head, looking at her incredulously. "Are you some kind of mind reader?"

"Oooh, dang! You figured me out."

"Really?"

"No!" she said, holding back her laughter. "I'm a social worker, remember? You can learn a lot about a person by the vulnerabilities they try to protect and the lengths they'll go to in protecting them. I'm sure it's probably part of human nature to not want to ask the hard questions."

"You think so?"

She shrugged. "Sure. It's hard on the ego to recognize you don't have all the answers. And in all fairness, I think lots of people are afraid of getting an answer that might cause them to change or think different. Most of us hold onto the ideas that formed our opinions, even when those ideas are proven false or flawed. Change is hard for all of us. We like to keep things easy and comfortable."

Charlie nodded, turning to Dr. Hermansen's note at the front of the notebook. Kate watched as he ran through each line with his finger as if he were looking for something specific.

"I've been thinking about this since yesterday:

Remember that the key to understanding lies in your own ability to ask hard questions—and in learning to expect real answers.

"That was helpful?"

"Yes. I'm not sure when it started, but looking back, I realized that somewhere along the line I stopped looking for answers."

"What do you mean? Isn't that why you kept going?"

"That's what I told myself, but..."

"But?" Kate repeated after a long silence.

"I didn't realize it until I was reading this notebook last night, but maybe I'm the same way Dr. Hermansen was."

"What way is that?"

"Skeptical in just about every way," he said with a laugh. "I realized last night that I haven't *really* been looking for answers. I didn't understand that until I read that bit you marked for me in your Bible."

"Wait, what?"

"That part you highlighted for..." He trailed off, recognizing she didn't know what he was talking about. He pulled the Bible from her bag and opened it to the note her father had written, pointing to the passage from James that she had discovered the day before.

"My dad marked that for me," Kate said. "I actually forgot the Bible was still in the bag when I gave it to you."

"So you didn't plan on me reading that?"

"No, I...why?"

He turned back to the Bible and read the words aloud. *"If any of you lacks wisdom, let him ask God, who gives generously to all without reproach, and it will be given him. But let him ask in faith, with no doubting, for the one who doubts is like a wave of the sea that is driven and tossed by the wind. For that person must not suppose that he will receive anything from the Lord; he is a double-minded man, unstable in all his ways."* James 1:5-8

"So, what did you think after reading that?" Kate asked after an awkward pause.

"Honestly, it totally ticked me off."

She nodded, not sure how to respond.

"But then I read that notebook and recognized she had the same brand of skepticism and cynicism that I had. Reading about that—in her own words—it made me realize that her attitude only kept her from finding real answers. It only kept her from opening up and seeing a bigger, brighter picture, didn't it?"

Kate nodded again, "But you know that she learned to listen?"

He nodded but didn't speak for a moment "I know it was none of my business, but I read that letter from your dad."

"Oh, that's okay. I'm sure I would have done the same."

"I think you and I grew up on totally different planets."

She smiled. "I'm sure you're probably right, but why do you say that?"

"That whole foundation thing your dad talks about—I'm pretty sure my parents never even thought about any of that. I don't remember ever thinking about a God who cared about any of my decisions. It just wasn't part of who we were."

"I'm sorry."

"What do you mean, *you're sorry*?"

"Charlie, I grew up believing there was a God in the heavens who knew me and loved me. I forgot that from time to time over the years, but having that in my life—knowing that foundation of love and grace and patience—it kept me..." She paused, recognizing the parallels between her upbringing and the gentle lesson Sammy had given her on the potter's wheel two days earlier. "It kept me centered."

"Centered? What does that mean?"

Kate nodded solemnly. "I'm just making sense of this now, but for the past few weeks, I've been trying to remember how to use a potter's wheel so I can teach my patients. I thought it would be like riding a bike, but it's been way harder than I remember it being in high school. I just couldn't get into the groove. The only things I've been able to make is a lot of dirty laundry and some very lopsided dog bowls."

"I tried that once back in high school. I had a friend who was taking a class and let me try once after school."

"How'd it go?"

"Let's just say it made me appreciate art forms where I don't have to get my hands dirty. It was really frustrating to see her making perfect vases and mugs and all I made was mud."

"Yeah, well, it takes some practice, but when you figure it out, it can be really satisfying to create something beautiful out of mud. Maybe, if you want, we could try it again sometime."

"Thanks, but I don't need any dog bowls."

"Yeah, neither do I. But I think I finally figured out what my problem was, with a little help from Sammy," she said, pointing to the notebook.

"Wait. You actually met him?" he asked, looking surprised.

"Yeah, just on Friday. He breezed through the studio and helped me understand what I was doing wrong."

"Huh? He does pottery too?"

"Yeah. You know that pencil vase on Isaiah's desk? He made that!"

"Really?"

"Yeah. The guy's got skill."

"And I assume all of this ties together somehow?"

"I think it does. Looking back on the last couple of weeks, I see that I really wasn't paying close enough attention to the centering process—I was rushing through things when I should have been more patient. I was anxious to get on with trying to raise the walls of the pot, and because of that, I was skipping through one of the most important steps. When Sammy showed me that I wasn't truly centered, I realized that no matter how bad I wanted it, it couldn't have gone any better. You can have the best clay and equipment in the world, but unless you get your clay centered, your pots will always be at least a little skiwampy and will never reach their full potential. I didn't think about it until just now, but maybe our lives are the same way. Maybe, without centering—without a firm, solid foundation—we don't have the ability to reach our full potential."

Charlie took a deep breath. "That's what Dr. Hermansen discovered in the end, isn't it?"

"I think so."

He looked out the side window for at least a minute before he spoke again. "That foundation that your dad talks about—if you could boil it down and put it in a nutshell, what is it?"

Kate smiled, remembering the many talks she'd had with her father over the years. "I think it all boils down to love, Charlie. My dad taught me that God's eternal love for His children is the only sure foundation he knows, that it is the only thing we could build our lives and our families on that would not fail or shift or fall apart. He taught me that keeping God's commandments would help me stay in a place where I could be constantly nourished by His love. My parents taught all of us that even though we might wander from God's love, it would be right there, waiting to embrace us every time we wanted to return."

"I guess I've always imagined that if there is a God, He's more interested in judging us than loving us. I think I'd prefer a god like you have, but the only thing I've got to go on is a lifetime of hard knocks and disappointments. It's hard for me to imagine a God who loves when life is so full of tragedy and heartache. I mean, do you ever doubt? Do you ever wonder if this is just a big galactic accident?"

"Doubt, yes. Galactic accident? Uhh, I can't say I've ever really considered that a reasonable possibility. But if you're asking if I wonder about the purpose of life then, yeah—all the time. Sounds like in spite of your aversion to the spiritual, you've been considering the purpose of life too."

He looked surprised. "Yeah, I've been trying to figure this out since I was eleven."

Kate nodded, remembering the story Andy had shared with her. "Was that due to an event or just a point of questioning in your existential development?"

"Probably both. My sister drowned...in a riptide."

"I'm really sorry," she said, putting her hand on his forearm.

"Yeah, well...I've blamed myself for it all these years. I was supposed to be watching her. I was supposed to take care of her. Where was God in that?"

She shook her head. "I don't know, Charlie. I'm sure I don't have the answers that would make any of that better. My dad used to say that he looked forward to the grand Q&A in the sky, where he hoped there would be satisfactory answers to some of his most difficult questions. I wish I had an answer for you, but the only balm I know is love. I can't say if it makes everything better, but I've found that it dulls the pain of mortality and offers light and hope when the world feels dark and unforgiving."

"I guess we all have to look for something, don't we?"

"I think so—or curse the darkness."

"Maybe that's where I've been for the last thirteen years—cursing the darkness. How have you been able to maintain your hope and beliefs in a world with so much chaos and darkness?"

She thought for a moment. "I guess it always comes back to that foundation of love. Growing up on a farm, hope and faith were sometimes the only thing we had to live on. You gotta have hope and faith to spend thousands of dollars and several weeks' worth of time to put seeds in the ground. We grew up praying over the fields and the animals. We prayed for rain. We prayed for protection from insects and hail and bad weather. Sometimes it felt like those prayers were the only thing that kept us alive physically, spiritually, and financially."

Charlie nodded, trying to imagine the world she was talking about. "Why does it have to be so hard?"

"What? Life?"

He nodded.

"I don't know, but it seems like life is really only hard when we're alone. I've never wandered very far from the foundation my parents built for me, and I've always come back to it when I have strayed. It's never been without its challenges, but I've lived long enough and seen enough of it to know that life without God's love is much darker and more hopeless. I know what being centered is. I know there is safety and the potential for growth there. I know enough about God's love to know that I want to stay connected to it—that I want to embrace it with all I have in me."

Belief is a wise wager. Granted that faith cannot be proved, what harm will come to you if you gamble on its truth and it proves false? If you gain, you gain all; if you lose, you lose nothing. Wager, then, without hesitation, that He exists.
Blaise Pascal

CHAPTER 31

EVIDENCE UNSEEN

The highest knowledge is to know that we are surrounded by mystery.
Neither knowledge nor hope for the future can be the pivot of our life
or determine its direction. It is intended to be solely determined by our allowing
ourselves to be gripped by the ethical God, who reveals Himself in us,
and by our yielding our will to His.
—Albert Schweitzer

Kate reached behind her and picked up the small photo album, setting it down in Charlie's lap.

"What's this?"

"It's the rest of that treasure map."

Charlie looked closer at the colorful sunset and ran his thumb across the word CALIFORNIA embossed on the glossy cover. "What is it really?"

"Go ahead and open it."

He opened the cover to a photo of hearts stamped into colorful concrete. "This is from the towers."

"Yeah. All of those pictures are. I know I'm no expert, but I was hoping that you'd let me tell you some of the treasure I've seen in Simon's work."

"You're trying to make a convert out of me?"

She shook her head. "I don't know enough to convert anyone. I only want to try to interpret the writing on the wall."

He took a deep breath, exhaling loudly. "At this point I don't have anything to lose, do I?"

"I don't think so. But there might be a lot to gain."

"You almost sound cocky."

"I don't mean to. But I do feel pretty confident that there's more to Simon's creation than you've allowed yourself to see."

"Is that right?"

"Yeah. What do you see in that picture?" she asked, pointing.

"Hearts."

"Which symbolize what?"

"Love," he said, rolling his eyes.

"That's pretty good for a boy," she teased. "The next several photos show some of the other hearts—the one at the far end of the complex, the one at the opening of the gazebo, the one above Simon's front door. As far as I can tell, hearts are one of the main motifs in his work, right?"

He nodded as he flipped through several photos of hearts. "So, what are you thinking?"

"You know that feeling you say you've felt but can't explain or find words to describe?"

"Yeah."

"I think that feeling is love. I think that's his sermon."

"Sermon?"

She nodded. "Isaiah told me that he thought Simon built the towers as a sermon—as an invitation to let your light shine. Considering that he used to hold church services there, it doesn't seem like much of a stretch to think that love and light would play a role in understanding his intentions—and his sermon. Both love and light are usually associated with the fruits of the Spirit."

"The fruits of the Spirit?" he asked, casting her a weird look.

"You've never heard that expression before?"

"No. Is that some kind of Christian thing?"

"Yeah, it's one of the basics—like probably one of the most important things there is in faith. Have you ever heard of Galatians?"

"Uh, doesn't that have something do with Greek mythology?"

"Really?"

"Yeah, I think she was a nymph or something like that…"

She shook her head. "Okay, stop for a minute. Is there such a thing as a nymph?"

"Well, I don't know. There is in Greek mythology."

"Yes, the Greeks were pagans, and they call it mythology for a reason."

He looked at her expectantly.

"They're all myths," she continued. "People just made that stuff up, probably to justify bad behavior in most cases."

"So what are the Galatians you're talking about?"

"They're the people from Galatia. I think it's part of Turkey today. Anyway, the Apostle Paul went there to try to straighten things out. After Jesus was crucified, the church kind of fell into chaos. People were doing all sorts of different things, basically muddying the waters by mixing in pagan traditions and falling away from the simple truths that Jesus taught."

She pulled her phone from the center console and handed it to Charlie, poking the screen until it opened to where she wanted. "This kind of outlines the two sides of life—the trappings of the flesh and the blessings of the Spirit."

"You want me to read this?"

"Please."

"What is it?"

"It's the fifth chapter of Galatians."

"Wait, you've got the Bible on your phone?" he asked incredulously.

"Thirty-two gigabytes of memory's got to be good for something, right?"

"You mean besides video games," he responded with a smile, raising the phone to his face. "What do you want me to read?"

"Start with verse nineteen there," she pointed.

"Now the works of the flesh are obvious, which are: adultery, sexual immorality, uncleanness, lustfulness, idolatry, sorcery, hatred, strife, jealousies, outbursts of anger, rivalries, divisions, heresies, envyings, murders, drunkenness, orgies, and other things like these; of which I forewarn you, even as I also forewarned you, that those who practice such things will not inherit the Kingdom of God."

"Well, I'm screwed," he responded, laughing. "I guess I'm better off not believing in God."

"You're not done," she said with a smile. "You haven't gotten to the good part yet."

"Oh, great, there's more hellfire and damnation!" he responded sarcastically. "Is it going to tell me I'm going to hell for making YouTube videos?"

"Just read it."

He shook his head, turning back to the phone. *"But the fruit of the Spirit is love, joy, peace, patience, kindness, goodness, faith, gentleness, and self-control. Against such things there is no law."* Charlie looked up at Kate, obviously surprised. He looked down again and reread the last verses silently. "Well, that's definitely not what I expected," he said humbly.

"I think that whole chapter is about the differences between the world of flesh and the things of the Spirit."

"So..." he responded, looking down at the phone again, "this peace, love, goodness...if those are the fruits...what spirit is this referring to?"

"You don't know?"

He shook his head. "I'm guessing you're going to tell me this has something to do with God, right?"

"Charlie, there's nothing to be afraid of," she replied, sensing his hesitation.

"You mean besides the fact that this challenges everything I've ever thought."

"Well, maybe it's time to think outside your box."

He shook his head. "You make that sound easy."

"Isn't it?"

"Kate, I've had twenty-four years of practice at this. This isn't something you're going to change in an hour."

"Well, I guess it's a good thing we have a couple of hours then."

He shook his head but smiled.

"Look, we've already established that you've got nothing to lose. Can you just try on this idea for a little bit and see how it feels? If it still doesn't work for you, I'll leave you alone and never bother you again."

"You'd give up that easy?"

"Charlie, I don't have anything to lose, but it's not like I have much to gain either."

"Then why do it? Why are you doing this?"

"Because of that," she said, pointing to the photo of the heart that graced the entry to Simon's gazebo.

"Because of love?" he asked incredulously.

"That's what I signed up for when I became a Christian—to love God and to love my neighbor as myself. Love is the first fruit of the Spirit. I felt it the first time I visited the towers, and I think you did too, even if you didn't know what it was. And I think that's what draws people in from all over the world whether they know it or not. Sure, the towers

Matthew 22:36-40

John 13:35

are beautiful and artistic, but they're in the middle of a run-down, unwelcoming slum. And that doesn't seem to stop anybody. People still come—tens of thousands of them every year."

"I know," he acquiesced. "Isn't that crazy?"

"No, it's a natural response. We're all drawn to light and love. We all need both in order to be happy. And most of us will go to great lengths to find it."

Charlie nodded knowingly. "In all my efforts to try and forget about it, I recognized last night that it's where I've experienced the greatest peace I've ever known. There's a part of me that wants to share it with the world, but another part of me wants to protect it—to hide it away and keep it safe."

Kate nodded thoughtfully before shaking her head. "That's not what Simon did."

He looked up.

"Simon didn't hide his light. He let it shine—big. He built a ladder and climbed to the top of it, and he turned his little light into a lighthouse. You don't do that—spending most of your life and your money—if you don't have something to share, something that you know people need!"

He nodded slowly. "So...love and peace and joy, huh? Not exactly things you'd expect to find in a slum, right?"

"No. But it's there. And maybe it glows brighter because it's there. Maybe that was part of Simon's genius—to create an oasis of light and love and hope in a desert of darkness."

"You believe that?"

"I do. Do you know what I mean when I say it's a city set on a hill?"

He gave her a look of uncertainty.

"It's from the Sermon on the Mount," she explained.

He looked confused. "And what's that again?"

"It's all about Jesus outlining the basics of his gospel of peace. If Simon was a preacher, he for sure would have known the Sermon on the Mount. In it, Jesus calls on the faithful to lift up their small lights so others can come to know of the love of God. I really believe that's what Simon's purpose was. That love—and the other fruits of the spirit that you and I have felt there stand as a witness that he accomplished what he set out to do."

Charlie nodded slowly. "You don't think those can be associated with other things—something other than God?"

"Haven't you spent the last five years trying to find an answer to that question?"

He let out a long breath, nodding slowly.

"If there's light, there has to be darkness, too. And I believe the dark side is pretty clever in making evil look and feel enticing. But Jesus taught his disciples how not to be fooled by counterfeits."

"Wait, he did?"

She nodded, pointing back to the phone. "I thought you might ask, so I highlighted it there." She touched the phone, opening it to the seventh chapter of Matthew.

"You want me to read this?"

"Please."

"*Beware of false prophets, which come to you in sheep's clothing, but inwardly they are ravening wolves. Ye shall know them by their fruits. Do men gather grapes of thorns, or figs of thistles? Even so every good tree bringeth forth good fruit; but a corrupt tree bringeth forth evil fruit. A good tree cannot bring forth evil fruit, neither can a corrupt tree bring forth good fruit. Every tree that bringeth not forth good fruit is hewn down, and cast into the fire. Wherefore by their fruits ye shall know them.*" Charlie looked up, surprised. "Do you really think it can be that easy?"

"I think that's what Simon learned. I think that's probably part of the message that he was trying to share."

"You think so?"

Matthew 7:15–20

"Charlie, Simon knew the dark side, right? You told me he spent at least a decade in a bad place. I don't think you can get out of that without learning to choose light over dark, without learning to sort out the good fruits from the evil ones. I think maybe it is that easy. I think the towers became a place where he could share his message of hope and mercy and redemption and grace."

Charlie sat silent for a moment. "So, if what you say about Simon's intent is true, I assume you've got a lot more to back you up than just these hearts?"

"You mean besides the fruits that you've already experienced?"

"I'm talking about evidence. I told you I'm a skeptic. I need to see more if you're gonna convince me. What else have you got to support your theories?"

She pointed to the album. "That album's full of evidence. Where do you want to start?"

He turned to the next photo—a picture of concrete that had been stamped all over with a simple flower design. "You think this has some deep meaning too?"

"I do."

He looked back to the photo, looking for what he had missed. "I'm guessing you know how he made these impressions."

"I'm a farm girl, remember? I've turned on many a spigot in my lifetime. It took me a minute, but I recognized the shape of the handle. And I think there's a deeper meaning behind them."

"You think this is also a symbol of love?"

"Indirectly. I did a quick search on the internet for flowers with six petals. I know it doesn't look exactly like it, but I think these might be an interpretation of daffodils."

"What do daffodils have to do with anything?"

"Flowers carry meaning. Roses often symbolize love. Violets symbolize faithfulness and purity. Daffodils are symbols of new beginnings, hope, and rebirth."

"Seriously?"

"Look it up if you don't believe me."

"No, I trust you," he said, taking a closer look. "I thought Simon was just filling space so he didn't have to do so much mosaic. It's gotta be a lot easier to just press a tool into the wet cement than to cover it with tile or glass."

"I'm sure you're right. There are lots of ways Simon could have cut corners, but that doesn't seem to be his style. If anything, he made things far more ornamented than was necessary. But he was Italian, remember. He would have grown up around art and symbols. I bet he was probably far more literate in symbolism than you or I will ever be. Symbols give different people a chance to see and understand different things, depending on where they are in life and what they know. From all that I've seen, he knew what he was doing. And everything he did played into expressing God's love." She looked over at the photo. "Even if those don't represent daffodils, even if they are just handles to turn on a hose, I can think of at least a couple of Bible stories that support my ideas."

"Like what?"

"Jesus once said, 'If any man thirst, let him come unto me and drink.'"

Charlie laughed after a moment. "Was he a bartender?"

"No," she responded with a smile, realizing she had set herself up for that one. "He wasn't talking about liquid refreshment. He was talking about truth and light. He was talking about hope, and he was talking about the Holy Spirit. Have you ever heard the story of Jesus talking to the woman at the well?"

"I'm sure I haven't."

"I think that might give you a better understanding of what it was Jesus was offering. He met a woman who had gone to a well to get water for her family, and he asked her to give him a drink. After she did, he told her that anyone who drank of that water would get thirsty again, but he told her that anyone who drank from the living water he had to offer would experience a symbolic source of water bubbling up into everlasting life and would never thirst again."

Charlie looked confused. "Wait, what kind of water was he talking about?"

"He was talking symbolically. He was talking about the Holy Spirit."

He nodded slowly. "Is that the same thing as the fruits of the Spirit you were just talking about?"

"Not exactly. One is the fruit, and one is the tree, symbolically speaking. The fruits of the Spirit are what you feel when the Holy Spirit is near you. The way I understand it, the Holy Spirit's job is to testify of things that are true. I grew up learning that when we experience the fruits of the Spirit, we are doing the right things or headed in the right direction—that sort of thing. My parents taught us that the fruits of the Spirit would help us stay on the path to happiness. If we were experiencing those fruits—love, joy, hope—regularly, we knew we were probably on the right path. But if we weren't, it might be good to look around and see if maybe we were lost and find our way back. I'm not sure if those impressions are a symbol of new beginnings or the living waters of the Holy Spirit—or maybe both—but either way, it feels like it definitely ties back to the hearts."

Charlie looked back to the album. "And this? You think there's

meaning behind this one too?" he asked, pointing to a picture of the frieze of wheat and grapes.

She invited him to turn to the next photo—a black-and-white picture of Simon standing behind the mold from which the frieze had been created.

"Hey, this picture's from the storyboards on the outside of the fence."

"I know. Hiding in plain sight. Look at his face. Look at the way he's pointing to the wheat. There's something there he's trying to say."

"What do you think it is?"

"I think he's trying to say that this is important. I looked up symbolic hand gestures related to Christianity, and that sign there is a variation on the hand gesture that Jesus is often shown making in Christian art throughout the world. He's pointing at the symbols of Jesus's Triumphal Entry, the Last Supper, the Cross, and the Resurrection. That one frieze holds symbols that tell all the stories that Christians consider most important to their faith. And Simon is pointing at them using a gesture that is symbolic of the Trinity—three in one."

Charlie held the photograph closer to his face as Kate explained the meaning behind the palm fronds, the wheat and grapes, the dogwood and the lily. She went on to explain with the aid of the next photo that the placement of this frieze above the deep basin was also significant since it was a place of baptism—a place where Christian covenants were made. But a photo of the deep basin itself with the archway rising from its floor also provided another significant symbol.

She had Charlie scroll to another passage of scripture on her phone, this one just above the bit he had read before: *Enter ye in at the strait gate: for wide is the gate, and broad is the way, that leadeth to destruction, and many there be which go in thereat: Because strait is the gate, and narrow is the way, which leadeth unto life, and few there be that find it.*

"That's the narrow gate, isn't it?" he asked, pointing to the concrete archway that rose from the middle of the basin.

"That's what I was thinking. Most Christians believe baptism is the entryway to the straight and narrow path." As she explained these things and the symbolism behind the photos she had selected, Charlie began to see many things he had walked past dozens of times over the last five years but had obviously missed.

"I couldn't decide if I wanted to start with the hearts or the ship," she said, pointing to the next picture.

"You mean the boat at the front of the complex?" he asked, looking confused.

"Yes."

"What about it?"

Matthew 7:13–14

"Do you see where it's sailing?"

"Yeah," he laughed. "Right into where the walls converge."

"Yes, but have you ever considered the cardinal direction that it's headed in—that the whole complex is oriented toward?"

"No. Why?"

"It's all positioned and pointing due east."

"And?"

"That doesn't mean anything to you?"

"Should it?"

"Many cultures tie symbolism to each of the cardinal directions. In the Chinese feng shui tradition, east represents things like compassion, love, and trust. The Celts believed it symbolized new beginnings, wind, and communication. Jews and Muslims build their mosques and temples with their doors facing east. So do many Christian churches, because we believe Jesus will return in his glory coming from the east. Even many Native Americans imbue the east with salvation. It's also the direction of the rising sun, of the hope that comes after a long, dark night."

Charlie shook his head.

"You don't believe me?"

"No, it's not that. I probably told you that Simon looked at several properties before he settled on this one, right?"

"Yeah, I remember."

"According to a woman I interviewed, this was the only one that would work for him. I always thought that he bought it because it was the cheapest—being on the edge of the railroad and such a weird shape for a lot. I guess I'm just realizing that maybe there's more to it than that. Do you think he would have known all these things?"

"Yes. I don't know if there's anything he did here that he didn't do deliberately. Even down to the shells," she said pointing to the next picture. There were several pictures of the sun-bleached clamshells that were embedded in the concrete and on the wall and that covered the structures. "There must be thousands of those," she guessed.

"I've actually heard that there are over *seventy-five thousand*."

"That's incredible."

"And you think there's meaning in those, too?"

"I do?"

He looked down at the photos. "Couldn't they just be cheap decorations—a way to cover big patches without spending a lot of money?"

"Sure, they could be, but that would be contrary to everything else he did. I believe there's deep meaning behind them." She pointed to her phone, trying to keep her eyes on the road. "Click on that."

"What's this?"

"It's part of the same Sermon on the Mount."

"Give not that which is holy unto the dogs, neither cast ye your pearls before swine, lest they trample them under their feet, and turn again and rend you."

"Rend you? That doesn't sound very good!"

"I think it means to tear to shreds."

"Awesome!" he proclaimed sarcastically.

"What is?"

"This just validated every concern I've ever had about making my film. I'm pretty sure I don't have the emotional strength to be trampled or torn to shreds—even metaphorically."

Kate laughed. "There's more to it than that. Look where Simon put the shells," she pointed at the photo. "I don't see any of them that could be easily trampled, do you? They're all off the ground, even climbing to the tops of the towers."

"So wait," he said, looking confused. "You're trying to tie Simon's clam shells to the pearls from what I just read?"

"Yes."

"That's gonna be a problem. I'm pretty sure pearls come from oysters."

Matthew 7:6

"Actually, I looked this up too. Oyster pearls are the most common, yes, but some clams also make pearls. In fact, all of the largest, most valuable pearls in the world have come from clams, including the very largest, which was worth ninety-three million dollars ten years ago."

"Seriously? For a pearl?"

"That's what Wikipedia said."

"Okay, but what was he trying to say with either clams or pearls?"

"In another chapter, Jesus compares the kingdom of heaven to a merchant seeking pearls, who, when he finds a very valuable one, is willing to sell all that he has in order to buy it."

"I don't know," Charlie said, looking unconvinced.

"Isn't that what Simon did? Didn't he give up the life he had before in order to build his towers—in order to share his message of hope and redemption?"

Charlie nodded.

"But the symbol of the clam has other meanings too."

"And let me guess—it's a symbol of love?"

"Good job! You're catching on. Scroll over to my photos," she said, pointing to her phone. He did, and she poked the picture she was thinking of. "Do you recognize that?"

"Uh, yeah, I think so, but I can't remember what it's called."

"That's Botticelli's *The Birth of Venus.*"

"And there's a connection between this and the towers?"

"What is she standing on?"

Charlie looked closer at the small screen. "Is that really a clamshell?"

"Yes."

"What does it represent?"

"This is a complicated one. Venus, of course, was a mythological Roman goddess—the goddess of love, in fact. But in astronomy, the planet Venus is known as the morning star. It's the third-brightest light in the sky and usually rises in the east shortly before the sun."

Charlie looked confused.

"In the book of Revelation, the last book of the New Testament,

Matthew 13:45

Jesus refers to himself as the Morning Star but also calls himself Alpha and Omega, which are the first and the last letters in the Greek alphabet."

"Sounds like he might have had an identity crisis."

Kate shook her head. "It's not like that. Jesus was talking metaphorically—symbolically. Among other things, he was referring to his life, sacrifice, and resurrection as the beginning of eternal life and the end of physical and spiritual death."

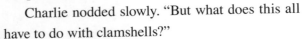

Charlie nodded slowly. "But what does this all have to do with clamshells?"

"That!" Kate said, pointing to Botticelli's Venus. "I did a little research and found out that Venus is a symbol of Christ, rising in the east, giving hope to those who wait for the long night of darkness to be over. The clamshell is still used today as a symbol of faith. In fact, pilgrims along the Camino de Santiago in France and Spain carry shells with them as symbols of their pilgrimage. In Christian art around the world, the shell is generally associated with James, one of Jesus's most loyal apostles, but it's widely considered to be a symbol of Christianity."

"This is starting to sound like a Dan Brown novel."

"I felt the same way as all of these things started coming together. I'm convinced Simon must have had a lot of help."

"Didn't I tell you? He built the towers entirely by himself."

Kate nodded. "I was actually talking about a different kind of help—more of a spiritual help."

"I don't know," he said, looking back down at the pictures in his lap. "I'm still not convinced. People see what they want to see."

"I won't argue with you. What do you want to see?"

"I want proof that Simon was thinking about what you say he was thinking."

"I don't know if you'll ever get that proof. Faith never works that way."

"Are you saying that your faith wouldn't be strengthened by some kind of physical proof of God's existence?"

"No, I'm not saying that at all. My uncle Ralph used to say, "All I have seen teaches me to trust the Creator for all I have not seen." Faith has never been based on what we can prove. It's seeing and *feeling* the hand of God in our lives. It's making connections, recognizing that he's leading us from step to step, giving us small nuggets of truth as we ask and receive and then ask for more."

"Now you really are sounding like Isaiah."

She laughed. "So anything you don't want to hear sounds like Isaiah?"

He grimaced.

"I guess it all comes back to those fruits of the Spirit for me," she continued. "I believe that only truth can feel true—that only the Holy Spirit, with its fruits of love, joy, and peace—can help us sort through life's questions and determine what's true and what's false."

"Doesn't that cut out the need for common sense and intellect?"

"I don't think so. I can't think of anything I believe in that runs contrary to common sense."

"Okay, how about this? You believe in a God who loves, yet the world is full of suffering and pain and death. How do you reconcile that?"

Kate shrugged. "Suffering is part of life. We learn to walk by falling down several hundred times. We learn who to trust by having a few people disappoint us. Everything has its opposite—good and evil—health and sickness—light and darkness. We learn in the choosing or, if we're lucky or wise, by watching others make choices and learning from their mistakes."

"But aren't you contradicting yourself? It doesn't take a genius to choose a better path after he's watched his friends do something stupid. Why do you need God? It seems like you can just be observant and avoid most of the challenges in life."

"You're probably right."

"That's it? That's all you got? You're not going to fight me on that?"

"What's the point?"

"Well, I just thought you…"

"Charlie, there are probably at least as many reasons for not believing in God as there are reasons to choose to believe, but for me, it all comes down to one question."

"What's that?"

"I've felt the undeniable love of God. I think you have too. The question for me is do I want to step closer toward that light or do I want to turn my back toward it and pretend it doesn't exist?"

Charlie nodded slowly. "It's that simple for you?"

"I can't think of a reason to make it any more complicated than that. Can you?"

He didn't answer.

"I guess there's another reason I choose to believe," she said after a moment.

He looked up.

"I know I need answers, and it's hard to imagine a better source for answers than the Creator of the universe."

"What makes you think he even cares?"

"You mean besides the love and joy and peace I've felt throughout my life?"

"Yeah."

She reached for the phone, and Charlie took the wheel for a moment as she found what she was looking for. She pointed to a passage that had been highlighted, handing the phone back to Charlie.

"You have an answer for everything?"

"No, but I believe there is an answer to everything—at least one."

He shook his head and turned back to her phone: *"Ask and it will be given to you; seek and you will find; knock and the door will be opened to you."* He glanced sideways before continuing. *"For everyone who asks receives; he who seeks finds; and to him who knocks, the door will be opened."*

Matthew 7:7

He looked up slowly. "You really believe this is true?"

"Yes, but you have to ask. Faith has always been a verb for me. If you don't ask, you can't expect answers. People get stuck because they give up. They stop knocking and asking and seeking. It happens to all of us, but this sounds like an invitation to get unstuck, right?"

He nodded slowly.

"There's more there if you want it," she said, pointing to the phone.

"What if I don't?" he asked, smiling.

"Then I guess you stay stuck."

He turned back to the phone. *"Which of you, if his son asks for bread, will give him a stone? Or if he asks for a fish, will give him a snake? If you, then, though you are evil, know how to give good gifts to your children, how much more will your Father in heaven give good gifts to those who ask him!"*

She was smiling when he finally looked up at her. "All good gifts begin with humility and a sincere question."

Charlie looked humble. "That's pretty much exactly what Dr. Hermansen said, isn't it?"

"Yes. There seems to be a pattern that's shared by everybody who gains any wisdom. You have to ask. And sometimes you have to continue to ask until the answers come. But that passage makes it clear that *somehow* they will come."

Matthew 7:9-11

"What else does this craving, and this helplessness, proclaim but that there was once in man a true happiness, of which all that now remains is the empty print and trace? This he tries in vain to fill with everything around him, seeking in things that are not there the help he cannot find in those that are, though none can help, since this infinite abyss can be filled only with an infinite and immutable object; in other words by God himself.   —Blaise Pascal

CHAPTER 32

A FIRM FOUNDATION

Heaven often seems distant and unknown,
but if He who made the road is our guide,
we need not fear to lose the way.
—Henry Van Dyke

"What else do you have in here?" he asked, thumbing through the photos, stopping at a picture of two tiles with peacocks carved into them.

"What do you know about those?" Kate asked, looking over at the album.

"I heard a tour guide say they were collectibles."

"Yeah, if you can find them. I saw a similar set that sold on eBay for twenty-five hundred dollars!"

"For a couple of tiles?"

"Yeah. They were made back in the twenties by a famous California tile maker—Batchelder, I think. They're super rare. But the symbolism is also cool."

"Don't tell me they're symbolic of love too?"

"Not exactly, but get this: peacocks are a symbol of the Resurrection and immortality."

Charlie looked down at the picture and shook his head. "Do you think Simon knew that?"

"I think he must have. Everywhere you turn, there's something to see that, I think, is supposed to prompt questions. I'm sure I've missed all sorts of good stuff."

"Okay, but you still haven't told me how you've been able to find the stuff you've discovered."

"I asked Isaiah if he had any advice for understanding what I was looking at. He suggested that I look through the lens of my faith." She looked down at the next photo. "You look at that and just see rocks, right?"

He looked closer at the photo and the next several photos, which showed images of volcanic rocks embedded in the walls, in the base of the second tower, and at the base of another structure that looked like a garden. "You're telling me you see something more than rocks?"

"Through the lens of my faith, yes."

He looked at the photos again, not seeing anything other than rocks. "I don't get it."

She smiled. "There's another verse in that same chapter that might help you understand," she said, pointing to the phone.

Charlie turned away from the photos and read the passage she pointed to:

Therefore whosoever heareth these sayings of mine, and doeth them, I will liken him unto a wise man, which built his house upon a rock: And the rain descended, and the floods came, and the winds blew, and beat upon that house; and it fell not: for it was founded upon a rock. And every one that heareth these sayings of mine, and doeth them not, shall be likened unto a foolish man, which built his house upon the sand: And

Matthew 7:24-29

the rain descended, and the floods came, and the winds blew, and beat upon that house; and it fell: and great was the fall of it.

"This is crazy," he said, shaking his head.

"What is?"

"Do you know what happened to the towers back in 1959?"

"No."

He shook his head as he made the connections. "A few years after Simon left, the city condemned the property. Some of the city engineers decided the towers had to be torn down."

"Why would they do that?"

"They thought they were dangerous. No one had ever seen anything like them. They created all sorts of arguments. They even had something like a week's worth of hearings, trying to decide what to do with them. A group of people who wanted to preserve them got another engineer involved. This guy figured the only way he'd be able to prove they were solid enough to not blow over in a windstorm was to put them up against a load test. The city demanded that the load be strapped up high on the center tower, believing it would just topple over and all the buttresses would bring everything else down with it."

"What?"

"Yeah. The engineers brought in a big crane; parked it across the street; and attached cables to the center tower, seventy feet up. While the neighbors gathered to either protest or encourage the destruction, the engineers applied ten thousand pounds of pressure to the side of the tower."

"Oh my gosh! What happened?"

"That's the crazy thing. They had over forty engineers betting the whole thing would just fall apart, but the towers resisted and stayed together. The cable actually lifted the crane off the ground before bending its arm."

"Did anything happen to the towers?"

"Yeah, one single shell fell off," he responded, laughing. "The engineers who'd shown up to see 'em fall went away feeling pretty stupid. It was decided that if they couldn't tear them down, they better do what they could to preserve them. All sorts of engineers and preservationists have tried to fix the small cracks that have shown up over the last sixty years. The crazy thing is, even with all the knowledge and know-how they've brought to the project, most of the repairs they've made have failed in months, where Simon's original work—as uneducated as he was—continues to last."

Kate smiled as she considered what she'd just been told. She glanced down at the photo of the second tower. *"And the rain descended, and the floods came, and the winds blew, and beat upon that house; and it fell not: for it was founded upon a rock,"* she mused, staring out at the road.

"So what does that rock symbolize?"

"What do you think?"

He looked at the three photos where the rocks were seen. "Do you think they all tie together somehow?"

"Yeah, I do."

He flipped back through the photos, stopping at the frieze of the wheat and grapes, recognizing the rocks that surrounded it. She watched as he flipped back and forth to the other photos of the rocks several times.

"What's the connection?" he finally asked.

"It might help if you back up all the way and look at the whole complex from across the street." She reached over and turned the page to a photo of the towers.

Charlie looked at the photo for nearly a minute before looking up. "What am I not seeing?"

"I think you do see it; you just don't know the symbolism." She turned back to the black-and-white photo of Simon pointing to the mold. "It has something to do with that."

He looked at the photos for a long time, searching for a connection.

"I don't think this was just his yard or just his church. I think this is a symbolic monument to the Godhead—to the Gods who saved him."

He looked confused. "Wait. What?"

"You've heard of the Trinity, right?"

"You're talking about that Catholic notion of the three-Gods-in-one stuff?"

"Yeah, but it's not just Catholic. Lots of different branches of Christianity teach some version of the idea that God is one but in the form of three persons: Father, Son, and Holy Spirit."

Charlie nodded thoughtfully. "I'll admit I haven't spent a lot of time thinking about this, but it sounds like a pretty confusing idea. Do you understand it?"

Kate shrugged. "I guess a lot of it is still a mystery for me, too. The Bible is both helpful and confusing about it, but looking at the towers..." she trailed off, glancing back down at the photo. "It's obviously highly symbolic, but I think this might actually clarify some of the things I've wondered about."

"Like what?"

"Well, some Christians teach that there is only one God who morphs into different apparitions when necessary. I guess it's always made more sense to me that the Godhead is united in a shared purpose but made up of three separate beings."

"This sounds familiar. I think I interviewed a woman who went to Simon's church who said something about this."

"Yeah, well, it seems pretty clear in some passages of the Bible, like when Jesus went to be baptized by John the Baptist in the River Jordan. There were three separate God-beings represented—Jesus in the water being baptized, the voice of God the Father speaking from heaven, and the Holy Spirit descending like a dove. It never made any sense that Jesus was some kind of a ventriloquist who could cast his voice into heaven and at the same time shave off a piece of himself to look like a dove while he's standing in the water being baptized. I mean, if we really are created in the image of God and we can't divide into three beings, why would God be that much different?"

Charlie laughed. "Don't look at me. I can't say I've ever even thought about it."

Kate smiled. "No, I guess not. It's just something I've tried to figure out over the years."

"And what have you come up with?"

"Probably something pretty similar to what Simon created."

"How do you mean?"

She pointed to the picture. "Each of the towers is different, but this one," she said, pointing to the third one, "is more different than the others for at least a few different reasons."

"It's smaller?"

"Obviously. But look at the color. Most of this tower is covered with green glass. I think this tower represents the Holy Spirit."

"Oh, right, because the Holy Spirit is also covered with green glass?" he responded sarcastically.

She shook her head, smiling. "If you're working with...what...glass, shells, rocks, cement, and tiles and you're trying to portray a spirit, it seems that it would make the most sense to use something transparent, right?"

He nodded.

"That's my first reason for thinking this tower represents the Holy Spirit, but there are probably at least a few others."

"Like what?"

She pointed to her phone again. "You already read some of the verses that referred to thirst, but read that one."

"*On the last and greatest day of the festival, Jesus stood and said in a loud voice, 'Let anyone who is thirsty come to me and drink. Whoever believes in me, as Scripture has said, rivers of living water will flow from within them.' By this he meant the Spirit, whom those who believed in him were later to receive.*"

Charlie set the phone aside, turning the pages in the album as if he

John 7:37-39

were looking for something until he came to a photo with an isolated view of the shortest tower. He ran his fingers over the hundreds, if not thousands, of green bottles covering the tower. "What was that bit you said about the woman at the well?"

She reached for the phone as he took the wheel. She found it quickly and handed it back to him.

John 4:14

"But whoever drinks the water I give them will never thirst. Indeed, the water I give them will become in them a spring of water welling up to eternal life."

"I think there's another cross-reference there," she said, pointing again to the screen.

1 Corinthians 12:13

"For we were all baptized in one Spirit so as to form one body—whether Jews or Gentiles, slave or free—and we were all given the one Spirit to drink." He looked at the passage for a moment before looking up. "What do you think that means?"

"I think it means that the Spirit unites all true believers—that it forms us into one body."

He looked confused. "How does that work?"

Kate paused, looking for an answer. As she did, another scripture came to mind, one she remembered from the cross-stitch that hung in the entryway of her family home. She poked at the phone as Charlie held it. "I think this is the answer."

John 13:34

He looked down and read, *"A new commandment I give unto you, That ye love one another; as I have loved you, that ye also love one another. By this shall all men know that ye are my disciples, if ye have love one to another."* He stared at the words, saying nothing for a long moment. When he finally did, his words were almost a whisper. "It always come back to love, doesn't it?"

"Yes," she replied, pointing back to the album. "I think those buttresses only support that idea."

He flipped the page to a photo of the first and second towers and the many arched buttresses that spanned the airspace between them.

"Those arches are different than the rest of the buttresses, aren't they?"

"You mean because of the hearts?"

"Well, yes, but more than that. I think most of the buttresses are probably for support—to tie the whole structure together and make it stronger."

Charlie nodded, thinking of the lower buttresses that spanned the promenade and tied into the outer walls.

"I think those are more than just support. Those look much more intentional, like they're an important part of the design. And the fact that there are twelve of them is also intriguing."

She watched as Charlie silently counted the spanning arms. "Twelve is kind of a big number in the Bible."

"Really?"

"I'm sure you've heard of the Twelve Apostles?"

He nodded.

"You might have also heard of Abraham, Isaac, and Jacob?"

"Maybe," he answered with hesitation.

"It's kind of a long story, but to make it shorter, they were the patriarchs of Israel. Jacob, Isaac's son and Abraham's grandson, had twelve sons of his own, and each of those sons became the leaders of their own tribes. They're known as the Twelve Tribes of Israel, and the Bible teaches that the House of Israel would be scattered and sifted into every nation of the earth. I think that basically means that everyone on the earth today has some portion of the blood of those patriarchs running through their veins."

Charlie looked confused. "So why would that have any significance to Simon?"

Kate pointed to picture of the second tower. "I think it has something to do with that. If I'm right, and that tower represents Jesus Christ, then that ring around the middle would have to represent his crown."

Charlie looked confused. "I thought Jesus had a crown of thorns."

"He did, but he was also known as the Prince of Peace. I think the only true way to have real, lasting peace is to have love, right?"

"What about those circles on the crown, the ones that are divided into four quadrants?"

"Oh, that's the internationally universal symbol for apple pie. Simon must have really liked his desserts."

"What?" he asked laughing.

Kate laughed too. "Those are actually eternal crosses."

"What's that?"

"There is one up there too," she said, pointing at the previous picture where the symbol hung above the hearts on the arched buttresses. "The cross in the middle is probably pretty obvious, at least to Christians, as the symbol of Christ's sacrifice, but the circle surrounding it is a symbol of eternity—think wedding rings. Together, the meaning is even more profound. Lots of people were crucified by the Romans, but only one of those—Jesus Christ, the Son of God—was an infinite and eternal sacrifice. Christians believe that Jesus's sacrifice paid for the sins of all mankind. It paid the debt of justice, making way for mercy and grace for all who believe and make covenants with God."

Charlie nodded, though he looked a little overwhelmed. "How do you know all this stuff?"

She shrugged. "When you grow up around it, seeing symbols in church and other places—and when you grow up reading the Bible, which is totally full of symbols too—you have to ask a lot of questions or you get lost."

"Okay, but who taught you these things?"

"I'm sure I picked up some of it from Sunday school and from my parents as we read the Bible at home, but to be honest, I think most of it came from just feeling my way through things."

"You mean that *feeling* again, right? About the... fruits?"

She nodded, turning back to the picture where the three towers stood proudly. "If what Isaiah told me is true—that you can only truly understand this through the lens of faith, then I think there are lots more secrets hiding in plain sight, waiting to be discovered and understood."

He lifted the album closer to his face.

"What are you thinking?" Kate asked

"You really think there's more?"

"Lots more. Everything Simon made has references to his faith. His work is his sermon. And all of it circles back to love."

"Is that really what your Jesus and your religion is all about?"

Kate nodded, glad to see he was finally getting it. She pulled up to the curb in front of the towers and turned off the car. She could see Isaiah standing near the gate as if he'd been waiting for them to arrive. "Can we finish this inside?" she asked.

He looked up from the album, suddenly recognizing where they were. "Lead on," he said softly. "Lead on."

"I was hoping you'd say that," she said with a smile. She reached behind him for the envelope on the back seat and handed it to him.

"What's this?"

"Open it."

He lifted the flap and looked inside, pulling out the note with the coin. He looked at the coin for moment before turning to Kate. "I don't understand. How did you get this?"

"It was given to me by someone who knew it would mean something to you."

IFF USE LURN OATROOTH— OATROOTH WIL SETCHUSE FREY!

He looked closer at the woman on the coin.

"Do you know what that is?" she asked.

"It's a fifty-cent piece, right?"

She shook her head. "It's an invitation."

"To what?"

She pointed to the top of the gazebo where the figurine sparkled in the sunlight. "That's Lady Liberty."

Charlie looked at the figurine, then back to the coin several times, making the connection. "Liberty...what the...heck?"

Kate laughed as she pointed to the crudely scrawled note. "If you learn the truth, the truth will set you free." She looked to Charlie's coin, then to the figurine at the top of the gazebo. "It's all here, hiding in plain sight. And listen to this." She reached for her phone and pressed the screen. *"Give me your tired, your poor, your huddled masses yearning to breathe free...Send these, the homeless, tempest-tost to me, I lift my lamp beside the golden door!"*

"What's that?"

"A poem that's inscribed on the base of the Statue of Liberty."

"Really? Read it again."

She read it a second time, emphasizing key words.

He shook his head, looking out at the small, simple lamp that stood tall and proud at the front of the walls surrounding the towers. "I haven't seen anything, have I?"

"Maybe not, but I don't know if that's what's most important."

"What do you mean?"

The New Colossus by Emma Lazarus

"You may have missed the details, but you felt something."

"Yeah, and a lot of good it's done me."

"Charlie, I think that feeling you've experienced probably did exactly what it was supposed to do."

"What, make me crazy?"

"No," she responded, smiling. She pointed to a patch of clamshells embedded in the outer wall. "It planted a golden grain of sand in your heart—it planted the seed of a pearl."

We have forgotten the gracious hand which has preserved us in peace and multiplied and enriched and strengthened us, and have vainly imagined in the deceitfulness of our hearts that all these blessings were produced by some superior wisdom and virtue of our own. Intoxicated with unbroken success, we have become too self sufficient to feel the necessity of redeeming and preserving Grace, too proud to pray to the God that made us.

Abraham Lincoln

CHAPTER 33

A NEW BEGINNING

You can't go back and change the beginning,
but you can start where you are and change the ending.
—C. S. Lewis

"You're late," Isaiah said, swinging open the gate to let them in.

"Kate told you we were coming?"

"No. He did," Isaiah said, tipping his head to Sammy, who was sitting in the same place he had been the last time Charlie had seen him. His eyes were closed as he faced the sun, his hands busy with the messages he was writing. They watched for a moment as the wind rustled the leaves of the eucalyptus before silently riding out across the lawn, parting the dandelions in its path. With a gentle grace, it picked up the small stack of Sammy's notes, lifting them higher and higher into the air before setting them free in all different directions. Kate smiled as she watched the notes disappearing, trying to imagine the people who would find them.

"Welcome home," Isaiah said, turning back to Charlie and clapping him on the shoulder.

Charlie smiled. "Why didn't you tell me about all of this?"

"Would you have heard it?"

He shrugged.

"I've been waitin' fo' you to ask. People come and go every day, but if they ain't listenin', they ain't gonna get much outta it. I've been waitin' fo' you to be ready—fo' you to believe there's more than what you've seen so far."

Charlie nodded slowly, looking humble. "Am I there yet?"

"That *all* depends on you, don't it?"

He nodded again, smiling at Kate before turning back to Isaiah. "So, do you have any advice for me?"

Isaiah's smile filled his face. "You just said the magic words."

THE END

You can find God if you will only seek — by obeying divine laws, by loving people, by relinquishing self-will, attachments, negative thoughts and feelings. And when you find God it will be in stillness. You will find God within.
Peace Pilgrim

ABOUT THE AUTHOR

Ben Behunin was born at a rather early age, and has lived most of his life at least 4000 feet above sea level. The oldest of eight children, Ben cut his imaginative teeth as a doodler, a daydreamer, a fortbuilder, a storyteller, and beginning at age fourteen—as a mudslinger.

Since 1996, Ben has made his living as a potter and a writer. Now the author of eight books, he still manages to work his way through 8-10 tons of clay each year while trying to keep up with his two teenaged children, Isaac and Eve. He also does his best to make sure his beautiful wife of twenty blissful, rambunctious and creative years, Lynnette, remains happy enough to stick with him for at least another twenty years. (She pretty much knows what she's in for, but he may still have a few surprises up his sleeve.)

In a recent interview with his children, they said of their dad, "He's basically a freak of nature. Yeah, like, a crazy man! Mom says it's just 'cause he's an exoshentric, or something like that. Nuh uh, I think its an extraterrestrial. (Laughter) He's probably one of those, too, but I think it's an ex-sentric. That means weird, right? Whatever. I don't even know.

Oh, and he likes to drag us all over the world with him to collect old bottle caps. But he's kinda fun, too. Yeah, I guess. But he's a weirdo."

Ben's only response to this was a silent smile.

The Behunins live in Salt Lake City, Utah, just feet away from the pottery/writing studio, where Ben is often found entertaining guests with what his children call his "pathetic attempts at yodeling." When he's not making pottery, writing, collecting bottle caps, or tormenting his children and their friends with bad jokes, Ben leads expeditions in search of the elusive Rocky Mountain Sasquatch. To book an expedition, you can contact him directly. And look for his forthcoming book, *How To Seduce a Sasquatch*, written in conjunction with National Geographic photographer, Harry Lederhosen.

Eve, Simon Rodia (shown actual size), and Isaac Behunin

VISITING WATTS TOWERS

Yes, it really exists! And one of my purposes for writing this book has been to encourage more people to visit Simon's masterpiece. I would highly encourage you to make it part of your next trip to Southern California, or make it a destination of its own. Consider taking the whole family. I've taken my family several times and we've all enjoyed it.

The Watts neighborhood is in south-central Los Angeles, and you will find the towers at **1727 E. 107th Street, Los Angeles, California 90002**. Your GPS should be able to navigate you directly there. If you have never spent any time in a big city, Watts might surprise you. It's a poor neighborhood, but it's as vibrant as it is gritty. It may not be a place where you want to build a summer home, but it's a great place to visit, and it's the only place in the world that has towers like these.

At the time of printing this book, tours are offered through the adjacent Watts Towers Arts Center, Thursday—Saturdays from 10:30-3:00 and Sundays from 12:30-3:00. The tours last 30 minutes and cost $7.00 for adults. $3.00 for seniors and youth 13-17 yrs, and children under 12 are free. You can find out more on their brand new website, www.wattstowers.org. The center offers a short video on Simon and the tower as a supplement to the tour.

Since the 70's, the towers themselves have been protected by a tall, steel fence that surrounds them. On the outside of this fence is a self-guided tour, posted on storyboards that you can visit anytime. These will give you a good introduction to the towers, but cannot compare with actually being inside the fence and taking the tour, so be sure to plan your visit on a day and time when the tours are offered. The half-hour tour is never long enough to see and experience it all. I have visited at least ten times and I discover new stuff each time I go back.

If you enjoy art and would like to make a day of it, consider visiting either the Getty Center of the Getty Villa on the same day. Both of these museums are free, but do charge for parking and may require a timed reservation during high visitation times. Check out www.getty.edu for more information. Enjoy!

Personalized books can be ordered
at www.potterboy.com.
There, you can register for the email mailing list
to receive updates about upcoming books, shows, and events.

Ben enjoys hearing from his readers.
You can reach him at benbehunin@comcast.net
or through snail mail at:

Abendmahl Press
P.O Box 581083
Salt Lake City, Utah 84158-1083

For speaking engagements including
book clubs, funerals and bar mitzvahs
call 801-883-0146

See the short video Quin Boardman created about Ben at
www.hiveseries.com

For design information, contact
Bert Compton at bert@comptonds.com

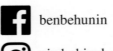 benbehunin

 niederbippboy

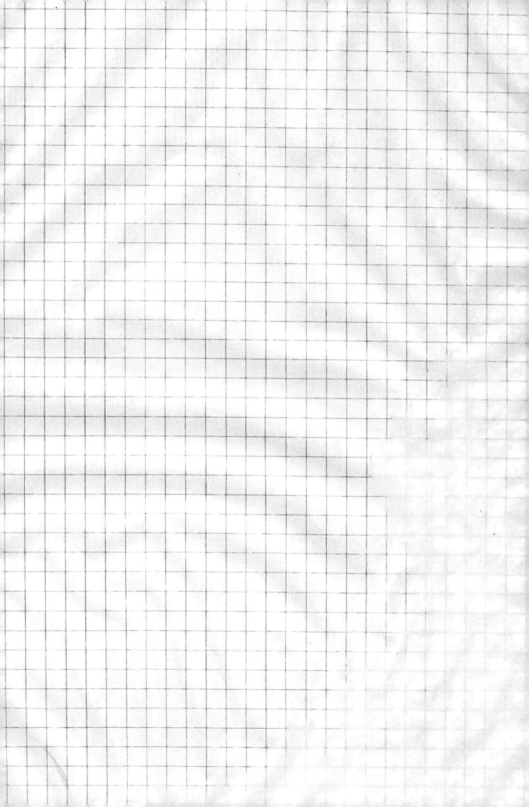

When we build, let us think that we build
forever. Let it not be for present delight nor
for our use alone. Let it be such work as our
descendants will look upon with praise and
thanksgiving in their hearts. —John Ruskin